The Coriddian Admiral

Shrouded King Book 2
by Sandell Wall

Books by Sandell Wall

<u>*The Runebound Trilogy*</u>

Rune Empire

Rune Destiny

Rune Legacy

<u>*The Shrouded King Series*</u>

The Tenth Reaver

The Coriddian Admiral

The First Champion

The Keeper of the Last Watch

The Shrouded King

<u>*The Shattered Son Trilogy*</u>

Rumor of Thorns

Binding of Souls

Blood of Druids

Thank you for reading my books!

Community:

Mail: sandellwall@gmail.com

My website: https://sandellwall.com/

The Coriddian Admiral © 2020 by Sandell Wall

Published by Sandell Wall

For my daughter, Verity. May your life be full of adventure and your future as limitless as the open sea.

Prologue

MAZAREEM STALKED THROUGH THE fetid swamp without leaving a mark of his passing. He was a shadow amongst shadows. Worm padded along at his side, pink tongue lolling out of the hound's grotesque mouth. Insects hungry for blood ignored both man and hound, and scaly predators that waited to drag the unwary to a watery grave slipped away at the first sign of their approach.

Three months of intense study and scrying followed by three months of hard travel had brought them here: an unnamed bog deep in the tropics far to the south of the Kingdom of Haverfell. Abimelech had given Mazareem the key to travel between realms but had not shown him the door. As always, the Lord of Dragons gave his blessings with a test.

Kaiser, the exiled tenth reaver, had escaped Mazareem against all odds. The memory still rankled Mazareem. Abimelech's reavers were Haverfell's greatest champions, but they were controlled through fear. Kaiser must be brought to heel lest the other reavers get it into their heads that escape was possible.

Unfortunately for Mazareem, Kaiser was far more than just a disgraced reaver. A simple reaver would be a trifling matter to deal with. Kaiser was more than a man now; he had been chosen as a champion of Abimelech's most bitter enemy, High King Rowen. That name twisted like a knife in Mazareem's guts. Rowen's blessing conferred terrible powers that made Kaiser extremely dangerous. Abimelech's will was clear: Kaiser must die, and Mazareem was the one set to the task.

Rotten ground beneath Mazareem's feet squelched with each step. Every few paces, he tested the trail with the end of his walking stick. The creatures of this place might want nothing to do with him, but Mazareem had no desire to sink up to his neck in stinking black mud.

Ahead of them, the foliage thickened, and a copse of oak and elm rose out of the swamp. Mazareem slowed his pace as the boggy ground gave way to solid earth. Strange, to find a thicket of hardwood at the heart of a great marshland.

"Stay alert, boy," Mazareem muttered to Worm. "This land has never known the rule of man. There's no telling what we'll find."

Worm's quiet growl meant that he understood. Together, the two of them crept forward. Mazareem pushed the tall ferns aside so that he could slip through, doing his best to leave the strange grove undisturbed. As they left the swampland behind, Mazareem's sense of unease grew.

The lush undergrowth thinned, and Mazareem and Worm stepped out into a clearing in the heart of the copse. Spears of obsidian stone stabbed up from the earth like teeth, the tallest twice the height of Mazareem. These jagged slivers of black stone filled the clearing, forming circles around the center. They decreased in height as they moved inward until the stakes in the middle stood only as high as Mazareem's knee.

In the center of the obsidian maw, a dark form slumbered on the ground. At their appearance, it stirred. Mazareem froze—Worm went motionless at his side. A sleek head rose into the air, supported by a long, scaled neck. Black wings unfurled, spreading wide to cast a long shadow. Eyes that smoldered like hot coals opened to regard Mazareem and Worm. It was a juvenile dragon prince.

This majestic and fearsome creature made Abimelech's dragon spawn seem pitiful in comparison. Pathetic, incomplete imitations of their patron, the dragon spawn took on the form of man, even using magic to appear human so that they could live amongst them. They served their master's purpose, but they would never be able to stand before a true dragon of the ancient blood.

For the first time in a thousand years, Mazareem felt the heart thudding in his chest. He dug out Abimelech's scale from beneath his cloak and held it before him. Twin points of fire, piercing in the way only the gaze of a dragon can be, considered the scale for a time. Apparently satisfied, the beast rose to all fours and walked a short way to the side, revealing the center of the obsidian stone formation.

Worm at his side, Mazareem started forward. The hound whined, hunkering low to the ground the closer they came to the dragon. Mazareem studied the creature as they approached. Its body was only slightly larger than a horse, but its long neck and wingspan made it seem much bigger. Based on its size, Mazareem guessed the dragon was no more than a hundred years old.

Visions and memories of riding at High King Rowen's side rose to the forefront of Mazareem's mind. In his zeal for conquest, the High King had hunted the race of dragons to the verge of extinction. Even Mazareem had believed that only Abimelech remained.

One juvenile dragon meant there would be more, perhaps many more. Mazareem struggled to reconcile this new understanding. Left unchecked, the age of dragons would return. Without the High King to wage war against dragonkind, humanity would be enslaved.

The dragon watched Mazareem with unblinking eyes. Mazareem passed in front of the creature, and a swirling green portal blossomed into existence in the middle of the obsidian stones. It spun like a lazy whirlpool, a tiny jade maelstrom that made no sound. Its presence did not even disturb the air. The draconic symbol carved into the scale in Mazareem's hand pulsed in time with the rotating vortex.

Mazareem took one last look at the dragon and plunged into the portal. Worm followed close behind. Reality coalesced into a single point of light, and Mazareem's entire being felt stretched across infinity. Sanity started to slip away. Amused, Mazareem let the sensation build for a time, and then when his patience wore thin, he took hold of his soul and defied the ravening nothingness that surrounded him. The forces of entropy held no power over Mazareem, and his master ruled over chaos. As if in response to his defiance, the world came rushing back. He stepped out of the portal on the other side.

Worm stumbled through behind him. Mazareem knelt to comfort the reeling hound.

"We're getting too old for this, aren't we, boy?" Mazareem said as he rubbed the dog's head. He looked behind them. No green portal swirled on this side—they would not be returning the way they came.

While Worm recovered, Mazareem stood and examined their surroundings. They were on a grassy hilltop in open country. A starry sky stretched overhead, although a touch of gray in the east heralded the rising of the sun. A vast openness which could only be the sea stretched across the southern horizon. Several miles away, the lights of an impressive city sprawled across the coast. From his perch on the hill, Mazareem saw a magnificent harbor full of ships, the smallest of which dwarfed the biggest vessel to ever sail from Northmark.

"Welcome to the realm of Praxis," Mazareem said to Worm. "Our quarry has a six-month head start. I suppose it's only fair to give them a sporting chance. Come, let's see what yonder city holds."

Mazareem and Worm descended from the hilltop and started towards the nearby city. He had no plan, only determination and need. If he returned to Abimelech empty-handed, his life would be forfeit. Mazareem corrected himself. His life was already forfeit; it was his soul that hung in the balance now.

Chapter 1

SORRELL STOOD ON THE deck of the C.E.S. *Indomitable,* a speck of woman braced on top of a leviathan of timber and iron. Three masts as thick as trees supported a phalanx of golden sails that captured the wind and harnessed the power of the sun. Rank upon rank of imperial artillery peered out of dark gun ports. Ocean waves surrendered before a hull strong enough to withstand point blank cannon fire. The ship was the will of the Coriddian Emperor made manifest.

The *Indomitable* sailed at the head of a line of thirty warships, each no less impressive than the first. They cut through the ocean with the inexorable weight of an empire's combined might. On the near horizon, a chaotic mass of sails fled before the *Indomitable* and her sisters of battle, baitfish trying to escape the swarming sharks. To the northeast, the coast of Linstall stood witness to the last stand of its nation's defenders.

Lieutenant Stone stood next to Sorrell on the deck of the *Indomitable.*

"Poor bastards," Stone said. "We're the last thing they expected to see."

"We'll have a fight, if we can catch them," Sorrell said. "But they'll have made a mess of our ships in the blockade. A needless waste."

"We have the wind," Stone said. "They can't escape us, and they can't turn to fight us. We'll slaughter them."

"You forget yourself, Mister Stone," Sorrell said, her voice firm. "Don't let your lust for battle overcome your sense of propriety. Today's enemies are tomorrow's allies."

Stone wisely remained silent as Sorrell raised a spyglass to her eye. Despite her reprimand of the lieutenant, Sorrell knew Stone was right. The enemy admiral had not anticipated breaking through the blockade only to run headlong into the massed strength of the entire Coriddian Fleet.

"They're trying to form their own line of battle," Sorrell said, the glass still held to her eye. "They're floundering. At this speed, we'll be on them within minutes."

Sorrell collapsed the spyglass with one swift motion and started barking orders. "Signal the other ships, Mister Stone. I'm going to pierce the middle of their line with the *Indomitable*. Have them follow us through. We'll cripple their formation before they've a chance to react."

"Aye, aye, admiral," Stone said. He turned from Sorrell and bellowed her orders out across the deck of the ship. Signal flags raced up and down the rigging, conveying her orders to the rest of the fleet. A smaller frigate, sailing parallel to their orderly line, mirrored the signals of the *Indomitable* so that the rest of the fleet behind them understood her orders.

All Sorrell could do now was wait. For the sake of her crew, which was about to sail into a storm of metal, blood, and death, Sorrell stood tall on the poop deck of the *Indomitable*. In her admiral's uniform—a long black coat with gold buttons and a black bicorne on her head—she liked to imagine she struck a dashing figure, but next to Lieutenant Stone, she felt tiny.

Broad shouldered and taller than Sorrell by two heads, Stone looked fit for an admiralty recruiting poster. His black uniform stretched tight over hard muscles. Sorrell had not told him yet, but after this voyage she intended to put him up for his captaincy. There was nothing more she could teach him.

A distant crack rang out over the water, signaling the start of the engagement.

"We're still half a mile out of range of their best guns," Stone said, shaking his head in amusement.

"Never underestimate the desperation of a doomed enemy," Sorrell said.

Sorrell turned her head to watch the signal frigate break course, sailing away from their line. A minnow compared to the *Indomitable*'s bulk, the smaller ship wanted nothing to do with the enemy's guns.

"After this, it's over," Sorrell said. "This is the final act of defiance of a defeated nation. When the guns fall silent today, the Coriddian Navy will stand unopposed."

"And its greatest hero will have her finest victory," Stone said with a grim smile.

Never wavering from her course, the *Indomitable* leapt across the sea. The guns of the enemy line started to speak with regular frequency. None of the shots came close enough to worry Sorrell yet, but that did not stop the slow burn of dread from igniting in the pit of her stomach.

Sorrell stuck her left hand inside her coat to hide its shaking. Her right hand gripped the rail of the poop deck so hard her knuckles turned white. Her hands might betray her fear, but her face remained resolute. Out of the corner of her eye, Sorrell saw sailors glance up at her, taking courage from her display of bravery.

"Mister Stone, make sure the marines are ready for boarding action," Sorrell said. "Once we break the enemy line, I intend to make straight for their flagship and bring the admiral to combat."

"Aye, aye, admiral," Stone said, dashing away to find the sergeant of the *Indomitable*'s contingent of marines.

The sound of the enemy's guns echoed across the water like rolling thunder. Sorrell heard the first whine of a cannonball tearing through the air. Above her head, a ragged hole appeared in one of the sails. Sorrell could not tear her eyes away from the sunlight streaming through the punctured etherweave.

"Four hundred yards!" a ragged voice shouted out from the prow of the ship.

Sorrell dropped her gaze back to the sea. The line of enemy ships stretched in front of the *Indomitable*. Clouds of smoke hung above the ocean as the hostile cannons belched fire. Sorrell's flagship bore the brunt of the assault, leading the way for the rest of the fleet that followed behind her.

"Two hundred yards!" the voice bellowed again.

That would be the last cry. Ruin came next. A cannonball skidded across the deck of the *Indomitable*, snapping legs and splintering wood—sailors fell away screaming, their skin shredded by the shattered timber. Sorrell flinched, but she did not move from her post.

The *Indomitable* shook as it soaked up the onslaught. She sailed at the enemy line head-on, presenting only her thickest armor as a target, but that did not stop them from trying to break her.

Lieutenant Stone returned to the poop deck just before they reached the growing cloud of stinking smoke that hid the enemy.

"Marines are ready, admiral!" Stone said, shouting to be heard over the din.

"Very good, Mister Stone," Sorrell said with a nod. "Sound the cry, if you please."

Stone gave her a maniacal grin, turned towards the deck with his hands cupped around his mouth, and roared into the chaos, "Hold fast, lads! If you find yourself at the gates of death, tell them you sailed on the *Indomitable,* and they'll send you back. The grave can't hold any who've sailed with the admiral!"

A cry of, "Sorrell!" and "Admiral!" went up from the crew.

Sorrell frowned at Stone's breach of protocol. She should reprimand him harshly—this moment must appear to be the culmination of the empire's grand conquest, not her pursuit of personal glory. But her heart soared at his words. Cannon smoke swallowed the *Indomitable,* and a fierce smile spread across Sorrell's face.

Sky and ocean disappeared in a shroud of suffocating silence. The deck of the *Indomitable* floated in a white cloud, and for a heartbeat, Sorrell could imagine drifting in serenity. And then the first gunnery sergeant bellowed the word that shattered the world.

"FIRE!"

Guns blazing, the *Indomitable* split the opposition's line, sailing between prow and stern of two enemy ships. Her three banks of imperial cannon spit destruction into the enemy's bowels.

Beneath Sorrell's feet, the deck of the *Indomitable* shuddered as her guns roared. The cannon crews timed their barrage with perfection. Each rank of guns fired only when the enemy could be seen through their gun ports. The gunners of the Coriddian Navy were the finest on the seas, and when their weapons spoke, carnage followed after.

Wooden hulls crumpled under the assault, and before the *Indomitable* cleared the smoke, both of her victims were already dead in the water. Enemy rifle fire swept the deck in front of Sorrell, but she never moved from her post. Next to her, Lieutenant Stone shouted orders over the din.

Smoke gave way to blue sky at the *Indomitable*'s prow, and she cleared the chaos as quickly as she had entered it. The ship slid out of the pandemonium with a whisper, clear sea and brilliant sky greeting Sorrell with the promise of victory. Tendrils of smoke clung to the ship's golden sails as if she had just burst forth from the mouth of the underworld.

Sorrell tore her eyes away from the open ocean. There was still a battle to be won. To the west, she spotted the enemy flagship trying to turn and run. The massive vessel floundered as it struggled to free itself from the doomed battle line.

"Hard to port, Mister Stone," Sorrell commanded.

"Aye, aye, admiral," Stone replied. He repeated her order to the helmsman, and the *Indomitable* changed course.

Admiral Finehorn commanded the Linstall fleet, and he had evaded Sorrell at every turn for the past three months. Finehorn was single-handedly prolonging the war. Linstall's rulers refused to surrender to the overwhelming Coriddian forces arrayed against them as long as their hero of an admiral still sailed with the fleet.

That ended today.

Sorrell reached for her flintlock and checked to make sure that the pistol was loaded. She had nothing to do but wait for the *Indomitable* to close the distance to Finehorn's flagship. Impatient and eager to end this engagement, Sorrell turned to survey the battle behind her.

Coriddian ships-of-the-line were pouring through the hole blasted by the *Indomitable*. The enemy was broken, all cohesion lost. Half of the Linstall ships were following their admiral's lead and turning to flee. The other half were trying to position themselves to fire a broadside at the Coriddian vessels. To Sorrell's experienced eye, the conflict was over. Now they just had to convince the enemy that the engagement was lost.

The sails of Finehorn's flagship billowed as they filled with wind, but he would never outpace the *Indomitable*. Above Sorrell's head, golden sails shimmered in the sun, the solar-powered etherweave granting her ship a swiftness that no vessel outside the Coriddian Navy could match.

"Why does he run?" Stone said at Sorrell's side. "He must know that he can't get away."

"In a few moments you'll be able to ask him yourself," Sorrell said. "Sound the boarding cry, if you please."

Lieutenant Stone cupped both hands to his mouth and shouted, "All hands, prepare to board yonder enemy ship. Admiral Finehorn himself walks her decks. Do your best to take him alive!"

Sorrell finally left her post on the poop deck as Stone's command was carried up and down the length of the *Indomitable*. She strode towards where the marines were gathered. While she moved, Sorrell stripped off her greatcoat and bicorne. She hung both items from pegs on the mainmast.

The marine sergeant nodded when Sorrell joined them. Their uniforms were black like hers and lined with gold braiding. A shako sat on the sergeant's head, a hat with a tall, flat top, but the rest of his men were outfitted with tricornes. They carried an assortment of pistols, blunderbusses, and sabers.

"Don't suppose I can convince you to sit this one out, admiral," the sergeant said when Sorrell stood beside him.

"Not today, not any day," Sorrell said, her voice hard.

"I didn't mean nothing by it, admiral," the sergeant said, ducking his head. "There's a foul wind blowing, is all. It would be a tragic shame to lose you on the last day of the war."

"Your concern is noted, sergeant," Sorrell said. "Now stow your pessimism and take that ship."

"Aye, aye, admiral," the sergeant said with a wry grin.

Admiral Finehorn had accepted that he would not get away without a fight and had turned his ship to face the *Indomitable.* Sorrell knelt with the marines behind a reinforced barricade as rifle and small-gun fire from the enemy flagship pelted *Indomitable*'s deck. Sorrell's sailors stayed out of sight, forced to weather the barrage as they drew closer.

Cannons thundered on the decks below, filling the gap between the ships with a killing storm of shrapnel. Finehorn's gunners kept their ports sealed against the assault. One cannon-blast full of nails could shred the flesh of an entire gunnery crew in the time it took to touch fire to fuse.

Stone appeared and knelt next to Sorrell. "We're within a hundred yards!" he yelled over the deafening noise.

Sorrell nodded and steeled herself for the battle to come. She felt a calm descend over her as she looked out over the deck of the *Indomitable.* The lower sails hung in golden shreds. A thousand wooden splinters hung in the air, kicked up by the hail of bullets pelting the ship. Hanging on the mast, Sorrell's greatcoat twitched as an enemy sniper poured shot after shot into it.

Two years of brutal conquest, and it came down to this. Sorrell closed her eyes and said a silent prayer. This battle was the grand realization of Sorrell's ambitions, the crowning jewel in a brilliant military career. Victory here meant she would have the power and influence she needed to see her ambitions realized. She refused to die when she was so close.

Hulls impacted with a grinding crunch that Sorrell felt in her bones. The *Indomitable* shook with the impact. The sergeant bellowed orders, and his men leapt into action. Grapple lines flew through the air, three-pronged iron hooks snagging and holding fast to the enemy ship.

Weapons in hand, the sailors of the *Indomitable* surged to the deck with a roar. Men with long-rifles revealed themselves in the high rigging, taking careful shots at the enemy sharpshooters. Ladders and planks were carried up from below and thrown across the gap between the ships.

Sorrell remained crouched behind the barricade as the marines charged up and over the railing. She counted to ten and then raised her head to look up into the rigging high overhead. At her signal, a length of rope dropped down out of the golden sails and dangled in front of her face. Designed specifically for this purpose, the rope ran through a pulley attached to one of the highest spars.

Forcing herself to act rather than hesitate, Sorrell wrapped the end of the rope around a forearm. With her free hand, she drew her rapier. She tugged on the rope to make sure it was secure. Confident that it would bear her weight, Sorrell jumped to her feet and sprinted along the deck parallel to the enemy ship.

At the same time, a team of sailors hauled on the other end of the rope. Sorrell leapt off the deck at the same instant they heaved upward, and her momentum carried her into the sky. She traversed the gap between the ships in a graceful arc, flying high above the smoke and chaos.

For an instant, Sorrell hung suspended above the battle below. She looked down at the men fighting and dying between the ships. The sound of gunfire and the clash of blades seemed so far away. She sucked in a deep breath of clean air. Her eyes were drawn to the brilliant blue of the open ocean on the horizon, and then gravity pulled at her—she plummeted towards the command deck of the enemy flagship like a bird of prey.

Sorrell landed on both feet, rapier out and ready to defend herself. Admiral Finehorn had seen her coming. He stood next to the ship's wheel with the biggest flintlock pistol Sorrell had ever seen pointed at her chest.

"The battle is lost, admiral!" Sorrell shouted. "Stand down your men, hand over this ship, and end this pointless fighting."

"We choose death over Coriddian shackles," Admiral Finehorn roared. He pulled the trigger.

Sorrell did not even have time to flinch. She saw the muzzle flash—the iron shot was so large she could see it speeding towards her. Finehorn disappeared in a cloud of black smoke. The bullet whizzed past her ear, missing her by only an inch. Finehorn cursed and scrambled to reload the hand-cannon. Two of his lieutenants rushed Sorrell to buy their admiral time.

In one swift motion, Sorrell drew her own pistol and shot the first lieutenant in the stomach. He fell away, clutching his bleeding midsection. She parried the attack of the second man with her rapier and danced away from his savage counter.

The man sneered at her. Behind him, Sorrell saw Finehorn finish loading his firearm. He raised the gun, only to find the back of his lieutenant between him and Sorrell.

"Step aside!" Finehorn bellowed.

Either the lieutenant did not hear his admiral, or he was intent on killing Sorrell himself. Whatever the reason, he pressed the attack rather than move out of Finehorn's line of fire.

Sorrell dashed forward to cross blades with her attacker. As long as she kept him in front of her, she was safe from Finehorn's pistol. Finehorn's marines tried to rush up the stairs and attack Sorrell from behind, but the riflemen in the rigging of the *Indomitable* made sure that none of them reached her.

Finehorn stepped towards her as he tried to get the attention of the lieutenant. Sorrell attacked the man with a flurry of quick slashes, doing her best to keep him focused on her instead of heeding Finehorn's shouting.

The lieutenant obliged, and Sorrell found herself fighting for her life as she withstood his assault. Her rapier flashed like quicksilver in the sunlight, every parry and attack accompanied by a deadly dance of footwork that kept her on the balls of her feet and facing her opponent.

Sorrell answered a vicious lunge with a riposte that put the lieutenant on his heels. Before he could recover his balance, a musket ball from the *Indomitable* ripped through his skull and sent him sprawling at Sorrell's feet. She tore her eyes from the corpse and stared in horror down the barrel of Finehorn's hand-cannon. He smiled at her in satisfaction.

Finehorn pulled the trigger. Fire sparked, and Sorrell heard the click of the firing mechanism, but nothing happened. Finehorn tried again, but the gun did not fire. In his haste to load it, he had fouled the barrel. He grimaced.

"The gods have spoken," Finehorn said. "A bullet would be too clean a death for you."

He tossed the useless pistol aside and drew his heavy saber. Sorrell took a step backwards. She could not cross swords with him — the thin blade of her rapier would crumple beneath his heavier weapon.

"Come on then," Finehorn said with a sneer as he flourished his sword. "Come and taste my blade."

Sorrell had shed her heavy coat and bicorne hat, but Finehorn still wore all the trappings of his admiralty. The thick folds of his great coat billowed in the wind as he strode across the deck towards her.

Pinned to his enormous hat, ribbons fluttered as they tried to wrench free of the medals they were attached to.

Finehorn did not give Sorrell any time to think. He came straight at her, his first swing powerful and clumsy. Sorrell ducked under the whistling blade of his saber and slashed at his midsection. Her sword bounced off the thick fabric of his coat.

"Pah," Finehorn spat in her face. "Your pathetic blade couldn't puncture the skirt of a fishmonger."

Midsentence, Finehorn reversed his swing and struck at Sorrell's throat. She lunged backwards, and the point of his saber nicked her skin. Sorrell slapped a hand to her neck—it came away covered in blood.

"That's a pity," Finehorn said, pausing his brutal attack. "I was aiming to open that pretty throat of yours."

"This is your last chance," Sorrell said. "Surrender this ship, and I'll let you live."

Finehorn's grin was sinister. "Here's your answer, you Coriddian whore."

Finehorn cocked his arm back, preparing to strike at Sorrell with all his strength. Sorrell anticipated this, as Finehorn had shown no restraint or technique thus far, preferring to force her back with a reckless but relentless assault.

Sorrell jumped forward inside Finehorn's swing. His sword arm descended, drawing the heavy blade with it—she slammed the point of her rapier between the buttons of his coat. Coriddian steel pierced the soft silken undershirt beneath. His forward momentum, combined with her desperate thrust, drove the blade deep into his chest and out his back on the other side.

Finehorn's mouth opened, but he made no sound. His heavy saber fell with a clatter. The two of them stood frozen like statues for a few heartbeats, Sorrell supporting the dying man's weight on her sword.

Finehorn slumped to the deck as the life drained out of him. Sorrell let him slide off her blade.

On the main deck of the ship, the sounds of battle were muted. It only took a glance for Sorrell to assess that they had won the fight for control of the top deck. Now her marines would have to root out any remaining resistance below. Out on the water, the thunder of cannon fire had ceased. The battle was over.

At Sorrell's feet, Finehorn gasped. He raised a bloody hand from his punctured chest, the trembling fingers reaching towards Sorrell. She knelt by his side.

"I never feared death," Finehorn said, his voice so weak that his words were almost lost in the wind. "I feared what I'd leave behind. I die as the last free man. Now the Coriddian empire will sweep across the world, unopposed and unchecked."

"We were enemies of circumstance," Sorrell said. "Your nation shouldn't have resisted us. You didn't need to die."

"Not so," Finehorn choked, struggling to speak. "We were your enemy by necessity. The spread of your empire's influence is the end of liberty, the death of dreams. Where the Coriddian flag flies, men have two choices: kneel or be broken."

Finehorn grasped Sorrell's arm in his bloody grip. Sorrell tried to pull free, but he still possessed surprising strength for a man on the threshold of the afterlife.

"Remember me," Finehorn gasped. "Remember me as the man that never bent his knee."

Sorrell did not answer. She watched as the life slipped from Finehorn's eyes and he slumped back on the deck. His hand fell from her arm, leaving bloody fingerprints on her black shirt. She stared at his still face for a long moment. Sorrell roused herself and reached down to pluck a medal from his gaudy bicorne for proof that she had bested the man in single combat.

"The ship's ours, admiral!" Lieutenant Stone called from below. "Word's spread that you killed Admiral Finehorn, and the rest of the crew surrendered."

"Very good, Mister Stone," Sorrell replied as she got to her feet. "See to it that enough sailors from the *Indomitable* transfer over to sail this ship. I'm taking it back to Coridal."

"Aye, aye, admiral," Stone said.

Sorrell moved to look out over the water. She rested her hand on the deck railing and surveyed the scene of her greatest victory. Clouds of dirty smoke clung to the surface of the sea. Here and there, ships burned, the doomed vessels reduced to nothing more than a wooden tomb for the sailors trapped inside. In the midst of it all, the golden sails of the Coriddian fleet shone like the glory of heaven, radiant even amidst the destruction of battle. The sight brought a fierce joy to Sorrell's heart.

With Admiral Finehorn slain and the remains of his fleet shattered, they had broken the back of the Linstall military. They had been defiant to the last, but now they would have no choice but to surrender. Sorrell smiled to herself. There was no one else for Coriddia to conquer. Now, at last, she could claim her reward.

Chapter 2

SORRELL TUGGED AT THE edges of her ceremonial uniform. The rich black cloth fit tight to her body. Medals of gold, silver, and copper spilled down her chest like a gilded waterfall. Her bicorne was festooned with ribbons and regalia. She felt beyond foolish. Every step, every minute movement, brought with it a tinkling and a rustling as if Sorrell had become some gaudy lawn ornament in the emperor's gardens.

None of the other admirals put on such a garish display. But as the only female officer in the Coriddian Navy, Sorrell's accomplishments were both her shield and her ammunition. They were proof that no one dared question her ability or stand in the way of her advancement.

The door to her private dressing room opened and Lieutenant Stone walked inside. He paused, taking in her appearance and the look of annoyance on her face. Stone wore the ceremonial uniform of the Coriddian Navy with the confidence and aplomb of a man born for spectacle. Like Sorrell's, his hat was tucked neatly beneath his left arm.

"Don't you dare smile, Mister Stone," Sorrell said.

Stone raised a hand to his mouth. "You look the part, if I may say so, admiral," Stone said.

Sorrell heard the amusement in his voice, but she let it slide.

"The chariot's outside, waiting for you," Stone said.

"Of course it is," Sorrell said in annoyance. "They afford me the highest honor, and yet somehow I still feel marginalized."

"These old, frail men—these white hairs that sit in cushy chairs and direct the war from afar, they've never sailed with you into battle," Stone said. "No one who's seen you stand unflinching on the deck of the *Indomitable* could ever doubt you."

"Indeed," Sorrell said, the corners of her mouth turning up in a smile.

Stone stepped aside and held an outstretched hand towards the door. Sorrell nodded to acknowledge the polite gesture and moved out of the room. Stone fell into step beside her.

"I'm told you're getting the rose," Stone said as they walked through the halls of the admiralty building. "The first one to be awarded in fifty years."

"People will say it's because of my family," Sorrell said, raising a hand to the medals on her chest. "I know the rumors that I'm just a royal brat playing at war."

"Come now, admiral," Stone said. "Even your cynicism cannot dim the honor of the Coriddian Rose. Who cares what others think? Those who know you know that you earned it."

"My ambitions don't end with the navy," Sorrell said. "Public opinion matters a great deal in the realm of politics."

"A pox upon politicians," Stone said. "You've had a glorious military career and you're not even in your prime yet. Why trade the thrill of battle for the petty infighting of the senate? Retire to a villa in the country and enjoy yourself. I'm sure you'd have plenty of suitors. You could have your pick of the young, eligible men."

Sorrell swallowed hard. "You forget your place, Mister Stone."

Stone glanced at her out of the corner of his eye. They had burned with unspoken lust for each other over the past few years, but Sorrell had refused to ever acknowledge it. And every time Stone hinted at it, she shut him down hard. Sorrell's military career was under too much scrutiny to risk it for a romp between the sheets with her statuesque lieutenant. To her continued frustration, this only seemed to encourage him.

"My apologies, admiral," Stone said, his voice amused.

"I'm going to put you up for your captaincy," Sorrell said to relieve the tension and distract Stone. "You're ready for your own ship, and with the war over, it's the perfect time to promote you."

Stone stopped short in surprise. Sorrell kept walking without even a glance back.

His footsteps echoed in the hallway as Stone ran to catch up with her.

"They won't give you the *Indomitable*, but you're ready for command," Sorrell said when Stone walked alongside her again.

"We'll never sail together again," Stone said.

"Not as officers of the same ship," Sorrell said.

Stone ran a hand through his dark hair. "Damnation, admiral. This is a shock. I don't know what to say."

"Say you'll serve the empire and do the *Indomitable* proud," Sorrell said.

"Without question or hesitation, admiral," Stone said. "Thank you."

"Don't thank me. I'd not recommend you if you didn't deserve it."

Stone's response died on his lips when they stepped out of the front door of the admiralty building. Automatically, they swept their hats up and onto their heads. The street outside was packed with sailors and officers in their best ceremonial dress. Sorrell had to return a hundred salutes before she made it ten steps. A cheer went up when the crew of the *Indomitable* spotted Sorrell, and she could not help but smile.

Together, Sorrell and Stone walked to a horse-drawn chariot that stood in the center of the street. The chariot only had room enough for a driver and a single occupant to stand. Resplendent in the morning sun, the golden chariot was an ancient affectation, a tradition that had somehow survived for hundreds of years. Hitched to the front of the chariot, twin white horses stood ready to transport Sorrell to the palace.

Stone stopped with a crisp click of his heels and gave Sorrell an immaculate salute. She returned the gesture before stepping up into the waiting chariot. The driver glanced over his shoulder. Sorrell gave the man a nod, and he snapped the reins in response. White horse flanks twitched, and the chariot started forward with a jerk. Sorrell gripped the rail to keep her balance.

On both sides of the road, the crowd stepped back to clear a path for the chariot. A cheer preceded Sorrell, and as she was carried to the main thoroughfare, every eye turned to witness her coming. The driver pulled the horse to a stop as they waited for the rest of the parade to form up behind them. Sorrell did not look back, but she knew the procession would stretch for at least a mile. Stone would be back there somewhere, marching at the head of the *Indomitable*'s crew.

On both sides of the wide street, people crowded the windows of the ornate buildings. Over the past decade, Coriddian architecture had shifted to the baroque, and the houses and business establishments of the empire's capital competed with each other to draw the attention of the passerby. Thousands of citizens lined the street, their shining faces turned towards the impending spectacle.

High overhead, the morning sun rose towards noon. Sorrell felt the heat of its rays and knew that before this day was over, she would be covered in sweat beneath her thick ceremonial uniform. She smiled to herself. Such a small discomfort was nothing compared to the heat of battle.

At some signal that Sorrell missed, the parade started. Reins snapped, and the driver of the chariot urged the horse forward. Sorrell took a deep breath, squared her shoulders, and stood tall as they began their journey to the palace. She gripped the rail with one hand and folded the other across her chest, hiding it underneath the unbuttoned flap of her coat.

The iron-banded wheels of the chariot clattered on the cobblestones, but the growing noise of the crowd soon drowned out all other sound. When Sorrell started to move, a cry went up that never abated. Chariot and driver carried her through the twisting avenues of the city, and the roar of ten thousand voices followed her wherever she went. Roses were thrown from rooftops to land in the street in front of her. Children darted into the road to scatter red petals beneath the chariot's wheels.

Sorrell observed the revelry with unflinching stoicism. She might be the conquering hero, but these people denied what was hers by right. They would celebrate her as long as she was content to stay in her place.

After traversing a meandering route through the streets of Coridal, the chariot turned down the wide highway that terminated in front of the Palace of the Eclipse. Even though Sorrell knew it was coming, her breath still caught in her throat when she entered the grand courtyard before the palace. City buildings fell away, and in their place stood hundreds of thousands of onlookers. It was too big to call a mob—it was an army, and it stretched across the huge, open space, every face turned towards her, and every mouth crying her name.

Unbidden, tears sprang to Sorrell's eyes. The chariot driver did not flinch, aiming the horse down the center of the Promenade of Victory. Despite the horde of people on both sides, not a single foot touched the brilliant white marble of the promenade. On either side of the marble lane, statues of the empire's heroes towered over Sorrell's head.

Here, the emperors and generals of antiquity stood guard against the future. Here, the glory of the empire, writ in blood and toil, was remembered by all who dared pass under the statues' gaze. In a gesture of both awe and reverence, Sorrell removed her hand from her coat and raised it over her head to salute the heroes who had come before her.

The roar of the crowd reached a new level of frenzy at Sorrell's gesture.

At the end of the Promenade of Victory stood the steps that led up to the Palace of the Eclipse. Perfect in their symmetry and geometry, the flawless stairs of white marble seemed to ascend to heaven itself. They stretched the length of the great courtyard, climbing towards the massive columns that supported the roof of the palace.

Above the palace, the greatest wonder of the world looked out over the city of Coridal. Commissioned four hundred years ago by Emperor Borellian, a colossal bronze statue of his divine likeness had been constructed over the imperial palace. One arm held aloft towards the sky, the metallic emperor held the entire earth in the palm of his hand. The edifice was constructed as such that, just after noon, the bronze globe eclipsed the sun and cast the courtyard below in shadow. Emperor Borellian had given the Palace of the Eclipse its name and decreed that, where other kings and emperors had likened themselves to the sun, none greater had come before him, for he eclipsed them all.

They entered the monument's shadow as the chariot left the promenade behind, and the driver turned the horse parallel to the steps so that Sorrell could climb out. The timing of her approach was not by chance, and Sorrell stepped to the ground cloaked in shadow. A hush fell over the crowd. On any other day, the cult of the emperor would gather in this holy shade to perform a sacred ritual of remembrance. Today, the eclipse touched only Sorrell, an honor only a few others had ever received.

Sorrell's pulse quickened as she raised her gaze to the top of the palace steps. Emperor Pyreshade stood alone. From this distance, the massive stone columns on his right and left dwarfed the emperor of the Coriddian empire. Behind Sorrell, the chariot driver snapped his reins and pulled away, leaving her to face the emperor on her own.

In the sudden silence, Emperor Pyreshade began his descent. Sorrell stood rigid in the center of the shadow cast by Borellian's monument. A hundred thoughts raced through her head. She tried and failed to still her racing heart. Sorrell had become the empire's greatest living hero. Her glory had reached its zenith. Her time was now.

She tried to keep her expression calm. It would do her no good for the emperor to read the naked ambition on her face. Behind her, the crowd cheered, and Sorrell let their adoration wash over her. To them, she was the embodiment of the emperor's will—a peerless servant of the Coriddian Empire. But she was no servant, and she only cared for the ambitions of the emperor as long as they aligned with her own.

Sorrell watched Emperor Pyreshade as he descended the last few steps. He was several years younger than her, his black hair swept back in the classic style of a Coriddian general. The emperor wore a simple white military uniform completely devoid of any ostentation. In an empire of black-suited subjects, he alone wore white. Yet while he might style himself after the commanders of his military, the emperor moved without grace or strength. Instead of squared shoulders, he stooped, and what should have been a stride of imperial confidence was more of a timid shamble. He flinched visibly with every roar of the crowd.

Emperor Pyreshade gave Sorrell a tremulous smile as he descended from the last step. Sorrell forced herself not to sneer in response. His features lacked the rugged quality that spoke of trustworthiness and competence. His pinched face and placid eyes were more suited to a clergyman or scholar than a leader of men. The emperor would not survive a single day on a ship-of-the-line. He tried to catch Sorrell's gaze for a long heartbeat, but when she did not shift her eyes to meet his, he looked away.

Disgusted, Sorrell made a conscious effort to not be the first to speak. She wanted this ceremony over and done with, but she would force the emperor to address her first. Emperor Pyreshade came to a stop in front of her, and for the first time, Sorrell noticed the object in his hand. He carried a Coriddian Rose.

A murmur rippled through the crowd as they made the same observation. The Coriddian Rose had not been awarded in fifty years, and the last man to receive it now stood as a statue on the Promenade of Victory. No man or woman could attain a higher honor from the emperor. No woman ever had.

"Hello, sister," Emperor Pyreshade said.

In spite of herself, Sorrell's gaze dropped to meet the emperor's.

"Hello, brother," Sorrell replied.

They stared at one another for a moment, and then the emperor indicated that Sorrell should turn to face the crowd. Sorrell complied, and Emperor Pyreshade stepped forward to stand by her side.

Together, they looked out over the sea of innumerable faces. To address so great a throng would be impossible, so the emperor simply raised the Coriddian Rose over his head and held it there for a long moment.

The rose itself was a thing of magnificence. Carved from colored glass and reinforced with glittering steel, it was a treasure beyond price. Gold lined each petal, and an unblemished diamond sat in the center of the unfurled flower. All the wealth that Sorrell acquired in her life would never match the value of that rose.

When Emperor Pyreshade knew the crowd could wait no longer, he turned to Sorrell. Moving slowly so that the people behind him could appreciate what he was doing, the emperor slid the Coriddian Rose into an open button hole on her jacket. This done, he stepped back and faced the crowd.

"Behold, the conqueror of Linstall!" Emperor Pyreshade shouted out over the parade ground. His weak voice did not carry far, but the throng did not need to hear his words to know what he said.

The crowd erupted. For a heartbeat, Sorrell feared that the statues along the promenade would crack and fall to the earth under the onslaught of sound. But the impassive stone faces only stared as the people cheered on. Under the gaze of these heroes of antiquity, the rest of the parade traveled down the promenade and turned to pass in front of Sorrell and Emperor Pyreshade.

Sorrell stood at attention as most of the empire's navy tromped by. At the head of the *Indomitable*'s crew, Lieutenant Stone snapped a perfect salute at Sorrell. She returned his salute, but not the huge grin that split his face.

The mile-long parade took the better part of an hour to expend itself. Her brother stood at Sorrell's side the entire time without speaking. He fidgeted as he observed the spectacle. Noon came and went, and the sun sank towards the western horizon. Sorrell watched with annoyance as the shadow of Borellian's monument stretched and slid eastward, leaving them standing in the midday heat.

Finally, the last soldier had passed in front of them, and Sorrell and Emperor Pyreshade were staring at the rearmost part of the procession. He turned towards the steps.

"Mother wishes to speak with you," Emperor Pyreshade said. He looked at her expectantly, waiting for her response before beginning his ascent into the palace.

"As well she should," Sorrell said. "This day has been long in coming."

Emperor Pyreshade frowned, but he did not respond. He waited for her to join him on the stairs before starting the climb upward.

The Coriddian Rose hung heavy from her jacket as Sorrell climbed the ivory steps to the Palace of the Eclipse. She glanced upward at Borellian's bronze, upturned face, and felt a rush of adrenaline as she passed into the palace. She would not be eclipsed. The time of her ascendancy was nigh.

Guards from the emperor's regiment of Royal Grenadiers stood watch between the great columns on the palace's porch. Their black and gold checkered vests and gleaming halberds were a marked contrast to the simple black dress of the navy. They glanced at Sorrell but did not salute.

Emperor Pyreshade picked up speed as they moved out of sight of the multitude below. Sorrell almost had to break into a jog to keep up. The thick fabric of her ceremonial uniform and the mountain of metals on her chest were growing heavier by the minute. She felt exhaustion creeping in, but she refused to acknowledge it. Sorrell could not afford to show any weakness in front of their mother.

Following in the emperor's footsteps, Sorrell traversed the grand halls of the palace, each one given over to a different type of art. In one, paintings the size of small ships hung on the wall. Another was devoted to statues of gold, every individual piece a study of the human form. As they progressed from one end of the hall to the other, the sculptures became more sensual, until the last few statues were intertwined in exotic and explicit displays of copulation.

Sorrell frowned. She knew the rumors about her brother. The officers of the navy were careful around her, but she would be a poor captain indeed if she did not know all that went on beneath the deck of her ship. They said that the emperor preferred to sequester himself away with his art collection rather than give himself to the task of governing the empire. More wealth went towards commissioning new artwork for the palace than any other civic or military endeavor.

To Sorrell's ire, her brother seemed intent on giving her a tour of the entire palace. Just when she opened her mouth to ask how much further, Emperor Pyreshade turned aside and passed through an open doorway. Sorrell followed him inside and found herself in a spacious but comfortable room that looked out over a private bay behind the palace. Bookshelves lined the walls, and supple leather chairs were arranged around an immense fireplace. In the winter months, she imagined this place would be quite cozy, but for now, the hearth lay empty and cold.

"Mother will join us soon," Emperor Pyreshade said, collapsing into one of the chairs with a great sigh. "I find ceremony so wearisome."

Sorrell perched herself on the edge of one of the leather seats. Her stiff ceremonial uniform prevented her from reclining further, even if she wanted to. She did not respond to her brother's comment. Her anger boiled at his laziness but now was not the time to antagonize him.

A serving girl appeared from the back of the room. She was a pretty young woman wearing a dress cut low enough to show off ample cleavage, and she carried a silver tray on her upturned palms.

Amber liquid sloshed in delicate crystal glasses as she sashayed across the carpet. Her brother took an offered glass, his awkward gaze looking anywhere but at the young woman.

Sorrell allowed herself to frown as the servant approached her. A tight satin dress did nothing to hide the woman's curves, and as she came close, Sorrell detected the scent of roses. Sorrell wondered if her brother ever took this girl to the hall with the fornicating golden statues. The girl's every movement whispered of seduction.

Head lowered in submission, the servant girl offered Sorrell the remaining drink. Sorrell said nothing and made no move to take the glass. Finally, the young woman looked up to meet Sorrell's gaze. Sorrell gave the girl a savage smile and was rewarded with a flinch.

"Must you terrorize the staff every time you visit?" a strong feminine voice said from the doorway behind Sorrell. "This isn't the navy where you can have someone tied to the mast and beaten just because they displease you."

Royal Mother Viatrix had arrived.

Emperor Pyreshade jerked upright in his seat, spilling his drink in his hurry to sit up straight. In front of Sorrell, the serving girl's eyes widened in panic, and she backed away, fleeing for the shadows on the edge of the room.

"Stay, Margaret," Viatrix said, stopping the serving girl in her tracks. "I'll need you momentarily."

Sorrell got to her feet and turned to face the door. Viatrix stood just inside the study, her silhouette framed by soft light from the hallway beyond. She stood as tall as Sorrell and possessed the same fierceness that her daughter had inherited. Viatrix's long brown hair was immaculate, spilling down her back in a cascade that shimmered when she moved. Despite her age, her pale skin was flawless and without wrinkle. In fact, to Sorrell's eyes, her mother seemed to grow younger every time she saw her.

Viatrix's eyes found Sorrell's, and Sorrell felt the familiar stab of fear. She had stormed the smoking ruins of fallen nations and battled every opponent of the empire into submission, yet the hard gaze of her mother still reduced her to a scared little child.

In Sorrell's memory, her mother's eyes were brown like her own, but when she held Viatrix's stare now, the royal mother's eyes seemed to shift from green, to blue, to gray. The prismatic effect startled Sorrell, and she struggled to recall if her mother's eyes had always been this way.

"I suppose I shouldn't be surprised at your behavior," Viatrix said as she looked Sorrell up and down. "You act as you look: like a brute. The years at sea haven't been kind to your figure, girl. I daresay, had I not known better, I'd have thought you a man from behind."

"As always, your words are a comfort," Sorrell said, doing her best to keep her voice emotionless. "I hold them close on those frigid nights in foreign waters, and they keep me warmer than any flame ever could."

Viatrix pursed her lips and did not immediately respond. "Must we do this now?" she finally said.

"I'm here at your summons," Sorrell said. "You already know my answer."

"So be it," Viatrix said. She raised a hand, summoning Margaret to her side. Viatrix whispered into the serving girl's ear for a moment, and then Margaret moved to where Emperor Pyreshade sat.

Margaret bent over at the waist and leaned in close to speak quietly to the emperor. The front of her dress fell forward, putting herself on display for his pleasure. Now Emperor Pyreshade did have eyes for her, and only her. Whatever she said to him caused the emperor to blush, and he allowed himself to be coaxed from his seat and led by the hand from the room. He never gave Sorrell a second look.

"There's no need to worry him with this," Viatrix said as she stepped further into the study. "You know he doesn't like it when we disagree."

Sorrell squared her shoulders as Viatrix sank into a leather chair with a sigh. Fifteen years of struggle, pain, and warfare culminated in this moment.

"It's going to concern him soon enough," Sorrell said. "I want the throne."

"I know you do, dear," Viatrix said, her response immediate. She closed her eyes and lay back in the chair.

"I'm not asking you anymore, Mother. I'm telling you."

At this, Viatrix's eyes snapped open and she sat up. "You're *telling* me, child? Do you think stomping around on the deck of a dirty ship for ten years somehow empowers you to come into my home and impose your will?

"Those medals and trophies you've bedecked yourself with mean *nothing*. Through every step of your career, I've opened doors and removed barriers. Without my intervention, you'd still be some pathetic midshipman, and probably fat with a bastard child. You're just a foolish girl who doesn't know her place. As long as you cling to this insane ambition, you put our family at risk. More than that, you put the entire empire at risk."

While her mother spoke, Sorrell plucked the Coriddian Rose from her jacket and twirled it between her fingers. The glass petals caught the torchlight of the study, shining like the surface of the sea. Her mother's words cut deep. In time, Sorrell's accomplishments had grown to match her ambition, and Viatrix's best defense was to claim that all her successes were due to her family ties.

"Laws of succession have changed before, and they'll change again," Sorrell said quietly. "The claim of the firstborn is stronger than that of sex."

"You would tear the empire away from your own brother?" Viatrix asked in disgust.

Sorrell looked at her mother overtop the gilded rose in her hand. "I'll make sure that he's not hurt. You'll be taken care of as well. Don't resist me on this. My legend has reached its apex. Were I to march from here to the floor of the senate, they would grant me anything I asked of them. You know this." After a brief pause, Sorrell said, "Do you truly believe that I'm not worthy? Look me in the eye and tell me that I'm not what's best for the empire."

Viatrix said nothing for a long time. When she did speak, her words tore at Sorrell's heart. "I should have killed you the day you were born. A firstborn girl is only good for bargaining in marriage, and you failed at even that. I let you join the navy because I thought you'd be ravaged, brutalized, and return home broken. I thought to cure you of this madness. Now my mercy is my undoing."

Sorrell suffered her mother's hatred in silence. The scars on her soul had long since rendered her numb to Viatrix's abuse.

"It will go better for everyone if you support my claim," Sorrell said. "Wheels are already in motion. If I'm not seen leaving the palace before sundown, Coriddia will erupt in bloody rebellion. Join with me, and you'll retain your title and position."

"Is this how you treat your own family?" Viatrix said, suddenly contrite, all hatred gone from her voice. "Come, dear. We're your flesh and blood."

"The navy is my family," Sorrell said. "I was an orphan the day I went to sea."

"Have a care, child. Casting aside the ties of blood is the first step down the road to damnation."

"Then I follow in your footsteps. Now give me your answer. If I leave here without one, I will count you as an enemy."

"It seems you leave me with little choice," Viatrix said with a scowl.

"Of course you have a choice," Sorrell said. "You can choose to keep a life of luxury and limited power or you can choose exile."

"If you're to be emperor, the first thing you must learn is that threats only serve to make you look petty."

"So you'll help me."

"The laws of succession are malleable, but to change them will take time. You need my influence and experience in the senate. Without me, you risk civil war."

"You forget I have the navy on my side."

"You're a hypocrite, blinded by your own ambition. You tell me you're what's best for the empire and then you threaten to tear it apart if you don't get your way."

"I knew talking to you would be a waste of time," Sorrell said. She got to her feet and made for the door.

"If I'm to help you, you must do something for me first," Viatrix said, a little too quickly.

Sorrell stopped. She trembled with the adrenaline coursing through her body. She had Viatrix in her pocket now. Above all else, her mother was a survivor, always willing to do whatever it took to hold on to her power. A little bargaining, a tiny bit of give-and-take, would allow Viatrix to save face as they moved forward into a new type of relationship. Old hurts would not be forgotten, but they could be ignored for the sake of mutual gain. Such was the price of the throne.

"It will take time to approach the senate with the idea of change," Viatrix continued. "While I lay the groundwork for a campaign of transition, perhaps you could take care of this... sensitive issue that has come up. It's a simple task, but one that requires a modicum of discretion. It's a matter to be handled by... family."

"I'm listening," Sorrell said, turning around to face Viatrix.

"You may show yourself," Viatrix said, her voice raised in such a way that made it clear she was speaking to someone else in the room.

Sorrell whirled to scan the shadows in the far reaches of the study. In the farthest corner, near the cold fireplace, a black shape detached itself from the wall and stepped forward. Sorrell's blood ran cold. This interloper had heard everything.

The man did not look human. He stood at least a head taller than Sorrell, and he wore a long black cloak that clung to his wiry frame. The man's ivory skin contrasted with the dark robe; his flesh was the perfect white of bleached bone. Spidery black veins stretched underneath his skin. Sorrell swore she could detect the pulse of each beat of the man's heart as his veins throbbed with black ichor.

He grinned at her, his hairless head bearing a striking resemblance to a skull. His eyes reminded Sorrell of her mother's— gray and cold, and yet somehow shifting across every color on the spectrum in some trick of lighting. Sorrell disliked the man the instant she laid eyes on him.

"This is Mazareem, one of my most trusted agents," Viatrix said when Mazareem stood next to her chair. "Don't fret about what he overheard. I would have told him everything soon enough."

Viatrix raised a hand, indicating that Mazareem should speak. "I'll let him explain what is asked of you."

"The royal mother is too kind with her praise," Mazareem said, giving Sorrell a smile that did not reach his eyes. "What her grace refers to is a delicate matter. Several months ago, a pirate ship that goes by the name, the *Golden Dawn*, raided one of the emperor's private storehouses. They stripped it bare, making off with some priceless pieces of art. This is insult enough and warrants swift and merciless retribution. However, in their ignorance, they made off with a commissioned work that is of great personal significance to the emperor."

Mazareem paused as he glanced at Viatrix. She gave no indication that she was listening, so Mazareem continued. "It's imperative that we recover this stolen property. Thus far, every attempt at tracking the *Golden Dawn* has met with failure. I fear we're running out of time. Soon, the pirates will sail beyond our reach or sell the last of the treasure and it will be lost to us forever."

Here, Viatrix returned her attention to the conversation. "I don't care how you get it done. You're the admiral, you figure it out. Complete this task for me and I'll support your claim."

"Peace is my first choice," Sorrell said. "So I'll do this for you. But if I return to find that you've betrayed me, there will be war. I'll not enter this palace as a subject of the emperor again."

"There's no need to be so dramatic, dear," Viatrix said.

"If you want me to go on a treasure hunt, I'll need to know what it is that we're seeking."

Mazareem smiled, revealing perfect teeth set in pitch-black gums. "I promise you, there's no mistaking it. It's an amulet—a golden pendant in the shape of a dragon."

Chapter 3

KAISER WADED OUT OF the cold surf and up onto the dark beach. The starless sky overhead was both a blessing and a curse. They were invisible to anyone who did not stumble onto them, but at the same time, they could not see more than a hundred feet in any direction.

Behind Kaiser, Lacrael and Brant climbed over the side of the rowboat, their feet splashing in the shallow water. Kaiser turned and grasped the prow of the little boat, and with their help, heaved it up onto the beach.

"I don't like leaving it out in the open," Lacrael whispered in the darkness.

"If we're not back here by sunrise, it won't matter if the Coriddian Emperor himself finds it," Kaiser said. "Signal the ship."

At Kaiser's prompting, Lacrael turned to face the open sea. She raised a palm, and with a thought, she summoned a small flame out of thin air. Lacrael let the fire flicker for several heartbeats and then closed her fist, extinguishing the light. After a moment, a second flame answered her signal far out on the water.

"That starts the clock," Kaiser said. "We have six hours. After that, they'll sail without us."

Brant stared at Kaiser with hate-filled eyes.

Kaiser ignored Brant's gaze. The man bothered him, but he was not about to admit it. If it were up to him, Brant would be locked in irons in the hold of the *Golden Dawn*. However, Gustavus refused to allow Brant to stay aboard with both Kaiser and Lacrael going ashore. Gustavus and his crew were terrified of Brant, and Kaiser understood their fear. Only Lacrael's insistence ensured that Brant retained his freedom.

"We have to move fast," Kaiser said, turning to hike higher up the beach. "Linstrad is still two miles away."

Lacrael spoke to Brant in quiet words while they moved. Kaiser listened intently, but as far as he could hear, Brant said nothing in response. Every day, Brant drifted further away from being human, yet Lacrael never stopped trying to get through to him. In Kaiser's opinion, Brant was a lost cause.

At the tree line, Kaiser turned east. He did not know the surrounding countryside, so the only way to ensure they did not get lost was to follow the coast. Kaiser hushed Lacrael, and the three of them hiked along the hard sand in silence.

Within a mile, the lights of Linstrad appeared on the horizon. The city was the capital of the war-torn Linstall Empire and had seen far better days. Pretending to be a trade ship, the *Golden Dawn* had been smuggling the rich and powerful out of the city and past the Coriddian blockade for weeks now. Linstrad was about to be gutted like a fat fish, and its wealth would flow back to Coridal on a tide of blood.

"I don't expect to encounter any guards," Kaiser said as they neared the city. "We're not visibly armed, so no one should give us trouble. Do your best to act like refugees and follow my lead."

Neither Lacrael nor Brant said anything in response. They both knew the drill. Kaiser knew they did not need to be reminded, but he was used to being a commander of men. Old habits died hard.

They had to pass through the Linstrad harbor to reach the city. Beneath the docks, they found a mob of homeless refugees. Entire families squatted in the wet sand. Little children peered up at Kaiser as he passed. The beach was littered with the remains of any animal unfortunate enough to wander too close.

A fleet of Coriddian ships floated out in the harbor. After the utter defeat of Admiral Finehorn, the city had offered its complete surrender. The vanguard of the Coriddian Empire's army would arrive within the week to occupy the ravaged city. Kaiser intended to be a thousand miles away when that happened.

Just as they were about to clear the shadow of the docks and ascend to the street, a small form shot out of the darkness and latched onto Kaiser's leg. Kaiser jerked to a stop—Lacrael jumped forward in alarm, hands raised to summon her fire.

Kaiser stood motionless, a hand raised to indicate that Brant and Lacrael should stand down. A small boy had wrapped his arms around one of Kaiser's legs. The boy buried his face against Kaiser's thigh.

The boy sobbed.

Gently but firmly, Kaiser pried the boy's arms from around his leg. The child looked up at him with eyes full of tears. Kaiser's heart seized when he saw the boy's face—in the poor lighting he could have been Saredon. Kaiser's soul ached at the thought of his son. He looked out over the harbor as tears sprang to his eyes.

"We can't help him," Kaiser said, fighting to keep his voice from quavering. "Tell him to run along."

The boy shook his head and wiped the tears from his eyes with the back of a sleeve as Kaiser pushed him away. The kid did not need to understand Kaiser's foreign tongue to know what he had said.

"He's a brave lad," Lacrael said. "Are you sure we can't—"

"No, we can't," Kaiser interrupted. "Look around you. There are hundreds of orphaned children, and there's not a damned thing we can do for them. We're here for one purpose, now let's get on with it."

Lacrael frowned but did not argue. She knelt next to the child and spoke to him in his native tongue. Of the three of them, Lacrael had mastered the local language the quickest. The boy sniffled, but he nodded his head and stepped back.

Kaiser ran up the stairs to the street, taking them two at a time. At the top of the steps, he glanced over his shoulder to find the boy watching them. He could only see Saredon staring back at him. Kaiser shook his head, angry at the tears in his eyes. As they stepped out onto the cobblestone streets of Linstrad, Kaiser said a silent prayer for his son's safety. It was a hollow gesture, for a man without faith, but he did not know what else to do.

The city above was far worse than the pitiful scene beneath the docks. Kaiser understood why families sought the limited safety of the beach. Every street they passed was overrun with desperate soldiers. Hungry eyes and sneers greeted the three of them on every corner, and bared blades glinted in the shadows. Lacrael attracted the most attention. Brant moved to walk close by her side, and he glared at any man who called out to her.

"Don't start a fight," Kaiser said as they passed near a large group of ragged soldiers loitering outside an alleyway. "I'll never hear the end of it if I have to slaughter an entire city."

Kaiser stared down the biggest thug in the crowd, daring the man to step forward. The ruffians looked the three of them up and down but let them pass without issue.

"Where are we supposed to meet our contact?" Lacrael asked after they turned the corner and moved out of sight of the soldiers.

"I've got the map memorized," Kaiser said. "Our destination should be two blocks ahead."

After one more block, they left the commercial district of the docks behind and entered a residential area. Mansions lined the streets. Some of the grand houses were locked tight and probably still in the care of their owners, but most had been torn open and looted. Discarded belongings littered the street. Once immaculate hedgerows had been hacked apart and trampled down.

"Up there on the left," Kaiser said as he stepped over an empty drawer. "See the mansion with the guards out front? That's our destination."

A trio of soldiers stood outside a locked iron gate. These men still had some fight in them. Armed with muskets and swords, they turned to face Kaiser, Lacrael, and Brant as the trio approached. Their uniforms still bore the insignia of Linstall's army. Light in the windows made it clear that the mansion they guarded was still occupied. Instead of a hedge, a tall iron fence lined the grounds.

Kaiser came to a halt before the nearest soldier. The man stared at him with barely disguised hostility. Before the guard could tell him to make himself scarce, Kaiser spoke the agreed upon phrase, "Coriddian wine tastes like cow piss."

The soldier blinked as he processed Kaiser's words.

Behind him, one of the other soldiers leaned forward and said, "That's the password, Lint. We're supposed to let them through."

"I know that, blast it," the soldier named Lint said. "I'm trying to decide if we can trust them."

"That's up to the general, not you," the second soldier said.

Lint scowled, and Kaiser thought the man was going to tell him to shove off, but the soldier finally stepped aside. Lacrael and Brant at his back, Kaiser made his way up the stone walk to the front of the mansion.

Kaiser had been in this realm for six months, but he did not ever think he would get used to the architecture. They built with wood and red brick instead of solid stone. One house contained more glass in the windows than the most lavish of castles in Kaiser's home of Haverfell. The mansion in front of them had a forest of peaked roofs and a great porch that circled the entire building. Ornate columns of carved wood supported the roof of the porch overhang.

The front door was a solid pane of etched glass. On the other side, Kaiser saw a flurry of frenzied activity. After a glance at Lacrael, he pushed the door open and stepped through.

Inside the mansion, an army of servants was in the process of jamming a mountain of clothes into several colossal trunks. Three young children ran squealing through the chaos, doing their best to get underfoot and trip the harried servants. Standing to one side, a regal looking couple oversaw the whole affair.

The husband noticed Kaiser, Lacrael, and Brant, and his face lit up as he moved towards them. He was unremarkable looking—handsome in a boring, average sort of way. His clothes were well-tailored, but they did not provide any clue about his occupation.

"Ah, you've come!" the man boomed. "I feared that you'd not make it through the insanity in the city. You're just in time. We're almost prepared to leave."

"I take it you're General Raither," Kaiser said.

"Indeed," Raither said. He looked the three of them up and down. "I must say, you're not what I expected. When I contacted the Golden Dawn, I anticipated receiving aid from... someone with more experience. By heavens, you're not even armed." Raither paused to glance over Kaiser's shoulder. "Captain Gustavus isn't with you?"

"The captain never leaves the ship," Kaiser said, turning towards the door. "Now, if you're ready to go, we must be away."

"All in the right time, my good man," Raither said. "My wife's trunks will be packed within the quarter-hour. We're only taking the most essential of items, you understand."

Kaiser froze mid-step. Slowly, he turned back to face Raither.

"Transport of your family isn't part of the contract," Kaiser said. "The agreement was you, and you alone. We've room for the clothes on your back, nothing more."

"Come now, we might have lost the war, but I'm still the greatest general Linstall has ever known," Raither said with a scoff. "Did you really think I'd abandon my family and slink away like a common vagabond? Everything's negotiable. Just get us to your ship, and I'll make it worth your captain's time."

"This is a lost cause," Kaiser said to Lacrael when Raither finished speaking. "Let's get back to the ship."

Kaiser took a step to the door.

"Wait," Raither said, holding up a hand towards Kaiser. "You can't just leave us here."

Raither's outstretched hand trembled ever so slightly, and Kaiser perceived the cracks in the man's confident act. Kaiser's gaze slid to the three children, who were now looking at their father in wide-eyed concern. He looked at Raither's wife, whose hands were clutched to her stomach in fear. Kaiser knew this desperation.

"Comply with the terms of the agreed upon contract or stay here and enjoy Coriddian hospitality," Kaiser said, making no effort to blunt the edge of his words. "I don't care which you choose, but if you want to remain a free man, you need to come with us, right now."

Raither's wife was suddenly at his side. "Go with them," she said. "We'll lose the house, but we'll survive. If you're free, there's a chance we can reunite somewhere safe. If you stay, you'll be taken prisoner and rot in a Coriddian cell, or worse."

Kaiser watched the inner turmoil play out on Raither's face. The man looked from his wife to his children. His gaze rested on Kaiser last. By the set of Raither's jaw, Kaiser knew the man would stay.

"Listen to your wife," Kaiser said. "She speaks the truth."

Raither opened his mouth to speak, but before he could get a word out, the door behind Kaiser crashed open. Acting as one, Kaiser, Lacrael, and Brant faced the sound and prepared to fight. Instead of an enemy assailant, they found a breathless soldier bearing the insignia of one of Raither's men.

"A squad of Coriddian Royal Grenadiers just entered the city," the soldier said between gasps. "They're coming here, general."

"They expect me to flee...," Raither said, all the color drained from his face.

"Only a fool would stay," Kaiser said.

"Go with them," Raither's wife pleaded with him. "Get yourself to safety!"

Raither's sorrow-filled eyes found Kaiser's, and Kaiser nodded. There was nothing left to say. Raither stepped forward and swept his wife into a fierce hug. She clung to him for a few long minutes. Kaiser cleared his throat, and Raither he let her go. He dropped to his knees and opened his arms for his children. They crashed into his chest, and Raither hugged them all at once, burying his face in their hair.

Kaiser looked away from the scene, unable to abide the painful memories of his own fractured family.

Raither released the children and climbed to his feet. "I put my life in your hands," he said.

Now with Raither in tow, Kaiser stepped through the door and back into the night. Lacrael and Brant took up positions behind Raither. At the end of the cobblestone path, Raither insisted on stopping to speak with the guards.

"My family isn't coming with me," Raither said to the three soldiers. "No matter what happens, watch out for them. Keep them safe."

The soldiers saluted as one, and after returning their salute, Raither nodded at Kaiser that they could continue on. Once in the street, Kaiser walked fast. He had no desire to encounter a squad of Coriddian soldiers between here and the beach.

For the sake of speed, Kaiser backtracked on the same route they had used to enter the city. They could not afford to get lost. Kaiser turned the corner onto the street with the rabble of soldiers, and he knew immediately that retracing their steps had been a mistake. The bored mob of soldiers was waiting for them, and they had found their courage.

When the first man spotted them, a cry went up. In just a few seconds, the road in front of Kaiser was blocked. Kaiser squared his shoulders and kept walking.

"Whatever happens, stay behind me," Kaiser said over his shoulder to Raither.

Kaiser came to a stop ten paces from the man who seemed to be the leader of the gang. He stood a head taller than the rest, and his heavily muscled arms and scars marked him as a brawler.

The big man spat into the street between them and crossed his arms. "I'll make this simple," he said. "Give us your valuables and the woman, and you can scurry off back to whatever trash heap you crawled out of."

Kaiser shook his head, able to understand the gist of what the man was saying, but he did not comprehend every word of the foreign Linstall language.

"Move," Kaiser said in the same language, one of the few words he knew.

The thug laughed. "We own this city, little man. You shouldn't have come back this way." He jerked his neck to one side, producing a loud pop. He took a step towards Kaiser, starting to work through the warm-up routine of a professional pugilist.

"After I kill the leader, the fight should go out of the rest," Kaiser said, his voice pitched so only his companions could hear him. He spoke with confidence, but he had a hard time judging the size of the mob in the darkness.

"Kaiser...," Lacrael said from behind him.

"I don't want to hear it," Kaiser said. "I can handle this."

Fists raised, the brawler stepped forward. He gave Kaiser a gap-toothed grin.

"Let's make this fun," the thug said. "I'll give you a fighting chance."

Kaiser let the man come. Still grinning, the brute advanced, hands up to protect his face. This man wanted to box. Maybe he was a good streetfighter, with an arsenal of dirty tricks, but Kaiser was a killer.

"I'm not going to stand here and watch this," Lacrael said from behind Kaiser. "Come on, we can go around while they're distracted."

Lacrael and Brant hustled Raither into the nearby alley. Kaiser let them go. All his attention was on the gang leader. He saw the first punch coming well before the man threw it. Kaiser took a single step forward to meet the blow, kicking out at where his attacker's leg would be as the man lunged into the attack. Kaiser's bootheel hit the man's knee with a sickening crunch. Kaiser ducked the now harmless punch and stepped back.

The gang leader howled and clutched at his ruined knee. Kaiser darted forward and slammed a fist into the brute's gut. With a grunt, the man dropped to the street, supporting his weight on his good leg.

Kaiser grabbed a fistful of greasy hair and snapped the thug's head back. He wanted to see the fear in the man's eyes. The taunts and calls from the gang had gone silent. One glance at the crowd told Kaiser that none of the ragged soldiers would come to their leader's aid.

"Look at me," Kaiser said.

The thug refused to obey.

"Look at me!" Kaiser shouted, giving the man's head a vicious shake.

Terrified eyes looked up at Kaiser's face. He smiled.

"Tell me what you see," Kaiser said. "Do you see mercy? Do you see compassion?"

Of course, the man did not understand Kaiser's foreign tongue, and he shook his head in confusion. Kaiser struck him. Delicate bones splintered under Kaiser's fist—his nose crushed, the gang leader sagged in Kaiser's grip.

Saredon's face flashed before Kaiser's vision, and he hit the man again. Red hot anger shot through him with a searing heat that felt real. For a brief instant, Kaiser gave his heart over to rage. His fist rose and fell like a hammer. When his vision cleared, Kaiser held a lifeless body. The man's face was a bloody pulp, and Kaiser's hand hurt. His grip on the brute's hair was the only thing keeping the body upright.

Kaiser let go, and the dead man slumped into the street. He looked at the rest of the gang over the body of their fallen leader. A hundred dirty faces stared back at him in horror. Kaiser stepped over the corpse and walked towards the mob.

No one spoke. The only sound was the shuffling of feet as they parted to let him pass. Kaiser walked through their midst, looking neither left nor right. No one challenged him as he passed through the crowd. On the other side, the empty street stretched away into the night. Kaiser picked up his pace, intent on catching up with the others. He did not look back.

Chapter 4

KAISER LEFT THE RAVAGED city behind without a second look. The very air itself stank of war. Once, the acrid tang of violence and suffering would have sent fire shooting through his veins, sparking a surge of adrenaline that would have carried him to bloody victory. Now, it only made him angry.

Wet sand squelched under Kaiser's boots as he hiked down the deserted beach. His mind registered the noise of the surf, but he did not really hear it. He massaged the knuckles of his aching hand. His thoughts were a world away. Apparitions swam before his vision in the pre-dawn twilight. Kaiser saw the face of his wife, watched for the thousandth time as the life left her eyes and the color drained from her cheeks. He saw a terrified Saredon, lost and alone, abandoned by a father who had sworn to protect him.

Tears filled Kaiser's eyes and threatened to spill down his cheeks. He swiped angrily at his face. For months he had been running from the truth, volunteering for any mission or task that would keep him too busy to face the turmoil in his heart. But the quietness always found him, and when it did, a small voice could be heard repeating the same few words over and over again.

In Kaiser's tortured memories, the voice hammered into his soul, each utterance a burning knife that stabbed into an open wound. The voice was his own, and it said, "You failed them. Mariel is dead and Saredon lost because of you."

Kaiser trembled as the pain of his wife's loss washed over him, as fresh as the day she died. Relentlessly, he replayed the events of that fateful day in his mind, trying to find his mistake, trying to find where he had stepped onto the path that led to the destruction of all that he loved. But the answer eluded him, and no matter how many times he relived that day in his memory, every choice ended with Kaiser cradling a dying Mariel in his arms.

A faint ringing in the distance caused Kaiser to raise his head. He could just make out the shadowy outline of the *Golden Dawn* as it made preparations to cast off. A single figure stood on the shore next to a rowboat. Still a mile away, Kaiser recognized the statuesque form of Gustavus.

Gustavus watched Kaiser come with his arms crossed. The massive captain stood at least a head taller than Kaiser. He wore only simple breeches and an open white shirt, but this did nothing to diminish his aura of command. On the open sea, Gustavus was second to none, and he demanded respect and obedience from even Kaiser as long as they sailed on the same ship.

Kaiser was in no mood to trade words with the captain, but if he wanted to sail out of here on the *Golden Dawn* he had no choice. He came to a stop ten paces from Gustavus and stared at the larger man. He knew what Gustavus would say.

"You killed again," Gustavus said.

"I'd like to get off this beach," Kaiser said.

"You're a thrice cursed fool. These excursions onto the mainland are dangerous enough without you killing anyone that looks at you funny. Vengeance isn't going to bring your wife back. How much blood do you have to spill to quiet your grief?"

"You know nothing of my grief."

"There's a saying on the islands of my birth," Gustavus said, the rumble of his voice carrying over the noise of the surf. "Your heathen understanding will mangle the true meaning, but I'll translate it for you. They say that a man who cannot let go of his pain has already dug his own grave."

"I've no use for the pitiful proverbs of some island shaman," Kaiser said. "If that's all you have to say, let's be off."

Gustavus frowned. He looked almost hurt. "By the blackest depths, man, there's not a day that goes by that I don't think about your wife and son. We all feel your pain, but you're not the only sad bastard on this venture who's suffered terrible loss."

Kaiser clenched his fists and looked at the surf. Helpless rage swelled in his breast. He watched the waves lick at the toes of his boots and bit down on the desire to lash out at Gustavus. Kaiser breathed deep. He could not release his anger, but he could control it.

"I'd like to get off this beach," Kaiser said again, raising his head.

Anger twisted Gustavus's countenance, but before he could speak, a voice called out across the water from the *Golden Dawn*.

"What's the hold up, captain?" the voice shouted. "We need to be away with the tide."

Gustavus glanced towards the ship and then back at Kaiser.

"Your recklessness puts the rest of the crew at risk," Gustavus said, his voice quiet despite the tension in his body. "I've marooned sailors for less. You may be the Shrouded King's chosen champion, but my patience has limits. Perhaps a month or two on a deserted island would give you time to get your head right."

A single spectral scimitar sizzled into existence while Gustavus talked. Kaiser absentmindedly inspected the weapon as Gustavus finished speaking.

"Make your threats, but be prepared for the consequences," Kaiser said.

Kaiser held Gustavus's gaze for a long moment. Gustavus finally turned away in disgust.

"Get in the damned boat," Gustavus said as he stepped into the small rowboat.

Gustavus settled on the bench and took up the oars in his huge hands. Kaiser set his shoulder against the prow of the small craft and shoved it off the beach. His feet splashed in the sea as he scrambled over the edge of the boat.

Head down to avoid Kaiser's gaze, Gustavus heaved at the oars. Muscles rippled beneath his flowing shirt as he propelled the rowboat across the waves. Kaiser sat facing Gustavus, but the captain never looked up.

Within minutes they were in the shadow of the *Golden Dawn*'s hull. Ropes were lowered and tied to iron rings embedded in the wooden planks of the rowboat. Kaiser gripped the bench beneath him as they were hoisted upward. Gustavus stood on his feet, unconcerned by the rocking and swaying of the boat.

The small boat cleared the *Golden Dawn*'s railing and swung out over the deck, and Gustavus jumped over the side without a second look at Kaiser. Kaiser waited to be lowered to the deck before attempting the same maneuver.

Lacrael was waiting for him.

"I'm sorry," Lacrael said. "I shouldn't have abandoned you. I just couldn't stand there and watch you slaughter someone else who only made the mistake of getting in your way."

"You don't have to apologize to me," Kaiser said as he brushed past. "You did what you were supposed to do."

Lacrael reached out, her fingertips brushing Kaiser's shoulder. He stopped and glanced at her face. She looked into his eyes, her dark pupils darting back and forth as she searched for something in his gaze.

"You can't... you can't go on like this," Lacrael said.

Kaiser took a shuddering breath. "I go forward, because I can't go back."

Lacrael looked like she wanted to say more, but Kaiser left her standing on the deck. Overhead, the rigging creaked as the sails filled with wind. The first rays of the new day's sun were shining on the eastern horizon, and Kaiser found that darkness suited him better than daylight. He made for the open hatch that allowed access into the bowels of the ship. Out of the corner of his eye, Kaiser spotted Raither engaged in a quiet conversation with Brant. Kaiser avoided meeting their gaze, having no desire to speak to either man.

Kaiser scrambled down the ladder into the lower decks. He was no sailor, but six months on a ship had forced him to find his sea legs. After climbing down past the gun deck, Kaiser stepped off the ladder and made his way through the crew quarters. Hammocks filled the cramped space, and here and there a few lockers were bolted to the deck. As special guests of the *Golden Dawn,* Kaiser and Lacrael enjoyed the privacy of two of the small cabins at the rear of the ship.

Inside the cabin, Kaiser found Tarathine hunched over a book. A single candle illuminated the faded pages. She looked up at the noise of his entrance. Her look of surprise quickly gave way to relief.

"Father, you've returned!" Tarathine said, closing her book and jumping up from the small table. She collapsed into Kaiser's chest, embracing him with a fierce hug that nearly squeezed the breath from his lungs.

Kaiser did not trust himself to speak. Instead, he wrapped his arms around his daughter and buried his face in her hair. Like the iron anchor that held the *Golden Dawn* fast against the turbulent seas, Tarathine kept Kaiser tethered to himself. He wept silent tears.

Tarathine leaned back in his embrace and looked up.

"You're crying," she said in alarm. "Were you hurt?"

Kaiser released her and stepped back. He smiled at Tarathine. The expression seemed so foreign that he felt like his face might crack. "I'm fine. I just need some rest. Why don't you take your reading above deck? The sun's almost out."

Tarathine looked skeptical, but she did not press him for answers. She gave him a quick kiss on his cheek, collected her book, and darted out the door. Kaiser stared at the open door for a long while as he contemplated his daughter.

In the six months since leaving Northmark, Tarathine had not let Kaiser see her grief. The girl was strong—stronger than he was, and her courage made his heart swell. He knew from a few brief conversations with Lacrael that Tarathine mourned in private, yet when she was with him, Tarathine was resolute. She had so much of her mother in her.

Exhausted, Kaiser snuffed the candle between his fingertips and lowered himself onto one of the two small cots. He did not even bother removing his boots. It seemed selfish, but Kaiser found himself grateful that he was too weary to think about Mariel and Saredon. Before he could dwell on that thought, sleep claimed him.

For a time, Kaiser drifted. No dreams interrupted his slumber, and a sense of rejuvenation and renewal suffused his being. He felt almost at peace. Despite the sensation of calm, Kaiser resisted it. He could sense a presence behind it, a will that was not his own. With this awareness came understanding, and in the next instant, he was no longer alone.

Kaiser found himself sitting on a green hilltop looking out over a sprawling city. Stars twinkled in the night sky overhead, and the lights from a thousand windows hung suspended in the darkness below. In front of him, a small campfire crackled. The hooded stranger sat on the other side of the fire.

For six long months Kaiser had waited for the mysterious stranger to visit his dreams. Day after day had come and gone and still the stranger did not appear, and each day that passed without a sign had only fueled Kaiser's anger. Kaiser had sacrificed everything, and the entity who set him on this path had abandoned him. He had resolved that should the stranger ever trouble his dreams again, he would demand answers—he would demand a reckoning. But now, in this place, his anger was held in check. The stranger prevented Kaiser from giving his rage a voice.

"I can sense your resentment and frustration," the stranger said from beneath his cowl. "It was not my intent to remain silent for so long. The enemy has found some way to enfeeble me in the spiritual plane. Ever since your escape from Northmark, the city has gone dark. A barrier obscures my vision, and an almost physical force repels me every time I try to draw near to the place."

"Saredon is beyond your reach," Kaiser said in a hollow voice.

The stranger bowed his head slightly. "For the time being, yes. But he isn't alone. One of my oldest allies watches over him. Have faith, Kaiser. Your son will endure."

"And live his life without a father," Kaiser said. "If your power wanes so do our chances of ever leaving this realm."

"I said I was weak, not impotent," the stranger said. "I still have much influence in this place. I've been invisible these past months, but I've not been idle. Events will soon come to a head, and the next champion will be revealed to you. All of you must be ready to act when the time comes. I cannot reveal too much lest you change the course of the future with the knowledge, but you're on the right path. My chosen one is very near."

"The crows take your cryptic babbling. It's Raither, isn't it? Raither is the next champion. We'll not be able to venture onto the mainland again. It's no coincidence that on the night we rescue him, you appear. It has to be him."

The stranger hesitated before responding. "You know I cannot tell you," he finally said.

"That's answer enough," Kaiser said.

From across the fire, the stranger stared at Kaiser from beneath his hood. Kaiser stared back, his gaze unflinching. He could see two pinpricks of firelight in the shadow of the stranger's cowl where the flames danced in the man's eyes.

"You must wake now," the stranger said at last. "I've tarried too long already. I may not be able to visit you again for a while but never doubt that I'm with you. As long as you can summon the powers I've given you, I remain strong enough to challenge the enemy. And Kaiser… please be gentle with Gustavus. He's one of my most loyal servants."

Kaiser said nothing. Seconds later, the stranger faded and disappeared before his eyes. The fire and landscape followed soon after, and Kaiser soon floated in a vast nothingness.

"There is nothing more for you here," the stranger's voice echoed from all around him. "Wake, Kaiser, the darkness is not your home."

Kaiser's eyes snapped open. He stared into the absolute blackness of his tiny room. The exaggerated rocking of the ship told him that they were well underway. Kaiser shook the last vestiges of the dream from his mind as he sat up. There was no knowing how long he had slept, but he felt more rested than he had in months.

Once out of bed, three quick strides took him to the door. Faint sunlight from a distant hatch lit the hallway outside. Kaiser's vision started to adjust to the light as he retraced his steps to the top deck, but he still had to squint and shield his eyes from the sun when he climbed out into the daylight. A quick scan of the ship showed no sign of Gustavus or Lacrael, so Kaiser made his way towards the captain's cabin.

The door to Gustavus's cabin was shut tight. Kaiser shouldered it aside without knocking. Inside, he found Gustavus, Lacrael, Brant, and Raither standing around the navigation table in the center of the room. They looked up in surprise at his sudden entrance, their conversation cut short.

Kaiser paused, looking at each one of them in turn. Gustavus glowered at him, but the other three stared back at him with a mixture of awe and fear on their faces.

"I've had a dream," Kaiser said.

These words produced a change of attitude in the cabin that was immediate and tangible. Gustavus crossed his arms and shook his head in resignation. Lacrael stepped around the table so fast that she struck her hip on the sharp corner. She winced and rubbed her thigh as she moved to stand in front of Kaiser. Brant hung back, but he waited eagerly for Kaiser's next words. Raither looked confused.

"He visited you again?" Lacrael asked. "Did he speak to you? Did he say why he waited so long? Did he tell you what we're supposed to do?"

Kaiser held up his hands to stop Lacrael's stream of questions. She ground to a halt and waited expectantly for him to speak.

"Yes, he came to me in my sleep," Kaiser said. "We spoke only briefly. He said that the enemy has found a way to weaken him. He didn't say what that meant, but it was clearly the reason he has been silent since we arrived in this realm."

"Pardon my confusion," Raither said from where he stood next to the table. "But what in the blazes are we talking about? Is this man some sort of seer?"

"A seer chooses to seek his visions," Kaiser said, making eye contact with Raither. "I wasn't given that choice. The stranger in my dream had more to say. He speaks only in riddles, but his meaning was clear enough. Raither will become the next champion."

Eyes wide, Lacrael turned to stare at Raither. Gustavus and Brant joined her inspection of the Linstall general. Raither took a step back, alarmed by this new scrutiny.

"What's the meaning of this?" Raither asked. "How can I have been a part of your sleeping vision?"

"It means that this little exercise was pointless," Gustavus said, nodding at the map spread out on the table between them. "I'm sorry, general, but we must break the terms of our contract. There's no port of safe harbor waiting for you. Willing or no, you're a part of this crew now." A slow smile spread across Gustavus's face. "As always, the Shrouded King watches over us."

"Now see here," Raither finally said, having recovered from his distress. "I paid you a small fortune to deliver me to safety. Now you're going to abduct me? Where's your honor? Do you now fly the flag of pirate instead of smuggler?"

"I'm no pirate," Gustavus growled. "There are powers at work here beyond your ken. You'll come around to our way of thinking. Give it time."

"You're in rare company," Kaiser said. "The good captain excluded, we're all here against our will, and it only cost us the people we loved the most."

Chapter 5

SAREDON CREPT ALONG A filthy alleyway. He did his best to avoid the puddles of greasy water, but somehow his feet always ended up soggy. High-walled warehouses crowded around on all sides. Bright eyes peered out at him from stinking sewer grates. Giant rats, probably. At least, that's what Saredon told himself. This early in the morning, the rodents were Saredon's only witnesses.

Braver street urchins worked the open markets in the center of Northmark. There, they had their pick of fresh-baked bread, fruit, and anything else their sly fingers could lift from beneath a distracted stall keeper's gaze. In the six months since his world fell apart, Saredon had done what he needed to survive, but he was a long way from having the courage to steal food in broad daylight in a public square.

On top of the dangers of being caught, there was the risk of being cornered by the other children that roamed the city. The orphans operated in gangs that usually reported to an adult. Ursais had warned Saredon that anyone who grew up in the gutter would recognize him for royalty the instant he opened his mouth. Saredon's obvious heritage would attract unwanted attention. So he stuck to the parts of the city where he could avoid being seen.

Saredon paused at the end of the alley. He looked left and right down a wide, cobblestone street. In the distance, he saw the forest of masts and sails from ships floating in the harbor. Two hours from now, this road would be crowded with laborers hauling goods to and fro, but for now, it was deserted.

Across the way, the nearest warehouse had a narrow crack in its foundation. When he was confident the coast was clear, Saredon darted across the street and wedged himself into this crevice. He had to suck in his chest to squeeze through, and the jagged stone scraped the sides of his head, leaving behind angry welts and scratches. In another few months, he would be too big to use this route.

Once through the walls of the foundation, the crawlspace of the warehouse opened up and he stood. The top of Saredon's head just brushed the floorboards above him. Wooden pillars thicker than he was supported the weight of the structure above. Saredon stepped gingerly in the near darkness. Beneath his feet, the remains of rotten fish littered the ground. He did not even wrinkle his nose at the smell.

Saredon shuddered at the memory of first finding this place. He had been on the verge of starvation. Back then, he had been able to slip through the crack without effort. That first time, he had been stopped short at the near physical stench on the other side. Saredon had fallen to his knees retching. When he had recovered enough to realize that the smell was dead fish, his hunger had taken control. Saredon had dropped to his knees and devoured piece after piece of the putrid, scaly meat. It had all come back up a moment later, but he knew he had finally found a source of food.

Since that day, Saredon had been coming back to the warehouse several times a week. He and Ursais had eaten almost nothing but dried fish for months. He had grown to hate everything about the

Northmark delicacy, but it took the edge off his hunger and kept him alive.

By memory as much as sight, Saredon made his way to a section of termite-ridden floorboards in the far corner of the warehouse. The bugs were making rapid progress, yet no one had attempted a repair. Saredon pushed the infested planks up and to the side. He hauled himself upward onto the main floor and crouched in the darkness, straining his ears to make sure he was alone. He had never encountered anyone here this early, but he would not risk being seen.

To his relief, the dark warehouse was quiet. When Saredon finally worked up his nerve, he pulled a tattered sack from his belt. He darted forward to where hundreds of fish were hanging on a line. These were the freshest, having been moved in from the sun the previous day. Saredon snatched six fish and stuffed them into his bag. In a warehouse so large, his minor theft would never be noticed.

It was funny how the weight of a few dead fish in his pack provided such comfort. That weight represented a few days of food, a few more days of survival. Clutching his precious burden, Saredon followed the familiar path out of the building. He hid the hole in the floor by carefully placing the insect-ridden boards back where he had found them. At the crack in the foundation, Saredon thrust his satchel out ahead of him as he wormed his way through the rough stone. Cuts and bruises were a cheap price to pay for a meal.

Saredon dashed across the street and into the safety of the dark alleyway. He had his prize. Now he needed to get back to the slums on the other side of the city. It would have been easier at night, yet Saredon could not bring himself to wander the dangerous parts of Northmark after the sun had gone down. He much preferred the still hours of the early morning when nothing stirred.

Fish tucked securely under one arm, Saredon jogged between the massive warehouses towards the nearest slums. Ursais had instructed him to avoid the nicer parts of town. It meant that it took Saredon longer to find his way back to their hiding place, but he did not mind. He could feel the stares of the well-dressed people when he got too close. In the slums, he was invisible.

As he left the shadow of the last warehouse, Saredon turned the corner and picked up his pace. He knew this section of town. He should be able to run for at least a quarter mile without drawing any attention to himself.

Instead of an empty street, he found a squad of the regent's own soldiers. Three robed Priestesses of Abimelech accompanied them. Shocked by the unexpected sight, Saredon stumbled to a stop. He stood and stared for a few heartbeats. His wits caught up with him before he was noticed, and he dived behind a row of barrels just as the soldiers turned in his direction.

Saredon held his breath. His heart pounded in his chest as he waited to hear the soldiers shout out that they had seen him. The cry never came. Instead, the squad moved closer to his hiding place. To Saredon's rising terror, the soldiers stopped next to the barrels he was crouched behind. He inspected the rivets on their boots between the crack next to his face.

"What a worthless assignment this is," one of the soldiers said, the voice coming from directly over Saredon's head. "Where the blazes are we even supposed to start? We're professional soldiers, not the fat constables who spend their worthless lives patrolling these slums."

A second soldier answered with a snort. "I didn't hear you voicing your opinion when the regent was giving the orders."

The first soldier did not reply.

"If the regent thinks the tenth reaver's brat is still in Northmark," we search until he says stop. We drew the short straw, so we start in the slums. Get over it. Now spread out and start kicking down doors."

"Remember, sergeant, everyone must receive Abimelech's sacrament," the feminine voice of a priestess interjected. "The sanctification of these unfortunates is just as important as your search."

"You heard the woman," the sergeant growled. "Go wake up some slum rats."

Saredon watched through the crack in the barrels as the black-armored soldiers spread out and started rousting the still sleeping denizens of the slums from their hovels. The words of the sergeant still rang in his head. They were looking for the tenth reaver's brat. They were looking for *him*.

Panic clawed at him. Saredon squeezed his eyes shut and tried to keep his breathing slow. He heard a rushing sound in his ears.

"Do you... do you sense something strange?" the priestess asked her companions, her words coming slowly as she looked up and down the empty street.

Beneath Saredon's dirty shirt, the dragon amulet felt warm against his skin. This awareness brought courage, and Saredon's thoughts cleared in an instant. He had to get out of here.

Not waiting to hear what the other priestesses said, Saredon crawled backwards as quietly as possible. There was a sewer entrance a few paces down the street that he could fit into. Saredon dropped to his belly and crawled towards the narrow opening. Without stopping to look back, he slithered headfirst into the damp darkness. It was almost as tight as the crack in the warehouse foundation. Saredon had to turn his head sideways to fit. In a desperate attempt to preserve the dried fish, he tucked the sack beneath his shirt as he fell. He winced as the heels of his feet clipped the top of the opening with a dull thunk.

Saredon landed with a splash in the filthy sewage. Foul liquid covered his face, and Saredon screwed his eyes and mouth shut. Bits and pieces of trash clung to his skin as the water dripped off him. He tried not to think about what the squishier chunks were. The fetid air was heavy with the stench of the sewer, and he held his breath until he was certain his lungs would burst. No cry of alarm sounded above. Saredon had escaped unnoticed.

Fingers seeking purchase on the slimy wall, Saredon pulled himself up. The water only came up to his ankles. He finally took a breath. Saredon gagged. One hand over his mouth and trying not to add the pathetic contents of his stomach to the city's sewage, Saredon pulled the bundle of fish from under his shirt. He smiled to find the pack still dry. The ancient stone tunnel stretched away into the shadows in both directions. Heading left would take him out of the city, so Saredon went right.

Ursais had demanded that Saredon never enter the sewers beneath Northmark's streets. The old man whispered of horrors released from the castle's dungeons, monsters that fed on not just a man's flesh, but also his soul. Saredon could not shake these dread warnings from his mind as he splashed along the dark passage. He decided that he would make his way back to the surface the first chance he got.

Soon, Saredon came across rusted iron rungs set into the stone itself. They led to a closed metal hatch in the ceiling of the sewer. Eager to be back in the sunlight, Saredon scurried up the ladder and tested the small door. It did not budge. Desperation began to creep into Saredon's stomach. He had no desire to descend back into the stinking water and search for another way out.

Determined to force the hatch open, Saredon put his back against the cold metal and braced his feet against the rungs. He heaved his slight frame upward, ignoring the pain as the pitted iron cut through his flimsy shirt. Rusted hinges squealed as the grate inched upward. Saredon gritted his teeth and pushed with all his might.

Saredon paused when he saw daylight. His body trembled with the effort of holding the sewer access open. He tossed his bundle of fish out of the hole and put his palms against the door. Summoning the last of his energy, he shoved upward until the hatch finally fell backward, carried by its own weight, to crash into the street with a terrible clang. He winced, hoping no one would come to investigate.

Once in the street, Saredon snatched up the fish and looked around. He was in a secluded alleyway. From the noises echoing off the nearby buildings, he guessed he was close to one of the open-air markets. He wondered if he should close the sewer, but one look at the open hatch chased that idea from his mind. Saredon did not think he could muster the strength to lift the metal door from the floor of the stone alley with just the tips of his fingers.

The sound of running footsteps caused Saredon to whirl around. Four children spilled into the alley from the direction of the market. They slowed when they spotted Saredon. Their clothes were just as threadbare as his, but where Saredon's garments were filthy, these kids' outfits were freshly washed. Three of them looked to be his size and age, but the fourth was a head taller and at least two years older. Obviously the leader, the bigger boy stepped out ahead of the others and made his way towards Saredon.

"See, Pickets, I told you I heard the sewer open!" one of the smaller boys said in triumph.

"Shut it," the leader snapped. "Now he knows my name, you dung brain." He stopped several paces from Saredon. His eyes darted between Saredon and the open hatch.

Saredon realized that the other boy was worried he might have friends crawling up out of the stinking tunnel.

"Only an idiot would cut in on Rames's turf without being straight with the boss," Pickets said, his words flowing fast in the common gutter slang. "And he didn't tell me nothin' 'bout newcomers, so what's that make you?"

"I-I don't know what you're talking about," Saredon said, taking a step back and trying to hide the stolen fish behind him. "I'm just trying to get back to the slums on the other side of town."

Pickets narrowed his eyes. "You don't sound like no slum rat. Are you some rich brat on the run? What's that you got behind your back?"

"It's nothing," Saredon said, wincing at how different his voice sounded. "Just some smelly old fish from the docks." He shuffled another step backward.

"Hey now, where do you think you're—" Pickets's question was cut short. Saredon turned on his toes and bolted toward the opposite end of the alley.

"Get him!" Pickets shouted.

Saredon flew across the cobblestones, his thin-soled shoes slapping against the street as he ran. The footsteps and cries of the other boys echoed off the walls of the alley all around him. Saredon turned at random, trying to lose himself in the maze of dark passages in the heart of the city.

Stamina fading fast, Saredon risked a glance over his shoulder. Pickets was right on his heels. A jolt of fear lanced through Saredon. He tried to push himself harder, but the flash of panic undid him. He tripped. Saredon went down hard, barely able to cushion his fall with his hands. He hit the rough stone and rolled. His palms and knees burned as the skin was torn away.

Saredon slid to a painful stop and rolled onto his back. His eyes filled with tears, and he sucked air into lungs that had been knocked empty. Pickets stood over him, a satisfied smirk on his face.

"You don't run if you got nothin' to hide," Pickets said, sneering down at Saredon. "The boss will sort you out. Now gimme that."

Pickets reached down and tried to snatch the bundle of wrapped fish out of Saredon's arms. Frantic to hang on to his prize, Saredon lashed out with his foot. His heel smashed into Pickets's knee. Pickets went down with a howl, and the three other boys swarmed Saredon.

Saredon curled into a ball as hard fists and shoes hammered into him. The street urchins screamed as they beat him, every blow followed by a curse or insult. Saredon squeezed his eyes shut and tried to protect the bag of fish from grabbing hands.

And then, for some reason, the abuse stopped. Saredon heard his assailants step backwards, and then an adult spoke from somewhere nearby.

"Enjoying a bit of sport, lads?" a ragged male voice asked. "Doesn't look like the fair sort to my eyes."

"What's it to you, old man?" Pickets said. "He's on our turf. He's our problem."

Pickets's words were bold, but Saredon sensed the fear behind them. Saredon opened his eyes and turned his head so he could look up at the source of the voice. He did not see much from where he lay on the street, but the man looked filthy. Dressed in tattered rags and covered in dirt, he was one of the thousands of homeless beggars that roamed Northmark. The vagabond's face was hidden in the shadows of a hood which was just a cloth sack with a hole cut in it.

"Your turf, is it?" the beggar said, shuffling forward. His words were garbled and strange as if his mouth could not form the sounds correctly. "You'd best check where you are, little man. You've wandered across the line you shouldn't cross."

For the first time since catching up to Saredon, Pickets glanced at their surroundings. He must have seen something he did not like, because he took a step back and motioned for his companions to move in closer.

"That's right," the beggar said. "I'm sure your boss told you about me. We have an understanding, he and I. Perhaps I should take your ears to remind him of it."

Pickets's face hardened. "We ain't afraid of you, old man. You ain't nothin' but a set of flapping gums. Ramses don't fear nobody and nothin'."

"He fears me," the beggar said. The man lifted his hands to his head and dragged the hood away from his face. Saredon watched in fascination along with the other four boys. Sunlight touched the man's face, revealing a twisted, broken horror. The entire right side of the beggar's head looked like it had been melted. An empty socket showed knotted flesh where an eye should have been. Saredon saw white teeth and bone through the ruined side of the man's jaw.

"L-l-let's get out of here, Pickets," one of the younger boys stammered. "We don't need no stinkin' fish anyhow."

"This isn't over, old man," Pickets spat into the street. Despite his tough words, he backed away in fear. Soon, Pickets and his three companions turned heel and ran back the way they had come. The beggar's terrible laughter filled the alleyway behind them.

When they had gone, the man turned his attention to Saredon. Saredon had struggled to his feet, and he stood trembling under the gaze of the beggar's one eye. Something about the dirty stranger seemed familiar to Saredon, but his terrified mind did not dwell on the why. The melted man stared at Saredon for a long time, and Saredon's sense of unease grew.

Finally, the man pulled the hood back up to hide his face. "Go on with you, then. They'll not be bothering you again today."

Without another glance at Saredon, the man shuffled away down the alley. Saredon watched him go, certain that the man had been about to say something else. He had lingered too long, and Saredon roused himself and crept along the alleyway in the opposite direction that Pickets had fled. His body ached, and tears spilled down Saredon's cheeks as he probed the tender spots on his body. He was certain to have some nasty bruises, but nothing seemed broken.

Fortune had been with Saredon. His mad dash through the backstreets had taken him closer to his destination. He soon found the main thoroughfare again, and he discovered that he was less than a mile from the slums where Ursais lived in hiding.

Rather than risk another run-in with the local gangs, Saredon kept to the populated paths like a good citizen. He ignored the odd looks he received, hoping that he did not turn a corner and walk straight into a squad of the regent's soldiers. Saredon breathed a sigh of relief when he reached the edge of the slums without another incident.

Chapter 6

SORRELL SAT AT A table across from Lieutenant Stone. Reserved for officers of the Coriddian Navy, the establishment was the one place in all Coridal they could enjoy a moment's peace. After yesterday's festivities, Sorrell relished the brief interlude of quiet. Tucked away in the back of the dim room, the two of them nursed their drinks. Stone was silent, still contemplating what Sorrell had told him of the mission from Viatrix.

"I don't like it," Stone finally said. "It's beneath you. Why send the navy's most prominent admiral to do the emperor's dirty work?"

She had anticipated this reaction from her trustworthy lieutenant. Stone saw her only as his admiral and captain. Sorrell had never included him in her scheming for the throne, nor revealed to him the dynamics of her family. She valued his honest, unbiased opinion of her based on her military accomplishments when everyone else saw her only as the emperor's sister.

"I know they seem far removed when out at sea, but the ties of family still bind," Sorrell said. "And the ties of my family weigh like anchor chain."

"Surely you can delegate this task," Stone said. "In fact, give it to me, and I'll have these brigands sorted within the month."

"I don't doubt that you would," Sorrell said, favoring Stone with a smile to soften her refusal. "But this is a task I must see to personally. That said, I did hope you would accompany me. One last voyage before we part ways."

Stone's face lit up. "Of course I'll sail with you, admiral! Come to think of it, chasing pirates is just the sort of vacation I need after winning the greatest naval conquest in history."

Sorrell suppressed a chuckle. From any other person, she would have taken Stone's comment as biting sarcasm. But from him, it was the honest truth. The man lived for the sea. And he was right, hunting bandits would be a welcome change of pace.

"We'll need to recruit a crew and obtain a ship," Sorrell said.

"The admiralty will give you anything you ask," Stone said. "You should have them give you the new vessel that just left the dry docks. The *Celestial.* It's like nothing I've ever seen. She's the size and crew of a sixth-rate, but with the hull of a corvette. I was just down there last night to look at it. They've developed a new material for the sails. It's so sensitive it can glean power from the moonlight on a cloudless night. Crescentweave, they're calling it."

"You know I don't like to use my influence to get special treatment."

"What influence do you mean? Oh, just the small matter of being a living hero of the Navy, the recipient of the Coriddian Rose, and the woman who defeated Admiral Finehorn in single combat? Come off it, admiral, people are going to be disappointed if you *don't* use your reputation to advance your career."

Sorrell frowned. "Don't let your drink go to your head, Mister Stone."

Stone paled, the use of the formal address for a lieutenant bringing him to his senses. "My apologies, admiral. I meant nothing by it. I was only trying to offer a suggestion."

"I'll consider it," Sorrell said, as she pushed herself away from the table. "We should be off. It's already late in the morning, and the admiralty is expecting us."

Together, the two of them made their way through the establishment towards the exit. Sorrell exchanged nods and smiles with the other officers at the surrounding tables, but the unspoken rule was that senior officers could only be addressed if they initiated the conversation. Sorrell was grateful for this, as otherwise it would have been nightfall before she had extracted herself from her navy brethren wishing to share in her glory. The entire capital was engaged in a riot of celebration that would last at least another week.

"To be honest, I'm relieved to have another mission," Stone said as they stepped into the street. "People are celebrating like there'll never be another war or conflict. Why, last night, I even heard a man saying that now we can disband the military and go back to a token peacetime force."

Sorrell snorted. "This empire was built on the backs of its soldiers. Without them, there is no Coriddia."

"You'd not think that to hear your brother talk," Stone said. He quickly corrected himself. "I'm sorry, I mean the emperor. He speaks of turning our ambitions now to art and science. That these are the rewards the might of conquest has purchased for the people of Coriddia."

"The throne answers to the senate, and my brother is not the man to defy them. Behind each senator is a host of men made wealthy by manufacture of arms and the support of soldiers. They're not soon to relinquish that source of power. Worry not, Mister Stone, you have a lengthy career in the navy ahead of you."

Stone fell silent as he contemplated Sorrell's words. They made good time as they walked through the city. The streets were empty of the normal hustle of business and commerce. At the emperor's decree, the day prior had been declared a national holiday, and everyone was sleeping off a late night of drunken revelry.

Filled with a sense of optimism she had not enjoyed in years, Sorrell relished the feel of her fresh uniform in the crisp morning air. Gone was the terrible weight of the medals on her chest and the thick, chafing fabric of her ceremonial dress kit. Today, she wore the same outfit she preferred at sea. It was the simple black and gold of an officer, without the ostentation befitting an admiral. Her face alone was proof enough of her rank.

After leaving the palace the day before, she had gone straight to her contacts in the city to inform them of the recent development. It had been a late, but profitable, night. The barons of military industry who she spoke of to Stone were no strangers to her. She had their full support in her bid for the throne, and now she had their assurance that if Viatrix was less than true to her word, they would rally behind Sorrell and subvert the senate with strong-arm tactics. However, there was no doubt that they much preferred Viatrix as a reluctant ally than a bitter enemy. Armed rebellion was a topic they danced around without ever actually suggesting it, but she had reason to believe that some of them would even go that far to see their wealth protected.

Stone wrinkled his nose as they approached the harbor. "I don't remember the air being this sour."

All around them, columns of pitch-black smoke stretched high above the rooftops, belching pollution into the sky.

"Coriddian industry never sleeps," Sorrell said.

"I think there are twice as many factories since I was last here," Stone said. "And that was only a few months ago."

"The supply of goods must keep pace with our expanding borders. Every territory we take under our protection brings with it fresh lines of supply, additional demands for resources, and a new market of customers."

"If you dwell on that thought, the navy almost seems like an arm of commerce for the empire."

"You're not far off the mark. We conquered Linstall for no other reason than there was money to be made."

Stone frowned. "You know I don't share your cynicism, admiral. There are many advantages for those who come under the empire's influence."

"I don't mean to discount your patriotic fervor, lieutenant," Sorrell said. "And you're right, those who fly our colors enjoy many privileges they would otherwise be denied. But don't let this cloud your vision regarding the impetus behind our conquests."

Sorrell stopped and raised her hand to gesture at the smokestacks spilling their waste into the air. "Look around you. We've become a system that exists to perpetuate itself. Which drives us, the need for tools to fight the war, or the need for war so we can make more tools?"

"That's the party line of those who would strip the military of its power," Stone said. "I didn't think to count you among them."

"And you shouldn't," Sorrell said, softening her tone. "But politics is the same as warfare. We need to understand our opponents to be able to combat them. I have a vision that will set us back on the path of glory. For too long, the men and women of valor who made us great have been at the mercy of those who hold the purse strings. I intend to correct this imbalance. There's a reason you'll not find statues of merchants on the Promenade of Victory."

Stone gave her a strange look that made Sorrell feel uncomfortable. She had never before come so close to revealing her true ambitions to her faithful lieutenant.

"Enough of this dour talk," Sorrell said, a little too forcefully. "On this day of all days, we should be celebrating with the rest of this magnificent city. After all, it's our exploits they drink to! Come, the admiralty building is just ahead. Let's attend to the business at hand and then find another navy tavern."

The thoughtful expression did not leave Stone's face, but he fell into step beside her. Sorrell cursed herself. At sea, life was simple. Here in the city, it was much harder to keep her roles separate and distinct. The last thing she wanted was to turn Stone into yet another sycophant to her heritage. Sorrell knew her life was about to undergo drastic and explosive change, but she hoped that her legacy in the navy would remain untarnished.

If Stone wanted to speak, he lost his chance when they entered the hustle and bustle of the harbor. The docks were crawling with stevedores and carpenters. Every berth was full, and the rest of the Coriddian fleet floated in the bay. With Linstall defeated, only a token force patrolled the seaways. For the next several months, the fleet would be operating at a third of its usual strength while the great ships-of-the-line were treated to some much-needed retrofitting and maintenance.

The *Indomitable* herself floated at the end of one of the long piers. Her massive guns were being slowly unloaded by crane in preparation for treating and cleaning the wood of the gun decks. A few of her golden sails still hung ragged, sunlight shining through the holes earned in the last battle. Sorrell felt a twinge of sadness when she looked at the glorious ship. Whatever happened in the next few weeks, that part of her career was over.

Its shadow almost touching the *Indomitable,* the admiralty building dominated the harbor, dwarfing even the mighty ship. Five stories high and running the length of the docks, it presided over the fleet, a physical manifestation of the navy's authority.

Sorrell had always found the structure distasteful. To her, the magnificence of the navy lay in its traditions and history. That was the glue that held a crew together. A ship and its crew had little need for ostentation. In stark contrast to this, the royal architect who designed the admiralty building had produced a palace fit for a despot.

On the harbor side, the building gleamed with a solid wall of stained-glass windows. Suspended in translucent color, the supposed greatest heroes of the Coriddian Navy looked out towards the sea. Every surface that wasn't glass shone with gold, the overlaid wood carved in intricate patterns.

Perhaps, Sorrell thought to herself as they approached, she would not have minded the gaudy display if the men portrayed in the glass merited the honor. But they did not. To have one's visage grace the opulent facade had become a matter of political influence or personal power. The faces changed as often as the tide, and even now, scaffolding on the far side of the docks indicated that someone new had paid enough bribes to have their likeness added to the scene at the expense of someone with shallower pockets.

"You'll be the first woman up there," Stone said with a nod towards the stained glass, breaking his silence as they entered the shadow of the admiralty building.

"I used to think that would mean something," Sorrell said. She did not give Stone the opportunity to respond. Without breaking stride, she pushed through the double doors, stepping into the lavish interior beyond.

Sorrell's boots were loud on the polished wood floor of the common area. She swept her hat from her head and tucked it beneath her arm. The junior lieutenant who had been drowsing behind the front desk nearly fell out of his chair when he glanced up.

"Admiral Sorrell!" the lieutenant almost shouted as he leaped to his feet in salute.

"Stand down," Sorrell said, returning the salute. "We're here to see the Lord Admiral. Is he in?"

"Yes, ma'am," the lieutenant said, his voice still too loud. "He's expecting you."

"Thank you, lieutenant. Carry on."

"Aye, aye, ma'am." Despite his acknowledgement of Sorrell's order, he remained standing as she and Stone moved towards the stairs.

"I suppose I shouldn't be surprised that word of our mission has preceded us," Sorrell said as they started their climb. "Although, I wish my mother had let me be the one to brief the Lord Admiral."

On a typical day, the place was a swarm of hectic activity. But at each landing, Sorrell glanced into the open work areas to find only empty desks and quiet. Apparently, the officers of the navy had joined the citizens of Coridal in their drunken festivities the night before. The Lord Admiral's office was on the highest level of the admiralty building. After five flights of stairs, even Stone was breathing hard when they reached the top.

Lord Admiral Corstan's office door was open, and Sorrell heard voices within. She paused, surprised that someone else had business with Corstan on this day. Corstan sounded annoyed. At the sound of the second voice, anger surged in Sorrell's chest. She knew that voice.

Sorrell stepped into the office. Lord Admiral Corstan, gone fat in his decadence, sat behind a desk that matched his bulk. Taken together, the pair would have sunk a small ship. A bushy gray mustache drooped below his cruel blue eyes. Those eyes jerked to Sorrell when she appeared and held her in a gaze that felt like cold iron shackles.

Across from Corstan's desk, reclined in a chair as if he did not have a care in the world, sat Mazareem, Viatrix's detestable agent.

"Admiral, at last you have appeared!" Corstan thundered. "This is highly unprecedented! I was roused from my bed at the arse-crack of dawn and ordered, *ordered* I tell you, to present myself in my office post-haste."

Frowning, she stepped to stand in front of Corstan's desk. Sorrell noted his disheveled state and bloodshot eyes. Mazareem gave her a bemused smile, which she ignored.

"My apologies, Lord Admiral," Sorrell said with a slight incline of her head. "I was not informed of this rude treatment."

"And this—this—*man*, demands that I do as he asks," Corstan said, spittle flying from his lips. He waved an irate hand in Mazareem's direction. "He says he speaks for the emperor and has a writ to prove it. Tell me, admiral, what do you know of this?"

Of all the people in the navy, Corstan was the one man Sorrell had spent her entire career trying to avoid. He perceived her as a threat to his authority, interpreting any hint of her family's influence as the intent to usurp his position of power.

Sorrell found the man's petty fear wearisome, and she considered briefly if now was the time to bring to bear the full weight of her imperial heritage. But she resisted the urge. Better to placate him for a while longer, better to wait until all the pieces were in place. Then there would be a reckoning for old Corstan.

Her gaze moved briefly to the colored glass behind Corstan's head. It was no mistake that a much younger Lord Admiral Corstan peered down at them from the window. The man was so vain that he had commissioned his likeness to stare into his own office. She decided that she would personally smash this part of the gaudy facade when she took complete control.

"I know nothing of this man," Sorrell said, gesturing towards Mazareem. "His business is his own, and I've no wish to intrude on it. However, I'm on a mission from the emperor himself, and I need your immediate assistance. So I must ask that he wait outside until our business is concluded."

"Ah, about that," Mazareem said, his quiet voice a marked contrast to Corstan's bombast. "It's best if I stay, I think."

Annoyed at having to address the man directly, Sorrell turned to Mazareem, and in her best admiral's voice she said, "Whatever influence you may enjoy in my mother's presence doesn't extend beyond the walls of the palace. Out here, you're subject to both the laws and regulations of the navy and my imperial authority. Leave this room. Now."

A slow smile spread across Mazareem's face. He made no move to comply. "Perhaps you'd best read yonder writ," he said, indicating a piece of paper on Corstan's desk.

Only with significant effort did Sorrell hold her rising fury in check. The man's impudence was abominable. Sorrell moved to the desk and looked down at the writ. She read it once, twice, three times, refusing to believe what it said.

Head spinning, Sorrell looked up into Corstan's grinning face. The fat pig could see that she was upset, and anything that bothered Sorrell pleased him.

"So you already know everything I'm going to ask," Sorrell said.

"It's all spelled out in the writ," Corstan said. His mood had improved remarkably after Sorrell's exchange with Mazareem.

Sorrell glanced at Stone, who looked in equal parts confused, concerned, and resolute. She smiled inwardly, thanking her patron deity for Stone while at the same time letting her rage fuel her next words.

"I want the *Celestial*," Sorrell said.

It took Corstan a moment to process her demand, after which he started sputtering. "Absolutely not! That ship is the navy's prize possession, not even yet commissioned on her maiden voyage. You forget yourself, admiral. You may be the emperor's sister, but this is *my* navy."

In response, Sorrell picked up the writ off the desk and began to read it out loud. "The possessor of this writ may request all resources, funds, and manpower to be placed at their disposal as if the emperor himself were making the request."

Sorrell lowered the paper and looked at Corstan. No one spoke. Corstan spluttered as his ire compounded upon itself. Unable to get a word out in his fit of indignation, the Lord Admiral's face turned as red as one of the bright panes of glass behind him. A single bulging vein on his forehead pulsed in time with his furiously beating heart.

"This mission is of great personal import to the emperor," Mazareem said mildly. "I'm sure he would be pleased to learn that the navy's best and fastest ship has been assigned to the task."

"Fine!" Corstan shouted, exploding like a boiling tea kettle. He surged to his feet, one arm extended, rigid finger pointing at the door. "Now take your forsaken writ and get out of my office. Might I suggest a visit to the privy next, where you can shove it up your pretty little royal arse."

Stone coughed and looked ready to speak.

"Come, lieutenant," Sorrell said before Stone could say anything. "We have a crew to recruit." Stone in tow, Sorrell stormed from the room without another look at Corstan or Mazareem.

Sorrell plunged down the stairs, trying to bring the building down with every step. Displaying a wisdom beyond his years, Stone kept his silence until they were outside the building.

"Pardon, admiral, but what was in the writ that has you so angry?" Stone finally asked.

"That man in the office, that was one of my mother's agents," Sorrell said. "His name is Mazareem. The language of the writ gives him ultimate authority over our mission."

Stone shook his head in consternation. "Politics and sailing don't mix. At least we'll soon be free of him."

"On that count, you'd be wrong," Sorrell said, making no effort to disguise the anger in her voice. "He's coming with us."

Chapter 7

LACRAEL SAT ALONE WITH Brant in the galley of the *Golden Dawn*. Neither of them spoke. The last few months had been a terrible struggle for the former merchant. He battled every night with the demon inside him, and upon waking, was almost completely consumed by the horrors of his nightmares. Lacrael sat with him every morning to offer what comfort she could.

To Lacrael's continued frustration, the crew of the ship avoided Brant as much as possible. Kaiser wanted to leave him on a deserted island, arguing that the monster inside Brant posed too great a risk to their mission. While Gustavus did not openly support Kaiser's extreme suggestion, Lacrael knew the ship's captain was not happy with Brant's presence. The only reason he was allowed to remain on board was because she demanded it.

She felt responsible for Brant's fate. Without Lacrael's interference, Brant would still be enjoying the simple life of a shopkeeper in his hometown of Oakroot. Thanks to her meddling, she had destroyed both the town and any hope Brant had of ever returning to that life. None of them knew what Mazareem had done to Brant in the Wraith Wood, but they had all experienced firsthand the awesome destructive power Brant possessed when not under the protection of the dragon amulet that hung from his neck.

Brant's once honest and open face was now marred by a perpetual scowl. He looked as if he was in constant pain. His hair hung long and ragged. Gone was his soft midsection, replaced by the hard muscle of strenuous work and lean diet. Brant was a giant of a man, but he walked with a stoop that made him seem small. The burden he carried weighed more than any physical strength could bear. In the rare instances when he did speak, his words were clipped and his statements short. Lacrael was the only person he would look in the eye.

There was no denying they had once shared a mutual attraction for each other. And they had grown closer during their time on the ship, but Lacrael had no idea what their relationship was now or if Brant would ever be whole again. Sometimes, in the quiet hours of the night, her thoughts drifted to how her fate could have been different. Her most pleasant daydream was a life of simple pleasures with Brant as her companion, away from all this insanity. These daydreams made her feel guilty.

The ship rocked gently back and forth, rattling the pots and pans that hung on the galley wall. Brant had not moved for at least half an hour, and despite her compassion for his plight, Lacrael's patience was wearing thin.

"I'm sorry last night was bad," Lacrael said. "You know if there's anything I could do to help, I would."

Head in his hands, crouched over the long table, Brant did not respond.

Disappointed, Lacrael got to her feet. She lingered at Brant's shoulder, hand resting on his back. He tensed under her touch, but he did not flinch away or snap at her. That, at least, was progress.

"I'm going above," Lacrael said. "If you need anything, you know where to find me."

She waited a moment to see if he would speak. He did not, and Lacrael left the galley in frustration. If this morning followed the usual pattern, Brant would wallow in his misery for a while longer before starting the day. When he had shaken off the terrors of the night, he was a reliable worker, a match for the *Golden Dawn*'s most experienced sailors. He threw himself into any task, grateful for the distraction.

Once on the deck of the ship, Lacrael moved to the starboard rail. Dawn's first light was creeping over the eastern horizon. She had been at sea for six months now, but the sight of the morning sunrise never failed to take her breath away. The ocean magnified the brilliance of the sun, transforming the waves into liquid gold. She was a child of desert wasteland. To her foreign imagination, the sea held a mystery and wonder that she hoped to never dispel.

"Now *that's* a golden dawn," a deep voice said behind her. Gustavus stepped up and joined her at the rail. Lacrael was a muscular woman, but the captain's prodigious bulk made her feel small. His mane of yellow hair was a stark contrast to Lacrael's black curls.

Lacrael turned and leaned her backside against the railing. Above their heads, the golden sails of the ship shimmered and gleamed in the morning light.

"The name fits the ship," Lacrael said.

Gustavus snorted. "It's supposed to be a metaphor. The golden dawn comes with the High King's return. But I like your interpretation better."

The captain bent over at the waist, resting his massive forearms on the handrail as he stared out over the water. "How's our tormented refugee?"

Lacrael frowned. "He's just as much a member of this crew as I am."

Gustavus waved a dismissive hand. "Don't you fret. I'm not going to dump him on a raft and leave him to rot."

"Every night is a struggle for him," Lacrael said. "He doesn't talk much about it, but I think darkness and solitude brings out the demon inside him."

"How can you be certain that Kaiser's wrong? How do you know Brant won't kill us all in our sleep?"

"Is the potential for violence enough to condemn a man?" Lacrael said angrily, the ready response fast on her lips. "Brant works hard and fights hard. If our cause is just, then Brant is our responsibility, because he suffers as a consequence of the High King's design."

"Peace, woman," Gustavus said. "It was only a question. Kaiser can be damned persuasive, as you well know."

Lacrael swallowed her anger. "I know. He's angry at the world right now. Brant's just an easy target. You and I chose to join the fight against Abimelech, but neither of them wanted this. Sometimes I worry that, despite everything they've been through, they'd still choose to go back to their old lives if they could."

"That ship has long sailed," Gustavus said. "And the sooner they come to terms with that, the better it will go for everyone. Maybe a visit to a tropical island will do them some good. We'll reach Spider's Cover in a day or two. With the war over, I've some business to attend to. A break from smuggling should provide everyone some much needed rest and relaxation."

"And now, if you'll pardon me, I've got to make sure we're still on course," Gustavus said, moving away from her.

Lacrael watched him go, frustrated by the man's confidence. He seemed to think himself the hero in his own legend. Whatever came next, Lacrael felt in her gut that it would not be a tropical vacation.

Chapter 8

MAZAREEM WATCHED THE MORNING sunlight blaze across the eastern sky. Beneath his feet, the prow of the *Celestial* cut through the sea with the effortless ease of a honed blade. Cold ocean spray sprinkled his face. Mazareem grinned. He could get used to this again.

The only stain on his pleasant mood was that Worm was not at his side. He had been forced to hide the hound in the basement of a deserted building on the outskirts of Coridal. Worm slept the sleep of the dead. Worm would wake at Mazareem's command or not at all.

He turned to observe the crew change shifts. Fresh from their hammocks below, the daytime sailors replaced the night watch. Sorrell and Stone had been true to their word, producing a list of ready volunteers in less than a day. Mazareem had scrutinized the process, curious to see if any of Abimelech's dragon spawn would try to infiltrate the hastily assembled crew. Their illusory magic made the two-legged lizards almost impossible to detect, but Mazareem knew how to identify them. He had seen none of the telltale signs of his master's minions in human disguise. Apparently, Viatrix trusted him to complete this task alone. He smiled to himself. What would Sorrell say, if she knew the true nature of her "mother?"

It had taken another day to ready the ship. Fortune was with them, as the *Celestial* had already been prepped for her maiden voyage. On the third day, they set sail. Everything was going according to plan. Now, all Mazareem had to do was find the *Golden Dawn*.

The crew of the *Celestial* avoided him as they moved about the deck. Sorrell made no effort to hide her displeasure at his presence, and in all things, her sailors mirrored the attitude of their captain. No matter. Mazareem was content to play this role for the time being. As long as Sorrell believed he was only an agent of her mother's, she was easier to manipulate. With that thought, Mazareem steered his path towards the captain's cabin. He had given Sorrell a day at sea to calm herself. Now, it was time to apply a little pressure.

Mazareem strode across the deck with the gait of a veteran sailor. He had earned his sea legs hundreds of years ago. There was no ocean he had not explored, in this realm or any other. He had to admit, the *Celestial* was a magnificent vessel. No expense had been spared. Above his head, the crescentweave sails flashed in the sunlight, shifting between pearlescent white and platinum silver as they rippled in the wind. Gold filigree covered every surface, and beneath that, a warm orange wood glowed with polish. While the ship was outfitted with the empire's best experimental guns, this was no warship. It was a statement of superiority and imperial wealth.

Abimelech could learn something from this realm's mastery of technology and magic. While the power of Mazareem's master was without question, his methods were antiquated. One of Abimelech's greatest failings was that he construed any human advancement as a threat. Free of the dragon tyrant's direct influence, science was flourishing in Praxis. The sails, in particular, were of great curiosity to Mazareem. He had never seen their like. He made a mental note to study them at the first opportunity. How they managed to propel the ship by the power of the sun in the absence of any wind fascinated him.

Sorrell and Stone were in quiet discussion in her cabin when Mazareem interrupted them with his abrupt entrance. They moved away from each other a little too quickly. Only a blind man could miss the romantic tension between the two, and Mazareem wondered if there was a way to exploit it.

"You've no right to enter this cabin without a summons," Sorrell said when she regained her composure. "Whatever your writ says, your authority is superseded by mine as captain of this ship while we're at sea."

"Forgive me, *captain*," Mazareem said with his best smile. He knew it gave him the look of a grinning skull, and he was rewarded with a grimace on Stone's face. Sorrell only frowned. He continued, "But we've been sailing for a day now, and it's time to discuss our destination."

"That's not a matter open for discussion," Sorrell said. "Lieutenant Stone and I have charted a course that will serve our purposes. Now if there's nothing else, you may leave."

"I'm afraid I'll need to see this course mapped out," Mazareem said, nodding towards the navigation table. "You understand, of course, that as soon as we return to Coridal I must give a full report. I'd never wish to challenge your authority as captain, but I have superiors I must answer to."

Stone stepped forward with his chest puffed out. "Now see here. The captain has given you a direct order. Insolence towards an officer of the Imperial Navy while at sea is a capital offense. You may turn around and leave of your own power or be dragged out and thrown into the brig."

Mazareem said nothing, content to wait while Sorrell contemplated his request.

Finally, she said, "Stand down, Mister Stone. It will do no harm for him to view our charted course."

"I applaud your wisdom and tact," Mazareem said, inclining his head towards Sorrell and favoring her with another smile.

Stone glowered at him. "You'd best watch yourself. I'll not suffer impudence on this ship."

"I said stand down," Sorrell repeated. "There's no need for that."

A spark of anger ignited in Mazareem's black soul. The man's obstinance combined with his adoration of Sorrell were grating. Briefly, Mazareem imagined tearing Stone's tongue out and showing it to him. But he forced such thoughts aside. Work must come before pleasure.

In two long strides, Mazareem reached the map table. He traced the charted course down the coast towards Linstall, making note of each destination as indicated by little colored pins.

"It's obvious you know what we're about," Mazareem said after a moment's contemplation. "However, you do appear to have missed one key port. I'm not surprised, as it doesn't appear on most maps."

"Between the two of us, we've sailed every sea, coastline, inlet, and bay this side of the world," Sorrell said, gesturing towards Stone. "Don't insult us. We missed nothing."

"Perish the thought. No insult is intended. But you view the world with a military mind. There are others of... less repute who don't share your zeal for conquest. This requires them to seek sanctuary away from your ever vigilant and expanding influence."

To punctuate his words, Mazareem placed a finger on the map, indicating a small chain of islands two days off the coast of Linstall. "It's only a small detour from the charted course to visit here, and we'd be remiss to ignore it."

"There's nothing there!" Stone said when he leaned over to view where Mazareem was pointing. "Those islands don't even have a name, which means they're uninhabited."

"That's because people pay good money to keep them hidden," Mazareem said.

"Don't be absurd," Stone said. "How could you hide a port in plain sight, this day and age?"

"No, he's right," Sorrell said, raising a hand to interrupt Stone. "I can't believe I forgot. There's a small smugglers town there. The navy turned a blind eye to it during the war, but maybe it's time we paid them a visit."

"Does it have a name?" Stone asked, accepting Sorrell's judgment without question.

"Spider's Cove."

Chapter 9

SORRELL SPENT THE REST of the day trying to work off her frustration and anger from the morning encounter with Mazareem. Her anger she understood, but her frustration stemmed from what the abhorrent man had interrupted. She was certain that Stone had been heartbeats away from kissing her, and she had been able to think about nothing else since then.

The barriers she had erected between the two of them seemed pointless now. And in light of the changes that would occur when they returned to Coridal, what risk was there in enjoying a pleasurable dalliance with her handsome lieutenant? He obviously wanted her. He always had. She was certainly no longer doing anything to dissuade his advances. It had gone unspoken between them so far, but they both knew this was probably the last chance for something to happen.

"Damnation," Sorrell said under her breath.

She stood alone in her cabin, but Stone's presence lingered. It took every bit of willpower Sorrell possessed to not think up some meaningless reason to request he visit her tonight. Instead, she forced herself to snuff the lamp and climb into her bed.

Fortunately, Sorrell was exhausted. Her hard work during the day had paid off, and she was soon asleep. However, she started to dream the instant slumber took her. She perceived no dividing line between waking and dreaming. One instant she was thinking about Stone, the next she was in another world.

In her dream, Sorrell stood on a vast and empty plain. It was a strange dream. She felt as if she were awake. A weak sun hung overhead, its silver, anemic light offering no warmth. The grass at her feet was the color of bone instead of a vibrant green, and as she looked around, she realized that there were no colors, only various shades of gray. Sorrell turned, scanning the horizons of her dream. As far as the eye could see, there was nothing. No undulation of hills, no canopy of trees, nothing to break the terrible monotony.

Forlorn, desolate, the place whispered echoes of fear and sorrow. Sorrell sensed there was something of great import here she should understand, but the meaning eluded her. The sensation of ruin slowly built in her soul, a creeping dread from which she could not flee. There was nowhere to hide on this desolate flatland.

"What a strange dream," Sorrell said to herself. To her surprise, she heard her own voice as if she spoke out loud.

Seemingly triggered by the sound of her words, another noise followed soon after. It started very faint, and Sorrell held her breath as she tried to identify its source. Indistinct in the distance, the sound grew slowly, building from a low rumble into the unmistakable staccato of falling hoofbeats.

Sorrell whirled, trying to find the direction from which the rider approached. Finally, after much frantic searching, she spied a horseman on the western skyline. From the silhouette, she identified the heavy armor of some ancient knight. Irrational terror overwhelmed her—she panicked. Sorrell turned and ran.

Beneath her feet, the lifeless grass flew by, but Sorrell did not seem to move from her spot. In that terrible way of nightmares, no matter how hard she struggled, she could gain no ground. Yet the rider moved no closer. A grave intuition, thrust upon her by the dream, screamed at Sorrell that the rider sought her. That intuition told her she could not run, could not hide, could do nothing to thwart the inevitable approach of the strange knight.

After what seemed like an eternity of horrible struggle, Sorrell's dream self had nothing left to give. She stumbled and fell, too spent to take another step. Silence filled the dream plain when she stopped moving. Sorrell rolled over and looked in the direction of the rider. He still sat on his horse, having come no closer. He watched her, and she recoiled from his gaze. She tried to wonder at this, but in another heartbeat, she slipped into a dreamless sleep.

Chapter 10

SORRELL WOKE THE NEXT morning filled with a sense of foreboding. Her nightmare clung to her, as did the feeling of isolation it brought with it. For no reason that Sorrell understood, her heart was heavy with sadness.

The dream was her first thought when she opened her eyes; her second was Stone. Sorrell's heart sank. She had gone to sleep consumed with romantic fantasies of her handsome lieutenant, but now, the courage and desire to face him again had fled. An uncharacteristic melancholy gripped her, and the last thing she wanted right now was to deal with Stone's advances.

Frustrated, Sorrell rose from bed and dressed quickly. An idea began to form in the back of her mind, and she chose a simple work uniform, free of any mark of rank or office. Hard labor would chase away her downcast mood, and it was high time she inspected the ship anyway. Satisfied with this plan, Sorrell strode from her room into the stillness of the early morning.

Outside her cabin, the dawn horizon was turning gray, but the sun had not yet risen. The officer of the night watch noticed her appearance and attended Sorrell immediately. He was a young man, a lieutenant several years subordinate to Stone. To her chagrin,

Sorrell did not remember his name. She took this as yet another indicator that she had been lax in familiarizing herself with her new command.

"A fine morning to you, admiral," the lieutenant said cheerfully.

"And you as well," Sorrell said, doing her best to not let her somber mood show. "Anything to report from the night watch?"

"No, ma'am. We made good time and encountered no difficulty. This ship could almost sail itself."

"Thank you, lieutenant."

The young man beamed at her. Sorrell felt her annoyance rising at his pleasant mood.

"I know the watch schedule is set for the next week, but I'd like to make a change to it," Sorrell said.

"Of course, admiral," the lieutenant said. "What are your orders?"

"I want Lieutenant Stone to take today's watch. It's short notice, but he's fit for the task."

"Aye, aye, ma'am. I'll inform him at once."

Sorrell winced as the lieutenant turned on his heel to go find Stone. She knew how Stone would take her orders, and he would not be wrong. This would keep him out of her hair while she went belowdecks. She could not delay their meeting again for long, but she needed time to think and clear her head.

Eager to get below, Sorrell began her descent into the bowels of the ship. The junior lieutenant had not been wrong. A ship like the *Celestial* could easily sail with less than a third of the crew they now carried. It was not designed to be a military ship, and the confines were cramped with the contingent of marines Sorrell insisted on bringing. Admiral Corstan had tried to block her from taking a squad of marines, but she anticipated boarding action. She would not hunt a fugitive ship without the means to force it to surrender.

Resolved to go over every inch of the vessel, Sorrell decided to start in the hold. This early in the morning, the ship was quiet. The change of the watch would not signal for another hour, and belowdecks, only the cooks in the galley were up and about. They were preparing a meal for the day watch, who would break their fast before taking over for the night crew. Sorrell reached the secured door of the cargo hold without encountering anyone.

The guard gave her a salute, but he did not question her presence. At her prompting, he unbolted the door and swung it aside. Sorrell removed a small, unlit lantern from the wall and turned the nob to feed the wick into the oil. She ignited a match using the flame from a wall mounted lamp and carefully eased it into the glass casing of the one she carried. It took a moment, but she finally got the wick burning brightly. Lantern in hand, Sorrell gave the man a nod and stepped inside.

Despite the brightly burning light in her hand, Sorrell could not see very far into the crowded hold. A narrow aisle split the piles of crates and barrels on both sides. Squeezing her way between the stacked cargo, Sorrell fought down a rising sensation of claustrophobia. The towers of wooden boxes were tied down, but she still imagined a sudden shift that would crush her under a mountain of supplies. Compared to the cavernous bellies of the ships-of-the-line, the *Celestial*'s cargo hold seemed cramped. Here, the sacrifices made to achieve the aggressive lines of the hull were most obvious.

The *Celestial* had been built for speed. Where a larger ship was prone to wallow in the sea, slowed down by armor plating and the need for storage capacity, the *Celestial* was designed to cut through the water. Even with the hold crammed full of food and equipment, they only had enough provisions to sail for two weeks without needing to resupply. To Sorrell, this limitation seemed terribly restricting, but she hoped the speed would compensate for the loss of range.

Although the ship was fresh out of dry dock, Sorrell still took painstaking care to inspect the hold for signs of leakage or rot. It was a matter of discipline, but it also provided the distraction she needed. She clambered up and over the cargo as she searched, performing the task of a lowly midshipman.

While she worked, Sorrell allowed her thoughts to turn to Stone. He was easier to ponder than the dream. Hard labor sharpened her mind, turning insurmountable problems into mere challenges to which she needed to find a solution. It was pointless to try and deny her affection for Stone. The man was stunningly attractive, loyal, and embodied all the traits she held most dear. He loved the navy and the empire more than his own life. And she suspected that he harbored a similar love for her. So why did she avoid him, even now?

At first, Sorrell thought it was simply the difficulty in lowering her resistance to his romantic advances. After all, she had been parrying his amorous thrusts for years. But as she contemplated this, she concluded her hesitancy went deeper than that. Sorrell was no stranger to the arts of love, even though it had been many long years since she had enjoyed the company of a man, but as she reflected on those experiences of the distant past, she started to understand why the prospect of embracing Stone made her uncomfortable.

Sorrell wanted to earn everything she achieved. As sister to the emperor, life could have been delivered to her on a silver platter. Anything she wanted was hers for the asking. This had driven her to the navy, and it compelled her to win the approval of men who despised her for who she was. Because when not even they could deny her accomplishments, Sorrell would know that her legacy was her own, and not the mere reflection of the imperial family's glory.

Dear, trustworthy Lieutenant Stone had always been her anchor in her navy career. He had been the youngest lieutenant on her first command, and he followed her to every ship after that. Sorrell believed that his respect for her was genuine, and that she had earned his ardent loyalty as his captain and admiral, but when she got to the root of the matter, she found that she did not trust his love. In the back of her mind, she feared that Stone only followed her because of her royal blood. In some ways, Sorrell realized, she would never be able to escape the reality of being the emperor's kin.

In moments of weakness, she considered bringing Stone into her inner circle. If he became her confederate in seeking the throne, perhaps then she might risk a romance. But she had never been able to bring herself to test his loyalty. He believed her to be the empire's champion. Sorrell did not want to shatter his perception of her by revealing to him how she conspired against her brother. He would learn soon enough, but by then, he would be captain on his own ship and far away.

Finally, covered in sweat and dust, and breathing hard, Sorrell reached the far end of the hold. She had to admit that the hull of the cargo hold was sound. She grinned at her silly admission. Of course it was sound, it was a brand-new ship. But while she worked, her misgivings about Stone had quieted, and the gloom brought on by her nighttime visions was receding. When the time came, she was ready to face Stone. She hoped to forget the dream.

Sorrell emerged from the hold to find that the guard had changed. Judging by the almost empty lamp she carried, her inspection had lasted several hours. The new guard was not surprised to see her. He set about securing the door as Sorrell brushed the worst of the grime off her uniform. Now that she had worked off her frustrations, Sorrell realized she was famished.

"Do you have the time, sailor?" Sorrell asked the guard.

"The midshipmen were just released to breakfast, ma'am," the guard said.

"My thanks," Sorrell said with a nod.

Tasked with morning chores while the others ate, and as a matter of decorum, the youngest officers of the ship were required to break their fast later than the rest of the crew. It was a benefit of rank and a sign of maturity to share the first meal with the veteran sailors and officers. This suited Sorrell. She had not yet introduced herself personally to the midshipmen. It was rather unorthodox for her to join them in the galley, but what was the point of being an admiral if you could not bend the rules a little?

Amused by that thought, Sorrell began her climb from the lowest deck of the ship up to the kitchen. She was excited to meet her midshipmen. This would be a brief voyage, but it would also be a prestigious one which would set up her crew for advancement in their careers. To make the most of this rare opportunity, Sorrell had gone out of her way to find female officer volunteers. There were precious few in the navy, and she wanted to give them the best opportunity to succeed. She knew from personal experience how hard it was for a woman to make lieutenant.

Conversation stopped when she stepped into the galley. A few sailors were eating late, and the midshipmen were seated around a small table on the side of the room. They all stared at her in surprise, food forgotten.

"Carry on," Sorrell said, gesturing that everyone should return to their meals.

The sailors mumbled, "Aye, aye," and resumed shoveling gruel into their mouths.

But the midshipmen remained frozen in shock. Ignoring their incredulous scrutiny, Sorrell collected a shallow metal plate and filled it with the morning hash. After grabbing a utensil, she made her way over to the midshipman's table.

When it became clear that Sorrell was going to join them, the midshipman clambered to make room for her. Sorrell frowned slightly. Two of the six were missing. In particular, Kayta, a young woman Sorrell had high hopes for, was not there.

"I do seem to recall that regulations require the midshipmen to eat together," Sorrell said as she took a seat. "Who wants to recite that section?"

In near perfect synchronization, the midshipmen squirmed in their seats. Sorrell's foul mood threatened to return. She understood that she was their captain and admiral, but these youngsters appeared too afraid to even respond to a direct order.

"Ma'am, we're dreadfully sorry—," a young man began, but he stumbled to a stop, his eyes going wide as someone new entered the galley. The rest of the midshipmen followed his gaze.

Mazareem had come to break his fast. Sorrell started to regret her decision. Better to eat in the officer's mess and avoid this sort of confusion.

To Sorrell's complete surprise, one of the midshipmen shot to his feet and made to run for the door. This blatant lack of respect turned her annoyance to anger.

"You will *sit down*, midshipman!" she said.

"But, but, captain, I mean admiral—ma'am!" the young man pleaded, a look of horror growing on his face.

"I said sit down!" Sorrell repeated it, her voice no louder, but the iron in it unmistakable.

Defeated, the midshipman slumped back into his seat.

"By the abyss, what's going on here?" Sorrell said, placing both hands on the table. "I've seen better behavior on a trash barge! Did you think this was a pleasure cruise?"

Again, no one volunteered an answer. The fear on their youthful faces was palpable. That did it. Sorrell would have every last one of these whelps up before Mister Stone. She was about to say exactly that when someone else entered the room.

Kayta and the other missing midshipmen had arrived. Sorrell decided to hold her peace until they joined her at the table. They had not noticed her yet and so were in for quite the surprise. She would dress down the lot of them at the same time.

But as Kayta and the other midshipman moved towards the serving line, they diverted their path towards where Mazareem sat. Sorrell watched, incredulous, as Kayta's partner in crime distracted Mazareem with a hand on the shoulder. The pale man looked up at the interruption. Behind Mazareem's back, Kayta slipped a lit firecracker into the gruel on his plate.

It happened so fast, and Sorrell was so shocked, that she did not think to cry out. Snickering, the two midshipmen stepped quickly away from Mazareem. Ignorant of the prank just played on him, Mazareem turned back to his food. Which promptly exploded in his face.

Sailors swore as they leapt up and away from the table. Kayta started laughing at Mazareem's distress. Mazareem sat stone still, the remains of his breakfast dripping off his bone white face.

"That was a mistake," Mazareem said, unfolding himself from his seat. He took a menacing step towards Kayta, and Sorrell had seen enough.

"Stop this madness!" Sorrell said as she jumped to her feet. Her voice echoed louder than the firework. "I saw the entire thing. I'll deal with this."

Mazareem paused and looked at Sorrell. His eyes snatched the next words from her mouth. Up to this point, she had perceived the man a spineless agent of her mother. But his glare punctured her like a stabbing blade. He blinked, and his placid stare returned. Sorrell shuddered. Had she only imagined the evil in his gaze?

"See that you do," Mazareem said. "I'd hate for my official report to include an indictment against your ability to instill proper discipline in your officers."

Sorrell ignored the barb. This time, it was justified. Mazareem wiped his face off, and with three long strides, disappeared through the door of the galley.

Now she understood the midshipman's fear. Sorrell's unexpected appearance had interrupted their prank. Kayta stood rooted in place, all the blood drained from her face. Behind Sorrell, the other midshipman did not move, did not speak, did not even breathe. Perhaps they hoped she would ignore them and punish the two perpetrators instead.

"All of you, against the bulkhead, *now!*" Sorrell said.

The six midshipmen jumped to obey. Utensils fell to the floor in the mad scramble to assemble themselves against the wall. While they fell over themselves to comply with her order, Sorrell did her best to bring her anger under control. As admiral and captain of this ship, she dare not be the one to mete out the punishment, or she would imperil the careers of these midshipmen before they even began.

"Have you forgotten that you're officers of the imperial navy?" Sorrell said. "Your conduct since I've entered this room has been deplorable. I'm ashamed to call you my crew, let alone my officers. Your actions put a blot on the reputation of every officer on this ship. And that includes me. Do you understand?"

"Yes, ma'am," the midshipmen said in unison.

"You will leave the galley, and you will report to Mister Stone at once, with my compliments," Sorrell said. "You are to request the most severe discipline befitting your station. If he has any questions, direct him to me."

"Aye, aye, ma'am," the midshipmen replied as one. They looked like they would rather be cashiered than face Lieutenant Stone's wrath. The youngest swiped at tears in his eyes. His lips trembled.

"Go," Sorrell said.

Under their pounding feet, the deck shuddered as the six of them bolted for the door.

Sorrell stared at the empty doorway for a long moment as she contemplated what to do next. Stone would see to it that the midshipmen could not sit comfortably for a week, and knowing him, that would be the least of their difficulties. Their poor conduct reflected on him as well as Sorrell.

She felt no sympathy for them. The navy was full of hard lessons, and proper conduct was one best learned early and fast. Sorrell winced, remembering her first caning. Back then, she had thought being the emperor's sister would protect her from that sort of punishment. She had been wrong, and she was better for it.

Mazareem would need to be placated somehow. Now that the moment had passed, Sorrell allowed herself to be amused at the prank. It was relatively harmless, and she understood why the midshipmen targeted Mazareem. But unfortunately for them and for Sorrell, the man was an agent of the throne for at least a little while longer.

"I can't believe I'll have to apologize to that ghoulish bastard," Sorrell muttered under her breath.

Chapter 11

SORRELL SPENT THE REST of the day sequestered in her cabin. Stone was busy with disciplining the midshipmen, and she needed to draft an official report to counter whatever Mazareem would write. She knew she should seek the man out to try to make amends, but she could not bring herself to rise to the task. Maybe tomorrow she would be able to swallow her pride and apologize for the poor behavior of her young officers.

Frustrated, Sorrell pushed herself back from her desk with a sigh. She had been at this for hours and made little progress. To distract herself from sour thoughts of Mazareem, she moved to inspect the navigation table. Their recent course correction had put them on the path to Spider's Cove. Barring an unforeseen storm, they would arrive within the week.

Not for the first time, Sorrell wondered about the true purpose of this mission. Her mother would not waste what little bargaining power and influence she had to recover a piece of stolen art, no matter how precious it was to the emperor. There were forces at play here that Sorrell did not understand. This made her uneasy. That mystery was one of the reasons she had accepted the task, hoping that she would learn more about Viatrix's true motivations.

It was possible that the mission was a ruse to lure Sorrell into a trap. Perhaps her mother had finally decided she was too dangerous to keep around, and an open grave waited for Sorrell in Spider's Cove. Whatever the real reason for this silly little quest, Sorrell could not act until Viatrix tipped her hand. Until then, all Sorrell could do was watch and wait.

Mazareem was an unknown and unforeseen complication. Who was he, and where had he come from? Sorrell had thought she knew the identity of all her mother's agents. In fact, she had made it her business to know. So how had Mazareem's existence remained secret for so long?

A knock at the door interrupted Sorrell's thoughts.

"You may enter," Sorrell said, not looking up from the map. Only Stone had the privilege and the courage to intrude on her personal time.

Stone entered the room and gently closed the door behind him. He approached the table where Sorrell stood with uncommon quietness. Even his footsteps were subdued. Sorrell could not bring herself to look at him, instead pretending to inspect some important detail of the map in front of her.

"I've disciplined the midshipmen, per your orders, admiral," Stone said after a long, awkward silence.

He was hurt; she heard it in his voice. Sorrell finally looked up. Rather than make eye contact, Stone stared across the table at the far bulkhead. He did not quite stand at attention, but his posture was rigid.

Tears sprang to Sorrell's eyes as a terrible sadness filled her. She sensed a rift between them, the start of a gulf that would drive them apart and spell the doom of their long friendship. Sorrell had always feared this day would come, but this was not how she wanted it to happen.

"Is that all you have to report, Mister Stone?" Sorrell said, matching his formal bearing.

Stone's eyes flicked to hers for an instant and then away. He was giving her the opportunity to say something, anything, to repair this breach between them. That she did not would only compound his emotional turmoil.

"I've nothing else, admiral," Stone said.

"Very well, you're dismissed," Sorrell said. "I'll see you in the morning with the rest of the officers."

For a moment, Sorrell thought that Stone had not heard her. He remained locked in his rigid pose, staring at the far wall. The longer he waited, the greater her hope grew that he would speak. Sorrell did not want their friendship to end this way, but she did not know how to prevent it. In this moment, she had never felt more like an admiral looking down on a lowly lieutenant.

Finally, Stone turned on his heel and marched towards the door. Sorrell's heart sank, and the tears threatened to spill down her cheeks. She did her best to hold them in check until Stone had left the room.

Instead of throwing the cabin door open and then slamming it behind him, Stone paused, his hand on the latch.

"Permission to speak, admiral," Stone said, his broad back still turned to her.

"Of course," Sorrell said, a little too quickly. She hoped Stone did not detect the tremor in her voice.

"You've been avoiding me today," Stone said. "I think we both know why."

"And why is that, Mister Stone?" Sorrell said. She wanted him to say it. She wanted him to finally admit what they had both felt for the past five years.

Stone turned from the door and took several steps back into the room. He paused between her and the front of the cabin, the stalwart lieutenant showing a rare moment of uncertainty. Sorrell saw unshed tears shining in Stone's eyes. His hands opened and closed at his side.

"Whatever you think of me, I'm no fool," Stone said. "I've served with you for five years now. For most of that time, I never left your side. I've shed blood with you. I've helped nurse you back to health when you've been injured. It has been my sworn duty to carry out your orders, sometimes without even asking you what those orders are. To that end, I know your comings and goings, your ambitions and plans, and your wants and needs. This is the service any good first lieutenant would perform for his captain. So when you hide things from me, I know.

"I know you have clandestine meetings that don't include me. Do you think I don't hear the rumors? I have played the role of dutiful lieutenant to your rising star in the navy because that was what you seemed to need and expect of me. I'm sure you have your reasons for not bringing me into your personal cadre. You have loyalties that extend beyond the navy, and I'm just a simple lieutenant. But I could be more for you. I want to be more for you."

Sorrell's sadness turned to elation as Stone spoke. She had never dared to hope that Stone might be recruited to her cause. However, the doubts remained. She had to be sure.

"I'm the last person who'd call you a fool, you know that," Sorrell said. "I couldn't have asked for a better friend and officer. And you're right, I won't deny it. I've kept you separate from the intrigues of my family because I didn't want to taint your love for the navy with the cynicism of the royal struggle for power."

"It's not the navy I'm in love with," Stone said.

To her surprise, Sorrell actually blushed. Suddenly, she needed to look anywhere but at Stone, who had finally found the courage to gaze into her eyes. Her thoughts went all fuzzy, as the yearning and attraction she thought she had mastered came rushing back. Sorrell's uniform felt hot against her skin.

"I-I need to be sure," Sorrell said. "You say that now, but you don't know what I'm planning."

"So tell me," Stone said.

Sorrell held Stone's gaze—here was the precipice. The truth was treason. And if Stone did not want to be complicit, he was duty bound to bring her to justice. But all the power in the world was useless without people you could trust. And she had precious few of those.

"I'm going to depose my brother," Sorrell said, plunging over the edge. "I'm going to take the throne and control of the empire."

Stone expelled a huge breath through his nose. Sorrell suspected he had been holding it.

"I knew what you were going to say, but hearing it is still a shock," Stone said.

"How could you know?" Sorrell said.

"It's the only thing that makes sense. I figured it out a year ago. I've been trying to get you to recruit me ever since."

"So you'll support me? You're not going to arrest me for treason?"

"Come off it, admiral!" Stone said, a grin finally cracking his face. "Haven't you heard a word I've said?"

"Sorry," Sorrell said. "This is just so sudden. I didn't mean to insult you by going behind your back. Asking a man to conspire against his emperor is no paltry thing."

"You're right, and I don't mean to make light of it. But never doubt that I'm your man, whatever comes."

The tension and awkwardness from moments before had been replaced with their old camaraderie. And a new sort of tension was growing. One that pulled them closer with an almost physical necessity. Now, Sorrell did not want Stone to leave the room. They grinned silly grins at each other while she racked her brain for something else to say, anything to keep the conversation going.

"I suppose you put the fear into the middies," Sorrell said.

"Damned near broke my cane," Stone said. "In ten years, when they're all lieutenants and captains, they'll still remember being bent over Lieutenant Stone's barrel."

"And you made sure to—" Sorrell tried to say, but Stone interrupted her.

"As long as we're on the subject of long suppressed truths, there's something else I'd like to say," Stone said.

Sorrell's heart leapt in her chest.

Without waiting for her to respond, Stone closed the distance between them in two long strides. Sorrell had to tilt her head back to look up into his eyes. She saw the need and passion in his gaze, but at the last instant, he held back. She felt it too. Years of navy conditioning, the rules of proper conduct, had been hammered into them. They teetered on the precipice of breaking those rules.

"If you don't kiss me, Mister Stone, I'll have you over the barrel next," Sorrell murmured.

Released by her words, Stone bent down and pressed his lips to hers. One of his hands came up behind her head, the other found her lower back. Gently, tenderly, he pulled her to him. Sorrell melted into the wondrous strength of his embrace—only the tips of her toes touched the floor.

Sorrell could not remember an enemy broadside that exploded with as much power as Stone's kiss. It sparked a powder-keg of desire in the core of her being. A fuse which had been smoldering for years. She pulled back from Stone, breathless.

"I'm sorry, that was—" Stone started, worry marring his handsome face.

"Hush, Mister Stone," Sorrell said. "Perhaps you should secure the door."

It took him a second to understand her meaning, but when he did, Stone's grin returned. He turned to do her bidding. Sorrell started to unbutton her uniform.

Cabin door locked, Stone turned back to Sorrell. He froze when he saw her undressing. The last article of clothing fell to the floor, and Sorrell stepped out of the pile, naked and on display for Stone. She met his hungry stare.

"Is this what you've been after, all these years?" she said.

For what came next, they did not need words.

Chapter 12

SORRELL COULD NOT REMEMBER being this happy. She lay in her bed, wrapped in sheets that still smelled of Stone. He had slipped away an hour ago. It was late in the night, but his presence would be missed if he did not make his midnight rounds. After a quick discussion, they had both agreed to keep their romance a secret from the crew. They would figure out how to announce it when the mission was over.

Sleep would not soon find her, and Sorrell was famished. She pulled the sheet around her shoulders and got out of bed. The ship's cook made sure to always prepare a fourth meal for her, just in case she woke in the night and needed a snack. Grateful for this, Sorrell crossed her cabin to the cabinet bolted to the bulkhead.

Her legs trembled as she walked. Muscles that she had forgotten she possessed complained about the recent, strenuous activity. Sorrell smiled at the vivid memory. She would get stronger with practice.

The cabinet yielded a plate of chilled meat and cheese with a hunk of dried bread. To Sorrell's hungry eyes, it was a feast. She took the plate to her small table and began to eat. Stone dominated her thoughts.

Sorrell knew she was in love with him. She did not quite know what that meant, because she had never been in love before. But what she felt matched what she thought love should be. Looking back, Sorrell realized that she had felt this way about Stone for years. It took the events of today to force her to admit it to herself. Whatever the case, Sorrell saw now that she had been foolish to wait so long to trust him.

Once she took power, Sorrell would need people she could depend on. More than that, she would need a new family to replace the one she was setting aside. Stone would be the start of that. Her own emotional and physical needs had never factored into her plans. For so long, she had taken them for granted. Sorrell understood now that such oversight was a mistake.

There were other lessons to be learned from Stone as well. In particular, Sorrell reflected back on the last few years and wondered how many friends and willing conspirators she had lost because of her unwillingness to let her guard down. To focus with such zeal on a single goal made her blind to other opportunities and possibilities. Sorrell made a commitment to herself not to fall into that trap again.

A quiet knock on the door intruded on Sorrell's contemplation. The door pushed open without waiting for a response.

For a heartbeat, she almost panicked. Sorrell was wrapped in a sheet and in no state to be seen. She laughed at herself. It could only be Stone. Sure enough, Stone stepped into the room and closed the door behind him.

Sorrell started to make a lewd joke, but one look at Stone's face stopped her short.

"What is it?" Sorrell said.

"Midshipman Kayta has disappeared," Stone said.

"What do you mean, 'disappeared'?" Sorrell said. In a dreadful premonition, she recalled Mazareem's hateful glare.

"I mean she's nowhere to be found on the ship. I spent the last hour looking with the help of the other middies. They last saw her scrubbing the deck right before the watch changed."

"There's a hundred places to hide on a ship like this."

"Trust me, we checked them all. And she's supposed to report to me, along with the other midshipmen, every hour for further discipline. She missed the last two reports."

"Are you saying you think she went overboard?"

"I'm saying I don't think she's alive."

"Come now, that's a bit extreme."

Stone shook his head. "Mazareem is a curse upon this ship. There's a reason the middies played the prank they did. The crew hates him. He haunts the lower cabins, appearing where he isn't wanted, and always muttering dark gibberish no one can understand. My gut's not often wrong about a man. He has murder written all over him."

Sorrell wanted to argue, but she found that she could not disagree with Stone's assessment. A worm of fear wriggled in her gut. Had she gotten Kayta killed because she neglected speaking with Mazareem immediately?

"Let me get dressed," Sorrell said. "I'll go with you to speak with him."

"Aye, aye, admiral," Stone said automatically. The formal response to an order seemed odd now, given what had transpired between them. "I'll wait outside."

It took Sorrell a few seconds to remember she was still naked, and when she did, she discarded the sheet and picked up her crumpled uniform from where it lay on the floor. She felt a pang of regret that this sudden emergency had stolen from them the frivolity of only an hour before.

Once outside the cabin, Stone fell into step with her as they strode across the deck. It was a moonless, starless night, and the near absolute darkness was only held at bay by a few flickering lanterns. The attitude of the sailors on deck was tense. Word of a missing crew member spread fast.

"No matter what we determine, they'll blame Mazareem unless we can prove otherwise," Stone said so that only Sorrell heard.

Neither of them spoke again until they reached Mazareem's cabin. Sorrell had assigned him a tiny room near the stern of the ship. She had intentionally kept him out of the suites intended for distinguished passengers. A sailor stood watch at the end of Mazareem's hall.

"He's not twitched a muscle since you set me to watch him, sir," the sailor reported to Stone.

"Very good, sailor," Stone said. "You may return to your duties."

"Aye, aye, sir," the sailor said, ducking his head with a salute before slipping away.

"I wanted to keep tabs on him in case he hadn't managed to get the body overboard yet," Stone said by way of explanation to Sorrell.

They stopped in front of Mazareem's door. Stone glanced at Sorrell, and she gave him a nod. Shoulders squared, face grim, Stone rapped his knuckles against the polished wood.

After a lengthy pause, Mazareem's voice echoed from inside the room. "You may enter."

Stone pushed through the door first, with Sorrell close behind. Inside, they found Mazareem sitting cross legged on his low bed. The strange man appeared to be meditating. He favored them with a smile that did nothing to improve his appearance.

"My, my, what a surprise," Mazareem said. "Admiral Sorrell herself is making cabin calls. And Lieutenant Stone, too. I apologize for my meager furnishings. I don't think I'm equipped to properly entertain you."

"You will stand in the admiral's presence," Stone said, his voice almost a growl.

"Of course, of course," Mazareem said. "After all, we're in her domain." He took his time stretching out his long legs and getting to his feet. Once upright, he was taller than Stone, although he was less than half the lieutenant's bulk.

"Are you aware that Midshipman Katya is missing?" Sorrell said.

Mazareem's eyes widened in mock surprise. "You're the first to tell me. How does one misplace an entire midshipman?"

The phrasing of that question bothered Sorrell.

"Did you have any contact with Midshipman Katya after your altercation in the galley this morning?" Sorrell said.

"I can't truthfully say," Mazareem said. "Your lieutenant here has had them running from stern to prow all afternoon. I may have bumped into her without knowing it."

Without warning, Stone stepped forward and strong-armed Mazareem up against the wall. Mazareem winced as the back of his skull smacked against the bulkhead.

"My apologies," Stone said, still holding Mazareem in place. "We must have hit a nasty wave. I lost my balance."

Sorrell opened her mouth to reprimand Stone, but the words died on her tongue. They did not feel right anymore. Boundaries for their new relationship had not yet been defined. How could she go on treating him like nothing more than her lieutenant?

Mazareem's calculating gaze missed nothing. Sorrell cursed her hesitation.

"Very interesting," Mazareem said, his cruel eyes dancing with amusement. "Very interesting, indeed. Katya might be lost this night, but I discern something else has been found. The unwashed lieutenant stinks of a woman's intimate juices. Don't you agree, admiral? Perhaps he tossed the midshipman overboard to cover up his forbidden tryst."

Stone snarled. Before Sorrell could stop him, he slammed a fist into Mazareem's stomach.

"That's enough, Mister Stone!" Sorrell barked, his sudden violence overriding her apprehension.

Mazareem doubled over, coughing. Stone released him and let him fall. After a few ragged breaths, Mazareem recovered and stood back up to his full height. What they had thought was coughing was actually laughter.

"Did you think to rough me up?" Mazareem said as his giggles subsided. "Slap me around a bit to put me in my place? Come on then, *boy*, is that the best you've got?"

"Stand down, lieutenant," Sorrell said before Stone could move. Next, she addressed Mazareem. "If you've no knowledge of Katya's whereabouts, we've no choice but to turn the ship around and search for her body."

Mazareem sobered immediately. "That, I cannot allow."

"You've no authority on this ship," Sorrell said. "As long as we're at sea, I'm in command."

"The writ says otherwise, and you know it. If your midshipman is overboard, she's dead and gone. We both know you'll never find her. A tragic loss, I'm sure, but not one that hinders the completion of our mission."

Sorrell swore under her breath. She had no proof of anything. Despite Stone's best assurances, Katya could very well be hiding somewhere on the ship even now.

"We will proceed to Spider's Cove," Sorrell said. "But you will remain confined to your cabin until the investigation into Katya's disappearance is finished. Right now, you're the prime suspect."

"As you wish," Mazareem said.

"Come, Mister Stone," Sorrell said, turning to the door. "This is going to be a long night."

"Ah, admiral, lieutenant," Mazareem said before they closed the door behind them. Sorrell and Stone paused to hear what he would say. "I won't forget this."

Sorrell followed stone down the hallway with Mazareem's hideous smile floating in front of her vision.

Chapter 13

LACRAEL STOOD ON THE deck of the *Golden Dawn*, her forearms resting on the side rail. Overhead, a brilliant tropical sun filled the world with warmth. It was the first time in her life that Lacrael had visited the equator of any realm. To her amazement, even the colors seemed brighter here. She had decided against wearing armor and was down to her tunic and pants. If it got any hotter, Lacrael would start wishing for the gauzy desert garb of her homeland.

On the near horizon, a chain of islands were silhouetted by the sparkling sea.

"The biggest island is the home of Spider's Cove," Niad said behind Lacrael's shoulder. "We'll make landfall within the hour."

Niad joined Lacrael at the rail. Her lustrous hair shone blazing red in the golden sunlight.

"It's been months since we had leisure time in a town that wasn't trying to kill us," Lacrael said. "I only wish it had a better name. I've had nightmares the past three nights of an island crawling with eight-legged monsters."

Niad smiled. "It's an ancient pirate port turned smuggler's town. They used to pick names that made their haunts sound inhospitable. They weren't too keen on unwanted visitors."

Lacrael tried and failed to return Niad's smile. The crew was taken with a cautious optimism that Lacrael did not share. No one was sad to leave the war-torn coast of Linstall behind. Over the last week, the mental burden of sailing in hostile waters was slipping away, and even the always grumpy Gustavus was showing hints of good-nature and high spirits. But long nights spent comforting a forlorn Brant kept the darkness of Abimelech's shadow at the forefront of Lacrael's thoughts.

"You're certain we don't qualify as unwanted visitors?" Lacrael said. "I feel naked without my armor but wearing it might kill me in this heat."

"Don't sweat it," Niad said, grinning at her pun. "Smugglers are our people. Over the years, the *Golden Dawn* has helped keep this port active. And besides, we're sailing well ahead of any news out of Linstall. Perhaps in a week or two, we might find a Coriddian ship here, but the captain is confident that we'll be well away before we have to worry."

"It's easy to forget that you and Gustavus led a different life before finding me and Kaiser."

"It does seem like a distant memory now. We've only been joined in cause for about a year, but everything that came before seems so... insignificant. The captain always said he was a Dragonslayer, and he would regale us with tales from his ancient order now and then, but none of us really believed him. We all thought it was just another part of the *Golden Dawn*'s legend that he loved to tell. A ruse to explain the magic he used to navigate between the realms."

"And you've no regrets that he was telling the truth?"

"I let go of regrets the day I joined this crew. It might be hard for you to understand, but this ship is my home. It's the home for every soul that hoists a sail, or mans a cannon, or chops onions in the galley. We're a part of this ship just as much as the planks and nails that hold it together. For most of us, the *Golden Dawn* is the only place we've ever belonged, the only purpose we've ever known."

Niad paused, her gaze drawn to the open sea. Lacrael waited patiently, not wanting to interrupt Niad's recollection.

"The captain recruited each and every one of us," Niad finally said. "Without him, the *Golden Dawn* doesn't exist. He's the patriarch of our family of misfits. So when he says we're going to sail to another world and beard a dragon, we say, 'Aye, aye, cap'n,' without so much as a 'What in the abyss is a dragon, sir?'

"None of us would think to question the captain. If he says aiding you and Kaiser is important, then it must be. He's not often wrong, and he's navigated more dangerous seas than these."

"You've still not told us *why* we're visiting Spider's Cove," Lacrael said.

"The captain keeps a storehouse there," Niad said. "He owns considerable property on the Linstall mainland, and the deeds are in a safe in that warehouse. He's hoping we can collect them and sell them at a discount before word of Linstall's surrender reaches this far. Once that news gets out, those documents won't be worth more than the parchment they're written on. And we could use the money. The last six months haven't been profitable for the *Golden Dawn*. With the funds they'll bring us, we'll be able to buy enough supplies to take Raither far away from here."

"He won't be happy about leaving his family behind."

Niad's good humor faded away. "He hasn't been told yet. The captain plans to keep him in the dark for as long as possible. He and

Kaiser are hoping that Raither will become the next champion before his attitude is a problem."

A shout from the bridge called Niad away before Lacrael could say anything more.

"I've got to make preparations for landfall," Niad said, turning away from the rail. "I'll find you again after we dock."

Lacrael turned her attention back to the ocean. They were close enough now that she could make out the details of their destination. The island itself was covered with jungle. Pristine beaches drew Lacrael's eye, and beyond the white sand, the dark green tangle of tropical forest sparked her imagination. She wondered what sort of animals stalked the deep shadows of the inner island. It put her in mind of her old home in Nogard forest. Would she have been able to survive here, if this were where the portal had dropped her?

Spider's Cove had been hacked out of the surrounding jungle in what appeared to be a losing battle with the encroaching trees. Brightly colored birds screeched at the offending settlement from the lush canopy, and as Lacrael watched, she spotted dashes of color as they flitted down into the streets to snatch morsels of trash.

On the edge of town, the oldest buildings were slowly being reclaimed by the island, ropey vines tearing apart foundations of stone like they were made of clay. Rather than repair these dilapidated structures, the occupants of the island seemed content to abandon them. The docks and those buildings nearest the water were sturdy enough, but they did not dispel the air of ramshackle desperation that hung over the isolated port. Lacrael had no trouble believing that this used to be a pirate hideaway.

There was a discernible line where the choppy ocean waves gave way to the still water of the cove. The *Golden Dawn* crossed this threshold and slid across the sheltered inlet without making a sound. From her spot on the deck, it seemed like they were gliding across a pane of glass. Lacrael was amazed at the quiet. She had taken for granted the constant churning of the open sea.

All activity on the docks had stopped when the *Golden Dawn* appeared. In fact, a crowd was gathering to watch her approach. To Lacrael's untrained eye, there was not a ship even half her size in the small port. Whatever Gustavus hoped to achieve here, it was certain that their presence would not go unnoticed. Lacrael said a silent prayer, hoping that Niad was right about a friendly welcome. They could use a turn of good fortune.

The *Golden Dawn* dwarfed every pier but one. Sailors scampered in the rigging above Lacrael's head, stowing sails as the ship coasted on a gentle path towards the dock. Ropes were cast down to dockhands, who quickly tied them off. There was a slight jerk as the lines were pulled tight and the ship came to a complete stop.

Gustavus appeared on the main deck with Niad at his side. In his greatcoat and tricorn hat, Gustavus towered over everyone else. Niad caught Lacrael's eye and beckoned her over. Lacrael tore her attention away from the crowd at the end of the dock and moved to join the captain and his first mate.

"I want you to come ashore with us," Gustavus said the instant Lacrael drew near. "I'm not expecting trouble, but I want you and Kaiser with us just in case. Kaiser will come with me to the warehouse, and you'll go with Niad to find us a prospective buyer."

"And by me, you mean Brant too," Lacrael said. It was not a question.

Gustavus frowned and looked away from her. "He's not staying on my ship while you go ashore. He's a big bastard. The locals will take him for an enforcer."

Lacrael sighed. "Should I put on my armor for this?"

"It's better we don't appear ready to fight," Gustavus said. "As far as these people are concerned, we're friends. I'd like them to believe that until we're long gone."

"I'll go find Brant," Lacrael said, turning away from Gustavus.

"I saw him cleaning the gun deck just a moment ago," Niad called to her back.

Lacrael passed belowdecks and headed for the gun deck. She did not mind having Brant accompany her every time she went ashore, but the lack of trust from Gustavus and Kaiser made her angry. They thought she had some sort of sway over Brant. She did not. The truth was, Lacrael was just as scared of him as they were. However, she refused to give into their pessimism. She had to believe that Brant could overcome the demon inside, and Lacrael knew he needed their help to do so.

She found Brant on his hands and knees, scrubbing the deck with a single-minded intensity. He was alone in this section of the ship. Where Brant went to work, the crew found every excuse to be somewhere else. His lank, long hair hung down, obscuring his face. Corded muscle flexed beneath the tanned skin of his forearms as he worked. He looked nothing like the meek, pudgy shopkeeper from Oakroot.

Brant noticed Lacrael before she spoke. His senses were keen, almost inhuman. He paused what he was doing and rocked back on his heels. Beneath Brant's open shirt, the golden dragon amulet glinted against his sweaty chest. Dead eyes stared at Lacrael.

Lacrael swallowed hard. The demon lurked just below the surface today.

"I'm going ashore," Lacrael said. "That means you're coming with me."

"As you wish," Brant said. His lifeless voice matched his gaze. Without another word, he dropped his brush into the bucket, got to his feet, and followed Lacrael back to the main deck.

Kaiser, Gustavus, and Niad stood on the dock below the *Golden Dawn*. Parnick, the ship's master-at-arms, had joined them. Lacrael and Brant navigated the gangplank and soon stood with the rest of the group.

Gustavus frowned at Brant, who had not even stopped to put shoes on his bare feet. Kaiser nodded a greeting at Lacrael.

"The harbor master has agreed to give us berth for a day and a night at a reasonable price," Gustavus said. "After that, he intends to bankrupt us. So let's be quick about our business. Niad, the three of you make for the Dripping Fang. Find us a land-hungry buyer. We'll meet you there in several hours, deeds in hand."

"Aye, aye, cap'n," Niad said. "Come on, you two." She motioned for Lacrael and Brant to follow her into the rundown little town.

Lacrael fell into step at Niad's side. Brant brought up the rear, glaring at the world from over their heads. Lacrael was accustomed to his creepy manner of following close behind, but Niad glanced over her shoulder now and then with a look of uncertainty.

The three of them made their way through a small crowd of gawkers at the end of the docks.

"Don't mind them," Niad said. "It's always a big event here when the *Golden Dawn* arrives."

Spider's Cove was decrepit. Buildings that had looked sturdy from the sea revealed themselves to be riddled with rot and patchwork repairs. Lacrael could not find a single piece of metal that was not pitted with rust. The structures that were not barred and boarded up were gutted and abandoned. Trash filled the gutter almost to overflowing.

"This place is a pit," Lacrael said as they made their way up a filthy street.

"Smugglers aren't the most civic minded," Niad said. "Just be glad it's not the middle of the summer. You think it looks bad? It smells worse."

They turned the corner onto what Lacrael guessed passed for the main street in this pathetic excuse for a town. While not clean, the cobblestones at least appeared freshly swept. The reason for this special care stood at the end of the road. It was the first building that did not look ready to collapse under its own weight.

"Behold, the Dripping Fang," Niad said. "Inn, tavern, and safe haven for smugglers in this part of the world. But don't let me paint a false picture for you. Inside, you'll find murderers for hire, gun runners, and worse. We've taken many a contract from here. Follow my lead when we get inside. They'll know we're coming and will be eager to learn what we're about. The captain's visits are never dull, and there's usually money to be made."

Three stories tall and boasting windows of clean glass, the Dripping Fang looked out of place in contrast to the rundown buildings that surrounded it. A porch with an overhang ran the length of the front of the inn, and a large wooden sign painted with a crude spider and the establishment's name hung from a pair of iron chains above the door.

Niad strode through the open door as if she owned the place. Lacrael followed the other woman into the tavern. On the other side of the threshold, she paused, wrinkling her nose and squinting her eyes. Lacrael could not decide which was worse, the stench or the shadows. Dark curtains covered the windows, and a few oily lanterns provided scant illumination.

Despite the time of day, the Dripping Fang was packed with customers. Furtive conversations were held around dingy tables.

Gold clinked as it changed hands. Curious eyes glinted in the shadows, no detail going unnoticed. One wall was covered in wanted posters and open contracts, which attracted significant attention from the tavern's clients. There was a lull in the room's conversation when the three of them entered, but activity quickly picked up again.

"They were expecting us," Niad said quietly.

At Niad's direction, Lacrael and Brant followed her to a table near the wall of posted notices. Niad sat where she could watch the room. Lacrael followed her lead and took a chair that allowed her to see the door. Brant paid no heed and sat with his back to both room and door.

"This table means we're selling, not buying or looking for work," Niad said after scanning the room. "Now all we have to do is wait for someone's curiosity to get the better of them. Oh, and take my advice: don't try the food."

Now that Niad had mentioned food, Lacrael noticed a distinct lack of it at the surrounding tables. Apparently, no one came to the Dripping Fang to fill their belly. As she inspected the people nearest their table, Lacrael instinctively looked for the reptilian features of dragon spawn. Thanks to their powers as Rowen's champions, only Lacrael and Kaiser could see through the magic that disguised Abimelech's agents. But she saw no sign of the enemy. Lacrael breathed a little easier and relaxed into her seat.

Sooner than Lacrael had expected, a shifty-looking man slipped into the one empty chair at their table. Clad in dingy leather armor and a ragged coat, with a battered scabbard hanging at his side, he looked the picture of a down-on-his-luck bandit. His greasy hair shone in the flickering lamplight. Pouty lips gave his face the appearance of a perpetual sneer.

Lacrael disliked the man instantly.

"Bartholomew," Niad said. From the tone of her voice, it was clear that Niad shared Lacrael's opinion of the man. "The last time I saw you, you were blubbering for mercy like a struck dog."

"Come now, beautiful, you know I hate that name," Bartholomew said, favoring Niad with a smile that revealed crooked yellow teeth. "Call me Bart. We're old friends, after all. Where's your high and mighty captain? I never did get to thank him for leaving me to die in the middle of nowhere."

"That was an act of mercy, and you know it. He should have killed you outright for what you did. How *did* you manage to survive?"

Bartholomew clasped his hands to his chest in mock piety and glanced upward towards the heavens. "I've been kissed by the goddess of the sea herself, I have. She pulls me to her watery bosom, but I always leave her satisfied, so she puts me back on dry land."

"You'd best clear off," Niad said. "If the captain finds you here, he'll finish what he started. And we've business to attend to that you've no part in."

"About that," Bartholomew said, an evil grin twisting his lips as he leaned towards them across the table, "if you'll take note of the rafters above your head, I've got three long rifles trained on you. Get out of your chair without my signal, and I'll be dragging you out of here with a hole for a third eye in your skull."

Alarmed, Lacrael jerked her gaze to the rafters. True to Bartholomew's word, she found the long barrel of a rifle trained on her. She guessed the other two men were behind her.

"You'll bring this whole place down on your head," Niad said.

Bartholomew shrugged. "And you'll be dead."

Beneath the table, Lacrael opened an upright palm and drew upon her power. A small flame sprung into existence and danced across her skin. Niad saw it out of the corner of her eye and gave Lacrael a quick but sharp head shake, indicating that she should not act.

Brant observed everything with his lifeless eyes, making no move to intervene.

"What do you want from us?" Niad finally said after weighing their options.

"I want you to get up from this table and follow me into the back," Bartholomew said. "Slowly, now. I'd hate to have to tell Gustavus that I spilled the brains of his saucy little first mate all over the Dripping Fang's floor."

Trapped in the sights of Bartholomew's guns, Niad stood up from the table.

"That's a good girl," Bartholomew said. "Tell your friends to come along."

Lacrael pushed her chair back and stood up. She placed a gentle hand on Brant's shoulder and knelt to whisper in his ear.

Lightning quick, Bartholomew's hand shot out and wrenched Lacrael's arm away from Brant. He stepped towards her at the same time, using his body to mask the movement from the rest of the tavern.

"None of that, missy," he hissed.

Lacrael jerked her arm out of his grip. Bartholomew raised a hand up towards the rafters, telling his men to hold their fire.

"Do that again, and you're dead," Bartholomew said, whispering into Lacrael's ear.

"Come on you," Bartholomew said to Brant. "On your feet."

"Listen to the man, Brant," Lacrael said. "Let's go with Niad."

Cleary disinterested, Brant got to his feet and stood next to Lacrael. Bartholomew observed Brant's odd behavior, confused at first, but then comprehension dawned on his ugly face.

Bartholomew snickered. "What's this? Is Gustavus so desperate he's recruiting idiots now? That's what happens when you leave your best man to rot."

Still grinning to himself, Bartholomew led them to the back of the Dripping Fang. Above their heads, Bartholomew's men tracked them the entire way. Lacrael glanced at the nearby tables, hoping that someone would come to their aid or at least raise the alarm. Instead, she found empty seats. The room, crowded just moments before, was now almost empty. They were on their own. No doubt word would reach Gustavus, but it would be too late.

Bartholomew stopped at a doorway in the rear of the room and ushered them through it in a sham of good hospitality. "This way, if you please, ladies and gentleman."

They stepped into a large storeroom at the back of the tavern. Lacrael got the impression of shelves and racks of foodstuffs, but none of that was important. What mattered were the three armed men waiting for them. Niad came to a stop, staring at the trio of raised pistols trained on her.

Confident now, and walking with a swagger, Bartholomew moved to stand in front of Niad. His grin grew wider.

"You always were a fool," Niad said. "Gustavus is going to—"

Bartholomew cut her off by slugging her in the mouth. Niad crashed to the floor, stunned by the violence of the blow.

"Do you know how long I've wanted to do that?" Bartholomew said, almost crowing with pleasure.

Lacrael surged forward, power at her fingertips, yearning to turn this wretched little man into a cinder.

"Don't," Niad said through her bloody lips. She raised a hand to stop Lacrael.

Only with tremendous effort did Lacrael let go of the inferno inside her. She knew Niad was right. She could roast Bartholomew, but it would be the last thing she ever did.

"Gustavus likes the fighters, doesn't he?" Bartholomew said, oblivious to how close he was to death. He stepped towards Lacrael.

"You won't touch her," Brant said. It was the first time he had spoken since landfall. The simple statement rattled Bartholomew. His eyes went wide when he looked into Brant's face.

"Pah, you won't be so tough in chains," Bartholomew said. "Come on, boys. We got our prize. Now truss them up. Gustavus will come looking soon enough."

Rough hands grabbed Lacrael from behind. A foot found the inside of her left knee, and she crumpled to the floor. Iron manacles clamped around her wrists, locking them behind her back. Matching restraints were fitted around her ankles and connected to those on her arms with a short chain. When they were finished, Lacrael lay on her side on the floor, hands secured behind her, and her legs wrenched painfully up towards her wrists.

Bartholomew's henchmen searched Lacrael, taking their time and enjoying her snarls as their hands lingered too long where they should not.

"Stay focused, lads," Bartholomew said. "There'll be time enough for that later."

The men leered at Lacrael but backed off at Bartholomew's orders. Quarry well in hand, the riflemen from the rafters had joined the rest of their gang in the storeroom.

From her vantage point on the floor, Lacrael watched as Niad and Brant were chained in a similar fashion. She breathed a sigh of relief when Brant submitted meekly to the restraints. But that relief turned to horror when the men spied the dragon amulet around Brant's neck.

"Hello, what's this?" one of the men said. He knelt down to inspect the golden jewelry. A knife flashed. He cut the leather thong and pulled the amulet from around Brant's neck.

Bartholomew and the other man gathered round to inspect the amulet, arguing over who should get to claim it. Lacrael ignored them, instead keeping her eyes on Brant's face. A knife twisted in her gut as she watched the change come over him. Brant's dead eyes came to life, but it was no longer Brant who looked out of them.

Lacrael summoned her power back into her fingertips.

This was not going to be pretty.

Chapter 14

LACRAEL WANTED TO LOOK away. She wanted to be anywhere else. The cruel groping of Bartholomew's thugs was easier to bear than to watch the monster take control of Brant. But she could not tear her gaze from his face. His features twisted, grotesque snarl shifting to wicked sneer and back again. Bound by his hands and feet, Brant's body shook with a seizure, rattling the chains.

Bartholomew soon noticed Brant's struggles.

"What's the matter, big boy?" Bartholomew said, his voice dripping with sarcasm. "Are the chains too tight for you?"

"We don't need him," one of the other men said. "Let's put a bullet in his skull and be done with it."

Brant was taking too long to act. At Bartholomew's prompting, one of the men approached Brant with a raised pistol. Lacrael could wait no longer. She called on her power and poured white hot fire through her fingertips into the cold iron around her wrists. The metal turned to slag and dripped to the floor.

"Don't you dare!" Lacrael shouted at the man with the pistol.

Stunned by her sudden outburst, he pivoted towards her. Lacrael's fireball caught him square in the chest, sending him crashing in the wall next to Brant.

"Sweet goddess!" Bartholomew said, leaping away in horror.

There was a mad scramble as Bartholomew and his men tried to understand what was happening. In the confusion, Lacrael rolled towards the door.

"Get out of the room!" Lacrael said to Niad, who was wrestling with her chains.

Niad heard the panic in Lacrael's voice, took one glance at Brant, and then started scrambling for the door.

The sudden violence and subsequent chaos was too much for Brant. He lost the battle for control. Howling with glee, the demon was unleashed.

Just as they were about to unload their pistols into Lacrael, Bartholomew and his men whirled to face the terrible noise behind them. Brant surged upwards, snapping the chains that bound him and standing to his full height.

"Kill him!" Bartholomew shouted, fear making his voice shrill.

Four flintlocks belched fire, filling the room with black smoke. Pistol shot punctured Brant's chest and stomach, but he took no notice. Dangling at the end of a chain, a manacle hung from his right arm. He struck out with this improvised weapon, the iron links cracking like a whip. The strength of the blow snatched one of Bartholomew's men from his feet. He hit the floor, dead before he landed, face fractured in a dozen places.

Bartholomew and his surviving men backpedaled. Hands went for swords, discarding spent firearms.

Brant roared as he bounded over the dead man at his feet. He lashed out with the chain again, this time wrapping it around a man's neck. Brant yanked. The man went down headfirst, his skull impacting the floor with the force of a cannon ball.

With a strangled cry, Bartholomew darted forward, thrusting his sword at Brant's exposed side. Brant twisted his body to avoid the blade, moving with a speed no human could match. Bartholomew's shout was cut off by a vicious backhand from Brant. Thrown backwards by the blow, Bartholomew crashed into the wall and did not rise.

Everyone paused, all attention on Bartholomew's crumpled body. It suddenly dawned on the four remaining men that this was a fight they would not win. The man nearest the door threw down his sword and turned to escape. Brant cackled in amusement. Again, the chain whipped out, wrapping around the man's ankles. He hit the floor with a thud. Terrified, the fallen man babbled near incoherent pleas for mercy.

Lacrael flinched. The thug had almost hit her when he fell. Niad had just made it through the door ahead of her, and Lacrael redoubled her efforts to flee the room.

Learning from their fallen comrade, the other three men closed ranks with their backs to the wall. Blades up, they presented a unified front against Brant and his murderous chain.

"We want no more of this," the biggest man said, the point of his sword wavering as he talked. "This was Bart's idea. He just paid us to be hired muscle. Let us walk out of here and we'll forget the whole thing. Do what you want with him."

Brant did not respond. Instead, he jerked the man on the floor towards him. Horror mounting, the man clawed at the wooden floorboards, desperately seeking purchase to resist the pull of the chain. His efforts were futile. A heartbeat later, the blubbering man was at Brant's feet.

"Leave off!" the big man with the sword said. "Let him up and let us go, and you'll never see us again."

Lacrael glanced back, hoping to see reason on Brant's face. He made eye contact with her. His mouth widened in a slow grin, madness dancing in his eyes. While Lacrael watched, Brant raised a bare heel above the fallen man's skull.

Unable and unwilling to see any more, Lacrael turned away and hurled herself the last few feet through the doorway. Behind her, there was a terrible wail, a violent crunch, and then a brief silence. The silence did not last long.

"What do we do?" Niad said. She was breathing hard. "He'll make quick work of those maggots and then come for us."

"First, we have to get out of these chains," Lacrael said. Heat flowed from her hands as she grasped the manacles around her ankles. Solid iron turned red hot and then sloughed away. Flames exploded on the wooden floor where the liquid metal touched.

"You next," Lacrael said. Thanks to her powers, Lacrael was immune to heat. Niad was not. Lacrael worked on removing Niad's chains, but she left the manacles in place. She took painstaking care not to melt Niad's skin along with the iron.

Lacrael tried to shut out the horrific sounds coming from the room behind them. It no longer sounded like a fight; it sounded like a slaughterhouse. The crunch and snap of breaking bones punctuated screams of dread. Above it all, Brant's maniacal laughing never stopped. She had no idea what she was going to do. How could she stop Brant without killing him?

A crash at the front of the Dripping Fang caused Lacrael to drop the last chain and spin towards the sound. Kaiser came hurtling through the door. Twin scimitars of blue flame glowed in his hands. Gustavus was close on his heels, flintlock and sword in hand.

Kaiser took one look at Lacrael and Niad, sized up the situation, and charged towards the room where Brant was finishing off Bartholomew's gang.

"Don't kill him!" Lacrael cried out, one hand raised in pleading as Kaiser barreled by her.

— —

Kaiser stepped through the doorway and stopped, stunned by the gore in front of him. In his role as Tenth Reaver, he had witnessed countless atrocities, but none worse than this. The remains of at least six men were scattered about the room. One man had been pinned to the wall, sword through his mouth, feet dangling a foot off the floor. Another was tied into a pretzel, arms and legs twisted at impossible angles. A third man lay almost headless, his skull exploded by some gruesome blow. Blood dripped from the walls and ceiling.

Some of the men still lived. Moans and whimpers penetrated Kaiser's disgust. At the rear of the room, Brant's broad back was unmistakable. He was bent over at the waist, intently focused on the body beneath his feet.

"Give me one reason not to cut you down," Kaiser said.

At the sound of Kaiser's voice, Brant went still. Slowly, he stood to his full height and turned around. Brant's face and chest were covered in blood. Puckered flesh on his chest and stomach marked the location of bullet wounds. He grinned. Brilliant white teeth shone through his crimson mask.

"Ah, the young reaver," Brant said in a voice that was not his. "I shall add your life's color to my little tableau."

That was the only warning Kaiser got. Brant lunged across the room. His bare feet slapped hard against the blood-slick floor. Kaiser knew from experience that he could not trade blows with the enraged Brant. Cursing Lacrael, he dismissed his ethereal swords at the last instant and shifted his body.

Kaiser parried Brant's grasping hand with a forearm, and with a quick turn, slammed his hip into the bigger man's thigh. Using

Brant's speed and weight against him, Kaiser flipped him on his back and stepped away.

Brant hit the floor and bounced back to his feet with a snarl. He whirled to face Kaiser, the chain on his arm spinning over his head. Brant lashed out with the chain. Kaiser ducked under the blow, darting forward inside Brant's guard. He slammed a fist into Brant's kidney, putting the weight of his entire body behind the strike. The punch would have dropped any other man. Brant only grunted.

Concerned now, Kaiser danced away and behind on the balls of his feet. This was not working. If Brant could not be subdued, he would have to die.

Rather than turn towards Kaiser, Brant spun the opposite direction, arm extended. Too late, Kaiser remembered the chain. Iron links cut through the air as straight as a blade. Unable to avoid the blow, Kaiser positioned himself to absorb the attack on the meat of his bicep. The chain slammed into his arm, wrapping around and cutting into his spine.

Kaiser's right arm went numb. It hung by his side, limp and useless. Pain shot through his back. He felt like an anchor had been dropped on him—Brant was on him in an instant.

Choosing that moment to make her appearance, Lacrael dashed into the room. But instead of blasting Brant with fire, she dropped to her hands and knees in a frantic search for something. Brant had not noticed her, and Kaiser did his best to keep the lunatic's attention.

Out of options, and reeling from Brant's assault, Kaiser summoned his spectral sword back into his left hand. Brant hesitated. Kaiser pressed the attack. Brant struck out with the chain again, but this time, Kaiser's smoking blade cut through the iron links with ease. The severed chain crashed into the wall behind Kaiser's head.

Brant took a step back, and then another. Kaiser's breath came in ragged gasps. If Lacrael did not act soon, he was going to lose the initiative. At the last instant before Kaiser's stamina ran out, Lacrael wrapped her arms around Brant from behind. She pressed the dragon pendant into the bare skin of his chest.

For a long heartbeat, time seemed to stop. Kaiser held the point of his weapon poised over Brant's heart. He watched Brant's face. If the demon did not recede, Kaiser would end it.

"Let him go," Lacrael was saying behind Brant's back. "By the power of this amulet, I banish you back into the darkness."

"His life is mine!" the possessed Brant said through gnashing teeth. "As will be yours, when I'm free of this accursed magic."

"But you're not free," Lacrael said. "And the magic binds you. Submit."

The demon did not go easily. It howled in rage and forced Brant to his knees with muscle spasms that wracked his entire body. Finally, at Lacrael's incessant demand, the demon inside of Brant slipped back into the shadows of his soul. Brant slumped, all the strength and fight gone out of him. Kaiser let out the breath he had been holding. He let the glowing blade in his hand flicker out of existence.

"We can't keep doing this," Kaiser said. "He's more dangerous than our enemies."

Before Lacrael could respond, Gustavus stepped into the room. Niad and Parnick were close behind. Gustavus let out a low whistle.

"Filthy reprobates, the lot of them, but they didn't deserve this," Gustavus said as he carefully avoided the blood and corpses. "The only way that man returns to my ship is in chains. He can sleep in the brig. And we're going to have a conversation about his future."

Lacrael looked angry, frustrated, and sad, but she did not argue. Kaiser glanced around at the butchered men. Perhaps after this,

Lacrael would have a new opinion of the former shopkeeper from Oakroot.

"You said Bart was behind this?" Gustavus said, addressing Niad.

"Aye, cap'n," Niad said. "He's on the floor over there, by the wall."

Gustavus moved to stand over Bartholomew's body.

"Black Bart, you stinking bottom-dweller," Gustavus said. "This is how you repay my kindness?"

Muttering under his breath, Gustavus bent down and flipped the body over. He rifled through the man's pockets. From inside Bartholomew's coat, Gustavus withdrew a folded parchment. He opened the document and inspected it.

"God's balls," Gustavus swore. "Ol' Bart here wasn't after revenge, he was after a bounty."

Kaiser moved close to read the notice over Gustavus's shoulder. It was an imperial decree from the Coriddian emperor himself. The *Golden Dawn* was named, as was Captain Gustavus. There was even an accurate drawing of the ship.

"Fifty thousand pounds sterling for our capture," Gustavus said. "I'm tempted to turn myself in for that sum."

"It doesn't make sense," Kaiser said. "We should be well ahead of any news out of Linstall."

"Look at the date," Gustavus said. "This was issued weeks ago. Someone's on our trail. Someone who knows we're in this realm."

"It was only a matter of time before the enemy found us," Kaiser said, saying what everyone else was thinking. "I'm surprised it took this long."

Gustavus folded the notice and tucked it into his greatcoat. "We're not safe here. And after this fracas, we'll not find a buyer."

To everyone's surprise, Bartholomew stirred at Gustavus's feet.

"Long time no see, cap'n," Bartholomew said, his voice so weak his words were almost a whisper. "Help an old hand out, would you? Don't leave me like this."

In one swift motion, Gustavus drew his sword and plunged it through Bartholomew's heart. The man jerked, eyes wide, He spasmed once, mouth open in a silent scream, and then slumped to the floor and went still.

"I learn from my mistakes," Gustavus said. He wiped his blade on Bartholomew's dirty coat before returning it to his side. "And turning a demon loose on my ship is not one I intend to make. Bind Brant or leave him here. You know which one I'd prefer. We're returning to the *Golden Dawn.* Spider's Cove isn't the haven I thought it would be. A bounty that big will make us a tempting target. Bart won't be the only one to come hunting. We'll buy what supplies we can and sail with the dawn."

Gustavus moved for the door, and Niad and Parnick followed. Lacrael searched the room for pieces of manacles and chains she could use to secure Brant.

"Help me, please," Lacrael said.

The defeat in her voice touched something in Kaiser, and despite his misgivings, he helped her bind Brant. He used his good arm to hold the chain together while Lacrael repaired it with her inner heat. She fused and molded iron like it was clay, working the metal into the shape she needed.

Kaiser had never considered the practical uses of their newfound abilities. He was amazed at Lacrael's ability to shape raw metal. A blacksmith would kill to be able to do what she had just done. He was about to say as much when he glanced at her face. Tears were streaming down her cheeks. Kaiser decided to hold his peace.

Lacrael worked slowly, but Brant's fetters were soon in place. She encouraged him to stand. He complied without raising his head to look at her. At Lacrael's gentle prodding, Brant shuffled from the room. He held his arms away from his body, avoiding the red-hot metal of the chains that had yet to cool. His bare feet left long bloody stains on the wood of the tavern floor.

Kaiser paused in the doorway, unable to resist one last look at the hideous spectacle Brant had left behind. Head shaking at the carnage, Kaiser exited the room. Now that the adrenaline was fading from his body, the pain in his arm was screaming for his attention. He suspected that it was broken. The ribs on his back hurt with every breath.

Outside, the street in front of the Dripping Fang was empty. Word of trouble spread fast in a place like this. Kaiser's thoughts returned to the bounty on the *Golden Dawn* as he followed Lacrael and Brant through the quiet town. For the bounty to have been posted before the fall of Linstall meant that Abimelech suspected their presence in the realm of Praxis. They had all been waiting for a sign of pursuit.

For six months, the *Golden Dawn* had operated in relative peace. No one suspected that Gustavus was harboring fugitives from another realm. That period of respite was coming to a rapid end. Events were progressing quickly now. Any day, Raither might manifest the powers of the next champion, and they could quit this realm and be on to the next. They only needed to stay one step ahead of the enemy until that happened.

Kaiser would not admit it to any of the others, but he considered the bounty a boon. Finally, their hand would be forced. He could not bear another month of waiting for something, anything, to happen.

Every day, the weight of his guilt and shame for abandoning Saredon grew heavier. Mariel's dying plea for Kaiser to believe in the cause of High King Rowen haunted him. She had not known what she asked. His wife would never have expected him to choose a path that required the sacrifice of their son.

If Kaiser knew how to navigate the portals between realms, and where to find them, he would have stolen away and returned to Northmark months ago. To his continued frustration, the only way back was forward. And in his heart of hearts, Kaiser suspected that the man in his dreams knew of this turmoil and approved of it. If not by design, it still served the stranger's purposes.

Whatever the case, Kaiser refused to think of the interloper into his dreams as High King Rowen. The rest of his companions were convinced, but Kaiser had seen no evidence, and the stranger refused to claim the title and name. And even if the man should do so, Kaiser was not certain he cared. He had made no oath of fealty to a high king.

Kaiser was in a dour mood by the time his feet found the gangplank of the *Golden Dawn*. He cradled his right arm with his left, his mouth set in a rictus of pain. Gustavus and his officers went straight to the captain's cabin. Lacrael guided the morose Brant belowdecks, no doubt heading for the doctor and then the brig. The wounds on Brant's chest had stopped bleeding, but they still needed tending. Kaiser headed straight for Tarathine.

He found his daughter in their shared cabin. Tarathine's face lit up when he pushed open the door. Pleasure quickly turned to concern when she saw he was hurt.

"Father, what happened?" Tarathine said, rising from the chair in which she sat.

"I had a run-in with an ill-mannered chain," Kaiser said. "Can you fashion me a sling?"

"Of course," Tarathine said. She moved to the trunk at the foot of the bed, rooting around inside until she found a long piece of cloth.

Gingerly, Kaiser sat on the bed. There was no way he was getting the shirt over his head. He called one of his scimitars into his hand and used it to slice away the fabric from his torso. He grimaced when he peeled the shirt away from his wounded arm. The blow from Brant's chain had left an ugly bruise that was turning his entire upper arm black.

Tarathine hissed at the sight of the injury. "It wraps around your back too," she said.

"I don't think it cracked any ribs," Kaiser said. "I just need a sling until my arm feels better."

"If it's broken, it needs treatment," Tarathine said as she worked to fold the cloth into a sling.

"We'll know in a day or two," Kaiser said.

Tarathine frowned but did not argue. Makeshift sling complete, she slipped it over Kaiser's head and helped him fit his arm into it. It took some work finding a comfortable position, but when they did, Kaiser breathed a sigh of relief.

"You should visit the ship's doctor," Tarathine said. "He'll know if it's broken or not."

Kaiser's reply was interrupted by the door to their cabin banging open. A young sailor stepped inside.

"Uh, sorry about that," the sailor said, looking sheepish after he realized that he had barged in without knocking. "The captain needs you topside immediately."

"Tell him I'm on my way," Kaiser said, too exhausted to reprimand the impertinent sailor.

After a quick nod, the sailor dashed back into the hall.

"You need to go to the doctor first," Tarathine said, her voice firm. She crossed her arms and gave him a look.

Kaiser smiled. She sounded so much like her mother sometimes.

"Right after, I promise," Kaiser said. He pulled her close and kissed the top of her head. "Thanks for the sling. I'm feeling better already."

Tarathine remained rigid for a heartbeat and then returned his embrace, careful not to aggravate his injured arm. Kaiser held her until she pulled away, and he gave her a smile before following the sailor topside.

Gustavus was waiting in his cabin, along with Niad and Parnick. They were standing around the map table in heated discussion.

"What is it?" Kaiser said. "What's so blasted important that you won't let me have a quiet moment alone with my daughter?"

"Just because we're in port doesn't mean we stop watching the sea," Gustavus said, ignoring Kaiser's tone.

"What of it?" Kaiser said.

"The lookout spotted sails in the southeast. They're a long ways off and strange looking, but he's certain it's a Coriddian ship. We have to assume it is. If we cast off right now, we can be away before they can challenge us. And there's no ship in the realm that can catch the *Golden Dawn* on the high seas."

"Have we had a chance to resupply?"

"We're scrambling to load what we can, but we're still a half-day's work from being back to fully provisioned. Have you heard anything from the High King? Can we depend on Raither to join us? If we're going to stand and fight, this is as good a place as any."

Kaiser bit off a bitter retort. He hated functioning as Gustavus's oracle. As he contemplated the question, Kaiser tried not to grimace at the pain throbbing through his chest and arm. He was in no state to wade into battle again so soon.

"We run," Kaiser said.

Chapter 15

SORRELL STOOD ON THE prow of the *Celestial*, spyglass trained on the ship that had just sailed from Spider's Cove. She could not believe their good fortune. This was to have been the first port among many they needed to check. If they had truly stumbled upon their prey so soon into the hunt, she would be back in Coridal within the fortnight.

"Is it the *Golden Dawn?*" Stone said from her side.

He had been the one to notice the large ship docked in the dingy port. Over the last hour, they had observed as it cast off and made for the open ocean.

"We'll know when the sun touches them," Sorrell said, her eye still glued to the spyglass. "If the reports are true, the *Golden Dawn* is the only ship outside the Coriddian Navy to hoist etherweave sails."

As if on cue, the clouds parted, and sunlight bathed their quarry. It could only be the *Golden Dawn*. Her sails gleamed with the magic woven into the best etherweave canvas. She was resplendent, the radiant golden light casting a heavenly glow on her pale deck.

"Possession of those sails is enough to warrant pursuit," Stone said, smacking the rail of the ship with an open palm. "It makes a mockery of the Coriddian Navy for a smuggler to sail under our colors."

"An hour and a half more and we'd have caught them with their anchor down," Sorrell said, finally lowering the metal tube. "Now we'll have to give chase."

"We'll have them before sundown tomorrow. Even with etherweave, they'll not outpace the *Celestial.*"

"That may be so, but they'll not come without a fight. Have the gunnery sergeant move a long gun up here. We'll start bombarding their rigging as soon as they're in range."

"Aye, aye, admiral," Stone said. He turned to obey her order.

"And, Mister Stone," Sorrell said.

Stone paused, looking back at her with a raised eyebrow.

"Please report to me in my cabin when the task is complete."

"I hear and obey," Stone said with a wolfish grin.

Sorrell turned back towards the sea to hide her own smile. In the past twenty-four hours, they had not been able to keep their hands off each other. They found every excuse to steal even just a few minutes alone together.

Stone had insisted Midshipman Katya was gone, but Sorrell had ordered an exhaustive search anyway. Katya was nowhere to be found on the ship. Sorrell had found no evidence to the contrary, so she had been forced to enter the incident in the logs as a tragic accident. Mazareem would no doubt find this amusing, and she was in no hurry to report her findings to the loathsome man. If it were up to her, Sorrell would leave him confined to his cabin for the rest of the voyage. Stone approved, arguing that it was for Mazareem's own safety. The crew was not happy about the young midshipman's disappearance.

To Sorrell's surprise, the tragedy had worked as a catalyst to drive her and Stone closer instead of apart. For someone who was so young and so full of promise to die such a meaningless death filled Sorrell with a sense of desperate immediacy, an almost physical need to take hold of life before it slipped through her fingers. It made her reckless, but she did not care. She found in Stone a willing outlet for this need.

But Stone was far more than just a vessel in which to quench her burning passion. He reciprocated Sorrell's yearning in every way, his desire a match for her own, and as they responded to each other's ardor, their growing love threatened to eclipse everything else, even the mission. Sorrell had never before found herself at the mercy of her own heart. It was both terrifying and exhilarating.

The sighting of their quarry pushed Sorrell's restless energy to new heights. Now the hunt began in earnest. Unable to banish thoughts of Stone from her mind, Sorrell left the prow and returned to her cabin. They had at least a night and a day before they were in firing range of the *Golden Dawn*. Sorrell knew exactly what she planned to do with that time.

Giddy with excitement, Sorrell closed the door to her quarters, shrugged out of her uniform, and slipped between the rumpled sheets of her bed. Not five minutes later, a soft knock on the door announced Stone's arrival. He slipped inside, not waiting for Sorrell to respond. A silly grin spread across his face at the sight of her already in bed, and he started adding his clothes to the growing pile on the floor. He almost tripped over his belt in his haste.

"The gun's being moved into place as we speak," Stone said as he slid into bed next to her. "I told the second lieutenant that we're not to be disturbed. He thinks we'll be coming up with a plan for the boarding action."

"I've some boarding action of my own in mind, but he's not going to hear about it," Sorrell said, drawing close to Stone.

For a time, everything but the bed and the small cabin ceased to exist. Sorrell let her worries and cares fade away as she gave every part of her being to Stone. Together, they soared on a crescendo of pleasure that seemed like it would never end. When it finally did, in an explosion of ecstasy, Sorrell lay back on the bed, panting and exhausted. Briefly, she thought of cleaning up, but she felt too good to move. Several minutes later, Stone's soft snores and the gentle rocking of the sea lulled her into a blissful slumber.

The instant Sorrell closed her eyes in sleep, a dream came to her. She found herself once again on the desolate plain, the dead sun lower in the sky this time. Her gaze was downcast, and beneath her feet, the pitiful pale grass wilted and died as she watched. To her surprise, she realized she was naked.

Disturbed by the dying weeds, Sorrell raised her eyes to scan the horizon. She found the strange horseman sitting not ten feet in front of her. Sorrell's dreamself screamed in fear and surprise. She took an involuntary step backward and tried to cover her nakedness with her hands. But she could not hide from the knight's gaze. His eyes, nothing but two dark holes in his helmet, never wavered from their silent regard of Sorrell.

The knight's armor shone like the dawn, resplendent in its magnificence. It was brighter than the weak sun overhead—Sorrell almost had to look away. He sat astride a horse of absolute black, and as she stared into that rippling darkness, Sorrell swore she saw the twinkling of a thousand stars. A shield hung from the knight's back, and a glittering scabbard was strapped to the side of his saddle.

Sorrell trembled. She was aware that she was dreaming, but she could not escape the vision. It felt real. There was no hiding from the knight's grim countenance on the empty dreamscape. Sorrell hated the fear that coursed through her. She wanted to challenge this dream visage. She wanted to banish it from her thoughts once and for all. Yet she could not bring herself to speak.

Somehow, Sorrell sensed that the knight knew of her fear and revulsion. Nothing was hidden from him. Slowly, the knight raised a gauntleted hand and pointed at Sorrell. No words were necessary. Sorrell understood. He had come seeking her, and he would not leave until she surrendered to his will.

Defiance won out over terror, and Sorrell opened her mouth with a snarl. Before she rebelled against the dream specter, he clenched his pointing hand into a fist and the dream ended abruptly. Sorrell woke in a cold sweat, disoriented and trembling. It took a moment to remember where she was.

She must have cried out, because Stone woke and pulled her into his arms.

"What is it?" Stone said, his voice a sleepy murmur. "Are you okay?"

Unaccustomed to being comforted and feeling diminished after her encounter with the knight in her dream, Sorrell pushed Stone away.

"I'm fine," Sorrell said. "It was just a dream."

"Oh," Stone said.

Sorrell had hurt his feelings. She held back a sigh of frustration and lay her head on his chest. After a moment, Stone's arms found her again.

"I'm sorry," Sorrell said. "I'm not used to waking up with someone in my bed."

Stone kissed the top of her head, which did more to tell her he understood than anything he might have said.

"I keep having this same damned dream," Sorrell said. "It's been hounding me since Linstall. My mother sees dire portents in the realm of dreams, but I've never put much stock in them. This one feels… different."

"Different how?" Stone said.

"I don't know. It seems so real, and at the same time, it feels like I'm in someone else's dream, not my own. There's this strange knight, and he wants something from me. Don't ask me how I know that, because he never speaks."

"Knight? As in, shining armor and valiant steed sort of knight?"

"One and the same. He's straight out of a children's fable."

"Are you already dreaming of my replacement?"

"Hush, you," Sorrell said, unable to keep a smile from her face. She did not have to look up at Stone's face to know he was grinning. Absentmindedly, one of his hands stroked her back, and neither of them spoke for a while. Stone would have to leave the cabin soon to avoid his overlong visit being noted by the crew, but neither of them were in a hurry to part.

"Where do we go from here?" Stone finally said, ending the comfortable silence. Sorrell had almost fallen asleep again.

Surprised by the seriousness of his question, Sorrell pushed herself up onto her elbows to look into Stone's eyes.

"What do you mean?" Sorrell said.

"We've not talked about what comes next," Stone said. "The *Golden Dawn* won't evade us for long, and after that, we sail back to Coridal. Are you still going to put me up for my captaincy? I'd like to think… I mean, I hoped that I've earned a place closer to your side. Not that I'd turn down my own ship, if that's what you need me to do."

"How does 'Lord Admiral' strike your fancy?"

Stone choked. He had to sit up to master his coughing fit.

Sorrell grinned. It took Stone a minute to recover from his spluttering. When he could speak again, he blurted, "Lord Admiral? I'm still a lieutenant!"

"I don't mean immediately," Sorrell said. "But I intend to replace that fossil Corstan, and in a few years, you'll be the perfect candidate. In the meantime, I'll make you captain as my adjunct. No one will question your sailing and combat experience. We'll find you a ship when the time is right, and you can take her out on your own to make it official."

Stone sat there stunned as he contemplated his new career trajectory.

"And there's something you should know, Mister Stone," Sorrell said, using her most serious admiral voice.

He looked at her, uncertain of what she would say next.

"As my adjunct, I expect you to be diligent in your duties," Sorrell said. "*All* of your duties."

Sorrell pushed him back down to the bed and straddled his chest, letting the sheet fall from her naked body. Stone looked up into her eyes for a long moment and then pulled her close into an embrace that made the rest of the world fall away.

Chapter 16

KAISER PACED THE DECK of Gustavus's cabin. The pain in his arm and side had receded to a dull ache. He wore a shirt with the right sleeve cut off to make room for the sling. Lacrael, Gustavus, Niad, and Parnick stood around the map table, watching him pace. They were waiting for him to speak.

"You said there was no other ship that could match the *Golden Dawn*'s speed," Kaiser finally said, coming to a stop and staring directly at Gustavus. "And yet it's been a night and a day, and they're still gaining on us."

"It's not an issue of speed," Gustavus said, finding refuge in a technicality rather than admitting he was wrong. "It's those gods-cursed silver sails. During the day, we outpace them. But in the night, their sails continue to shine as if the sun still hangs overhead, and they gain on us. They have some new sort of magic sail that works around the clock."

"Why they're going to catch us isn't important. What matters is that we're not going to get away from them unless we do something drastic. Can we toss the guns overboard to lighten our load?"

Gustavus gestured to the table where scattered parchments were covered in hastily scrawled calculations. "By our best estimates, even if we jettison all our guns and cargo, we'd only delay the inevitable. Without the power of our etherweave sails at night, we're at the mercy of the wind. If we hit the doldrums, they'd be on us before sunrise."

Kaiser resumed his furious pacing. The cramped quarters did not offer much range of motion, forcing him to turn on his heel every few steps.

"So we fight," Kaiser said. "But the question is, do we make our stand at sea, or try to make for land?"

Gustavus, Niad, and Parnick all shared a look. Kaiser did not miss the silent exchange.

"If you've something to add, speak up," Kaiser said.

Gustavus nodded to Parnick, indicating he should speak.

"There's no way we'd survive landfall," Parnick said. "Without a port and a dock, we'd be forced to anchor off-shore and row in by boat. In the time it took to do that, the enemy would be on us. They'd blow us out of the shallows like fish in a barrel. If we're going to fight, it has to be on the water."

"And we can't afford to be drawn into trading broadsides," Gustavus said. "The *Golden Dawn*'s guns are a means of last resort. She's a sleek hunter, a thing of beauty, not a plodding brute like a warship. One well-aimed barrage of cannon fire, and we're crippled."

"But you obviously have a plan," Kaiser said. "Why didn't you just say so instead of letting me ramble on?"

"Because you're a damned prickly customer," Gustavus said. "You tend to be more agreeable when we let you reason it out yourself first."

Kaiser almost tore into Gustavus as he would have an upstart young reaver. He stopped himself at the last instant. Upon quick reflection, he realized that Gustavus was right. Kaiser was still treating his companions as if they were soldiers and he was their supreme commander.

"Don't hold your breath for an apology," Kaiser said, his voice almost a growl. "If you've a solution to our problem, out with it."

"You see what I have to suffer on my own ship?" Gustavus said, in mock appeal to the others. "Yes, we have a plan. It stands to reason that our pursuer is a bounty hunter, most likely a privateer commissioned by the Coriddian Navy itself. That being the case, they'll want to board and capture us. They'll consider the *Golden Dawn* a part of their reward, which means they'll avoid damaging her if at all possible.

"Tomorrow, we'll reduce our speed to allow them to catch us a little after daybreak. When they're within range, they'll fire a warning shot to indicate we should stow our sails and allow ourselves to be boarded. We'll comply, which is when you and Lacrael will convince them to stand down. I've never seen the like of the ship that's on our tail, but it's the size of a sixth-rate. They'll have twice our number if they're carrying marines. So it's on the two of you. Force them to surrender with as little bloodshed as you can manage. It's too late for Raither to be of any use, even if he does turn to our cause in the night."

"One good fireball, and I can probably sink them before they get close," Lacrael said.

Gustavus shook his head. "It's too risky. I've seen your aim. If you miss, they'll fall back and shred us with long-range artillery. And if you wait till they're alongside us, they'll respond with a full broadside into our hull. I want to sail away from this unscathed. And anyway, if we can take their ship without sinking it, we'll have solved our supply problem."

"It lacks the refinement of military strategy, but it will have to do," Kaiser said.

"You can stick your military strategy up your pompous backside," Gustavus said. "Now, before you get your britches in a twist, there's something else we need to discuss."

Kaiser clenched his teeth so hard his jaw hurt. He was out of his element here, and Gustavus knew it. It was not a sensation that Kaiser enjoyed.

No one spoke, and Gustavus continued, "Something has to be done about our guest in the brig. He's chained, barred, and under the influence of the protective amulet, but he's thwarted such measures before. All it takes is him deciding to remove that leather thong from around his neck and we've got an unstoppable killer in our midst."

A shadow fell across Lacrael's face. She looked ready to mount a vehement protest.

Gustavus held up his hands to forestall any outburst. "Now, don't let it be said that I'm not a compassionate man. I feel for the boy, I really do. He's been dealt a dead hand from a rigged deck. But we can't risk that his misfortune becomes our own. Our cause is more important than the fate of one man, no matter how unfair that sounds."

"What are you saying?" Lacrael said, her voice trembling with barely controlled fury. "That you want to fill his pants with cannon shot and toss him overboard?"

"I'm open to other suggestions," Gustavus said with a shrug.

"I have an idea," Kaiser said.

Kaiser did not trust Brant any more than Gustavus did, but he wanted to get one over on the smug captain. That, and to his surprise, he did not want to see Lacrael forced to stand by as someone she cared about was murdered.

"At Spider's Cove, you molded metal as if it were putty," Kaiser said to Lacrael. "It put me in mind of a master smith, although I didn't say anything at the time. What if you were to do the same thing again, but this time, you fashioned a harness for the dragon amulet? A harness that he could not remove himself."

Lacrael's face lit up as she contemplated Kaiser's words.

"I could do that, easily," Lacrael said. She turned to Gustavus. "Would that be enough? Would yet another set of chains ease your mind and buy an innocent man his life?"

"It wouldn't be right to kill him, cap'n," Niad said quietly. "He's innocent, as she says, and he's saved our lives twice now."

"By thunder, now you turn on me?" Gustavus said. He pounded his fist on the map table. "Have it your way. Craft your harness. And don't forget, I'll hold the two of you responsible for any of my crew he harms. Champions of the high king you may be, but there are lines on my ship that you don't cross."

"Like it or not, *captain*, he's a part of your crew," Lacrael said. "Niad and Parnick see that, why won't you?"

Lacrael did not wait for an answer. She strode from the cabin, letting the door slam against the outside wall and making no effort to close it.

Gustavus rubbed a large hand across his face. "The fire burns hot in her. I'd save the boy if I could, but that's beyond my power. Does his single life weigh on the balance equal to the lives of the entire crew?"

"Balance isn't the same as justice," Kaiser said. "If we murder an innocent man to increase our chances of success, how are we any different than the enemy we're trying to defeat?"

"What I saw in that room at the back of the Dripping Fang wasn't the work of a man," Gustavus said. "He isn't human anymore. Are you going to stand there and tell me you believe Brant to be the same naïve soft-belly you found in Oakroot?"

"No, I can't make that claim," Kaiser said after a long pause.

"Then you'd better hope your sense of justice doesn't get us killed," Gustavus said. "Because Brant's a powder keg primed to go off. And I don't want to be anywhere close when he does."

Chapter 17

SORRELL WATCHED THE *GOLDEN* Dawn through her spyglass. Their quarry's behavior was different this morning. The *Celestial* had gained ground on her prey all through the night, and with the dawn, Sorrell had expected their target to start pulling away as on all previous mornings. But this morning, the *Celestial* continued to close the gap.

"They're slowing down," Sorrell said to Stone, who stood at her side with his own spyglass raised to his eye.

"They've done the same calculations we did," Stone said. "They know they can't get away, and making for land would be suicide. Their only option is to surrender or fight."

"Which will it be, I wonder."

"They're smugglers. They've no taste for battle. My guess is they'll try to bribe us."

"They'd have better luck loading their coin into a cannon and firing it at us."

Stone chuckled. "Shall I give the order to fire a warning shot?"

"If you please, Mister Stone," Sorrell said.

"I serve for the admiral's pleasure," Stone said, giving her a perfect salute.

They had moved past the awkwardness of addressing each other by their naval rank. Now they enjoyed the delicious irony when they slipped into their formal military personas. Their only trouble was remembering to hide the truth from the junior officers.

Sorrell turned her attention to the splendid sunrise. The morning sun rose on the eastern horizon, and the waves of the ocean were tipped with the shining fire of its rays. Several miles away, the coast of the mainland stretched out of sight, a thin green line atop the cerulean sea. A cool breeze caressed Sorrell's cheek, the last gasp of the night's chill before it gave way to the warmth of day. She smiled. This was her place. Sorrell might take the throne, might become the ruler of an empire, but where she belonged would always be on the deck of a ship, sailing the high seas.

Her heart had never felt more full. Her relationship with Stone was showing her that life did not have to be only duty and achievement. There could be pleasure too. Even joy. For the first time in her life, Sorrell was genuinely looking forward to each day as it came, instead of always setting her sights in the distant future and making whatever sacrifices were necessary to reach it.

The resonating boom of a long gun yanked Sorrell's thoughts back to the present. She tracked the shot as it hurtled towards the *Golden Dawn*. It splashed into the sea only a few boat-lengths behind the *Golden Dawn*'s stern. She would have to commend the firing squad on the excellent shot.

Their target seemed to have anticipated the warning shot, because the *Golden Dawn* began to slow immediately. Sorrell felt the familiar surge of adrenaline, and she said a silent prayer of thanks that today would be a simple affair. As an afterthought, she also asked that it be bloodless. The crew of the *Golden Dawn* would have no choice but to surrender before Sorrell's contingent of marines, although they might take some convincing first.

Stone returned to her side, slightly out of breath from his trip around the deck.

"It appears our quarry is inclined to be reasonable," Stone said. "I told the gunnery sergeant to hold off on a second shot. I also rallied the marines. They'll be ready to board by the time we draw near."

"Very good, Mister Stone," Sorrell said. "It comes to my mind that we've not visited our... *guest* below in some time. He's certain to have heard the cannon fire. If you please, could you go inform him of the imminent military action, and also, instruct him to remain in his cabin for his own safety?"

"Aye, aye, admiral," Stone said.

Sorrell could not fail to see the gleam in Stone's eye as he moved away. Whatever he had in mind, she hoped he went easy on Mazareem. The man still had the ability to make their lives difficult.

Chapter 18

MAZAREEM SAT CROSS-LEGGED on the cot in his cabin. He had used the past few days of isolation to meditate and rest in preparation for the work to come. It would soon be time to end this charade, and the anticipation was working its magic on him. For the first time in recent memory, Mazareem actually felt excited.

A single muffled cannon shot shattered the stillness of his little cabin. Mazareem smiled. So it began. He stood up from his bed and stretched his long limbs. Sorrell would send someone to check on him, he was certain. It did not matter who it was, but Mazareem hoped it would be Stone.

Not for the first time, Mazareem regretted the absence of his black robe. He could conceal much beneath its shadowy folds. But the garment would have been cumbersome in the close confines of the ship. Instead, he wore a simple black outfit, much like the kit the admiral preferred. This required him to store most of his tools in a pack instead of on his person.

Moving quickly, Mazareem stepped to the dresser where his pack lay and removed a needle he had prepared in the night. Careful not to prick himself, he hid it between the forefinger and thumb of his right hand. The poison that coated the tip could weaken even Mazareem's inhuman constitution.

Footsteps in the hall announced Mazareem's visitor. He forced the smile from his face—Stone's heavy tread was unmistakable. The big lieutenant did not knock, instead pushing his way through the door as if he wanted to catch Mazareem in some criminal act.

Mazareem did his best to play the part of a feeble, frightened old man.

"Lieutenant, how good of you to come!" Mazareem said, creeping towards Stone as he spoke. "I heard cannon shot and my heart started racing. Tell me, have we caught up to our quarry?"

"Aye, we're moving to intercept as we speak," Stone said. "You're to remain here until the conflict is over."

"We may have our differences of opinion, but I'll not deny your navy's usefulness," Mazareem said, doing his best to look relieved. "I'm no swashbuckler. Heroic adventure on the high seas is a bit too dramatic for my tastes."

Stone made no effort to hide the disgust on his face. "At the first sound of battle you turn coward. I told the admiral you were craven. You've got no fight in you if you're not terrorizing young women."

Mazareem smiled his most placating smile. Stone had no idea that his news had signed his death warrant. "You really should let that go, lieutenant. Your own admiral acquitted me on the account of there being no evidence."

"I don't need evidence to know the truth," Stone said. "You'd best watch your back if you want to return to Coridal alive. You've been confined to your cabin for your own safety. The crew is ready to string you up, even if it means defying the admiral."

As Stone talked, Mazareem took another step closer. He was only a few feet from the lieutenant now. If he drew any nearer, Stone would become suspicious.

"And I suppose you've done everything you can to quench the flames of the crew's righteous indignation?" Mazareem said, hoping to keep Stone talking.

"If it were up to me—" Stone started to say, but he never finished the sentence.

At that instant, a large wave jostled the ship. Stone put his hand on the door jamb to keep his footing. This was the opportunity Mazareem had been waiting for. The deck pitched slightly towards Stone—Mazareem allowed himself to stumble forward.

Instinctively, Stone put up his hands to prevent Mazareem from crashing into him. Quick as a striking viper, Mazareem's right hand flashed towards the exposed skin above Stone's collar. The needle pierced Stone's flesh. Stone slapped a palm to his neck as Mazareem stepped back.

"You filthy bastard!" Stone said, inspecting his hand for signs of blood. "What've you done?"

Mazareem stood to his full height. "Extract of sea scorpion. The first thing to go will be your balance."

Right on cue, Stone sagged against the door frame, hands clutching at the wall to keep his feet.

"Here, let me help you," Mazareem said.

Revealing a fortitude that Mazareem had kept hidden until now, he slid one shoulder under Stone's arm and half-dragged, half-carried him towards the bed. Stone tried to resist Mazareem's assistance, but his strength was fading fast.

"The next thing to go will be your muscle control," Mazareem said as he laid Stone on the cot. He arranged the lieutenant's arms and legs in a comfortable resting position. "Don't worry, I limited the dosage so that you'll keep breathing. You may soil yourself. Don't be ashamed if you do. It's a perfectly normal reaction. You get used to that sort of thing in my line of work."

While Stone struggled to accept what was happening to him, Mazareem moved to check the hallway for any witnesses. There were none. Confident that he had Stone to himself for the immediate future, Mazareem closed the door and turned back to the cot.

To be certain the poison had time to run its course, Mazareem waited a full minute. He watched Stone intently. Stone flopped his head toward Mazareem, the anger on his face stolen by the enfeebling poison. Only Stone's eyes still burned with his hatred for Mazareem.

"What're you doin' to me?" Stone said, his voice weak and his words slurred.

"I'm killing you, my dear boy," Mazareem said.

Stone struggled to process this. Mazareem patted the boy's shoulder and then bent down to rummage through his pack. In short order, he produced several round, leather disks, and a small but extremely sharp knife. He gave each disk a sharp tap on the bottom, and they popped open to form small bowls.

"You-you-you can't do this," Stone said, panic giving him a surge of strength that quickly faded. "You'll... never... get away... with it."

Mazareem pulled up the room's one tiny stool to the edge of the bed. He looked down at Stone. The rage in the poor man's eyes had been replaced with a mounting terror. Mazareem sighed. Stone had annoyed him, even angered him, and Mazareem had wanted to savor this moment of triumph. But when it came down to it, he felt sorry for the man. Stone was a victim of circumstances and powers he would never understand. There had been no contest here, only a brute beast being led to the slaughter.

"Unfortunately, there are some lessons we don't survive," Mazareem said as he worked. "This was never your story. I'm not even certain it's mine, but this is where your role in it ends."

Working with the efficiency of long practice, Mazareem dangled Stone's arm over the edge of the bed, placed one of the leather bowls beneath his wrist, and sliced open his vein. Stone's lifeblood gushed out into the small vessel.

"You should feel no pain," Mazareem said, patting Stone's knee. "I'm not a monster, after all."

The first bowl soon filled to almost overflowing. Deftly, Mazareem swapped it for a new bowl. Careful not to spill a drop of the precious blood, he poured the red liquid into a small glass bottle and sealed it with a stopper. This he stowed in a padded satchel at the bottom of his pack. It clinked against a dozen other matching bottles.

"It's only a small comfort, I know, but you should die with the knowledge that your life force is a precious resource that won't go unused or unappreciated," Mazareem said. "Katya, while possessed of a certain youthful vitality, only produced enough to sustain me for several days."

Stone stared at the ceiling. His lips moved, but he lacked even the strength to speak now. Mazareem leaned over Stone's face to catch his last words. Such things should be documented. The faintest whisper touched Mazareem's ear. Stone was repeating one word over and over. It was a name. He was calling out for Sorrell.

"Ah, the admiral," Mazareem said, pulling back from Stone's face. "You love her, no? Death is more potent when love dies with it. But don't you fret. She'll join you in the afterlife soon. Perhaps the two of you will think of me now and then, maybe put in a good word?"

Mazareem chuckled at his joke.

After filling six more bottles, Mazareem had no choice but to stop his gruesome harvest. The remaining blood would rot and be wasted, but he could carry no more.

Footsteps in the hallway interrupted Mazareem's work. Annoyed, he snatched the small blade into his hand. A sailor crashed through the door, Lieutenant Stone's name on his lips. Without rising from the stool, Mazareem turned and whipped the dagger toward the offending sailor. Four inches of steel pierced the man's eye and embedded in his brain. He collapsed on the floor, dead where he lay, his momentum carrying him into the room.

Mazareem stood and dragged the body into the cabin before securing the door a second time. He yanked his dagger from the man's skull and wiped the blade on his victim's shirt. When he returned to Stone's side, the lieutenant was dead. The poison in addition to the blood loss had been too much.

"You see what you did?" Mazareem said to the slain sailor beneath his stool. "I didn't even get to say goodbye."

Mazareem hated the taste of human blood. He was beginning to think Abimelech's gift was actually a curse. A man's vital fluid, when mixed with the tyrant's dragon scale, could sustain him, yet it did nothing to slake Mazareem's thirst for dragon's blood.

Only one thing took the edge off his craving—the flesh of a fresh heart. Mazareem cocked his head, listening for sounds of battle overhead. He heard nothing, which meant they had not drawn close enough to the *Golden Dawn* for boarding action. Perhaps he still had time for a brief indulgence.

Whatever sympathy Mazareem felt for Stone had died with the man. Eager for a treat, he cut open Stone's shirt and made one last incision on his chest.

Chapter 19

SORRELL WAS WORRIED. STONE had not returned, and there was no sign of the sailor she had sent looking. She needed Stone to lead the assault. It would be just like Mazareem to cause trouble at the worst possible time.

The marines were assembled on the deck, bunched up behind their wooden barricades. Floating less than a hundred feet away, the *Golden Dawn* was rapidly closing the distance between the two ships. At this point, Sorrell had no choice. She would lead the attack herself and find Stone afterwards.

Frustrated, Sorrell swept the length of the *Golden Dawn* with her spyglass. At least they seemed inclined to come peacefully. Their deck was empty, save for three figures watching the *Celestial* approach. Sorrell could find no snipers hiding in the rigging. Prudence demanded caution, however. They could easily be hiding a counter-attack below decks.

Stowing her small telescope with a snap, Sorrell strode from the poop deck towards where the marines were gathered.

"Bring me my sword and pistol," Sorrell said to a junior lieutenant. "I'll be leading the boarding party. And if you see Lieutenant Stone, tell him to report to me immediately!"

"Aye, aye, admiral!" the young lieutenant said before dashing away.

To Sorrell's surprise, she recognized the marine sergeant. It was the same sergeant from the last battle for Linstall.

"I didn't expect to see you again, sergeant," Sorrell said as she joined the marines who were hunkered down behind a barricade.

"When I heard the call for volunteers, I couldn't resist," the grizzled sergeant said with a grin. "Besides, this is naught but a pleasure cruise, if you don't mind my saying so, admiral."

Sorrell wondered if the sergeant's grin was a bit too knowing. If the man had winked, she would have been certain he knew about her and Stone. Sorrell swore under her breath. She did not like this constant second-guessing of her interactions with the crew. If he noticed her hesitation, he did not remark on it.

"Do you think they'll fight, admiral?" the sergeant said, nodding towards the *Golden Dawn*.

"They're making every appearance of coming in peacefully," Sorrell said. "Let's hope that holds true."

"I second that, admiral. This lot is as green as a frog's arse. Half of them have never seen action. I put the youngest in the rigging with orders not to fire."

Alarmed, Sorrell glanced upwards, trying to spy the hiding marines.

"Never fear, admiral," the sergeant said. "There's more than enough of us to handle some spineless smugglers."

"I admire your confidence, sergeant," Sorrell said. "But I didn't know half your contingent was inexperienced."

"They're here by order of the Lord Admiral himself," the sergeant said. He spat on the deck to show his opinion of Lord Admiral Corstan.

The young lieutenant appeared at Sorrell's side, her weapons in his hands. "No sign of Lieutenant Stone, ma'am."

"Very good, lieutenant," Sorrell said. "Return to your station."

"Aye, aye, admiral!"

Sorrell buckled on her sword belt and checked that her pistol was loaded.

"Twenty feet to contact!" a voice yelled out.

"We have to give them every chance to surrender," Sorrell said. "Tell your men that I don't want an offensive charge. We will show ourselves, make it clear that we're armed, and then attempt an orderly crossing to their ship. Is that clear?"

"Aye, aye, ma'am," the sergeant said. He turned to his corporal with instructions to convey Sorrell's orders to the rest of the marines.

"Contact!" the voice called out a second time.

The shout was followed by the crunch of the two hulls coming together. Sorrell felt the shock of the crash reverberate through the deck beneath her feet. As soon as the ships touched, marines tossed grapple lines across to the *Golden Dawn*. Rope after rope unfurled through the air, metal hooks biting hard into the wood of the captured ship. Marines worked fast to tie the lines tight, anchoring them to the *Celestial*'s deck.

"She's not going anywhere now, ma'am," the sergeant said.

"Very well, sergeant," Sorrell said. "Let's show ourselves."

Marines at her side, Sorrell stepped from behind the barricade. Heavy wooden planks were being wrestled into place to bridge the gap between the two ships. Rapier and pistol in hand, Sorrell mounted one of the planks the instant it was in position. Balanced above the waves below, she moved out onto the makeshift bridge. A great gust of wind tore at her coat and threatened to snatch the bicorne hat from her head. She ignored these distractions, intent on the prize. Sorrell boarded the *Golden Dawn*.

Other than the three people standing in the middle of the deck, the *Golden Dawn* was deserted. Sorrell approached the trio. She recognized Captain Gustavus by description. His sheer size and head of yellow hair were hard to miss. He was flanked by what must be his officers.

On Gustavus's right stood a man with his arm in a sling. Despite this injury, Sorrell sensed an aura of menace. The man had the appearance and bearing of a hardened soldier, but his eyes marked him as a leader. Though he stood no taller than Sorrell, he looked down on her. He assumed she was subordinate to his will. Sorrell knew that look. She had been shoving it back down men's throats for years.

To the left of Gustavus, a foreign-looking woman watched Sorrell approach with interest. Her dark skin and hair marked her as belonging to the people of the sand, a rare sight in the Coriddian Empire. The woman did not appear to be a sailor or a soldier, and she certainly did not seem afraid.

In fact, between the three of them, there was a distinct lack of concern about being boarded by the Coriddian Navy.

Sorrell came to a stop several paces from Gustavus. He watched as the marines fanned out behind her.

"In the name of the Coriddian Emperor, this vessel is under arrest for crimes against the throne," Sorrell said. "Surrender all arms and command of the ship, and I'll personally see to it that you're treated with respect, and I'll petition the court for leniency. Resist, and we will have no choice but to take control by force."

Chapter 20

SORRELL WAITED FOR GUSTAVUS to respond. Something was wrong, but she could not place her finger on what it was. With every step she had taken onto the Golden Dawn, her sense of unease had grown. For reasons she did not understand, she felt afraid. The fear brought to mind her recurring dream, quickly followed by visions of Stone. Annoyed at the churning of her thoughts, Sorrell forced the battle calm to wash over her. Whatever happened next, she was ready.

A look passed between Gustavus and his officers. Gustavus stepped forward to give an answer to Sorrell's challenge.

"I'm afraid we're going to have to decline your very courteous invitation," Gustavus said. "However, we do have a counteroffer."

It took a moment for Sorrell to digest his words. This was not going how it was supposed to.

"You misunderstand," Sorrell said, giving an edge to her voice. "This isn't a negotiation. You surrender, or we storm your ship. Unless you've got several hundred marines hidden belowdecks, I'd advise against the latter option."

"You know we don't," Gustavus said, stepping to the side. "We've got something better." He looked at his two officers. "Show them."

Sorrell tightened her grip on her weapons, preparing to fight. "Now hear this! You will stand down, and—"

The words were snatched from her mouth by two events that happened almost simultaneously. An impossible flame blossomed from the desert woman's upturned palm, and in an immediate answer, the report of a long-rifle sounded from the *Celestial*'s rigging.

Sorrell watched in stunned disbelief as the bullet caught the dark woman high in the shoulder and spun her around. Blood from the wound trailed in the air as she crashed to the deck.

"Sergeant, tell your men to cease fire!" Sorrell shouted.

But it was too late. Suddenly, Gustavus had saber and flintlock in hand, and with a bellow, he summoned the army of angry sailors who had been hiding below.

At Gustavus's signal, the deck of the *Golden Dawn* exploded into a violent melee. Swinging swords and brandishing pistols, sailors swarmed the deck, climbing out of every hole and hatch. Sharpshooters, who had been expertly hidden in the sails above, opened fire. Gustavus and his remaining officer surged forward. Sorrell's marines answered their charge, flowing past her in a wave of black uniforms.

Sorrell reached deep to summon the strength to wade into the fight. It did not come. She found herself rooted in place. Her head throbbed. Nausea swept over her. The sense of wrongness that had been building now threatened to bring Sorrell to her knees. Above the terrible noise of the battle, Sorrell swore she heard the sounds of hoofbeats ringing in her ears.

An enemy sailor spotted Sorrell. He charged in her direction, cutlass raised. His attack was sloppy, and Sorrell's well-honed reflexes took over. She might be on the verge of passing out, but she could still fight. Sorrell danced away from his first swing, parried the next, and stabbed her riposte into his unprotected belly. The man dropped his blade and lurched backwards, hands clutching his bleeding midsection.

A passing marine slashed the sailor in the neck, finishing off Sorrell's attacker. It was the sergeant. He paused only long enough to salute Sorrell with his sword.

He did not wait for Sorrell to respond—the sergeant turned and joined the melee. His body disappeared from view as he hacked his way into the enemy. This skirmish should have been over as quickly as it began. Sorrell had forty experienced marines at her back, not counting those providing covering fire from the *Celestial*'s rigging and the one hundred and twenty sailors of her crew. A sloop the size of the *Golden Dawn* should have no more than seventy crew in total. And yet, somehow, the enemy sailors were pushing Sorrell's black-clad soldiers backwards.

Cursing her sudden malaise, Sorrell forced herself to move. She followed the sergeant into the fray. He had disappeared into the mass of bodies, and she twisted herself, slipping between two of her marines, trying to get to where the fighting was the thickest.

A bullet plucked the hat from Sorrell's head as she plunged into the chaos. In an instant, she was surrounded by friend and foe alike. Her foot slipped on the blood-slick deck—the press of bodies kept Sorrell on her feet. Something in the middle of the deck was driving Sorrell's marines back, but there was no room left, and fighters were still streaming across from the *Celestial*. The battle had been reduced to a deadly wrestling match.

Six inches from Sorrell's face, a young marine grunted with effort, straining to find the leverage to skewer the enemy sailor he grappled with. She found herself pressed up hard against his back.

Sorrell tried to bring her pistol to bear on the marine's attacker, but someone had grabbed the barrel. There was no room to get her own blade around the marine's broad shoulders.

She watched, helpless, as the marine in front of her lost the lethal contest of strength. His sword arm gave out, collapsing against his side. He cried out as the enemy's cutlass slipped between his ribs and deep into his chest. Blood filled his mouth and bubbled down the front of his uniform.

The point of the blade pierced the dying man's body and out his back—Sorrell hissed as the cold steel split the folds of her coat and stung her skin. Realizing Sorrell was pinned, the burly enemy sailor gave her a wicked grin over the marine's shoulder. He put his full weight against the hilt of his cutlass.

Unable to free her firearm and out of options, Sorrell pulled the trigger. Whoever was trying to wrench the weapon away from her got more than they asked for. Shouts of surprise and pain followed the violent explosion. For a heartbeat, Sorrell had the space to move.

Snarling now, Sorrell swung the discharged weapon up and around the dead body between her and her attacker. Still smoking, the barrel struck the man on the side of the head. He staggered to the left, and the weight on Sorrell's chest disappeared. The dead marine slumped to the deck and Sorrell was free.

Determined to keep the initiative, Sorrell slashed left and right with her sword, carving a path forward. The sailors of the *Golden Dawn* had no stomach for a proper fight. They fell over themselves to get clear of her blade.

Sorrell finally reached the center of the deck, and once more, she found herself in the company of her marines. But they were stalled. Frustrated by the mounting losses of what should have been a simple operation, Sorrell pushed herself through the ranks of her fighters. Whatever had them stymied, she would deal with it.

What Sorrell found brought her to a stumbling halt.

The man with his arm in a sling, one of Gustavus's officers, was singlehandedly holding the deck of the *Golden Dawn.* He fought like a demon, even with his injured arm held close to his body. In his good hand, he wielded a sword unlike any other Sorrell had ever seen. It flashed a brilliant blue in the sunlight and made no sound when it struck.

Around the man's feet, black uniformed bodies were piling up. Sorrell won free of the melee just in time to see the marine sergeant cut down. He lunged forward in an attempt to catch the killing blue blade on his own. Despite his courage, the sergeant never had a chance. The ethereal sword cut right through the sergeant's saber and sliced open his chest. Gutted like a fish, the sergeant flopped on the deck, his torso split from throat to belly. Bile rose in Sorrell's throat at the ghastly sight of exposed ribs.

For the first time in her life, Sorrell had no idea what to do. Nothing about this mission was as it seemed. A squad of imperial marines were getting slaughtered by a one-armed smuggler. After the sergeant fell, no one else stepped up to challenge the enemy swordsman.

Sorrell's head was pounding—she shook it violently to stop the sky from spinning. If she did not act, the morale of her marines would fail and the battle would be lost. For the hundredth time, Sorrell wished Stone were at her side. But the stalwart lieutenant was nowhere to be seen. She took a deep breath to steel herself, cast aside her spent pistol, and stepped forward with her sword raised.

The enemy swordsman gave Sorrell an appraising look, the sort an expert fighter gives his opponent before attacking. In the immediate vicinity, the sounds of battle ceased as all heads turned to watch the confrontation. Sorrell knew that the contest for the *Golden Dawn* rested on the outcome of this duel.

A shifting of the man's weight was the only warning Sorrell got. He danced forward, blue blade slashing through the air. Sorrell jumped back. She had learned from the sergeant's fatal mistake. Her sword was no match for the strange ethereal weapon. In her sluggish mental state, Sorrell struggled to think of a way to attack the man. If she came within striking distance, she died.

Before the swordsman swung again, the dark-haired woman, the second of Gustavus's officers, appeared at his back. Her shoulder bled from the gunshot wound. In her outstretched hands, fire swirled above bare skin. Anger flashed in her eyes, and she stepped forward, hands raised towards Sorrell and the *Celestial*'s marines.

Sorrell stared, dumbfounded. She knew she should move, but something held her back. Her sword arm dropped to her side, the strength and will to fight gone in an instant. The throbbing pain and haze that had confounded her thoughts was gone, replaced by… nothing. Sorrell felt a terrible emptiness inside her. For a heartbeat, she forgot who she was. She could not even recall her own name. It was as if her identity had receded like the tide, leaving her high and dry without it.

Was this what it felt like to face her own death?

Her vision flickered, the dreamscape from her recurring nightmare replacing the deck of the *Golden Dawn* and then disappearing in dizzying flashes. A profound sensation of being in two different places at once almost undid Sorrell. On the desolate plain of her dreams, she could move, but in the real world, she was frozen in place. Sorrell cried out in the false reality, trying to banish it from her mind.

Instead, the delusion only grew stronger. Sorrell decided she had gone mad. The two enemy officers attacked in what seemed like slow motion. One heartbeat they were rushing at her, the next she was alone on the empty prairie. Sorrell watched, unable to even raise her sword in response as they struck in unison. Behind her, the *Celestial*'s marines realized she was doomed, and they put up a cry as they surged forward to her defense. But they were too late.

In the next instant, Sorrell's insane vision stole reality from her again, and the strange knight reared in front of her. This time, he was so close that Sorrell could *feel* his gaze. He reached down and placed a gauntleted hand on her shoulder. Before she could scream or fight back, cold like Sorrell had never known flowed into her. Ice poured from his hand and consumed her body, talons of frost stabbing into every pore. It felt like the knight's touch had frozen her soul.

The deck of the *Golden Dawn* came crashing back. Sorrell could do nothing but watch the enemy come. With a flick of her wrist, the dark woman hurled a fireball through the air at Sorrell. The enemy swordsman stepped forward, pivoted on one foot, and slashed his spectral blade at Sorrell's neck. Sword passed through flame, and the flame clung to it, wreathing the weapon in fire.

At the last second, Sorrell found the will to scream. And with her scream, strength rushed back into her body. In Sorrell's dream world, the knight released her, and she sensed his approval. Raw, untapped power replaced the void in her soul. She felt full to overflowing. Time seemed to stop. The mystical vision receded, and Sorrell knew she was once again firmly rooted in reality. She heard the unmistakable sounds of hoofbeats reverberating across the open sea.

Sorrell's sword hit the deck. She raised both hands to ward off the oncoming assault. Possessed with an intuition she did not understand, Sorrell tapped into the newfound power surging in the core of her being. It responded to her need, her desperation.

A shield of solid ice exploded into existence in front of Sorrell. It curved over her head like a half-formed sphere. The enemy swordsman's weapon hit the frozen wall and bit deep, but his deadly slash was blocked. Ice hissed and steamed as it melted under the fire on the blade.

Arms outstretched, Sorrell stood, unable to comprehend what had happened. The deck had gone silent. She could not tear her eyes away from the ice wall she had summoned. A figure appeared at her side, and too late, Sorrell realized the enemy swordsman had darted around her barrier. But his glowing weapon was not in his hand.

Before Sorrell could react, something hard hit her in the back of the head and the world went black.

— —

Kaiser caught the enemy captain as she slumped to the deck. He discarded the wooden pin he had clubbed her with. At the same time the woman lost consciousness, her ice shield splashed to the planks in a puddle.

"Gustavus, you'd better tell these men to stand down!" Kaiser shouted.

With his good arm, Kaiser dragged the enemy captain towards where Lacrael stood. The black-clad marines were still too shocked to move, but when they recovered, they would no doubt try to rescue their leader.

Gustavus landed on the deck next to Kaiser with a solid thud. The *Golden Dawn*'s captain had been high overhead in the rigging. He held a long-rifle in his huge hands. Its barrel was still smoking.

"What's the plan?" Gustavus said.

"She might damn well be the next champion," Kaiser said between grunts as he pulled the woman across the deck. "We can't give her up."

Gustavus contemplated this, and in the span of five seconds, formulated a plan of action. His deep voice boomed out over the ship in the language of the Coriddian Empire. Kaiser understood just enough to be able to follow along.

"We've taken your captain captive," Gustavus said. "If you wish her to live, stand down immediately. Return to your ship and we'll negotiate her release. Refuse, and we'll be forced to kill her. The rest of you lot will be next. You've now seen the power of my officers. Do any of you want to test them where your captain failed?"

One of the enemy marines, a corporal by his insignia, stepped forward.

"Of what use to us is the word of a smuggler?" the man said. He spat on the deck to show his disdain for Gustavus's trustworthiness.

"You want collateral?" Gustavus said. "Fine. We'll stay tethered to your ship until negotiations are complete. If you're not happy with the outcome, you can blow us out of the water."

The corporal did not look happy about it, but he had little choice. He raised a hand to point at Sorrell.

"She's no mere captain, boyo," the marine said. "That's Admiral Sorrell, the pearl of the Navy. You harm a hair on her head, and you'll bring down the wrath of heaven on your miserable souls."

Kaiser looked down at the woman in his arms in surprise. No one on this side of the world had not heard of Admiral Sorrell. He had not expected she would be so young.

"We've no wish to hurt her," Gustavus said. "But if you don't clear off my ship, you'll leave us little choice."

The corporal stared at Gustavus like he wanted to resume the fight. Finally, he turned, and with a shout, ordered the rest of the marines back to their ship. Kaiser stood with the surviving crew of the *Golden Dawn* and watched as the enemy dragged their wounded and dead away.

Gustavus barked orders, rallying his men and women to take care of their own injured and slain. A quick tally was taken, and Gustavus shook his head in sorrow and fury.

"By the stinking abyss, this isn't a butcher's bill we could afford to pay," Gustavus said. "They've cut our number by a fourth."

"We took twice as many from them," Kaiser said. Certain that the immediate threat of retaliation was gone, he lowered Sorrell to the deck.

"A fool's comfort," Gustavus said. "The empire's numbers are limitless. We've only got the souls on this ship. And… I knew every one of them by name."

In a rare display of emotion, Gustavus turned away from Kaiser and looked out over the ocean.

Kaiser let the captain of the *Golden Dawn* have a moment alone. He turned his attention to Sorrell. Lacrael knelt next to him.

"How's the shoulder?" Kaiser said.

"The bullet missed the bone," Lacrael said. "Bled like a stuck pig, but it should heal easily."

Together, they made a cursory search of Sorrell's clothing to make sure she was not hiding any weapons.

"She's got to be the next champion," Lacrael said. "There's no other explanation. That ice *felt* like our powers, and when she summoned it, I felt a sort of kinship with her, didn't you?"

"I felt something," Kaiser said with a frown. "But I don't know if I'd call it kinship. If she's who we've been looking for, then your high king has led us on yet another idiotic errand with Raither."

"Maybe from one perspective," Lacrael said. "But we'd never have been in Spider's Cove if we hadn't thought Raither was our man. We were on the right path for the wrong reasons."

Kaiser sat back on his heels. "I don't like it. Riddles and subterfuge stink of manipulation to me. If your high king is so honorable, why doesn't he reveal himself and give us clear instruction?"

"You said yourself that he told you he can't. He aids us as best he can without revealing himself to the enemy."

"If the two of you are finished, we need to discuss how to get out of this mess," Gustavus said, cutting off Kaiser's angry retort. "I'd wager we have about two hours before the admiral's crew come looking for blood. If we show even the slightest notion of cutting ourselves loose, they'll fill our belly with hot iron and try to take Sorrell by force. Even if we hold them off, it would spell our demise. We'd be dead in the water."

"We can't surrender her," Kaiser said.

"So you've said, and I'm of a mind to agree with you. But unless you're going to take that fancy sword of yours and clear out a ship full of angry marines, I don't see any other options."

"Bring some salts from the sick bay. If we can get Sorrell awake, maybe we can convince her to negotiate on our behalf."

"What's she going to tell them? 'Sorry, old chums, I've been chosen to go on a mystical quest to worlds far away. Off you go back to the emperor. Tell him everything's fine, and I'll write when I can.'"

Kaiser got to his feet. Gustavus's disagreeable attitude was wearing his patience thin.

"What do you want me to say?" Kaiser said. "That your high king has spoken to me and shown me the path to victory? He hasn't. He's the one who got us into this, assuming he's even who you claim. If you've no solution forthcoming, then get on your knees and pray. Maybe he'll listen to you, because he certainly doesn't hear me."

Chapter 21

MAZAREEM WAS BRIMMING WITH energy. The sustenance provided by Stone's body was just the rejuvenating tonic he had needed. Who said you could not squeeze blood from a Stone? He grinned at his pun.

Above his head, the sounds of fighting had gone quiet. Mazareem waited another fifteen minutes just to be sure the conflict was over. It was time to reveal himself, but when and how he made his entrance was critical. There were two possibilities.

The first, and best outcome, was that Sorrell and her marines had somehow managed to kill or capture the two magi on Gustavus's ship. They were, after all, the entire reason Mazareem was in this realm. Once he made sure they were dead, he would kill Sorrell per his agreement with Viatrix and then vanish without a trace.

The second, and more likely outcome, was that Gustavus and his pet magi had overcome Sorrell and her crew, who had not been expecting much in the way of resistance. If this was the case, Mazareem had to proceed with extreme caution. They would not suspect his presence, and he had only one chance to strike from the shadows. If he managed to kill just a single magus, Mazareem would consider this venture an unmitigated success.

While Mazareem considered these options, he worked quickly to buckle several belts around his lanky frame. One went around his waist, and another looped across his chest and around his back. These belts held a multitude of little vials and bottles, most of which swirled with dark liquids or colorful gases. In a few of them, fearsome looking insects scrabbled against the glass walls of their tiny prisons. Mazareem took extreme care in securing the last vial, even though it appeared to hold nothing more than a bit of dust.

Once the belts were secure, Mazareem removed his small dagger from his pack and then slung the small burden over his shoulder. He inspected the blade with a frown. It had been a long time since he was forced to employ such crude martial means. They lacked the elegance and efficiency of a carefully crafted magic sigil, but without his staff, and in these close quarters, he was forced to improvise.

Confident that he had waited long enough, Mazareem eased the door open and scanned the hall through the crack. It was deserted. He slipped through the door and gently shut it behind him. Unfortunately, he had left a mess in his cabin. Mazareem suspected his hosts would be less than pleased.

His long legs carried him quickly and silently to the stairs that led to the next deck. Mazareem paused before making his ascent, straining his ears for even the slightest sound above. He heard nothing.

On the next level, Mazareem moved from room to room, ready to strike and kill, but finding no one. The next deck was the gun deck, where he was sure to encounter sailors.

Mazareem stopped at the next set of stairs. The *Celestial* was a twenty-gun ship, with five men to a gun crew. In this sort of engagement, they'd need to man only half the guns, so Mazareem could expect to encounter fifty sailors on the gun deck.

After making this quick mental calculation, Mazareem plucked a glass bottle from his belt. It was the one he had treated with great care. He held it up to his eye, inspecting the little pile of gray dust. No doubt, the sailors would not let him pass without a challenge, and he would prefer not to have to kill all fifty men. Better to scare them into compliance, if possible. He needed to get by them, and fast.

Taking the steps two at a time, Mazareem ascended to the gun deck. He stopped at the top of the stairs momentarily to confirm that his guess about the number of men had been correct. The gunnery sergeant on the nearest cannon noticed him immediately. He barked a word to his crew and gestured towards Mazareem. They stepped away from their gun and into Mazareem's path.

"Well met, my good sirs," Mazareem said with a genteel smile. "Am I correct in surmising that the battle is won? I've not heard a gunshot for the past half hour."

The gun crew muttered amongst themselves, slightly put off by Mazareem's cordial address. By this time, the rest of the gun deck had turned to watch, although they did not leave their posts. The five men in front of Mazareem had come to some sort of agreement, and the sergeant stepped forward.

"You got a lot of moxie, showing yourself up here," the swarthy sergeant said. "Fancy words don't change nothin'. None of us have forgot what you done to poor Katya."

Mazareem dropped his act.

"I'm in a pleasant mood, so I'll give you one warning," Mazareem said. "Step aside or suffer the consequences."

The sergeant sneered. "There's fifty of us and one of you. What're you gonna do, push us all overboard like you did Katya?"

At this, the crew started to advance towards Mazareem. Four of them brandished crude cutlasses, with the fifth holding the cannon ramrod like a halberd.

"So be it," Mazareem said.

In one swift motion, Mazareem threw the glass bottle in his hand so that it smashed beneath the feet of the gun crew. He covered his nose and mouth at the same time. Poison had little effect on him, but this one was more of a… stimulant.

Surprised, the sergeant and his crew stopped short and looked at the shattered glass. Nothing happened. The sergeant threw back his head and laughed. And laughed. And kept laughing. His gun crew joined in, and within several heartbeats, their laughter had become the sound of madness. Faces twisted into snarls, and still they laughed.

In the midst of a fit of deranged cackling, the sergeant turned and buried his sword in the throat of his nearest mate. Blood spurting from his severed neck, he slashed at the sergeant's face and chest, carving great gashes in the sergeant's skin. The other three men of the gun crew turned on each other, their lunacy reaching new heights as they set into one another in frenzied glee.

Stunned, the rest of the sailors on the gun deck watched in horror, too surprised to even petition the gods for mercy. Mazareem waited impatiently for the little quarrel to run its course. In the end, only the man with the ramrod remained standing.

Still laughing hysterically, the man was using the ramrod to grind the head of his sergeant into paste against the deck.

"There's nothing left of his skull to load into the cannon," Mazareem said to the man. "How about you try mine instead?"

The man jerked his head up at the sound of Mazareem's voice. His laughs were nothing more than a choked wheezing at this point, but still, he could not stop. He abandoned the sergeant's mangled remains and stumbled his way towards Mazareem. Mazareem let him come.

Another step, and the sailor was within striking distance—he thrust at Mazareem with the ramrod. Mazareem easily stepped around the clumsy blow and jammed the blade of his dagger up through the soft skin beneath the man's jaw. Instead of letting the body fall to the floor, Mazareem held the dying man up on the point of his blade. The man's body spasmed—the ramrod fell to the deck. He wanted to make sure the rest of the sailors on the gun deck did not give him any trouble.

"Take it from an experienced alchemist," Mazareem said. "Steel and brain matter don't mix well."

Mazareem jerked the dagger out, and the man crumpled to the floor, dead where he lay. Under the terrified gaze of the remaining sailors, Mazareem knelt and cleaned his weapon on the dead man's shirt. He took his time to let the impact of what had just happened sink in. Finally, he stood, and he turned his attention to the next nearest gun crew.

"Now, who's going to be a good man and tell me the outcome of the battle?" Mazareem said.

Knees trembling, the gunnery sergeant stepped forward. "We, ah, uh... th-the..." He stumbled to a stop, unable to tear his gaze from the dead men on the deck at Mazareem's feet.

"Do try to stay focused," Mazareem said. "While I appreciate the admiration of my handiwork, I'm rather pressed for time at the moment."

The sergeant gulped and tried again. "The b-battle is over... sir. The enemy captured the admiral, and we're waiting t-to negotiate her return."

Mazareem smiled to himself. Leave it to fate to find a third option he had not anticipated. So they were at a stalemate. He wondered what he could do to break it.

Five quick strides took Mazareem to the gun port of the now unmanned cannon nearest him. He leaned his head out into the opening to peer at the *Golden Dawn*. The *Celestial* sat higher in the water than the other ship, which put the gun port almost level with the *Golden Dawn*'s main deck. An idea came to Mazareem as he stared at the pristine wood of the *Golden Dawn*'s hull.

"Split your crews enough to man this cannon," Mazareem said to the sailors of the gun deck, patting the iron armament at his side. "I want all ten guns on this side loaded and fired into the *Golden Dawn*'s belly."

"You're mad," the sergeant said. "You'll get us all killed."

"Judgments about my sanity are to be reserved until later," Mazareem said. He plucked another glass bottle from his belt and cradled it in his palm where the sailors could see it. "Now, do you wish to obey, or should I demonstrate another of my concoctions?"

The sergeant's eyes flicked back and forth between the bottle and Mazareem's face. Mazareem watched as the man contemplated resisting and then thought better of it. Finally, the sergeant's shoulders slumped, and the fight went out of his eyes.

"Come on, lads," the sergeant said. "Let's do as the man says. Maybe the admiral can escape in the confusion."

"A wise decision," Mazareem said. He moved to stand in the center of the gun deck, giving himself the vantage point to supervise each crew. The glass bottle gleamed in his open palm, a promise of swift retribution if any man faltered or hesitated.

Now under Mazareem's command, the surviving sailors leapt into action. Sergeants barked orders as the cannons were loaded, primed, and winched into place. Men grunted with the effort of lifting the heavy guns so that they were pointed down into the *Golden Dawn*'s bowels. Wooden chocks were placed under the rear of the iron barrels to hold them on an incline.

Mazareem watched the gun crews work with growing anticipation. He had not had this much fun since his five hundredth birthday.

When the last gun was loaded and in position, the nearest sergeant looked to Mazareem for the order. Mazareem could not help from grinning as he spoke the command.

"Fire all guns!"

Chapter 22

LACRAEL WAS STANDING IN Gustavus's cabin with Kaiser, Niad, and the unconscious Sorrell when the deck beneath her feet exploded. One moment, they were in tense conversation about how to get away from the enemy, the next, they were scrambling for the door as the floor heaved and bucked beneath their feet.

Gustavus scooped up the limp form of Sorrell and dashed for the door. Lacrael, Kaiser, and Niad followed close behind. The terrible thunder of the broadside lingered, and Gustavus had to shout above the ringing in Lacrael's ears.

"Those miserable whoresons!" Gustavus shouted. "They've ruined us!"

Sailors stumbled up from belowdecks, too stunned to speak. Lacrael saw men missing hands and arms, women covered in blood, all of them people she had learned to call friends over the past six months. A cold fury gripped her heart.

"If they want fire, I'll show them fire," Lacrael said as she stepped towards the enemy ship. Flames ignited from her clenched fists.

Before Lacrael had taken two steps, a panicked cry sounded from below her feet.

"Fire belowdecks!" a sailor shouted. "It's in the magazine!"

"Cap'n, we're done for," Niad said, her voice strained.

"Gods below... not like this," Gustavus said in almost a whisper. His next words were a bellow that shook the ship almost as much as the enemy cannon fire. "Abandon ship! She's gonna blow!"

Lacrael whirled to the big captain. "We can't—"

"There's no time, woman," Gustavus said, cutting her off. "You don't want to be standing here when that magazine goes."

Gustavus and Niad were already moving towards the starboard rail.

"Brant's still locked in the brig!" Lacrael said.

"Tarathine," Kaiser said.

Kaiser did not wait for a response. At the thought of his daughter trapped belowdecks, he bolted towards the nearest hatch.

Gustavus ignored Lacrael's plea for Brant. He tossed Sorrell overboard and dove in after her. Furious at the captain for leaving Brant to die, she chased after Kaiser. Lacrael dove through the hatch—she almost missed the wooden rungs of the ladder in her haste.

— —

Kaiser charged through the billowing smoke on the gun deck. An image of Tarathine trapped in their cabin filled his mind. He could see nothing else. The cries of dying sailors barely registered.

Daylight flashed by as he sprinted past the gun ports. At the stair down to the third deck, Kaiser came to a stumbling stop. He was coughing now, tears and mucus streaming from his eyes.

The stairs were almost completely hidden beneath the roiling black smoke. Kaiser did not see any flames yet, but he knew the deck below must be engulfed. To venture any further was probably suicide. Kaiser did not care. He was not going to lose another child.

Hand over his mouth, eyes screwed shut, Kaiser plunged down the stairs. He lost his balance after the third step and tripped, falling painfully the rest of the way. Kaiser lay sprawled on the floor of the third deck. He opened his eyes as he gasped for breath.

Over his head, the charcoal smog clung to the ceiling. There was still a small gap of fresh air close to the deck. He had recovered enough to move again, and Kaiser scrambled along the wooden planks on all fours, keeping his head down below the deadly smoke. Pain shot through his injured arm every time he put weight on it, but Kaiser ignored the protests.

The cabin he shared with Tarathine was on the opposite side of the ship from the enemy broadside. Kaiser refused to consider what had happened if a cannon ball had penetrated that far. Although the brig and the powder magazine were on the next deck down, their cabin was almost directly above both.

Kaiser crawled towards the rear of the ship. He felt the heat of flames he could not see. Sweat poured from his body. His already depleted stamina was fading fast. In the back of his mind, a little voice told him that he did not have the strength to swim if they won free of the burning ship. Kaiser shut that voice out. All that mattered right now was saving Tarathine.

Finally, he reached the door to his cabin. He had also found the fire. A carpet of flames covered the door and wall. The heat was almost unbearable. Fortunate for Tarathine, the door had been closed.

"Get away from the door!" Kaiser shouted over the roaring fire.

Kaiser covered his head with his arms and charged through the door. Flame weakened wood splintered under his weight. Kaiser felt the fire's blistering kiss as he fell into the room.

He found Tarathine huddled in the far corner of the cabin. She flung herself at Kaiser the instant he entered the room. Kaiser hugged her close to his chest. Both of them were crying.

"We can't go back that way," Kaiser said between ragged breaths. "There's only one way out."

Kaiser pushed Tarathine to the side and summoned one of his spectral blades.

"Get ready," Kaiser said. "We'll have to swim for our lives once I make the cut."

Tarathine only nodded.

Kaiser moved to the bulkhead, and with three quick slashes, carved a man-sized opening in the hull of the ship. The ethereal sword sliced through the hard wood without noise or resistance. Water sprayed through the first cut and started to fill the room as Kaiser worked.

"Get behind me!" Kaiser shouted, motioning for Tarathine to move to his back.

Their cabin was not completely below the water line, but the last cut would free the heavy section of hull to come crashing into their cabin. With his injured hand around Tarathine's, Kaiser made the last incision.

Ocean water came spewing through the opening, carrying the piece of hull with it. The water only came up to Kaiser's waist, but the flow of the inward current almost knocked him off his feet and carried him back into the hall. His damaged arm wrenched in its socket as Tarathine held on for dear life.

Shouting in pain, Kaiser pulled Tarathine to his chest, and together, they cast themselves into the sea.

— —

Lacrael's feet hit the gun deck running. The brig was next to the powder magazine. If the magazine blew before Lacrael could reach it, Brant would be vaporized. Black smoke billowed up from below. Dead and dying sailors lay scattered on the bloody deck. Feeble hands reached up toward Lacrael as she dashed by. Kaiser was nowhere to be seen.

"I can't help you, I can't help you," Lacrael repeated over and over as she left friends to die. Tears were streaming down her cheeks now. Her debt to Brant made his life paramount. She must save him above all others.

The stairs down to the third deck almost did Lacrael in—smoke filled her lungs and blocked her vision. She found her way down by gripping the guide rail. When she cleared the last step, Lacrael fell to her hands and knees, hacking and coughing. Mercifully, on this side of the ship, the gaping holes that had been blasted in the hull were venting much of the black fumes.

Lacrael pulled herself to her feet. The devastation on this deck was horrible. Entire rooms had been obliterated by the point-blank fusillade. Lacrael forced herself not to see the mangled bodies and disembodied limbs scattered through the wreckage. Everywhere she looked, the shattered wood was slick with blood.

Brant was one level lower, on the very bottom of the ship. Lacrael descended the last landing and found herself face-to-face with an inferno. Left unchecked, the fire was devouring the *Golden Dawn* from within. Lacrael felt the terrible heat, but it did not hurt her. The problem was the smoke.

Issuing a silent plea to her dead grandfather that this would work, Lacrael raised her hands and added her own fire to the blaze. The force of the power flowing from her palms drove the conflagration back and cleared enough space in front of her that Lacrael could breathe.

She fought fire with fire. Lacrael moved down the long hallway in the underbelly of the ship towards where Brant was held. Within a few steps, flames surrounded Lacrael on all sides. She walked in the heart of the cataclysm.

Brant's cell reared out of the smoke sooner than Lacrael had expected. She checked the fire shooting from her fingertips lest she be the one to incinerate him. Relief flooded through Lacrael when she found Brant still alive. He was lying on the floor to keep himself below the smoke. In another minute or two, his prison would be consumed.

Lacrael grasped the already hot iron lock—it melted it into liquid between her fingers. The door swung open, and she rushed in to kneel beside Brant. His terrified eyes found hers.

"Come on," Lacrael said. "I can push the fire back with my own."

Before Brant could reply, an explosion rocked the ship. The powder magazine, separated from the brig by a single wooden bulkhead, had started to detonate.

Brant rose to his knees, never breaking eye contact with Lacrael. She raised a hand and caressed his cheek. In Brant's fear, in his imploring look for salvation, Lacrael saw something of the old Brant that she missed so much.

"We're out of time," Lacrael said. "I'm sorry... for everything."

They only had one chance, but Lacrael expected it would kill them both. She pulled Brant to her in a fierce embrace. The dragon amulet, now secured around his chest and shoulders with links of chain, bit hard into her breast. Lacrael kissed the top of his head and called to the fire within her like she had never done before. A swirling orb of flame surrounded them, pushing out in all directions. If the *Golden Dawn* was dying, this would finish it off.

At the same instant, the powder magazine exploded. Lacrael screamed, throwing everything she had against the violence of the hostile blast. In the belly of the *Golden Dawn*'s erupting corpse, Lacrael and Brant clung to each other, riding out the destruction in the center of a newborn star.

Chapter 23

SAREDON MISSED HIS FAMILY. An emptiness clawed at his soul where a mother, father, and sister should be. Every day brought with it a growing sense of despair and dread. In the quiet hours of the night, when Ursais slept, Saredon huddled in the dirty corner of their hovel and cried. It was the only way he knew to grapple with the torment in his heart.

Even to Saredon's childish awareness, it was clear that Ursais's health was fading fast. The old man no longer ate what meager scraps of food that Saredon could pilfer or scrounge from the streets. Ursais would consume only the blood of Abimelech from the priesthood's sacrament, and he demanded Saredon find more and more of it.

In the past week, Ursais had rarely felt well enough to speak. And when he did, his maddened ramblings terrified Saredon. Rather than take comfort in his protector's presence, Saredon fled their hiding place when Ursais started raving.

Saredon had hidden the dragon amulet behind a brick in the crumbling wall of their dingy dwelling place. Ever since his encounter with the priestesses of Abimelech, he had been too scared to carry it with him. They seemed to be able to sense him when he wore it.

Outside the slums, the city of Northmark was finally starting to return to stability. The return of a daily, normal routine for most citizens caused problems for Saredon. He had been invisible in the chaos of the past few months, just another orphan trying to find his family. But now that things were settling down again, people started to notice his comings and goings.

This afternoon, Saredon returned almost empty-handed. He had ranged far, hoping to find the remnants of a fresh catch on the docks. But the presence of one of the street gangs had scared him away from his target. After his beating in the alley, he learned to stay away from the other organized orphans that roamed the city.

Beneath his shirt, Saredon hid a few pathetic bread crusts and part of a half-eaten carrot. He had devoured the prize of the day, a rotten apple, and was bringing the rest for Ursais. What the old man refused, Saredon would eat as well. Ursais would be furious with Saredon for not bringing any of Abimelech's blood.

Saredon's arms trembled with the effort of carrying his tiny load. He was sickly and growing weaker by the day. On the rare nights when nightmares did not haunt him, memories of the feasts he enjoyed as a son of the tenth reaver dominated his dreams.

Careful to avoid the patrolling guards, Saredon darted across the last street and passed through the gate into the city's trash heap. He and Ursais had been forced to move their hiding spot when the priesthood started searching for them. They had not intended to stay in the dump, but that was before Ursais lost the ability to walk.

At the very back of the stinking heaps of refuse, hard up against a brick wall that separated the trash from the city, Saredon ducked into a little hole. On hands and knees, he crawled through a maze of broken furniture, discarded clothing, rusted tools, and dripping yuck to reach the small cave they had carved out of the garbage.

Saredon pushed aside the filthy leather hanging that served as a door. He paused. Above the stench, he detected another smell. It was the stink of death.

Not wanting to see, but forcing himself forward, Saredon crept toward the alcove where Ursais lay. Ursais's wheezing breath had gone silent, and his aged face looked almost serene, freed from the delirium that had twisted it in the last few weeks of his life. The old man was dead.

Distraught, Saredon sat down hard. The food he had gathered for Ursais tumbled to the ground. Ursais was the last adult that knew Saredon still lived, and the old man had given him no instruction, no last words of insight or comfort. He was just dead, breathing his last while Saredon was out scrabbling for scraps in the gutter. And now Saredon was completely alone.

There were no more tears to shed. Saredon felt hollow. Mechanically, he gathered the food from the dirt, shoved it into his mouth, and started to chew. When he finished eating, Saredon did not know what to do next. So he curled up into a ball on the cold ground and went to sleep.

Dreams came. Nightmares where Ursais rose from the dead, screaming for more of Abimelech's blood in his gibbering madness. The black clad priestesses hunted Saredon through his fitful slumber, until at last, he found merciful peace in the arms of his mother. This was Saredon's favorite dream. In it, he found himself in the lap of his mother, his head cradled in her arms. She rocked him gently as she sang to him.

If Saredon could have stayed asleep forever in that dream, he would have. But hunger woke him. It always did. After waking, the comfort of his mother's presence stayed with him, and Saredon could think clearly for the first time in days. He looked around the pitiful hiding place—nothing remained for him here. Ursais was dead, and Saredon saw no reason to stay. He did not know where he could go but anywhere would be better than here.

Saredon felt strange leaving Ursais's body where it lay. They had been each other's only friend and companion for the past six months. Saredon sensed that there should be something said or done to mark the old man's passing. But he did not know what that should be, and so after one last look at Ursais's wizened face, Saredon got on his hands and knees and crawled toward the door.

A memory tugged at him, and Saredon hesitated. He glanced at the shoddy brick wall where the dragon amulet lay hidden. Something inside urged him to take the charm with him. Saredon found himself resisting this internal prompting. The crazier Ursais had become, the more Saredon's fear of the trinket grew. Ursais had ranted about strange powers and dreadful prophecies. The amulet acted as the centerpiece in all his demented stories.

After Ursais became bedridden, Saredon had waited expectantly for the old man's prayers to be answered. Ursais had believed so fervently, and begged for intercession so relentlessly, that Saredon fully expected a divine savior to come to their aid and right all the terrible wrongs they had suffered. But a savior never came, and now Ursais was gone. Whatever power the amulet was supposed to have, it had failed.

This realization brought memories of Saredon's father to the forefront of his mind. Kaiser had been diligent in teaching them that they should be the source of their own strength and confidence. He had taught them that each person's gods existed in their own mind, and that the strongest mind did not need them. Saredon felt foolish for forgetting his father's lessons.

Confident that his father would approve, Saredon left Ursais and the dragon amulet behind. It was still evening outside, which left him with some daylight to figure out what to do next. Having eaten the food meant for Ursais, his belly felt content with the double portion. Saredon would not go hungry this night, but he needed to find a safe place to sleep.

The only hiding spot that sprang to mind was the smelly warehouse of dried fish on the outskirts of the docks. Saredon was sure he could still squeeze through the crack in the foundation, and if he had to, maybe he could widen the gap a bit. No one would think to look in the basement of that putrid building for a lost orphan. And if he was lucky, he might be able to pilfer breakfast without having to venture into the city.

Before leaving the dump, Saredon searched until he found a filthy satchel. It had a rip in one side, but if he hung it around his neck with the hole against his leg, no one would notice the damage. In a rare moment of clarity, Ursais had told Saredon that traveling the streets was easier if you looked like you had a purpose. Since then, Saredon always carried something to make it look like he was on an errand.

However, pretending to be on an assignment was not enough to hide him from the watchful eye of the priesthood's hunters. In the downtime when he was not searching for food, and to avoid Ursais's ramblings, Saredon spent long hours watching and listening to the city, always careful to stay out of sight. He knew that any boy close to his age found alone on the street was snatched up, and those that disappeared were not seen again. The orphan gangs traveled in force now, desperate to stay out of the priesthood's clutches. Those gangs searched for Saredon too, hoping to stop the relentless kidnappings if they captured and delivered Regent Trangeth's quarry.

Saredon did his best to shut out these thoughts as he made for the docks. The entire city was against him, but over the past few months he had been learning to survive. While they filled Saredon with terror, the priesthood and Trangeth's soldiers were predictable in their patterns. So far, they had proved easy to avoid. He darted down the street and ducked into an alleyway. Saredon felt like a little mouse trying to find his way to safety through a den of hungry cats.

A companion to the gnawing hunger, fear was a constant part of Saredon's life now. During the first two weeks of hiding, he had been too afraid to venture outside. But the aching emptiness of his stomach had taught him a harsh lesson. Like the mouse, he moved or he died.

Saredon paused at the other end of the alley and peered around the corner. At the nearest intersection, a bored-looking soldier in the black plate mail of Trangeth's personal guard scanned the citizens passing by. Saredon needed to sneak by under this soldier's nose; otherwise, he would have to take a lengthy detour that would find him arriving at the docks after dark. Despite his growing courage on the streets, Saredon had no desire to be outside after nightfall. The very thought sent a shiver of apprehension down his spine.

This late in the evening, the thoroughfare was jammed with merchants returning from the market. In another half hour, the intersection would be deserted, but right now, it was crowded with people. Saredon watched and waited, and when he saw his opportunity, he stepped out and joined the procession of a street vendor who was heading home after a long day.

Four dirty children helped the man wrestle his crude cart over the cobblestones. Saredon walked close enough behind them that he looked a part of their group, and the soldier's gaze slid right over him without a second look. He was just another child laborer, following after his master.

When they reached the other side of the intersection, Saredon ducked into another alleyway lest the merchant discover him tagging along. He waited for a moment to see if anyone noted his absence. His heart pounded in his chest. He had been certain that the soldier would see through his ruse. To his relief, no one followed, and no cry went up, and Saredon hurried on towards the fish warehouse.

Night had almost fallen by the time Saredon reached the docks. Twilight gave way to the long shadows of darkness, and he was eager to find the safety of a roof over his head. The gap in the foundation of the warehouse was a tight fit, but Saredon forced himself through. On the other side, the familiar stench of dead fish was almost comforting. At least it was something he recognized.

Saredon curled up in a ball next to a dirty wooden pillar and closed his eyes. He was exhausted. His body trembled, and he struggled against the desperate urge to cry. Thoughts of his family filled his mind. He no longer expected to see them again. The agony of absolute abandonment made Saredon forget about his hunger, and he fell asleep trying to summon the dream of his mother.

But Saredon found no comfort in his dreams. There was no escaping the city that was now his prison. He wandered through the streets in his sleep, every daytime fear magnified tenfold in his nightmares. Monsters lurked in the sewers, and the priesthood's guards hounded his steps. Saredon ran through the city, calling out for his father to save him, yet Kaiser never appeared. Above it all, the sound of Ursais's maniacal voice echoed in the gray sky.

Hours later, Saredon woke to a noise in the warehouse overhead. He felt like he had not slept at all. His body ached from the hard ground. The memory of his nightmares clung to him, and he could scarcely bring himself to breathe as he strained his ears to listen.

"It stinks worse than cat's piss in here," a surly voice was saying.

"Of course it does, it's a warehouse full of dead fish," someone answered. "Now stop your whining and help me lift."

Through the gaps in the floorboards, Saredon peered up at two men who were wrestling with a crate. Torchlight filtered through the cracks in the boards, and Saredon pushed himself deeper into shadow in case one of the men glanced down.

The men carried crate after crate out of the warehouse, talking amongst themselves the entire time. Saredon listened intently. Their easy friendship and playful banter nourished some part of him that felt desolate. The urge to reveal himself was overpowering, but in the end, the fear kept him silent.

When they were almost finished with their task, the two laborers took a moment to rest right above Saredon's head.

"Give it a minute," the first man said. "The boss won't notice if we take our time with the last crate. Let's see him lug these blasted fish. Heavy as rocks, they are."

"That last box gave me a splinter," the second man whined as he sat down hard and inspected his hand.

"I told you to wear gloves, you idiot."

The second man murmured an insolent reply while he picked at the splinter. A minute later, he said, "Say, did you hear about that statue they found in the dockside slums?"

"What of it?" the first man said, his response quick and his voice guarded.

"Hey now, there's no need to get short with me. I was just asking if you'd heard about it, that's all."

"Yeah, I know of it, and I'll tell you what I told the last fool that mentioned it: I don't want to talk about it."

"Oh, come on, who's going to hear us in here? They say it's the spitting image of the tenth reaver's dead wife—what's her name? Do you think some of the rebels survived?"

At the mention of his mother, Saredon's heart quickened.

"I'm done talking to you," the first man said. "Get back to work. And if you've a speck of sense in your head, you'll forget that blighted statue unless you want to rot inside a cell."

The second man grumbled, but he got to his feet and went back to work. Saredon did not hear another word they said. Only one thing mattered now—there was a statue of his mother in the nearby slums. Who would create such a thing, and why? Surely, anyone who would honor the memory of his mother would care for Saredon as well.

Saredon decided that he had to see this likeness of his mother immediately, if only to look on her face one more time. And the more he thought about it, the greater his resolve became. It gave him a purpose, a goal. The dockside slums were dangerous but small. He should be able to search through them in a day, and he knew how to stay out of sight.

As soon as the warehouse above went silent, Saredon scrambled for the crack in the wall. In his haste, Saredon did not even think to eat. It was still dark outside, with only the faintest hints of the dawn visible over the eastern rooftops.

The section of the slums that pressed up against the dockyard was not far. Most of the stevedores that made their living hauling cargo in and out of the ships that frequented Northmark lived in the filthy shanty town. It was a violent place that Saredon usually avoided. This early in the morning, however, he should be able to wander the rooftops without being noticed.

Flitting from shadow to shadow, Saredon moved through the streets without making a sound. At the edge of the dockyard ghetto, he clambered up onto a low roof as quietly as possible. An unbroken plain of rooftops stretched out before Saredon. The shacks and huts were built so close to each other that they shared walls, and in between them, the alleyways were so narrow that he could jump over them.

Silent as the mouse he imagined himself to be, Saredon scurried across the tops of the flimsy hovels. He paid careful attention to where he placed his feet. It would do him no good to come crashing down into the bed of an angry dock worker.

Saredon had a good idea of where the statue must be. There was only one place in these slums where it might go unnoticed by the priesthood for a time. In the poorest and most dangerous quarter, nearest the salty spray of the sea, not even the regent's guards patrolled. Saredon considered this fact even as he made his way in that direction. The hope of seeing his mother's face pulled him onward.

Beneath his feet, Saredon could hear men and women stirring as they rose to get ready for another day of hard labor. He picked up his pace, determined to find the statue before he had to find a hiding spot to wait out the morning rush. So far, he had seen no hint of it, and he was fast approaching the water.

Shoes slipping as he scrambled up a particularly steep incline, Saredon reached up with his hands and hauled himself to the peak of the roof. He paused at the top and peered down into a dead-end alleyway. It was the last line of shacks before the sharp drop into the ocean. And there, in the dirt street in front of them, was Saredon's goal. The statue sat against a blank wall, positioned to look out into a small circular gathering area. It was the size of a child, no bigger than Saredon. At the stone figure's feet, a few bright flowers provided a splash of color to an otherwise dreary scene.

From his vantage point on the roof, Saredon could not make out the details of the statue. The thought never entered his mind that it might not be his mother. He wanted it to be. He needed it to be. This close to a physical, tangible memory of her, his breath came quick and his heart started to hammer.

Saredon slid down the sloped roof and lowered himself down into the dirt street without a thought about how he would get back up. All that mattered was seeing his mother's face. He approached the statue. It was her. Carved from cold stone, Mariel's smiling face gazed at Saredon, level with his own. Fingers trembling, tears streaming down his cheeks, Saredon raised a hand to touch the lifeless visage of his lost mother.

"You shouldn't have come, boy," a grating voice said from behind Saredon.

Startled, Saredon whirled to face the voice. A man in a ragged, hooded cloak stood between him and the only way out of the alley. He had wide shoulders and the look of a soldier, but his back was stooped and the shadows of his hood hid his face. Saredon was certain he had seen the man before.

The man gestured at the statue with a clawed hand. "It's a trap, set for anyone who might remember her fondly. But most of all, they were hoping to lure you."

"You won't take me," Saredon said through his tears. His own defiance surprised him—he felt himself drawing strength from the image of his mother.

"Easy, lad," the man said. "There are still those who remember your father and mother with love."

At that, the man reached a hand up and pulled back his hood. The right side of his face was ruined, melted almost to the bone. It was the same beggar who had saved Saredon from the gang in the alley.

"Don't you know me?" the man said.

Saredon shook his head. At the sight of the man's face, his courage had fled.

"I suppose I'm not what I once was," the man said, his hand rising to touch his ravaged face. "I bounced you on my knee when you were just a babe, I trained you to fight, and I... I failed you at the last. By thunder, it's me, boy, it's Garius! I've been watching this statue for days, just in case you learned of it and came looking."

For several long heartbeats, Saredon did not respond. It was Garius, former captain of Kaiser's guards. The man who should have kept them safe. Anger, confusion, sorrow, and elation all battled for prominence in his soul. In the end, the understanding that Garius was a friend won out. With a shuddering sob, Saredon hurled himself at Garius with his arms outstretched.

Garius gathered Saredon into a close embrace. The man's arms were thin but still strong.

"Hush, lad," Garius said. "We're not in the clear yet. There was an agent of the regent watching this statue. I killed him when I saw you on the rooftops, but his relief will be here soon, and the alarm will go up. We need to be away before that happens."

Saredon nodded, his face still pressed into Garius's chest.

"I've got another cloak that should fit you," Garius said. "These mark us as diseased. A useful deterrent against those too curious for their own good."

Garius helped Saredon don the stinking, ratty garment.

"If you walk with a hunch, it adds to the effect," Garius said as he stepped back to inspect Saredon. "Maybe shuffle a foot now and then. Show people what they expect to see. Can you do that?"

Saredon nodded again.

"Come now, have you forgotten everything I taught you after a few months on the streets? That's no way to respond to a request."

"Yes, sir, I can do it," Saredon said.

"I know you can, now come on. I've a place we can hide until this blows over."

Now disguised as one of Northmark's most unfortunate denizens, Saredon followed Garius through the twisting, narrow alleys of the dockyard slums in a daze. For six months he had been on his own, save for the dying Ursais. The sudden appearance of Garius was too much to process.

Saredon cast one last glance over his shoulder at the statue of his mother before they turned the corner. Even in death, she still watched over him. Saredon smiled at the thought and rubbed the tears from his face as he turned back towards Garius.

Chapter 24

SORRELL WOKE AS IF from a nightmare, yet she could not remember dreaming. She was lying flat on her back on a hard floor. Above her, she recognized the planks underneath a ship's deck. Beyond these immediate, innate observations, thoughts and memories would not come. Sorrell remembered her name and that something terrible had happened, but anything else eluded her.

With a groan, Sorrell rolled over. She found iron bars next to her face. Brig. She was in a brig. This thought produced a thread of memory which she traced back to its source. This was the brig of the *Celestial,* her ship. Lieutenant Stone was her first lieutenant and lover. And with that thought, everything came rushing back.

Alarmed, confused, Sorrell sat up a little too quickly. Her head swam, and she almost collapsed to the floor again. The back of her skull throbbed in pain. Gingerly, she probed the wound with her fingers. There was no blood, and as she thought about it, she remembered getting knocked out by Gustavus's demon swordsman.

And before that... Sorrell looked down at her hands. She had summoned a shield of ice out of thin air. It had saved her life. Somehow, she knew the power was still there. Sorrell felt it filling in the parts of her being that she had not even known were empty. What was happening to her?

The dream of the horseman came back to her. Sorrell detected his presence lurking in the power inside her, even stronger than before. The meaning was clear—the powers were a gift from the knight in the dream. But why? Every child in Coridal grew up learning the legends of powerful magi, but they were just myths and fairy tales.

Despite her condition and the circumstances in which she found herself, Sorrell felt a slight thrill when she remembered a particular story about the ancient warlords of Coriddia. Legend had it that in the old days, the gods chose who would lead, and they bestowed their favor on their chosen by giving them special powers. Were the gods themselves blessing her claim to the throne?

Sorrell shook her head carefully to dispel these musings. First, she needed to figure out what was going on. To find herself a prisoner in her own brig could only mean one thing. Mazareem had made a move for control while she was unconscious. It was past time for a reckoning with that man. Sorrell made up her mind that she would get out of this cell, find Stone, and return to lock Mazareem behind these same bars.

Confident that she could convince any sailor that appeared to release her, Sorrell sat on the single wooden bench and waited. From the way the ship rode the sea, she knew that they were close to land and anchored, which seemed odd. If Mazareem had ordered the *Celestial* to the coast, he had overstepped his bounds to the point of treason.

Minutes stretched into hours, and Sorrell began to grow concerned. No one appeared to attend to her, and she did not hear sounds of activity on the deck above. The ship seemed to be deserted.

Frustrated, and beginning to worry that the situation might be more serious than she initially thought, Sorrell got to her feet and moved to the bars of her cell. A few minutes of inspection revealed no obvious weakness, and picking the lock was beyond her, even if she had the tools.

At some inner prompting, the image of using her new powers to break out sprang unbidden into her mind. Sorrell stepped back from the bars and considered the idea. Could ice bend iron?

Curious now, Sorrell raised an upturned palm and concentrated on it. An icicle started to take shape, and it grew to the length of a javelin before she let go of the thought. Sorrell hefted the frozen weapon in her hand. It was frigid, but the cold did not bother her. On the contrary, it felt wonderful. She tested the point and pulled back her finger with a hiss. Razor sharp.

Sorrell raised the ice spike over her head and slammed the point into the lock on the cell door. Her hands slipped with the impact, robbing the strike of most of its force. The improvised spear left a wicked scratch on the iron but did no real damage. To Sorrell's surprise, the tip of the icicle did not shatter.

Frustrated, Sorrell tossed the ice to the floor. It landed with a clatter and did not break. To her surprise, the stuff was at least as strong as iron and almost weightless, but Sorrell did not have the strength and leverage to use it to force the door.

Again, a vision filled her mind. This time the picture was more specific. It showed her the ice shield she had summoned on the deck of the *Golden Dawn*. Sorrell did not know if she could reproduce that feat. She did not know how she did it in the first place.

After taking a deep breath to calm herself, Sorrell raised both hands towards the cell bars and called on the power she felt inside her. A wall of solid ice sprang into existence in front of her. She gasped in surprise and almost let it go.

Sorrell poured more and more of her power into the ice. The shield grew and morphed. It quickly reached the limits of floor and ceiling and started to press out towards the iron bars. Sorrell tired quickly. She had not expected there to be a limit to this newfound power—she felt like she had just spent an entire day scrubbing the deck.

Iron bars did not stand a chance against the expanding ice. Sorrell winced as the metal gave way with a terrible creaking and then a loud series of pops. Wood splintered, and the bars of the cell ripped free of the deck. Panting, Sorrell let go of the small iceberg she had created. It turned to water and splashed to the floor in a puddle. The door and wall of the cell followed it down with a crash.

No one appeared to investigate the noise, and the hallway outside the brig was deserted. Sorrell started to march towards the stairs to the deck above, but she had to stop and lean against the wall when her strength abandoned her. Not only did using her new powers leave her drained, but she was also famished. Sorrell suppressed the gnawing hunger in her belly. Food would come later. First, she needed to find Stone.

On the landing of the next deck, Sorrell realized that Mazareem's cabin was only a few doors away. Intuition suggested she give the room a look. She needed information about what had happened, and perhaps she would find evidence in Mazareem's personal things. And if she found the bastard, Sorrell would confront him right now.

Sorrell crept along the hallway towards Mazareem's door. To her annoyance, she felt like an intruder on her own ship. The door was open a crack, and when Sorrell pushed on it, she discovered something blocking it on the other side. She put her shoulder to the door, and with a grunt of effort, she pushed her way into the room.

A dead sailor lay sprawled on the floor; his legs had been obstructing the door. Dried blood covered the wooden planks around the corpse. Sorrell gagged at the stench. She recognized the man—it was the runner she had sent after Stone.

No sign of Mazareem, but there was no question in Sorrell's mind that this was his handiwork. When she finally tore her gaze from the slain sailor, Sorrell saw another body on the bed. She stepped forward, careful to avoid the mess, to get a better view.

It took a long moment for Sorrell to register what she found. It was Stone. His face looked peaceful, as if he were in deep slumber, but it was deathly pale. Sorrell's eyes moved down his body, refusing to believe the truth. Stone's right arm hung from the cot, his fingertips almost touching the floor. His wrist had been opened, and Sorrell realized that most of the blood splattered on the cabin deck was Stone's. Her stomach lurched.

Sorrell raised a hand to her mouth, fingers trembling. Stone's uniform had been wrenched open. A bloody incision gaped beneath his ribs. It looked as if someone had torn the heart out of his chest. At this discovery, Sorrell lost control. She fell to her hands and knees next to the cot, body heaving as her empty stomach forced bile into her mouth. Stone's blood stained the palms of her hands red.

The fit of retching passed, and Sorrell crawled to the top of the bed to cradle Stone's head in her arms. Tears spilled down her cheeks, and she pressed her wet face to his. Unable to stop herself, Sorrell kissed his cold lips, tasting the salt of her own tears.

Sorrow crashed over Sorrell. She was defenseless before it. Pain in her chest stabbed like a physical wound—it felt like it would split her in two. Whoever had cut out Stone's heart had torn out Sorrell's with it. For what seemed like hours, Sorrell could not muster the strength to move. If she stayed here in this moment with the last vestige of Stone's presence, perhaps she could cling to him forever. Sorrell could not bring herself to stand up and walk out into a world where Stone was dead.

While she wept, Sorrell's mind churned. Mazareem had done this. What sort of monster was he? Was this another of Viatrix's hideous lessons, a punishment for the demands Sorrell had made of her mother, or was this the first death in the war that was to be between them?

Sorrell cursed herself. For years she had held Stone at arm's length, knowing the risk of becoming attached to anyone. She had let her guard down. This close to taking the throne, she had thought herself untouchable. And her infatuation with Stone had distracted her from the danger. He had paid the ultimate price for her hubris.

"I'm sorry," Sorrell said through her tears. "I knew better than this."

If Mazareem's boldness was any indication, Viatrix might even now be preparing to move against Sorrell's conspirators in Coridal. Sorrell sensed the world unraveling around her. This mission had been cursed from the start, but she had pushed on anyway, determined to overcome any challenge.

In the blackness of her despair, Sorrell's fingers tingled with cold, reminding her of her newfound powers. Here was something Viatrix had not—could not have—anticipated. If Sorrell reunited with her forces on the mainland, she had a chance. Thousands would rally to Sorrell's standard if she demonstrated she was blessed by the gods. She still had time; Viatrix would have no choice but to wait for word from Mazareem before taking action. If Viatrix wanted war, Sorrell would give her war.

But first, Mazareem must die.

Sorrell got to her feet. She stared down at Stone's serene face for a long time, etching it in her memory, and she hoped that in whatever afterlife waited for them all, he was happy.

"Maybe I'll see you again, someday," Sorrell whispered.

Eyes wet with unshed tears, Sorrell turned away before she started crying again. It was time to harden herself. She would grieve later. Now, it was time to honor Stone by avenging him. Sorrell did not look back as she stepped out of the room. She set aside her sorrow and focused on the rage that gripped her soul with the chill of death.

Confident that the lower decks were empty and that she could move about undetected, Sorrell reached the gun deck quickly. She paused on the last landing of the ascending stair to catch her breath.

The use of her power combined with fatigue from her ordeal on the *Golden Dawn* had left Sorrell extremely weak. Part of her started to worry that if Mazareem resisted her, she would not have the strength to fight back. But the only other option was to wait for him to come for her in the brig. Mouth set in a grim line, Sorrell climbed the last few steps to the next deck.

At the top of the stairs, she peered around the corner to check for sailors. Sorrell froze, stunned by what she saw. Her mouth fell open. The gun deck was devastated. Emanating from the gun ports on the starboard side, the deck and ceiling were blackened in long, narrow streaks that reached the middle of the ship. It looked as if terrible fingers of fire had reached in and clawed at the *Celestial*'s guts. The cannons on that side of the deck had been melted to slag, the tips of their now cool barrels melted over the edge of each opening.

It was clear that the *Celestial* had been attacked by some sort of explosive weapon, but Sorrell could not imagine what would cause this much damage. As she crept along the deck, she found outlines of human bodies that were nothing but ash. What had happened here?

Sorrell climbed towards the main deck, worried about what she would find. The top of the ship would have no protection against whatever caused the destruction below. Sure enough, when Sorrell raised her head up above the deck line to check for watchers, she discovered a ravaged and crippled *Celestial*.

The entire top deck had burned. A forest's worth of pristine timber had been reduced to ugly, charred wood. Two of the three main masts had been snapped off at their base, and the one that still stood was missing half its length. A few pitiful sails hung limp from the ragged rigging on the surviving mast. Sorrell cataloged the damage in a glance. It would take weeks to make the ship seaworthy again. If they could get a makeshift mast up, they might be able to limp down the calm waters of the coast, but the ship would be at the mercy of the open ocean.

Barrels of supplies had been lugged up from below and tools were scattered around the deck. From over the side of the ship, Sorrell heard the rhythmic chopping of axes and pounding of hammers. The repair effort was already under way. Sorrell crawled to a nearby stack of crates, wedging herself between them. Making sure she was well hidden, Sorrell peered over the edge of a wooden box.

Sailors were hard at work clearing the debris and patching up the *Celestial*. Here and there, Sorrell spotted the black uniform of a marine. She saw no sign of Mazareem. Sorrell was just about to reveal herself when she noticed one of her junior lieutenants heading in her direction. His name was Eggard, if Sorrell remembered correctly. She waited for him to pass near her hiding spot, and when he did, Sorrell hissed to get his attention.

Startled, the young man stopped short and looked around. Sorrell hissed again, and he looked in her direction. His eyes nearly popped out of his head when he saw Sorrell. After a furtive glance towards the shore, Eggard knelt down out of sight next to her.

"Admiral, you're awake!" Eggard said. "We'd almost given up hope."

"Report, lieutenant," Sorrell said. "Tell me exactly what happened."

"No one rightly knows, ma'am. We were conferring to negotiate your release from the *Golden Dawn* when our cannons fired without orders. Mazareem slaughtered a gun crew to force them to attack.

The broadside must have lit the *Dawn*'s powder magazine, because she went up like she had a hold full of munitions. I'd have never guessed a ship that size would carry so many explosives. That blast damn near ended us."

"Where is Mazareem now? Why was I in the brig?"

Eggard looked haggard. "None of us were happy about that, ma'am. We tried to protest, but he's got an official writ of authority from the emperor."

"Never mind that, answer my questions," Sorrell said.

"Yes, ma'am," Eggard said with a nod. The routine protocol of obeying an order seemed to put the young man at ease. "You've been unconscious since yesterday. After the *Golden Dawn* sank and we put out the fire, we started fishing survivors out of the ocean. We found you roped to a barrel, so someone over there wanted you to live. After we pulled you from the sea, Mazareem appeared and took command. He took one look at you and started acting very strangely. He accused you of madness and sedition, deeming you unfit for command. None of us believed that for a second, but we were still in shock, and no one wanted to stand up to him right then.

"Mazareem tried to order us to take you below and put you in the infirmary where he would treat your injuries. He was adamant that he needed solitude to revive you. That was one demand too much, and we threatened to mutiny. None of us trust that creepy blighter. So we reached a compromise. We'd lock you in the brig until you woke up, and Mazareem would stay ashore and well away from you. Now that you're here, you can put him in his place… ma'am."

"You've done well, lieutenant," Sorrell said. "I've no doubt you saved my life. Mazareem has already murdered Lieutenant Stone. No doubt, I was next on his list of targets."

"That rotten bastard needs to die," Eggard said.

"That's what I'm about. Here's what I want you to do. Find me a long-rifle, bring it here, and then go ashore and draw him into range. Do that, and I'll put a bullet through his skull."

"Easy said, easy done," Eggard said with a nod.

Sorrell rested her head against the wooden crate as Eggard dashed away to find a gun. She closed her eyes to preserve her quickly fading strength. If she managed one good shot, it would be a miracle. In her weakened state, there was no way Sorrell could confront Mazareem face-to-face.

Eggard returned in what seemed like an instant. Sorrell jerked in surprise and realized she had fallen asleep. The young lieutenant placed the loaded rifle in Sorrell's hands.

"This is Minty's gun, he's the best shot in the whole crew," Eggard said. "It's loaded and primed."

"Very good, lieutenant, now go ashore and bring Mazareem close," Sorrell said.

"Aye, aye, ma'am," Eggard said, giving her a quick salute before disappearing again.

Sorrell waited and listened as Eggard shouted orders at the nearby sailors, directing their repair efforts to the other side of the ship. Soon, Sorrell was alone on the stern of the *Celestial*. When she was certain she had given Eggard enough time to get in a rowboat and start towards land, Sorrell crept from her hiding spot.

The landward window in the remains of her cabin would provide the perfect sniper's perch. Moving as fast as her body would allow, Sorrell crawled through the blackened doorway. Once inside, she stood and slid a chair over to the window. That done, she rested the rifle against the back of the chair to steady it. She made sure to stand back from the opening. In the light of day, Mazareem would not see her even if he looked directly at the window.

Through the small portal of sunlight, Sorrell scanned the nearby shore. The surviving sailors were hard at work felling trees and hewing them into parts to repair the *Celestial*. Off to one side, those too injured to help were recovering on the small beach.

Eggard's small rowboat appeared, the young lieutenant straining hard at the oars. Sorrell watched him run the prow of the boat aground and then hop out and head into the trees at a brisk trot. She slowed her breathing in preparation for the shot.

Mazareem in tow, Eggard returned to the beach only minutes later. The lieutenant gestured towards the *Celestial* with exaggerated concern, no doubt having lured Mazareem here under some pretext of a repair problem.

Sorrell stilled herself and lowered her cheek to the rifle's stock. She sighted down the long iron barrel, waiting for the perfect opportunity. The ship rocked easily beneath her, and Sorrell let the motion become a part of her, using it to guide her aim rather than resisting it. Mazareem stepped forward to look up at what Eggard was pointing to. His pale face was dead center in Sorrell's window.

Stone's presence looked over her shoulder. Tears in her eyes, Sorrell breathed out and squeezed the trigger.

Chapter 25

MAZAREEM FOLLOWED THE INCOMPETENT lieutenant through the trees. The inability of these military minds to think for themselves beggared belief. Without an order from a superior officer, they did not act. To Mazareem's mounting frustration, he needed every able body for the time being. She might be crippled, but the *Celestial* would make far better time down the coast than he could on foot. For that to happen, the repairs must be finished first. And his prize still waited in the brig.

One look at the unconscious Sorrell and Mazareem had known she was a magus. The scent of enchanted ice was strong on her, a new power the other two did not possess, and the fact that they had tied her to a barrel was evidence enough of her importance to his prey. In addition to these observations, there were the eyewitness accounts from the surviving crew. They claimed Sorrell had summoned ice from thin air.

What a stroke of good fortune that Mazareem had acted when he did. For the *Golden Dawn* to have sailed away with a third magus on board would have been maddening. It would also probably have sealed Mazareem's fate before Abimelech.

The only trick now was figuring out how to get near enough to Sorrell to finish the job. Understandably, the sailors did not trust Mazareem. Nor did they believe his accusations against their revered admiral. Ever since placing Sorrell in the brig, two of the crew's best fighters shadowed Mazareem's every move. If he tried to approach the ship, they would sound the alarm and attack.

After he ordered the surprise broadside, the blast from the *Golden Dawn* had penetrated into the *Celestial*'s gun deck in a firestorm that melted flesh and iron alike. Every sailor manning a cannon had been incinerated in an instant. Mazareem had only survived by hurtling himself to the deck at the last second, and even then, he had suffered terrible burns down one side of his body. For the first time in his undead life, he actually hurt.

Mazareem knew he was not thinking clearly. His pack, along with the blood harvested from Stone, had been lost in the chaos. He needed to feed; he needed time to restore himself, and denied both, he was suffering and at risk of permanent damage. Leaving Sorrell asleep in the brig was dangerous, but he had no other choice.

He could have probably killed Sorrell when she lay unconscious and sopping wet on the deck of the *Celestial*, but with a mob of angry sailors pressed close around, it felt too much like suicide. While he had no choice but to obey his master, Mazareem had no desire to die for Abimelech's cause.

"As you can see, the surviving mast isn't tall enough," the lieutenant was saying. The man had not stopped babbling since accosting Mazareem and dragging him out of the cool shadows of the forest.

Mazareem forced himself to pretend to be interested in the lieutenant's observations. Anything to speed up the repair efforts. Hand raised to block out the sun, Mazareem stepped forward and looked up at where the man was pointing.

A gunshot rang out over the water—an iron musket ball tore into Mazareem's left eye and exited through the back of his shattered skull. He found himself on the ground, but he did not remember falling. The lieutenant stood over him, sword in hand.

Dazed and in tremendous pain, Mazareem struggled to his knees. Something was missing. The world looked all wrong. He raised a pale hand to his face. His left eye was gone, the only remnants a bit of ocular jelly that came away on his finger when he scraped the socket.

Horrified, the lieutenant stared down at him, mouth agape. Around them, work stopped as every eye turned towards the gunshot. When they recovered from their shock, Mazareem did not doubt they would rally to finish him off.

Mazareem snarled. He lunged to his unsteady feet, open hand lashing out towards the lieutenant's face. Mazareem was slow and weak, but he still struck too fast for the man to parry. Cartilage and bone crunched under Mazareem's palm, and the man fell away with a crushed nose.

And then Mazareem did something he had never done before. He turned and ran. A cry went up. Another shot rang out from the ship, but the aim was bad. A plank of wood exploded to Mazareem's right.

Sailors closed in, axes and saws trying to fell Mazareem now instead of trees. His balance was off and he felt blind, but his long legs and waning strength did not fail him. He tripped once, sent sprawling by a log he did not see on his blind side. Fortunately, the *Celestial*'s crew gave only a half-hearted pursuit. None of them wanted to be the first one to actually catch Mazareem.

Mazareem ran until he no longer heard the sounds of a chase. He stumbled to a stop, and the urge to find a quiet, dark place to sleep was almost irresistible. Flies buzzed around the hole in his head, eager to fill the damp emptiness with maggots. Mazareem swatted at the insects. A restorative coma would heal him, but at this point, it would take years before he awoke. He did not have years. Sorrell was free; he might only have a few days to redeem this situation.

Fingers trembling, Mazareem plucked a glass bottle from his belt. The searing heat from the *Golden Dawn*'s fiery death had boiled the contents of many of his phials, rendering them useless. A few were now too dangerous for even Mazareem to open. There were precious few that retained a safe potency. He swirled the ochre liquid once, raised it to his lips, and drank it down in one gulp. Impatient to move on, Mazareem forced himself to wait for the potion to take effect.

Augmented strength flowed into his limbs. It would be enough, for now. Mazareem resumed his trek through the forest. The first thing he needed to do was figure out where he was.

Chapter 26

KAISER WATCHED THE ATTACK on Mazareem from the distant trees. The shock at recognizing Abimelech's dark agent had been quickly replaced by a surge of hope, and then disappointment, when Mazareem survived being shot through the eye. Briefly, Kaiser considered tracking Mazareem through the forest and finishing him off, but the man had fled in the opposite direction, and he was moving fast. Kaiser had already been searching for hours. He needed to report back.

Moments after Mazareem disappeared, Sorrell appeared on the charred deck of the *Celestial*. A cheer went up from the crew on the shore. Kaiser breathed a sigh of relief. Sorrell still lived. All was not lost, provided they could convince her to see reason.

It had been a day and a night since the battle. Ever since reaching the shore with Tarathine, Kaiser had been scouring the beach for survivors. He had found precious few. Anyone still in the ship when it exploded had been devoured by fire along with it, and most of those who made it clear had still been burned severely.

Time was of the essence. Kaiser turned away from the *Celestial* and headed north along the coast. The living crew of the *Golden Dawn* were at least an hour's hike away.

Kaiser frowned to himself. Lacrael was not saying much about what had happened in the hold, and Brant was in a coma, but everyone knew that it was not the powder magazine alone that had caused such a massive explosion. While Gustavus had not yet outright accused Lacrael of being responsible for the deaths of his crew and the destruction of his ship, Kaiser suspected the big captain was thinking it.

Losses were regrettable, but death was no stranger to Kaiser. All that mattered at this point was that Tarathine had survived. However, her and Kaiser's fates were linked with the rest of the crew for now, which left him with no choice but to work towards a common end no matter how much it rankled him.

Sand crunched under Kaiser's feet as he walked. The injury to his right arm was healing slowly. He exercised it as he hiked, working the muscles and tendons to avoid losing range of motion. Hopefully, in a day or two, Kaiser would no longer need the sling. Brant had been unconscious since reaching shore. He replayed his last encounter with the enraged Brant in his mind, and Kaiser decided that he would not mind if the man never woke up.

Evening was fast approaching when Kaiser finally reached the survivors' camp. At this point, he did not expect their number would increase. All told, Tarathine, Gustavus, Niad, Lacrael, Brant, Raither, and twenty-two sailors had made it to shore alive. Gustavus, Niad, and most of the sailors were all suffering from varying degrees of burns. Some of the men probably would not last the night.

Gustavus noticed Kaiser first, and the big captain moved to the edge of the camp to intercept him. In the face of losing everything he cared about, Gustavus's usual disagreeableness had been replaced with hardened resolve. Kaiser had to admit a begrudging respect for the man, now that the steel beneath was showing through. That, and Gustavus was now starting to defer to Kaiser when it came to decisions of leadership. Kaiser knew the man was still in shock, but this new arrangement suited him.

"You're alone," Gustavus said. "I expected as much, but I still hoped."

"I've not seen a body on the beach in hours," Kaiser said. "Others may have survived, but they could have drifted for miles to the north or south."

"Have you... has *he* spoken to you?" Gustavus said as if he had not heard Kaiser speak. He wanted to hear from his "high king," not Kaiser. The captain looked haunted. The limits of Gustavus's faith were being tested, and Kaiser had no pious platitudes to offer in comfort.

"You know he hasn't," Kaiser said. "Not since we found Raither."

Gustavus looked away, the doubt and frustration clear on his face. "Did you find the *Celestial?*"

"She's about an hour south of us. She's torn up, but they're starting repairs. And that's not all I found. Come on, the others should hear this."

Kaiser stepped past Gustavus and moved to the center of the little camp. Lacrael sat with Brant's head in her lap. She looked up at Kaiser's approach and gave him a tired nod in greeting.

Tarathine got up and moved to Kaiser's side, pressing herself tight against his uninjured arm. He hugged her to him as he spoke.

"We're in bad shape," Kaiser said, addressing the ragged band of survivors. "But we're not dead yet. I found the *Celestial* a short hike down the coast to the south. She's torn up but still seaworthy. Sorrell survived. I spotted her on the deck directing the repair efforts."

The news that Sorrell still lived proved little comfort. Gustavus stared out over the sea, stone faced and silent. Lacrael said nothing. She listened to Kaiser, but her attention was on the comatose Brant.

"That's not all I saw," Kaiser continued. "Mazareem was on the *Celestial.*"

That information provoked a reaction. Lacrael's head jerked up. Gustavus swore under his breath.

"I watched Sorrell and her crew chase him off," Kaiser said. "He survived a bullet through the eye and fled into the forest."

"Curse his maggot-ridden hide," Gustavus said. "He's got to be the one behind the bounty. He knew the *Golden Dawn* was in Praxis, but he had no way to find it. No one else had any reason to hunt us until after Linstall, and even then, I'd wager Raither here wouldn't warrant the effort. No offense."

Gustavus's last statement was directed at Raither, who did not respond. The former Linstall general listened intently, but it was clear that he was lost.

"I thought the same," Kaiser said. "And now that he's escaped, we have to assume he'll resume the hunt or bring back reinforcements. Either way, we don't have much time."

"We have to take the *Celestial,*" Gustavus said. "That's our only chance. We don't even need to convince Sorrell. If we can commandeer the ship with her on it, we can be out of this realm before she has any idea what we're doing."

"You can guide us to a portal without your maps?"

"The gateways between realms won't be marked on common maps," Gustavus said. He paused, opened his mouth to say more, and then changed his mind. In an attempt to divert attention from his blunder, he said, "But I've the location of a few memorized, for occasions just like this."

Gustavus was holding something back. He had been about to say something else and decided against it.

"Your hesitation doesn't inspire confidence," Kaiser said.

"I don't need your confidence," Gustavus said, a hint of his surly nature returning. "I can get us to a portal, but there might be... complications. We'll deal with them when the time comes."

This satisfied Kaiser. Any plan was better than none, and even the best plan must be adaptable. They could not sit here and solve every contingency. They needed to act while they still could.

"Can I speak?" Raither said. He stepped forward, indicating that he intended to address the group no matter how they answered his question.

Kaiser glanced at Gustavus, who shrugged in response. They had both been waiting for Raither to make his case. It was obvious what the man wanted, and Kaiser, most of all, could not blame him.

"If you must," Kaiser said.

Raither cleared his throat before continuing. "I don't know what sort of madness you lot are mixed up in, and I don't want to know. You've held me prisoner against my will, and now you've almost got me killed several times over. It's only by the mercy of the gods that I survived to stand on dry land again.

"It's clear from listening to you that I'm not who, or what, you thought I was. That being the case, of what use to you am I now? Let me go. I know this coast. This is Linstall, my homeland. Release me, and I can return to my family. I won't tell a soul what I know of you. You have my word on that."

Gustavus and Kaiser had already agreed that Raither must stay with them until they reached the portal to exit this realm. To let him go before that was too great a risk. He might go with the best of intentions, but should Raither fall into the clutches of the enemy they would make him talk no matter how strong he thought his will to resist.

"Believe me, I understand your desire to go to your family," Kaiser said. "Stay with us for a little while longer, perhaps until we've taken command of the *Celestial,* and I promise, we'll let you go. Right now, we need all the able-bodied help we can get. We can't afford to lose you."

Raither's shoulders sagged, but he did not argue. The man was a shadow of his former self. To look at him, Kaiser would never have placed him as the general of an entire nation's military. Kaiser did not think Raither would run, but the temptation to try to escape must be growing. He made a mental note to make sure Raither never stood night watch alone.

"Anyone else have anything to say?" Kaiser said, looking around at what was left of the *Golden Dawn's* crew.

The only response was the shaking of a few heads.

"I don't think the *Celestial* will be fit enough to move until tomorrow at the earliest," Kaiser said. "But just to be safe, I'll hike back down there and stand watch through the night. If they try to leave, I'll stop them. At sunrise, the rest of you follow. When you arrive, Lacrael and I will force the ship to surrender."

They should leave now, but Lacrael had been adamant that she would not abandon Brant. And Kaiser suspected that Gustavus and Niad would feel the same about their injured sailors. He hoped that the night brought change; otherwise, come sunrise, Kaiser would be storming the *Celestial* on his own.

Accepting Kaiser's words, the others turned away from him to talk amongst themselves. Kaiser took Tarathine's shoulders in his hands and looked down into her eyes.

"The only way back is to go forward," Kaiser said, speaking as much for his daughter as for himself. "The only way to return home is to venture further away from it."

Tears welled up in Tarathine's eyes at thoughts of home. Kaiser pulled her to him, and she returned his hug with surprising strength.

He finally pushed himself free, and he gave her one last smile before turning to trek back down the beach towards the *Celestial*.

Chapter 27

LACRAEL STARED AT KAISER'S back as he marched away across the sand. Soon, he disappeared into the shadows of the dwindling twilight. She felt guilty for not going with him. Together, they could have taken the *Celestial* tonight. But Brant needed her. After everything Lacrael had done to save him, she was not about to walk away and let him die.

According to Gustavus, Brant had saved Lacrael's life. She remembered nothing after the firestorm she had summoned in the wreckage of the *Golden Dawn*. The next thing she had known, she was waking up on the beach next to a passed-out Brant. Gustavus said that Brant had swum her to shore, had lain down next to her, closed his eyes, and then did not rise.

That had been almost a full day ago. Since that time, Lacrael had not left Brant's side. His head lay in her lap, and absentmindedly, Lacrael brushed the hair away from his brow. Her other hand was pressed against his chest, fingers splayed wide. Through this connection, she filled Brant's body with heat.

Without this warmth, Lacrael feared that Brant would die. This unusual sickness he suffered from stole the heat from his body every time she withdrew her power. He was covered in burns, and in a terrible twist of fate, the metal chains and the dragon amulet had become fused with his flesh. Lacrael had tried to pull them away from Brant's skin, but they were stuck fast.

Lacrael was too exhausted to cry. Her shoulder throbbed underneath a dirty bandage. The bullet was still in the wound. She had listened to Kaiser but had nothing to contribute. If Brant did not improve in the night, she would be faced with an impossible choice in the morning. She sensed Gustavus's trial of faith, and it was hard not to question the high king herself after what happened. Why did he seem powerless to help them in their times of greatest need? Surely, all this death and destruction could not be a part of his design.

Visions of her grandfather filled Lacrael's mind. She recalled Garlang's sacrifice. He lost everything dear to him to stay true to his faith in the high king. In the end, it cost him his life and earned Lacrael banishment from her family and home. Was her faith that strong? Her grandfather never witnessed evidence of the high king's return, yet he had never wavered. Lacrael possessed undeniable proof, and still, she found herself doubting. She felt ashamed.

Too tired to think any more, Lacrael slumped over Brant and tried to rest. Darkness stole over their meager camp. Gustavus and Niad built a small fire and offered what little aid and comfort they could to the dying sailors.

Hours passed. Lacrael's hand on Brant's chest ached with the effort of holding it up so long, but she ignored the pain. He struggled to breathe and sweat covered his brow. Either he would soon find victory over his mysterious ailment, or he was about to die. Lacrael cursed her helplessness. She could only watch and hope.

Sometime in the night, Lacrael woke with a start. She had fallen asleep. Her hand had slipped from Brant's chest. Panic filled her, and she jerked upright, certain she would find Brant cold and dead. Instead, she found him sleeping soundly.

Lacrael put a palm to Brant's forehead. She found no fever, and he no longer felt like ice. Daring to hope the danger had passed, she inspected the rest of his body. To her surprise, Brant's burns were gone, healed completely. His skin was unmarred, perfect even. Even the scars from old injuries had vanished.

On Brant's chest and around his shoulders, the chains and dragon amulet were sunken into his skin, but she saw no blood or irritation. They had simply become a part of him. Lacrael touched the amulet embedded in his chest with the tip of a finger. At her touch, the eyes of the golden dragon blazed orange, and Brant's eyes opened.

Lacrael snatched her hand back, startled.

Brant stared up into her eyes. He did not move or speak.

Something about his gaze was different. The pain behind his eyes had receded. A shadow of violence no longer haunted his countenance.

"Brant?" Lacrael whispered.

"Hey," Brant said, his face splitting with a weak grin.

"Is it—is it you?"

"It's me."

Overcome with relief, Lacrael wrapped her arms around Brant's head and pulled him close. For a long time, they sat that way, drawing strength from each other's touch. Curiosity finally got the better of Lacrael, and she pulled back and asked the question she had to ask.

"What happened?" Lacrael said.

"I only remember bits and pieces," Brant said. "After pulling you out of the ocean, the demon inside tried to take complete control. In my weakness, I couldn't resist him. But your fire in the brig did something to me. It seared the amulet into my chest and made it a part of my being. Instead of losing myself to the demon, I passed out. I remember absolute blackness and chains of fire. The demon was there, but he was fighting someone else. I was just watching. It was doing battle with a knight. I remember the knight's armor; it was so radiant it almost blinded me.

"The high king," Lacrael said, her voice quiet with awe.

"I could feel your power flowing through me. It saved my life, and it gave the knight the strength to defeat the demon. The fire seemed *alive,* and he used it to bind the fiend to the amulet burned into my chest. Now I control the monster."

As he spoke, Brant raised a hand to the amulet and felt along the chain that had been grafted into his torso.

"It's still in there, and it's angry," Brant said. "But as long as you lend me your power to keep it chained, it serves me and not the other way around."

Lacrael smiled for what felt like the first time in years. "If it's fire you need, you've come to the right woman."

Chapter 28

SORRELL WORRIED THAT SHE was losing her grip on reality. Too much was happening that defied explanation. The events of the last few days were beyond her wildest nightmares or imaginings, and she wondered how she could ever get back on a path towards normalcy.

Stone's death still hung over her. His absence was like an open, bleeding wound in Sorrell's heart. At least once every hour, she would turn to say something to him only to discover he was not at her side, and the grief would crash over her again as if he had just died. Sorrell did her best to hide her tears from her beleaguered crew.

Her fantastic new powers had taken up permanent residence in her being. Sorrell could never quite forget about them. They lurked beneath the surface of her mind, demanding an answer to their presence and purpose. The longer she went without summoning the enchanted ice, the more energy she felt being stored up. This growing power demanded release, almost as if it had a will of its own. That sensation troubled Sorrell.

Mazareem had survived what should have been a mortal wound. Sorrell replayed the shot over and over again in her head, certain she had blown out his eye. The sailors who had given chase swore that Mazareem had a hole clear through his skull, but that did not stop him from getting up and fleeing into the woods. What manner of creature could survive such an injury? Could he even be killed?

After attacking Mazareem, Sorrell had passed out. She had slept for the remainder of the day and for most of the next night. Her crew had stood watch over her, and when she woke, they cooked her a meal she desperately needed.

For the first time in days, Sorrell felt alive again. Now, she stood on the deck of the *Celestial* with her few surviving officers. They were discussing their plan of action in the dawn's early light. Poor Lieutenant Eggard had not survived Mazareem's assault, which left Sorrell with two lieutenants and three midshipmen.

"We should be able to get a crude mast up by noon, ma'am," Lieutenant Chartrand said. "After that, it's short work to hang some rigging. We can start making our way down the coast before nightfall. There's a strong northern wind blowing."

"By my best estimate, we're on the coast of Linstall somewhere below Linstrad," Sorrell said. "If Mazareem travels west until he finds a road or town, and assuming he obtains a horse, he can reach Coridal in seven to eight days. With some emergency repairs, we should be able to make better time, but we have to set sail today. We *must* reach the capital before he does."

"Aye, aye, ma'am," the officers replied as one.

"Forgive me for belaboring this point, but it must be clear what we face," Sorrell said. "There's no doubt in my mind that Mazareem is making for the emperor with the news that I'm a traitor. I think, short of killing me, that was his plan all along. If you stand with me, that makes all of you traitors as well. But you're also the only living witnesses to what occurred here. If we can beat Mazareem to Coridal, we'll have a chance to give the true accounting of the past two days. I can't guarantee what will happen after that. I don't know what's transpired since we set out on this doomed voyage."

"We're with you, admiral," Lieutenant Chartrand said. "To a man, there's not a member of this crew who'd not follow you into the black pit itself. Mazareem is a monster, and we'll do whatever it takes to expose him as such."

"Thank you, lieutenant," Sorrell said. "Now, we must turn our attention to—"

A cry of alarm from the shore cut off Sorrell's next words. She moved with her officers to the rail to see what had prompted the shout. On the beach, the *Celestial*'s sailors were rushing to form a mob. They brandished axes, shovels, and saws at the new threat that had just appeared from the trees.

Sorrell and her officers looked down at a band of about thirty battered sailors who had stepped out of the forest to the north of the *Celestial*. At their head, Sorrell recognized the imposing form of Captain Gustavus, and at his side, the two officers from the battle aboard the *Golden Dawn*.

"It appears that our quarry did not go down with their ship," Sorrell said.

"We've got them outnumbered two to one," Chartrand said. "And we've got sharpshooters up here. Let's give them a warning shot and see how they react."

"Belay that, lieutenant," Sorrell said. She had not forgotten the strange powers that Gustavus and his people wielded. Better to try the peaceful approach first. Sorrell could suffer no delay, and she needed every sailor she had left.

"Tell them we'll parley aboard the *Celestial*," Sorrell said after a moment of thought. "Gustavus and his officers only. The soldier with the injured arm and that dark, exotic looking woman. I want them separated from their crew."

"Aye, aye, ma'am," Chartrand said.

"One of you midshipmen, summon the acting master-at-arms to my cabin," Sorrell said. "And offer their sailors what aid we can. They look to be in bad shape. A gesture of good faith might help our case."

Lieutenant Chartrand gave her a sharp salute before moving off to do her bidding. The other officers followed after him to arrange for the care of the *Golden Dawn*'s crew. Sorrell watched them go, deep in contemplation.

Of course, Gustavus would want to see to the safety of his crew. But would he want more than that? Was there a threat of violence here? Sorrell could not deny that she was curious about the powers his officers had shown. They seemed similar to her own. Was there a connection?

Try as she might, Sorrell could not think of any reason Gustavus would wish further conflict. In fact, perhaps she could enlist him and his crew to her cause. She would offer a full pardon, on the condition that they help her put down Mazareem and take the throne.

Confident that she had the other captain's measure, Sorrell moved into her now cleaned-up cabin in preparation for meeting with him. Within minutes, the master-at-arms joined her.

"I want you to muster as many armed sailors as you can find in five minutes and bring them here," Sorrell said to the man. "I don't expect a fight, but I want to be prepared."

"Aye, aye, ma'am," the man said.

Sorrell hoped she was making the right decision. Soon, the room was filled with sailors, some with loaded flintlocks on their hips, while others carried curved sabers. They took up position behind Sorrell against the back wall. In all, the master-at-arms had found ten men. That should be more than enough. Sorrell turned to address them.

"The captain of the *Golden Dawn* and two of his officers are coming here to parley," Sorrell said. "I intend to make a common cause with them and avoid conflict, but you're here to remind them of the consequences should they try anything stupid. Ignore their captain and watch his officers. If they make any sudden moves or threats, draw your weapons and prepare to fight."

As one, the sailors acknowledged her orders. Outside the cabin, voices and the sound of boots on the deck signaled the approach of the party from the *Golden Dawn*. Sorrell positioned herself facing the door and struck a commanding pose. In her ragged black uniform and missing her hat, she no longer looked like an admiral of the Coriddian Navy, but she could at least act like one.

Gustavus was the first person through the door. He took in the armed sailors at a glance, and his instant and obvious dismissal of them annoyed Sorrell. His two officers followed close behind, the soldier with his arm in a sling entering second, and the tall, exotic woman coming third. Sorrell frowned. This woman had dark red hair. She was certain she remembered black hair from the battle. But that had been right before she was knocked out, so perhaps her memory was faulty.

Sorrell's few remaining officers filed in last and moved to stand behind her. Already, the attitude in the cabin was tense. Gustavus had the disposition of the aggressor, not of a fallen captain who had just lost his ship and more than half his crew.

"Welcome to his excellency's *Celestial*, the finest ship in the Coriddian Navy," Sorrell said, making a formal start to their negotiations. "She's a little worse for wear at the moment, but we'll have her seaworthy again in no time."

"That's a different tune than the one you were singing on the deck of the *Golden Dawn*," Gustavus said.

"As you're well aware, circumstances have changed. Whatever crimes you've committed are no longer my concern. In fact, I've called you here to offer a full pardon, and perhaps much more, if you'll make common cause with me and my crew. As a gesture of good faith, your men and women are already being tended to with what aid we can offer."

"You blow us out of the water and now you want our help? The depths take your 'gesture,' woman, and you along with it."

At Gustavus's irate tone, the sailors behind Sorrell bristled.

"At ease," Sorrell said, raising her hands for calm. "I understand your anger, captain. But I didn't order the destruction of your ship. I was betrayed. I think I was the target, more than you, and the traitor who orchestrated the attack has now fled."

"Mazareem," Gustavus's male officer said.

"You know this man?" Sorrell said, taken aback. How did these people know of Mazareem?

Gustavus and his officers shared a look.

"You should dismiss your men," Gustavus said. "I don't think you're going to want them to hear what I have to say."

Sorrell stiffened. "Absolutely not. All that remains for us to discuss is whether you'll join with me or not. I warn you, refuse, and we'll leave you stranded here."

"So be it," Gustavus said. "Order your men to stand down. We're taking control of this ship. We'll make common cause with you, but the cause will be our own."

Sorrell was too perplexed to laugh. "You can't hope to overpower us," she said.

"I don't need to," Gustavus said. He nodded toward the window. "Take a gander at the shore and tell me what you see."

Uncertain now, Sorrell moved to the small cabin window and looked out. Her heart almost dropped out of her chest. Legs spread wide, arms outstretched, the raven-haired woman Sorrell remembered from the battle stood facing the *Celestial* on the bank. Swirling above the woman's hands, an orb of living fire burned. As Sorrell watched, the fireball grew to the height and width of a man, obscuring the dark woman completely. A giant, bare chested man stood at her side. The meager crew of the *Golden Dawn* surrounded the pair in a tight circle.

"She'll scuttle this ship with a thought," Gustavus said. "I'd not recommend firing on her. That fire will melt a musket ball in a flash, and she's already angry about the first time you shot her. And if you do manage to harm her, I promise you, that brute next to her will take this ship apart with his bare hands."

"What's the purpose of this?" Sorrell said, stepping away from the window and back into the room. "We should be allies, not enemies. Is this about revenge? Join with me, and I'll give you vengeance. I'll not rest until I have Mazareem's black heart in my hand."

"As tempting as that offer is, we're not after him—we're here for you," Gustavus said. "His time will come."

"You think to strike me down in my own cabin?" Sorrell said, her hand going for her sword. "I'll die before I surrender."

Faster than should have been possible, the man at Gustavus's side lunged forward. In two quick strides, he stood before Sorrell. In the time it took her to blink, a smoking, ethereal blade appeared in his hand. He held the weapon pointed at Sorrell's chest, and from the look in his eyes, she knew him perfectly capable of ending her life on the spot.

Voices raised in surprise and anger, Sorrell's officers and sailors alike drew their blades and raised their firearms. The entire room was poised on a knife's edge, ready to explode into violence.

"I think you'll remember Kaiser from your failed boarding action," Gustavus said. "Those sailors behind you might kill me and my first mate here, but they won't touch him. And you're right—you'll be the first to die. The choice is yours, admiral."

Sorrell's head was spinning. This had gotten out of hand fast. Despite her bravado, she had no desire to perish here. She owed Mazareem a great debt of pain, and she had spent too much of her life working towards the throne to throw it all away.

"What is it that you want?" Sorrell asked, doing her best not to stare at the spectral sword poised an inch from her chest.

"Stand your men down, turn over all your weapons, and we'll let them go," Gustavus said. "Any man who wishes to join my crew may do so, but he'll first swear an oath that will bind his soul to me. You, of course, will stay with us. You sank the *Golden Dawn,* and I'm taking the *Celestial* as a replacement. Once she's fit, we're taking her far away from here."

Sorrell could find no way out that did not end in bloodshed. And she did not intend to die this day. Her entire body tingled with power demanding to be unleashed, but she did not know how to use it to save herself. Instinctively, Sorrell drew on the power anyway, desperate for a way to strike back.

Ice began to form around her hands, the air around them crackling with energy.

"Don't," Kaiser said.

She met Kaiser's gaze, and in it, Sorrell saw her death.

Defeated, infuriated, her shoulders slumped. She released the power inside, and the ice vanished.

"As you wish," Sorrell said. "The *Celestial* is yours."

"Admiral, no!" a sailor behind her said.

"Stand down, sailor," Sorrell said. "There's been enough death here already. Let's not add any more blood to the water."

"You've saved many lives this day," Gustavus said. "Now, as I asked you before, dismiss your men."

Sorrell ordered her crew from the room with a gesture. That she did not speak the order was a message to her crew. She expected navy discipline to hold strong, even in the midst of adversity.

"Leave your weapons on the floor," Gustavus said.

There was a long moment of silence, and Sorrell started to worry that the men would disobey her, but in the end, discipline won out. After the first sword hit the deck with a thunk, the rest soon followed after.

"Niad, arm yourself, and stand watch over this lot," Gustavus said to the red-haired woman. "And give Lacrael the signal that we've taken the ship."

Niad nodded, collected a flintlock and sword from the floor, and followed Sorrell's sailors out of the cabin. Sorrell, Kaiser, and Gustavus were the only people left in the room. Kaiser stepped back and dismissed the strange sword from his hand.

"There's a lot to say and very little time to say it," Gustavus said. "And I suspect much of it will be wasted on you right now. Whatever you may think, we're not your enemies. You've seen the evidence of true evil in Mazareem. Until you manifested your powers, you were never his target—we were. You were just collateral damage.

"Kaiser and Lacrael are the same as you, chosen as champions, and given great powers, to do battle against Mazareem's master. That won't mean anything to you, as this realm has long forgotten the legends of High King Rowen and the tyrant Abimelech. But the agents of evil are at work even here, though you don't recognize them.

"The entire reason we're here is to find you, the next champion. We paid a... we paid a damned high price to do so." At this, Gustavus broke off from speaking and looked away.

To Sorrell, Gustavus's words sounded like madness, and the captain did not seem certain that he believed what he was saying. It had the ring of a rehearsed speech, and behind it, the stench of indoctrination. Sorrell knew of cults that existed on the periphery of the empire. She was not surprised to find a ship of smugglers consumed by mysticism.

"He'll fill your head with insanity, if you let him," Kaiser said. He spoke with a thick accent that Sorrell had never heard before. "The simple truth is this: you've powers you didn't ask for. Be they gift or curse, they've changed your life forever. Your best hope for survival is with us. This will become clear, in time."

Kaiser's reaction was telling. He never took his eyes off Sorrell, and she returned his stare without flinching. He made no attempt to disguise his disdain for what Gustavus was saying. They made a strange pair. Both wanted to lead, neither intended to follow. Gustavus spoke like a practitioner of the occult, while Kaiser, the man whose presence validated his supernatural claims, wanted nothing to do with them.

"I'm your prisoner now, what choice do I have?" Sorrell said. She had thought to give these brigands the slip at the first opportunity. Now, she was worried it would not be that simple.

"None," Kaiser said. "I hope you can appreciate that we must bind you for a time. Until you're ready to listen, we cannot risk you escaping."

Sorrell kept her mouth shut to stifle an angry outburst. These bastards had tricked her. They had bested her only because they tried a suicide gambit. She should have known better than to expect to find a shred of honor in a band of pirates. Sorrell made a promise to herself that if they harmed a single one of her crew, she would have their heads on a plate next to Mazareem's.

Chapter 29

MAZAREEM SUFFERED. HIS WORLD had become pain. Every step produced a fresh agony. The blessings of undeath carried with them a curse, allowing the body to endure what would kill a normal mortal. Almost, Mazareem found himself wishing for death. He could feel his body deteriorating as it tried and failed to heal itself. Rot was spreading, and it would grow dangerous if left unchecked for much longer. If Mazareem did not feed soon, he would be beyond even his formidable power and knowledge to save.

He had pushed the bits of skull and brain that he could salvage back into his head and then wrapped the wound in a strip of his black shirt. The fabric provided a makeshift patch over his empty, gaping eye socket. Already, his body had filled in the empty space the bullet had made, but he was far too weak to regrow the eye or bone.

After tending to his injury, Mazareem paused only to perform the summoning ritual for Worm. No matter how far from his master he slumbered, the hound would come. Mazareem was almost ashamed to admit that he missed the beast.

Careful to ration what little of the stimulant potion remained, Mazareem made good time through the forest. He headed due west until finding a road, and upon discovering this evidence of civilization, turned south. Day and night he walked. Time was his greatest enemy now.

Mazareem had one chance to rectify this situation—he had to return to Coridal before Sorrell. It would be easy enough to brand her a traitor, which was Viatrix's plan all along, but Mazareem had to get there first to tell the royal mother what had happened. There was still time to catch Sorrell's allies unawares. However, Sorrell being a magus now was an added wrinkle that they could not ignore.

At the back of Mazareem's mind, a lurking presence watched his struggles with amusement. Mazareem recognized the dark signature of Abimelech's shadow. No doubt, the explosion of enchanted energy unleashed in the *Golden Dawn's* obliteration, combined with the emergence of a new magus, had drawn the lord tyrant's attention. Failure under Abimelech's gravid gaze would mean certain damnation. Mazareem tried not to dwell on this.

Finally, after almost a solid day of walking, a small city appeared on the horizon. Deserted up until this point, the road started to fill with travelers coming and going from the town. They took one glance at Mazareem and moved far to one side of the highway to let him pass.

Mazareem saw the signs of war as he strode into the city. Injured and dying men lay in the street, beggars now instead of soldiers. Shop windows were boarded up. Doors were closed and secured. There was a distinct lack of women and children. Based on these signs, Mazareem guessed this was a border town, situated somewhere close to Coriddian territory. From what he had heard, the interior of Linstall had not seen much combat. The conquest had been decided at sea.

In one of the glass shop windows, Mazareem caught a glimpse of himself. He had seen better looking corpses. In fact, he looked like he should be dead. He adjusted the black cloth wrapped around his head. Best to keep the wound hidden. The last thing he needed was to be chased out of town by a torch-wielding mob.

As he suspected, Mazareem found a Coriddian military garrison in the center of the city. The town hall had been fortified, repurposed into a fort for the empire's legions. Banners of Coriddian black and gold hung from the roof, each proudly displaying a black orb eclipsing a blazing sun.

Anticipating being refused entry, Mazareem fished out the emperor's writ from beneath his shirt. Document in hand, he did his best to stride confidently up to the soldiers guarding the door. To Mazareem's ire, it was more of a determined shamble.

The two soldiers shared a look as Mazareem approached. He did not need a second eye to read the disgust on their faces.

"Shove off, old man," one of the soldiers said. "You'll find no handouts here."

"Please pardon my ghastly appearance," Mazareem said, deciding to adopt a tactful approach. "I've suffered grievous injury. I'm an agent of the emperor on a critical mission. Here's my writ of authority as proof. I need to see the captain of this garrison immediately."

The soldier guffawed. "That's a new one on me," the soldier said. "You hear that, Mason? He's a bleedin' agent of the bleedin' emperor himself."

"I really must insist," Mazareem said, proffering the document.

Rather than take the piece of paper, the soldier shoved Mazareem back.

"I won't tell you a third time," the soldier said with a snarl. "You stink like a corpse. Get out of here before I spill your guts in the street."

"What if he's telling the truth, Rame?" the soldier named Mason said.

"You want to read this idiot's paper?" Rame said. "Fine, go ahead, and I'll tell you what, if it's a writ from the emperor, I'll lay a turd in the general's helmet."

"Let's have it," Mason said, beckoning for Mazareem to hand him the document.

Mason's eyes widened as he scanned the parchment.

"It looks like he's the real deal," Mason said. "The captain will be able to verify this signature."

Rame blanched.

"Follow me," Mason said after handing the writ back to Mazareem.

On any other day, Mazareem would have taken his amusement at Rame's expense. Instead, he shuffled past the mollified soldier without even a nod. Rame looked anywhere but at Mazareem.

Inside, the seat of the local government had been turned into a combination of a barracks and an armory. Cots filled the largest rooms, and weapons and armor were stacked in the corners. They passed what used to be a small office where a blacksmith was hard at work hammering dents out of a breastplate.

Mason obviously felt the need to make small talk as they made their way to the captain.

"We've not seen any fighting for weeks," Mason said. "What you see here is an occupational force only. And now with the emperor on his way, most of us are about to march out to meet him."

"The emperor's coming here?" Mazareem said.

"Oh, aye. There's a grand campaign on its way from Coridal. The emperor himself is going to plant the flag of conquest on Linstall soil."

Mazareem pondered this as they entered the captain's office. Viatrix would no doubt accompany her son on such a grand occasion. That would mean his journey could be shortened by precious days. Not to mention the fact that Sorrell might return to the capital and find her brother and mother missing.

The garrison captain sat behind a desk meant for more civic-minded purposes. Instead of city documents, it was scattered with military dispatches and reports. The captain himself wore a well-used suit of armor as if he expected to be called into battle at any moment. In this age of gunpowder, the Coriddian legions still preferred to wear a light mail, and the links rattled when the captain moved.

"Corporal Mason reporting, sir." Mason snapped a smart salute to the captain and stood at attention in front of his desk.

Annoyed at the interruption, the captain looked up from the parchment he had been reading.

"Yes, what is it, corporal?" the captain said. The man's eyes widened slightly when they found Mazareem.

"This man says he's an agent of the emperor," Mason said. "He's got a writ of authority that looks legitimate. He asked to see you immediately."

Mason handed over Mazareem's writ for the captain to inspect. He returned to rigid attention while he waited for the captain's verdict. Mazareem did his best to wait with an air of patience. The truth was, he was famished and had little time for these pointless formalities.

"This does appear to be authentic," the captain said. He looked up from the paper. "You're dismissed, corporal."

"Yes, sir!" Mason said. He gave another salute, spun on his heel, and marched out of the room.

The captain turned his attention to Mazareem. "I'm Captain Pierce, commander of this garrison and ranking officer in this city. I don't recognize you, and I had no knowledge of our agents still operating on Linstall soil. This means, I suspect, that you'll tell me little to nothing about your true purpose. So why have you come to me?"

Mazareem dropped the act of false humility. This sort of man would see right through it. "Three days ago, the ship I was sailing on was attacked by pirates," Mazareem said. "We went down with all hands. I managed to swim to shore and make it here on foot. What I need from you is a horse and some supplies. There can be no delay. I must report back to the emperor as soon as possible."

"Pirates, this close to Coriddian waters?" Pierce said. "I know they've grown bold after Linstall fell, but I was certain our navy was protecting the coast."

Mazareem struggled to still the trembling of his hands. "Yes, yes, it was an unfortunate encounter, but I really must get on the road again."

"Are you well?" Pierce said. He leaned over the desk and looked Mazareem up and down. "You look fit for the grave."

"My health is none of your concern, captain. However, a horse and supplies are. Can I assume both will be forthcoming?"

Captain Pierce frowned. "So, it's going to be like that? Very well, follow me. I'll take you to the stables."

Pierce got to his feet, made his way around the desk and headed out the door. Mazareem fell into step beside the captain. Together, they made their way down a long hall towards the rear of the garrison.

"The corporal mentioned that the emperor himself is on his way to Linstall," Mazareem said. "What is his route and currently expected position?"

"His excellency is taking the path of least resistance, traveling along the Coriddian grand highway," Pierce said. "The procession is ceremonial in nature, which means they don't move quickly. At the moment, they should be somewhere near the city of Togen, several days to the southeast."

Pierce motioned for Mazareem to wait in the hall, and he ducked into a supply room. He returned a moment later, carrying a fully kitted infantry pack. The captain handed the burden to Mazareem.

"This is the best I can offer on short notice," Pierce said. "There should be enough hard rations to last you a week, along with basic survival gear and ammunition."

Mazareem reached for the pack, and Pierce dropped it at the last second, forcing Mazareem to lurch forward to prevent it from dropping to the floor. Pierce watched Mazareem struggle with a smirk on his face.

"It should be sufficient," Mazareem said. He swung the pack around to his back and tightened the straps around his shoulders. His tired body almost sagged under the added weight. The bandolier of glass bottles dug into his back beneath the load. He would transfer them to the satchel later.

Neither of them spoke again until they reached the stables at the back of the garrison. The stalls were full of the cavalry's stallions. Mazareem swallowed hard at the sight of the warhorses. He and horses did not get along. The skittish animals sensed right away that Mazareem was not quite human, and he could never get one to trust him. Only great urgency could force him onto the back of a horse.

Mazareem tried not to let his relief show when the captain marched past the great destriers and stopped next to a packhorse that had been tethered to a pole.

"The cavalry mounts aren't mine to give away," Pierce said. "And seeing as you won't tell me what you're about, I can't very well demand they give me one. This nag will have to do. She'll get you to Togen, at the very least."

"She's adequate for my needs," Mazareem said. "Your assistance is appreciated, captain. I'll make sure to mention you in my official report."

At this, Pierce's attitude improved. For his name to appear in a report that might find its way into the emperor's hands could advance his military career beyond his wildest imaginings.

"No hard feelings, hey?" Pierce said. "I'm just trying to do my job here."

"Some coin would go a long way in helping me forget your lack of hospitality," Mazareem said. "What little I carried is resting at the bottom of the sea."

Pierce contemplated this request for a moment, and upon reaching a decision, took the pouch from his belt and handed it to Mazareem.

"That should get you where you need to go with plenty left over," Pierce said. "Remember me, when you're talking to the emperor."

Mazareem hefted the small leather bag in his palm. It had a satisfying weight to it, and inside, he heard the tinkling of coins.

"Much obliged, captain," Mazareem said.

Pierce only nodded. There was nothing left to say. Mazareem untied the horse from the post and led her out of the stables into the street. He waited until he turned the corner and was out of sight to pause and rest—the dizziness was getting worse. A hand on the horse's neck was the only thing that kept him standing. Mazareem needed to feed within the next hour, or his body was going to shut down.

Chapter 30

MAZAREEM DID NOT HAVE the strength or the time to hunt down his prey. His only option was to lure someone into his clutches. Beneath his shirt, strapped hard against his skin, the scale of Abimelech provided a constant reminder of the curse he was under. Without that scale, not only would Mazareem starve, he would also be trapped in this realm with no way to leave.

He muttered a dark deprecation against his master as he moved down the muddy street. Mazareem made for a nearby inn. In an occupied city like this one, there were sure to be men of a certain type looking for work. Mazareem intended to hire such a man for a very important service.

Outside the inn, Mazareem tied his newly acquired nag to the hitching post. His was the only horse in front of the building. He thought briefly about leaving the heavy infantry pack with the animal but decided against it. A horse and a laden pack together were too tempting a target for a thief.

Strength fading fast, Mazareem forced himself to stand tall, climb the steps, and walk through the open door of the inn. The main room was dimly lit. Mazareem stopped on the threshold to let his single eye adjust to the darkness. True to his expectation, the tables were crowded with an assortment of unsavory-looking characters.

The murmur of low conversation stopped when Mazareem appeared. Every grizzled face turned in his direction. The inn's customers looked like a mixture of mercenaries looking for work and disgraced Linstall veterans who had survived the war. To a man, they were all armored and armed. None of them looked happy to see Mazareem.

"We're out of rooms and food," the innkeeper said from behind the bar at the back of the room. "You'd best look elsewhere."

"On the contrary, I think you have exactly what I need," Mazareem said.

Ignoring the predatory stares from the men scattered around the room, Mazareem entered the inn. At the closest empty table, he slid a chair back and sat down. Confident that he had everyone's attention, Mazareem tossed Pierce's money pouch onto the table in front of him. It landed with a solid *thunk.*

"I'm in need of a bodyguard," Mazareem told the men watching him. "I've got to reach Togen in a few days' time, and the roads aren't safe for an oldster like me. Is there a man here willing to earn his keep for a few days honest work?"

All eyes had gone to the bag of money. This was a gamble, but Mazareem was out of time. If he did not walk out of here with a guard, he would be followed, mugged, and probably killed. He waited as a table of five rough-looking mercenaries muttered amongst themselves, discussing his proposition. The other men in the room glanced at this group of mercenaries and then quickly away. No one spoke until the five had reached a decision.

Finally, an ugly man with only one ear and a scarred face stood up from the table of mercenaries. He tried to smile at Mazareem, but he seemed to have forgotten how. It was more of a sneer.

"We've got what you need, old man," the man said. "My name's Cagen, and these boys are my crew. One of us can get you where you need to go. But we don't talk business in front of the competition. We've got a room upstairs. Come with us, and we'll hammer out the contract."

Mazareem contemplated Cagen and his crew. He tried not to laugh at their transparency. It was obvious that the room upstairs would be his end, and his possessions their plunder. However, this new opportunity sparked an idea in Mazareem's mind. Perhaps he could turn this to his advantage in more ways than one.

"How kind of you, my dear Cagen," Mazareem said, hoisting himself up from his chair. "If you'll lead, I'll follow."

"Come on, boys, you heard the man," Cagen said to the men seated at his table. "Look lively. We got ourselves a client."

Cagen went first up the stairs, and Mazareem followed close behind him. Cagen's crew took up the rear. Mazareem glanced at the innkeeper as he passed by the bar, and the man gave Mazareem an almost imperceptible shake of his head. Mazareem smiled and nodded at the man, pretending to be oblivious to the warning.

At the top of the stairs, Cagen turned left and walked until they reached the second door. He glanced back at Mazareem, and then he pushed open the door and stepped into the room. Mazareem moved aside and gestured for the rest of Cagen's crew to enter before him. He was not about to step into the room with them behind him.

There was an awkward moment where the four mercenaries in the hall were not sure what to do. Mazareem wondered if they would assault him right there in the open.

"Get in here, you louts!" Cagen said from inside the room.

At Cagen's bidding, the men shuffled by Mazareem and through the door. None of them would look him in the eye. Mazareem followed the last man inside. He closed the door behind him.

Sparsely furnished, the room held three beds and a table with two chairs near the door. Battered leather packs, clothes, and dirty dishes littered the floor. Cagen and his companions were all standing facing Mazareem.

"Will you permit an old man to sit?" Mazareem said, cutting off Cagen who had opened his mouth to speak.

Mazareem did not wait for an answer. He lowered his tired body into a chair with a sigh.

"Ah, that's better," Mazareem said. "I understand we're to discuss a contract?"

"Here's the terms," Cagen said. "You hand over your money and that pack, and we'll let you walk out of here alive."

"How shortsighted," Mazareem said. "You haven't even heard what I'm offering as payment. There's more in this for you than this tiny sack of coins, if you can get me where I need to go."

"I don't care; the terms are the terms," Cagen said. "Either way, I get what I want."

"Does he speak for all of you?" Mazareem said, eyebrows raised.

"Who made you boss, all of a sudden?" one of the men behind Cagen said. "What about what *I* want? Let's hear what he has to say."

Cagen whirled, fury twisting his ugly face. "I'm the boss because none of you've got the guts to say otherwise! If you've found your spine, step forward. I'll tear it out and beat you with it."

While Cagen faced down his lackey, Mazareem slipped a bottle from a loop in the bandolier on his chest. He gave it one quick shake to make sure the occupant was awake and then pulled the cork. Before Cagen turned back around, he placed the open bottle mouth down on the table in front of him.

"What's this, then?" Cagen said when he turned his attention back to Mazareem. He eyed the upturned bottle with suspicion.

"This, my good man, is a lesson," Mazareem said. In one quick motion, he lifted the bottle up and away. Beneath it was what looked like a tiny, black thorn.

"In its native habitat, they call it a reaper flea," Mazareem said. "Like its smaller cousin, the standard flea, it's almost impossible to kill. It prefers to ambush its prey, lying in wait disguised as a simple thorn. But that thorn isn't just for show. It's strong enough to burrow through thick hide. I'd stay very still if I were you. This one's pregnant and in dire need of a host. They hunt based on movement, and I promise you, you don't want to feel this flea's bite."

On Cagen's unsightly face, confusion gave way to disbelief as Mazareem spoke. His eyes flicked back and forth between Mazareem and the thorn on the table. Mazareem stopped talking, and there was a tense pause as Cagen and his men waited to see if anything would happen. Nothing did.

Cagen laughed. "You're a crazy old man, I'll give you that."

In one smooth motion, Cagen drew his sword and stepped forward.

"Now, about that contract," Cagen said.

In the silence following Cagen's statement, there was the faintest of *clicks* as the flea launched itself from the table. Cagen tracked the insect's arc through the air, his eyes widening in surprise. His mouth hung open, his next words forgotten.

The reaper flea landed on Cagen's tongue and immediately jumped again. Its chitin thorn plunged into the soft flesh of his upper palate. Cagen gagged, hurling his sword away and clawing at his mouth. He dropped to his knees. A terrible, keening wail escaped his lips.

Tearing into soft, pink flesh, the flea burrowed—Cagen lost control of his body. He flopped onto the floor. Blood poured from his mouth as he screamed. His howls turned to moans as the flea found his brain. In a few heartbeats, his moaning stopped, and all that was left was the random twitching of his limbs.

Cagen's demise had only taken a few seconds. Mazareem had not moved. The four surviving mercenaries looked up from Cagen's body, their faces ashen.

Mazareem gave them the best smile he could muster. "There's still money to be made, if you're willing. Or you can join your friend on the floor, if you'd prefer."

The men trembled in fear, too terrified to even speak.

"Once it's found a host, the reaper flea won't attack again," Mazareem said. "She'll fill his head with eggs and then die. In a few weeks, this place is going to have a flea problem. I'd encourage you to be far away by then."

"We'll take your work," the man who had stood up to Cagen said. "Just-just don't kill us!"

"You're already showing better sense than the last man in your position. Now, I've changed my mind about needing a bodyguard. Here's what I want you to do instead."

Mazareem described Sorrell, Kaiser, Lacrael, Brant, and Gustavus to the four men. He gave them instructions to watch the town. If any of the targets appeared within the next few days, the mercenaries were to find a way to ambush them. Killing was preferred, but slowing them down was acceptable too.

"Divide this amongst yourselves," Mazareem said, tossing the entire money pouch to the new leader. "And mark my words, if you run off without fulfilling your end of the contract, I'll know. When my current business is concluded, I'll track down each one of you and introduce you to pain worse than your former boss suffered."

The man caught the pouch and tucked it away in one deft movement. "We'll honor the agreement," the man said.

"See that you do," Mazareem said. "Now leave me for a spell. I desire privacy, and this room will do."

Careful to avoid touching Cagen's corpse, the men filed past the table and out of the room. By sheer force of will, Mazareem sat straight in his seat and waited patiently for the men to leave. If they had tested him, if they had known how close he was to collapsing, they would have killed him and been done with it.

Finally alone, Mazareem waited to a count of ten before acting. He could delay no longer—he lunged out of his chair towards Cagen's body. He snatched his knife from its boot sheath and set to work on his grim harvest. The first four bottles of blood he drank straight away, grinding a bit of Abimelech's scale into each to create the tonic that sustained him.

Mazareem slowed his feverish pace as the burning ichor spread through his body and started its rejuvenating work. The desperation of fatal hunger faded. Mazareem took his time, filling every empty phial with blood. He even emptied a few of their now useless contents to make room for more of the life-sustaining liquid. Mazareem stowed the newly acquired crimson potions in his new pack.

"That was a near thing," Mazareem told the dead Cagen. "Between me and the fleas, your blood will not go to waste. But there's one more thing you can give me."

Mazareem slid the blade of his dagger down into the socket of Cagen's right eye. With a sharp twist of the wrist, he severed the nerves behind the eye and scooped it into his waiting hand. He held the bloody, fleshy sphere up to inspect it. A light blue iris stared back at him.

"Not my color, but beggars can't be choosers," Mazareem said.

Gingerly, Mazareem lifted the bandage that covered his empty socket and slid the stolen eye into his skull. It took a few seconds for his body to respond. When it did, he smiled at the delicious sensation of the nerves and muscles intertwining with the newly adopted organ. It would take several days for his full vision to return, but soon, he would be whole again.

Feeling better than he had in days, Mazareem collected his pack and prepared to depart. It did not really matter to him if the four mercenaries kept their end of the bargain. His real purpose had been fulfilled in Cagen. If they managed to slow down any pursuers, that was a stroke of good fortune but not absolutely necessary. In a few days, Mazareem would reach Viatrix, and Sorrell's fate would be sealed.

Chapter 31

SAREDON'S BELLY WAS FULL. He had almost forgotten what it felt like. Granted, it was full of stale bread and gruel, but that did not make the sensation any less wondrous. For the past two days, he had relished having three meals a day, a bed, and a roof over his head. These basic comforts made him feel human again. Saredon's perception of himself as a dirty street mouse started to fade into memory.

Garius was staying with a washerwoman named Liv in one of the poor districts of Northmark. It was not the slums, but it was as close to them as you could get without living in them. Liv was not happy about housing and feeding Saredon, and she let Garius know every chance she got. While Garius was out, she refused to speak or even look at Saredon.

Just that morning, Garius and Liv had argued about Saredon. He had listened from where he pretended to sleep. The shouted words were still fresh in his mind.

"We're on the precipice of privation!" Liv said. "And you bring in another mouth to feed? Tis madness, I tell you. Tis no time for charity, even if he's naught but a helpless little waif."

"I'm not putting him back on the street!" Garius thundered. "I won't hear any more of this talk, woman. He's staying with us, and that's final."

"Tis *my* house, you half-faced dog, or did you forget? I took *you* in, not the other way round!"

"You only kept this place thanks to my wages. Don't you dare imply I haven't earned my keep."

"You can stuff you blighted wages! And you can keep your twisted cock in your pants. As long as the boy's here, you stay out of my bed. If you desire warmth and comfort, go sleep with the dogs."

The only sound Saredon had heard in response was the slamming of the front door.

Before arriving at Liv's house, Garius had been adamant that Saredon must keep his identity a secret. Liv had no idea who Garius was, and despite the strange affection he had for the woman, Garius did not trust her with that knowledge. The story was that Saredon was a street urchin Garius had rescued from being harassed by a gang. Garius and Liv would give Saredon a place to sleep until it was safe for him to return to the streets.

The actual plan, according to Garius, was for the two of them to lie low until the regent relaxed his search for Saredon. Right now, it was impossible for any adolescent boy to leave the city unless his parentage could be verified. Once it was safe, Garius said that the two of them would escape into the countryside and disappear. Every night, Saredon dreamed of green forests and rolling hills.

Garius and Liv both worked during the daylight hours, which meant that Saredon was stuck in the small house all day by himself. To maintain the deception, and at Garius's insistence, he was not supposed to step foot outside. This left him with nothing to do, and after two days, he was full of pent-up energy.

There were no books to read, no toys to play with, no yard to exercise in, and no one to talk to. On the first day, Saredon had searched every nook and cranny of the house thrice over. He found nothing to capture his interest. On the second day, he grew more daring, and he started pulling things out of the cabinets to play with, although he was careful to return them to their places before Liv came home.

On the afternoon of the third day, Saredon was playing a game that required him to avoid touching the kitchen floor. He had arranged all the chairs in a row, and was jumping across them, when the door to the house banged open.

Liv was home from work early. Startled by Liv's entrance, Saredon lost his balance and tripped. He caught himself on the back of a chair, but the piece of furniture toppled and smashed against the wall. The force of this impact jolted the dishes that were hanging on the wall from their hooks, and they crashed to the floor. Painted pottery shattered into a thousand tiny pieces.

Frozen where he had fallen, Saredon stared up at Liv. Her eyes blazed with fury. Saredon did not know which made her angrier, the broken dishes or the fact that she had acknowledged his presence.

"Now you've stepped in it, you little brat," Liv said. "I won't stand for this, not in my own home. I'm leaving, and you'd best not be here when I get back."

Liv spun on her heel and stomped back out the door. It rattled on its hinges with the force of her slamming it. Stunned, Saredon sat up, wondering what he should do. Garius would be home soon. He would know how to fix this. In the meantime, Saredon swept up the ruined dishes and returned the chairs to their places.

Saredon felt strange stuck in the house waiting for Garius. For the past six months, he had been responsible for himself. There had been no one else to look out for him. After Liv's outburst, Saredon's first instinct was to seek out a place to hide, to search out a nook that no one could find or reach and wait for the trouble to pass. He felt trapped in the house, exposed in a way that he did not like.

But instead of running, Saredon forced himself to calm down and sit patiently at the kitchen table. He wanted so desperately to stay with Garius. Tears welled up in his eyes at the thought of returning to the streets. Saredon wanted a home again and people that cared about him. Suffering Liv's anger was preferable to being an invisible gutter rat.

By the time Garius came through the door, Saredon had worked himself into quite a state. He knew he was in trouble, and he was certain that Liv would force Garius to put him out of their home. Lower lip trembling, tears starting to spill from his eyes, Saredon scrambled down from his chair and launched himself at Garius. He wrapped his arms around the man's waist before Garius could react.

"Ho, lad, what's this?" Garius said. Gently, Garius pushed Saredon away and looked down at his face.

"I broke the dishes and made Liv mad," Saredon said through his tears. "Please don't let her send me away! I don't want to be alone again."

Garius glanced at the now empty wall where the dishes used to hang. He frowned, which looked more like a grimace on his ruined face.

"She was here?" Garius said after a moment. "She saw this?"

Saredon only nodded.

"I knew it wasn't meant to last," Garius said, shaking his head. "I know you heard our fight this morning. I don't think we can stay here any longer. I was a fool to bring you in the first place. I had thought... well, never mind what I thought. Liv's mind is made up, and I'm not about to change it."

"Where can we go?" Saredon said.

"Don't you worry about that. I'll think of something. Let me gather a few items and we'll go. Maybe later, I can come back and explain myself to Liv."

Saredon stood in the kitchen while Garius gathered a pack and started stuffing supplies into it.

"I've paid for half of this stuff, so I'm entitled to it," Garius said while he worked. "I'm no thief."

Within minutes, the pack was almost full, and Garius stood next to Saredon trying to remember anything else they might need. The front door swung open. In walked Liv, her anger still burning hot.

"Going to loot my home and make a run for it, is that it?" Liv said when she saw the pack in Garius's hands.

"This food is mine as much as yours, and you know it," Garius said. "You want the boy gone, so we'll leave."

"It's too late for that," Liv said.

"Don't make a fuss. There's no need to argue about it. We're leaving, and that's that."

"I don't intend to argue." Liv stepped aside to clear the doorway.

Through the open door, three soldiers stepped into the house. They wore the dull black plate mail of Regent Trangeth's personal forces. Each of them had a sword buckled to their hip. In the lead, a short, weary-looking soldier walked in front of two hulking brutes. The shorter of the three soldiers looked bored, but the other two scanned the dwelling with greedy eyes. Their gaze lingered on Liv, eyes roving up and down the full length of her body before moving on.

"What have you done?" Garius said, the question almost a shout. He reached to his hip for a sword that was not there.

"What I should have done two days ago," Liv said with a smirk. "They're paying a month's wages for any orphan boy you can deliver. And if he happens to be the brat they're looking for, I'll never have to work another day in my life."

"Yes, yes, a grand reward and all that," the tired looking soldier said. "Come here, boy. Don't make me have to send Clodd and Ticus over there to collect you."

"You can have the tyke, sergeant," one of the big soldiers said. "We'll take the woman."

The soldiers at the sergeant's back grinned at each other.

Saredon's hand found Garius's.

The sergeant's eyes narrowed. He peered at Garius's face. "Are you the boy's relation?"

"I already told you, he's not," Liv said. "He's just some street filth from the slums."

"Interrupt me again, and I'll hand you over to my men for their sport," the sergeant said.

Liv paled, and for the first time, seemed to sense that she was not the one in control of the situation.

"Do you know the boy's parentage?" the sergeant said, still addressing Garius.

Garius did not speak for a long moment. Finally, when he was at risk of his silence alone being answer enough, he gave Saredon's hand a squeeze and said, "As she said, he's just an urchin from the slums. I'd never laid eyes on him before three days ago."

Saredon did not understand what was happening. The only two facts that he could grasp were that he was terrified of the black-armored soldiers and that Garius had lied. Liv had recovered from her apprehension and looked triumphant again. Garius pulled his hand out of Saredon's. Saredon stared up at his former mentor, but the man did not look down.

"Go with the soldiers, lad," Garius said. "There's nothing more we can do for you here."

The sergeant beckoned to Saredon with a gauntleted hand. Saredon felt dead inside. The tears that had been threatening to fall, even the fear, had vanished. Six months of avoiding capture, and he had been given up by the one person he should have been able to trust.

It did not matter that even Saredon's immature mind could understand that for Garius to attack the three soldiers would have been suicide. The former captain of the guard should have done something, anything, to deliver them from the enemy. He should have acted as the hero Saredon always thought him to be.

Saredon did not move—Garius gave him a gentle push forward. Once he started walking, Saredon did not stop. He felt like he was not in control of his body. From very far away, he watched himself cross the room and stand before the sergeant. A black gauntlet grasped Saredon's shoulder, armored fingers digging in hard.

"If he's the boy we've been seeking, you'll be contacted about the reward," the sergeant said. He jerked Saredon around and made to leave through the door.

"What about my finder's fee?" Liv said. "I demand my payment for bringing the boy to your attention!"

"Give her a few coins," the sergeant said.

One of the other soldiers dug into a pouch on his hip and tossed a few coppers at Liv. The coins fell to the floor with a dull thud.

"Do I look like a beggar to you?" Liv said, her voice approaching a shriek. "That's not enough to buy a hunk of rotten meat at the market. You promised me a month's wages!"

"Clodd, explain it to her," the sergeant said.

Before Liv could open her mouth to complain again, Clodd's giant hand came up and wrapped around her throat. He lifted her feet off the floor and slammed her up against the wall. Liv hung in his grasp, gagging and clawing at his armored arm.

"See here, wench," Clodd said. "The finder's fee required you to deliver a boy to us. But you dragged us out here to this stinking hovel, so we're taking that time out of your payment. If you don't like it, there are *other* ways you can earn the difference."

To make his meaning clear, Clodd grabbed Liv's chin with his other hand and kissed her violently on the mouth. Liv flailed, but she was helpless in the man's grip. Clodd pulled back, laughing. He let Liv drop, and she crumpled to the floor.

Garius never spoke or moved from the spot where he stood. Saredon tried to make eye contact with him, but he refused to meet Saredon's gaze. The sergeant gave Saredon a hard shove, and he was forced out the door and into the street.

Clodd and Ticus followed the sergeant out, slamming the door shut on the miserable scene. The three soldiers towered over Saredon. They conversed amongst themselves as if he were not there, but the sergeant's iron grip on his shoulder never wavered.

"The two of you are disgusting," the sergeant said. "That woman probably bathes in the sewer. Kissing her is like swapping spit with a diseased roach."

"You're just jealous that she liked me and not you," Clodd said with a sneer. "She tasted mighty fine. And she had some sass in her. I like that in a woman."

"I'm sure she'd be flattered. Now, get the collar. I'm tired of holding this kid."

In response to the sergeant's command, Ticus unclipped a leather loop from his belt. He unwound the long leather leash that was wrapped around it. That done, he snapped open the collar and leaned close to fit it around Saredon's neck. Saredon tried not to breathe. The man's breath was terrible.

Ticus secured the restraint and gave it a vicious tug to tighten it. Saredon choked as the hard leather bit into the soft skin of his throat.

"Run, and it'll squeeze the life out of you," Ticus said, inches from Saredon's face.

"Do you think he's the one?" Clodd said as Ticus stood up.

"You ask that every time, and every time it's not," the sergeant said.

"Why are you always such a wretched whoreson? We could split the reward three ways and be rich. A fella can dream, can't he?"

"I dream of a day when we're not babysitting orphans for the priesthood. The tenth reaver's get is either dead or long gone by now. This is a waste of time. Come on, let's get moving."

The sergeant set off down the street. Clodd and Ticus fell into step behind him. Ticus yanked Saredon so hard he almost lost his feet. His captor's long stride meant that Saredon had to run to keep up. It was that or be dragged.

People stopped and stared at the strange sight of three soldiers escorting a leashed child. Saredon wanted to shrink from sight. He would have happily taken the dirtiest hole in the trash heap if it meant he could hide. Now the tears came. Saredon sniffled, trying not to let the men in front of him hear his crying.

They passed out of the poor district and were soon marching through the crowded market. The mob parted without being told before the determined step of the sergeant. Saredon searched the throng for a face of sympathy. He saw curiosity, indifference, and disgust, but he could not find one person that appeared concerned. Saredon thought he had been alone before. But now, being led through hundreds of people who did not care one whit about his fate, he had never felt more abandoned.

Unbidden, thoughts of his father filled Saredon's mind. Why did he not come? Saredon had done his best. He had survived against all odds, expecting every day for Kaiser to appear and make everything right again. Now, as Saredon stumbled along with a leash around his neck, he began to accept that no one was coming to save him.

After leaving the market behind, they entered a part of the city Saredon had avoided for the last six months. Here, the wealthy and the elite built their homes, and here the cathedral, castle, and arena, dominated the skyline.

The sergeant made straight for the Tarragon Cathedral. A monolith of dark stone and twisted metal, the cathedral filled Saredon's heart with dread. Its many spires clawed at the sky like talons, and terrible monsters carved from rock leered down at them from a hundred different alcoves.

Saredon rubbed at his eyes, trying to wipe away the tears. The soldiers dragged him into the cathedral's courtyard. Their crude banter had gone silent as they passed into the shadow of the cathedral's ominous towers. Ticus and Clodd stopped outside a grand stone archway. Saredon waited behind them as the sergeant ventured inside.

In the center of the courtyard, a grotesque tree spread its branches over an ancient tomb. Saredon could not look away from the tree. Instead of bark, it looked like it was covered in sickly white skin. A snarl of pale roots clutched at the sarcophagus at the foot of the tree, and a dozen grinning skulls peered out from the shadows between those roots.

To Saredon's disgusted fascination, he was almost certain that he could see blood pulsing through veins beneath the tree's translucent surface. Seven swollen fruit hung from the outstretched branches, each piece as big as Saredon was tall. A strangely sweet scent filled the courtyard and made his head ache. He shuddered. The tree *smelled* evil.

The sergeant returned moments later with a priestess of Abimelech. They exchanged a few quiet words, and after accepting his payment, the sergeant ordered Ticus to hand the leash over to the woman. Their business concluded, the three soldiers left the courtyard as quickly as possible.

Saredon inspected his new captor. The woman was beautiful, statuesque in her long black robe. She smiled at Saredon, and the brilliance of her affection felt like the warmth of sunshine after a long winter's day.

"Come to me, child," the woman said. Her voice matched her beauty. She knelt so that she was eye level with Saredon.

Unsure of himself, but wanting to believe the woman was a friend, Saredon took a tentative step forward. He glanced at the woman's chest where a picture of the wicked tree was embroidered in silver. That gave him pause. Surely, someone so pretty could not be evil?

"It's okay to be shy," the woman said. "I won't hurt you."

Her words were a comfort and a salve for Saredon's confusion, and he took the last few steps to stand in front of the woman. She looked deep into his eyes and traced the contours of his face with her gaze.

"I knew your mother," the woman said. "And I believe... yes, I'm confident."

The woman reached up and unfastened the collar around Saredon's neck. She cast it to the ground, a look of disgust on her flawless face.

"Those soldiers can be so cruel," the woman said. "I'm sorry you had to endure that."

Still smiling, she stood up to her full height and extended an open hand to Saredon.

"Welcome, Saredon, son of Kaiser. We've been waiting for you."

Chapter 32

KAISER SAT ON THE shore next to the *Celestial* and watched the sun go down. He was exhausted. After taking control of the ship, they had worked hard for the rest of the day to get her seaworthy again. Most of Sorrell's crew had chosen to vanish into the forest and find their way back to friendly territory. To Kaiser's surprise, eight of the Coriddian sailors decided to join Gustavus.

Gustavus did not trust these new recruits, and he and Kaiser were certain they only joined up to try to rescue Sorrell, but they were not about to turn away skilled workers. If they proved to be traitors, they would be dealt with when the time came.

All told, the crew now had thirty capable souls, along with several who were still injured. By Gustavus's estimate, they would be able to set sail in another day or two. They could limp their way to a safe harbor where they would have time to fully repair the damaged ship.

A small fire crackled in front of Kaiser. Raither sat next to him, lost in quiet contemplation. Together, they were sharing the first watch of the night. On the other side of the fire, Sorrell lay in the sand, trussed up and unable to move. She had refused to speak since they captured her.

It had been Kaiser's idea to keep Sorrell on the beach and her former crew on the ship for the night. As long as they were separated by water, it made any attempt of a midnight escape almost impossible.

Kaiser heaved himself to his feet. Raither glanced up but did not say anything. Kaiser walked around the fire and knelt to check Sorrell's bindings for a third time. The firelight shined in her eyes as she watched him. Gustavus had cut strips of crescentweave sail to bind her with. According to the captain, the magic infused cloth would not freeze, which ensured Sorrell could not use her new command over ice to break free.

A few quick tugs on the makeshift rope reassured Kaiser that Sorrell was not going anywhere. Satisfied, he returned to his place on the other side of the fire. The last faint flickerings of the day's light were glowing on the western horizon. Darkness crept across the beach.

"You're not saying it, so I will," Raither said. He tossed a twig into the fire as he spoke. "We've taken the *Celestial;* you've got the woman you were after. You don't need me anymore. Why can't I just disappear into the forest?"

"I've got a family too," Kaiser said, staring into the flames.

Raither looked sideways at him.

"My daughter, you know," Kaiser said. "Her mother died only recently, and I've got a son…"

Kaiser did not continue, and Raither cleared his throat.

"What I mean to say is that I understand your desire to return to your family," Kaiser said. "Of all the people here, I respect that the most. You're just going to have to trust me that you'll see them again. Wait a little while longer, and you'll be free. You have my word. And the Coriddian military is probably still hunting you. You might be safest with us."

"Of what use to me is the word of a pirate?" Raither said bitterly. "Your captain has proven himself to be a brigand. I should never have trusted him with my safety."

Kaiser did not respond. He had nothing to say that would appease Raither. Let the man stew a while. Maybe it would keep him silent. Yawning hugely, Kaiser stretched his arms wide and flexed his tired shoulders. Sleep would be more than welcome when this watch was over.

Night shadows danced in the firelight, and Kaiser found himself mesmerized by the rhythmic undulation of light writhing against the darkness. He watched, almost in a trance, as a human shaped shadow detached itself from the forest's edge and stalked across the ground towards where Kaiser sat. He observed this strange apparition with a detached curiosity, not thinking to remark on the oddity of a free-moving shadow until it was almost on top of him.

At the last instant, when it dawned on Kaiser that this shade seemed to be more than a figment of his weary imagination, he tried to jump to his feet. But he was too slow to act. The shadow lunged across the distance between them, elongating and twisting into an inhuman form as it sped across the ground. It disappeared when it touched Kaiser's feet. A cry of alarm died on his lips as the claws of irresistible slumber dragged him into unconsciousness.

For a time, Kaiser floated in nothingness. He was aware that he was asleep, but no matter how hard he tried, he could not force himself to wake. Soon, a dream began to take form around his disembodied awareness. The beach returned, and he found himself sitting in the same spot. However, in his vision, Raither, Sorrell, and the *Celestial* were nowhere to be seen. He was alone on an empty shore in front of the small fire.

A heartbeat after Kaiser made these observations, the air rippled around him. The dream world shuddered and shifted. When the disturbance ceased, a hooded figure was sitting on the other side of the fire. To Kaiser, it felt like he had blinked and missed something, but he had not closed his eyes.

Kaiser knew immediately that this was not the same stranger that had visited his dreams before. This new interloper stared back at Kaiser from beneath his hood. Eyes that burned with an unquenchable fire watched him from across the campsite. The apparition had the form of a man, but Kaiser sensed, in the way of dreams, that this was no ordinary oracle.

"Your thoughts are open to me, son of Northmark," the stranger said. "You're a long way from home. You may call me Umbris. Speak and learn. You'll find I don't answer in riddles."

The voice made Kaiser wince. Umbris's words tore at the fabric of his dream, every utterance lancing across his awareness like the dragging of a knife's tip. Kaiser tried to meet Umbris's gaze, but he could not bring the figure on the other side of the fire into focus. Without appearing to move, Umbris kept sliding to the edges of Kaiser's vision, indistinct almost to the point of being invisible.

"You stink of evil intent," Kaiser said. The words only came with significant effort. "Get out of my head."

"Alas, I cannot change my nature," Umbris said. "And unlike others who have visited you in this way, I'll make no claims to be something I'm not. I present myself to you as I am, without deception. I'm only here to warn you, young one. Don't go to your doom clinging to a false hope."

"Lies are no better than riddles," Kaiser said. "If you've a point, then out with it. Otherwise, leave me be."

"I see why he chose you," Umbris said, the hint of a smile behind his words. "Very well, I'll be brief. You're being used. Every step of the way, every facet of your journey since that day in Oakroot when you gained your powers, has been manipulated towards one end.

You've been told your purpose is righteous, and your companions hold to this faith, but you doubt, and rightfully so. I told you I'd not speak mysteries, but there are truths that even I am not allowed to utter here. You must see the meaning behind my words for yourself.

"Think on this. The one you name enemy, my... master, did not set you on this path. You grieve daily for your dead wife and lost son, but who is it that should answer for your suffering? The one who called you would sacrifice Mariel a dozen times over to realize his ambitions."

"You're wasting your time," Kaiser said. "I put no more stock in your dire prophecies than his. Go bother someone who believes in your gibberish."

"Belief isn't a requisite," Umbris said. "That of which I speak will be made manifest whether you believe it or not. Don't be so foolish as to think that your actions are without consequence. The ignorant man is far more dangerous than the one equipped with proper knowledge."

"Perhaps I'm ignorant, but I'm no fool. Maybe the one who gave me my powers is as evil as you are, but that doesn't make you my friend. The enemy of my enemy can still be my enemy."

"Truly spoken. But if forced to choose between two enemies, wouldn't the wise man prefer to be on the winning side?"

"If you were confident of that, you'd not be here annoying me."

Umbris laughed. The sound reverberated through the dreamscape, distorting the scene and almost warping it beyond comprehension.

"Very well, child," Umbris said. "Trust in your own strength for a while longer. We shall see how far it takes you. Now sleep and do not wake. When you rise, remember what I've said when you see the evidence of your frailty."

Umbris's hooded form faded back into nothingness, and with him went the dream. Kaiser struggled against the fatigue that flooded him, but he could not overcome Umbris's influence. Kaiser slept.

— —

Sorrell held her breath as the odd shadow crept across the beach towards Kaiser. The hair on the back of her neck had stood on end when she noticed it detach itself from the dark tree line. Silent as it slipped across the sand, the thing attached itself to Kaiser and disappeared from sight. A few seconds later, Kaiser's head slumped and his body went limp.

Lost in thought, Raither had not noticed. Sorrell waited for a good five minutes before acting. Kaiser started to snore softly, and she knew she would not find a better opportunity.

"Pssst," Sorrell hissed, trying to get Raither's attention without waking Kaiser.

Raither glanced up.

"He's asleep," Sorrell said, nodding at Kaiser.

Sorrell waited for Raither to understand the implications. That understanding came quickly, and Raither surged to his feet and started toward the trees.

"Wait!" Sorrell said. "Cut my bonds and let me go. Don't leave me here a prisoner in the hands of these criminals."

Raither paused several feet from Sorrell. "I don't want to give them any reason to come after me. If they have you, they'll forget about me."

"I can help you," Sorrell said, thinking fast. "You're General Raither, right? I recognize you. If you let me go, I can report to the Coriddian army that you're dead. They'll stop hunting you. You'll be free to return to your family and make a new life in peace."

Sorrell held her breath. If Raither abandoned her here, she would probably not get another chance to escape. Finally, after an excruciating pause to mull over Sorrell's offer, Raither knelt next to her and went to work with his knife.

Crescentweave did not cut easily, but Raither was able to free Sorrell's hands so that she could go to work on the knots. The entire time, she kept glancing at Kaiser, expecting him to wake up any second. But he remained sound asleep and blissfully unaware.

Raither helped Sorrell get her legs untied, and she scrambled to her feet. Together, they sprinted for the cover of the dark forest. Dangling crescentweave slapped at Sorrell as she moved. She would get the rest off when they had put some distance between themselves and the water.

They ran until they were out of breath, imagining the footsteps of pursuers as they dodged tree trunks in the darkness. Mercifully, the forest floor was flat and easy to navigate. A nasty fall could have ended their mad dash in painful frustration. Sorrell gave up trying to estimate the distance they covered once she was certain they had traveled at least two miles.

A few minutes later, Raither stumbled to a stop. Sorrell stopped with him and sagged against a tree. Chests heaving, they stared at each other, unable to speak until they had their wind back. Sorrell recovered first.

"That's a few miles between them and us, at least," Sorrell said. "They'll not easily track us in the night. We should be able to get a good lead on them by morning."

"This is where I leave you," Raither said when he could talk. "If you travel due east, you should reach a road by morning. Head south, and you'll find a border town called Parda within a few days. From there, your fate is in your hands. Don't forget to tell your army about me. I died when the *Golden Dawn* went down."

"I won't forget," Sorrell said. "And thank you for what you did back there."

Raither gave her one last nod, turned, and vanished into the shadows. Before moving on, Sorrell wrestled with the last of the crescentweave still clinging to her. Once she removed it, she almost tossed it on the ground. At the last second, she realized that to do so would leave a blatant sign that she had passed this way. With a curse, Sorrell stuffed the shreds of fabric down the front of her shirt. She could dispose of it later, when it would not give her away.

Sorrell pressed on, heading east as best she could. Dawn would show her how good her sense of direction was. She spurred herself to greater speed, certain that Kaiser would have awoken by now. Would they set out in pursuit right away? Would they seek her at all?

Gustavus had the *Celestial* now, and while the man was clearly beset by mystical delusions, Sorrell had a hard time believing that he would commit valuable manpower and time to a mad chase through the countryside. That said, Kaiser concerned her. The man's motivations were murky, but one thing was certain, he needed Sorrell for something important, and he was not about to let her go easily.

Thoughts in turmoil, Sorrell tried to formulate a plan while she moved. She had set carefully executed strategies in motion when she sailed away from Coridal, but she had no idea what had happened since then. The mission had been a complete failure. Sorrell was returning alone, without a ship and a crew. That in itself could prove to be a terrible blow to her ambitions.

Viatrix was not an idiot. Mazareem would inform her of Sorrell's strange powers. Her mother would see the risk, and Viatrix would start working at once to undermine any advantage they might give Sorrell.

Everything had gone so wrong. If there was a way to salvage this, Sorrell could not see it.

Mazareem had a day's head start. If he found a horse, he would reach the capital well ahead of her. Armed with Mazareem's lies, Viatrix would brand Sorrell a fugitive. She had no doubt about that. And the royal mother's allies would have no qualms about arresting Sorrell.

Sorrell's only hope was that enough of her conspirators remained loyal and alive to make a play for the throne. Through Mazareem, Viatrix had dealt her hand. Single-handedly, the man had crippled Sorrell's chances, but she was not dead yet.

The furious churning of her mind slowed, and all Sorrell was left with was the memory of Stone. In the solitude of the night, alone under the shadows of the trees, Sorrell allowed herself to grieve. In her sorrow, she remembered.

She remembered Stone's easy laugh and silly smirk. She remembered his unimpeachable character and his love for the navy. Stone had been the embodiment of everything Sorrell valued, and in him, she had found a love and acceptance on her merit alone that she thought could not exist.

Tears spilled down Sorrell's cheeks as she walked. The last few days with Stone had been more wondrous than all the years of her life prior. She had been a fool for refusing his advances for so long. If she had taken him as a lover and companion at the first, maybe things would have gone differently. Maybe he would still be alive.

Sorrell clenched her jaw. She would not tarnish Stone's memory with regret. Better to cherish the time they had together than to let despair rob her of the happiness he had given her. As Sorrell dwelt on this, the immense and immediate pain ripping at her soul receded to a dull ache. Stone's presence stepped back, and so too did her overwhelming grief; although, Sorrell suspected the aching of his absence would stay with her for years. Perhaps for the rest of her life.

Sorrow gave way to rage as Sorrell contemplated the life stolen from Stone. He had been robbed of everything he had ever dreamed of. No longer would he stand on the deck of his own ship. He would never make admiral. He would never bounce his own son on his knee. He would never again feel the warmth of the sun and the spray of the sea on the open ocean.

The black-hearted creature who had taken these things from Stone still lived, and that was a travesty of justice that Sorrell intended to rectify. Let Viatrix and Mazareem plot and scheme. With or without the power of the throne, Mazareem would die by her hand.

Soon, the first rays of sunlight filtered down through the treetops, and Sorrell was encouraged to discover that she had been traveling east through the night. Within the hour, the road Raither promised appeared. It was a wide dirt highway cut out of the trees that encroached on both sides.

Sorrell turned south, moving fast now in the light of day. Somewhere up ahead, the town of Parda waited, and beyond that, Coriddian territory. Every step strengthened Sorrell's resolve. The events of the last week had cost her almost everything she loved in the world. No more. She would wear no more chains and submit to no man. Like the Coriddian emperors before her, she would ascend to eclipse the sun.

Chapter 33

KAISER WAS FURIOUS. HE had slept through the night. The next shift of the watch had discovered him asleep and Sorrell and Raither escaped, and they had tried and failed to wake him. Instead of sending an immediate search party after Sorrell, Gustavus had decided to wait until morning to determine what to do. Now, Kaiser, Lacrael, Brant, Gustavus, and Niad were holding a tense conference in the captain's cabin of the *Celestial*.

"You'd best explain yourself, *captain*," Kaiser said. "Your inaction has cost us dearly. We'll be hard pressed to catch Sorrell, even if we're right about where she's heading."

"Point your anger elsewhere, because I won't have it," Gustavus said. "You're the one who fell asleep on watch. Or have you forgotten that little detail? I'm still the captain of this ship, and I made the decision I thought best."

"We've been searching for Sorrell for *six months!* Tell me, in what way does letting her escape help us?"

Gustavus exchanged a look with Niad before continuing. When he started speaking again, he became animated, gesturing with his hands for emphasis. He spoke quickly, as if to forestall any objection from Kaiser.

"Swallow your ire for a moment and hear me out," Gustavus said. "I've been doing a lot of thinking, ever since the *Golden Dawn* went down. Gods below, that wasn't a price I ever expected to pay. Every man and woman that went to the depths with her was like losing a brother or a sister."

By the tone of Gustavus's voice, Kaiser guessed where he was heading. For days, the big captain had walked around in a daze. When they had confronted Sorrell, Kaiser had heard the bitterness and doubt in Gustavus's voice when he spoke about their quest. The man had reached a turning point in his crisis of faith.

"I don't like where this is going," Kaiser said.

Gustavus pressed on. "Why would the high king mislead us about Raither? Why would he be silent for six months and then put us on a course that ended with the loss of my ship and half its crew? Is he so powerless to protect us, or, dare I say it, did he intend for the *Dawn* to sink?

"I can't answer those questions. But I can see the boon that has been given us in the *Celestial*. She's a mighty fine ship. She'll rival even the memory of the *Golden Dawn* when she's fit again. We've just enough crew to sail her. We can start over. Let Sorrell go back to her blasted empire. What did finding her bring us in the first place? And if we do go after her, and by some miracle win her back, we'll just have to abandon everything we've earned here and travel to another forsaken realm to find the next champion."

Lacrael looked pale and Brant concerned. Niad was looking everywhere but at Kaiser. Gustavus stopped talking and looked to see if his argument had been convincing.

"Let me get this straight," Kaiser said, his voice tight. "You've suffered some personal hardship, and now you want to quit? Do I have the gist of it?"

"Have a care with that tongue of yours," Gustavus said. "I've gutted men for less. You're not the only one with a burden to bear. We've suffered your griping for half a year now. You walk around here acting as if no one else has scars on their soul to match yours. Get over yourself. I've got a crew to think of, where you've only yourself."

Kaiser's initial reaction was to answer Gustavus's anger with his own, but before he lashed out, he realized that the man did not have the support of anyone else in the room. In attacking Kaiser, Gustavus had even lost Niad's approval. She stood with her arms crossed, frowning at her captain.

"Let's recount the cost *I* paid," Kaiser said. "This being you call the high king took *everything* from me. I lost my family, my home, my wealth, my reputation, even my country. You've dragged me into this realm and told me that our cause is just, that we're out to defeat an evil that not only threatens all of mankind but also watches over Northmark ensuring I can never return unless it's defeated.

"Now you know the stakes. Now you share in the loss we've all experienced. Lacrael has no home to return to. Brant's entire village was destroyed. Did you expect to get through this unscathed? Take this path, and the legend of the *Golden Dawn* will remember her captain as a coward!"

Kaiser's words echoed in the small cabin. No one spoke into the silence that followed. Gustavus only stared, and in his eyes, Kaiser saw the same haunted look from earlier on the beach. He understood then. Gustavus was afraid, perhaps for the first time in his life.

"You know my doubts about your 'high king'," Kaiser said. "I can't restore your faith in him, and even if I could, I don't know that I would. What I do know is that we've got to fix what's broken. I have a son I'm going to rescue and a home I intend to return to. I expect Lacrael and Brant feel the same, in their own way. And you, you're the one who set us against Abimelech. Do you think he'll just ignore you now if you decide to return to the life of a simple smuggler?

"You'd never be safe. Mazareem's still out there. I've a feeling in my gut that this conflict won't end until we win or die. You can't just walk away and pretend none of this happened. You said you're still the captain of this ship. Act like it. Be the hero they sing of in those ridiculous legends you spread."

While Kaiser spoke, Gustavus stood up taller. He squared his shoulders. The look of bewilderment left his eyes.

"Damn your hide, you're right," Gustavus said. "Who'd listen to a song about Captain Gustavus, who abandoned his quest? The *Golden Dawn* might be at the bottom of the sea, but we can honor her memory by making sure her sacrifice wasn't in vain.

"By my soul… it wasn't supposed to happen this way. That ship was more than metal and wood to me. I loved her like she was my own wife, I did. I'd never thought there'd come a day when she wasn't somewhere out there, sails full of wind and shining like the dawn's sun."

"None of us wanted any of this," Kaiser said. "But we find ourselves here, and the only way home for any of us is to press on. Are you with us, captain?"

Gustavus got control of his emotions, took a deep, shuddering breath, and stuck out an open hand towards Kaiser.

Kaiser grasped Gustavus's massive forearm, and the captain returned the embrace.

"I'm with you," Gustavus said. "For the *Golden Dawn*, and for my crew. If we ever find him, the high king will answer for both."

"There will be an accounting, mark my words," Kaiser said.

Gustavus released Kaiser and stepped back. "If we're going after Sorrell, we should leave at once."

"She's certain to be making for Coridal," Kaiser said. "I'm sure we can find her. The problem is getting out once we do."

"If you track her on land, I'll bring the *Celestial* down the coast," Gustavus said. He moved to the table where a map of the Linstall and Coriddian coast was tacked down. Gustavus traced his finger along the coastline until he reached Coridal. "Each night, we'll anchor in a cove or inlet. Here, I'll make a sketch for you to carry with you."

Gustavus dug a piece of parchment out of a drawer and went to work with a charcoal pencil. Within minutes, he had produced a crude copy of the map, with each night's planned stopping point clearly labeled.

"Now, if you run into trouble, you know where to find us," Gustavus said, handing the drawing to Kaiser. "By my reckoning, on day seven you should reach Coridal. If you don't appear that night, what do you want us to do?"

"If we don't make the rendezvous, we'll either be dead or captured," Kaiser said as he inspected Gustavus's hand-drawn map. "In either event, you should make for the open ocean until you find out what became of us. There's no reason to risk the ship by lingering in enemy territory for too long, and you'd have no hope of mounting a rescue."

"Who's this 'we' you're talking about?" Gustavus said. "Who's going with you?"

"I don't expect Sorrell to come easily," Kaiser said. "I need Lacrael with me. Together, the two of us might have a chance."

"Brant's coming too," Lacrael said, the tone of her voice leaving no room for argument.

Kaiser had suspected as much. He looked at Brant, who had said nothing up to this point. There was no denying that a change had come over the man. Ever since waking up on the beach, Brant had seemed close to his old self again. The only new quirk being that he no longer wore a shirt.

The bruise on Kaiser's injured arm ached, reminding him of what had happened the last time Brant had ventured off the ship. Kaiser stepped forward to stand in front of Brant. He had to tilt his head back slightly to look up into the bigger man's eyes.

"Lacrael thinks you've gained an upper hand on the demon inside you," Kaiser said. "But I want to hear it from you. Are you whole again? Will you put us at risk if we take you with us?"

Brant winced, his gaze finding Kaiser's wound. He raised a hand to brush the dragon amulet embedded in the flesh of his chest. "I'm sorry I hurt you. With Lacrael's fire and the magic of this amulet, I'm in control of the demon. It won't threaten us again. And… I can feel the thing's power burning inside me. If you take me with you, I can help."

"He's certainly not staying here!" Gustavus said. "That pair already cost me one ship. I'll not have them blowing up another."

"I'd like to believe you," Kaiser said. "But there needs to be an understanding between us. If you show any hint of succumbing to the influence of the demon, I'll have no choice but to kill you."

Lacrael frowned. She opened her mouth to speak, but Brant cut her off.

"It's a hard thing to say, but… I'm okay with that," Brant said. "I'd rather die than be in its clutches again."

"Remember that, if the time comes," Kaiser said. "Now if there's nothing else, we've already wasted enough daylight."

"There's only the matter of Sorrell's sailors," Gustavus said. "She ran off without taking them with her. Do we continue to trust them?"

"Treat them as allies until they prove otherwise," Kaiser said. "But watch them carefully."

Gustavus nodded his agreement.

None of the others had anything to add, and Kaiser beckoned for Lacrael and Brant to follow him. The three of them left the cabin and went to scrounge what little supplies they could for their inland trek. Within the hour, they had returned to shore and were making their way east.

Chapter 34

LACRAEL HIKED THROUGH THE trees at Brant's side. Kaiser walked a few steps ahead of them. No one had spoken for the first hour of their journey. Kaiser set a brutal pace, but by this time, Lacrael and Brant were used to it.

In the pit of Lacrael's stomach, a tension was growing. After Kaiser and Gustavus's argument on the *Celestial,* she had been replaying their words over and over in her head. Lacrael had resigned herself to Kaiser's cynical attitude regarding the high king, but to see Gustavus, who had seemed so stalwart in his faith, begin to doubt, made her concerned.

Unlike the others, Lacrael had been raised to believe in the high king. And unlike the others, she had been raised from a young age with a constant awareness, and daily reminders, of the evil that opposed the high king's justice. Garlang, her grandfather, had shown her time and again how Abimelech had ruined their world and kept their people in subjugation. Those were lessons she would never forget.

Surely, if Kaiser and Gustavus had similar experiences, they would believe as she did. But Lacrael did not know how to communicate to them the strength of her faith and the conviction that drove her. This inability almost made her despair. If only they understood how Lacrael felt, their doubts and fears would vanish.

Gustavus's perception of the high king was built on heroic legends passed down through his dragonslayer heritage, and he had started to question his faith in their cause at the first sign that reality did not match the myth.

Kaiser was a lost cause. Lacrael had given up talking to him about the high king. He accepted that someone had given them powers and turned their lives upside down, but he refused to believe that they were a gift from High King Rowen. It was still a source of frustration for Lacrael that Rowen chose to communicate with Kaiser and not her. She told herself it was a test of faith, but that idea proved little comfort. That, and perhaps Rowen was working to convert Kaiser.

"What did you think of what Gustavus said?" Lacrael said to Brant, quiet enough that Kaiser could not overhear.

"What in particular?" Brant said. "I sort of tuned them out when they started jumping down each other's throats."

"He implied that the high king is either powerless or dishonest, to the point of doubting in the righteousness of our cause."

"Oh, yeah. I think Gustavus fancied himself the hero, and in the stories, the hero doesn't lose his ship and half his crew. He needs someone to blame, and unless he wants to take responsibility, the high king is the only other option. It can't be Abimelech, because that's the evil we're supposed to defeat. You can't blame your enemy for trying to destroy you, so Gustavus lays it at the high king's feet."

"I just can't understand that. His false vision of reality comes crashing down but instead of accepting that his perception was wrong in the first place, he lashes out against the very belief that brought him so far."

"I went through something similar, after Oakroot. I was furious, and I needed someone to blame for what had happened to me. Life as I had known it was over. At first… that target was you. But over time, I accepted that you had never intended to cause me harm. After the Wraith Wood, after what Mazareem did to me, I nurtured a hatred against the world. I don't know if it was the demon inside me, my own pain and anger, or a combination of the two, but I wanted everyone to suffer as I had."

"I'm sorry for what happened to you. There's not a day that goes by that I don't regret it."

"Save your regret. I've made peace with it, and Gustavus will make peace with his anger, in time. It's a terrible lesson to learn, but we can't control what happens to us. The only thing we can control is how we respond. If we let the bad things define us, allowing regret and anger to shape the rest of our lives, it's as if we tear open the wound fresh every day. Better to move on and let it heal, even if it leaves a nasty scar."

"More than any of us, you've the right to be angry. You're just able to let that go?"

Brant gave her a half-grin. "Before you helped me lock the demon away, I was forced to do battle with it every day. I learned that to get the upper-hand, I needed to find a weakness I could exploit. Turning my back on my anger made the demon furious, and it gave me strength. Denied my rage, the monster struggled to find a foothold from which it could control me."

They walked in silence for a few minutes while Lacrael contemplated what Brant had said. She stared at Kaiser's back without really seeing him.

"Do you believe in the high king?" Lacrael finally said.

"A week ago, I didn't," Brant said. "I'd never given him much thought. But I *saw* him chain the demon. He was with me, standing at my side just as real as you are right now. Gustavus and Kaiser can say what they want. The high king is real, and he saved my life."

Reassurance in her faith and affection for Brant surged in Lacrael's heart. She could not stop a smile from spreading on her face.

"I'm glad you're back," Lacrael Said.

"Me too," Brant said.

Lacrael glanced at Brant's muscular torso out of the corner of her eye. "Aren't you going to put on a shirt?"

Brant chuckled. "With your fire burning in the amulet, I feel warm all the time. I'm more comfortable without one on."

Together, they walked in happy silence for about a mile. Lacrael spent most of that time wondering how Brant would react if she reached out to take his hand. Before she could muster up the courage, Kaiser dropped back to walk next to them.

"There's something we need to discuss," Kaiser said. "I didn't want to bring it up back there on the ship because Gustavus wasn't in the right frame of mind to handle it. I didn't fall asleep on watch last night. I was... visited by a dream. It knocked me out like a blow to the head. One minute, I was sitting there talking to Raither, the next, I was unconscious."

"The high king spoke to you?" Lacrael said, unable to contain her excitement.

"Not quite," Kaiser said. "It was someone, or something, different. Someone new. He called himself Umbris, and he claimed to be a servant of Abimelech. He offered a warning. He said that the high king is manipulating us towards an unknown end."

"He lied," Lacrael said.

"The best lies contain an element of truth. But I don't trust his words more than any other invader of my dreams. I believe his true purpose was to let Sorrell escape. This is the first time our enemy has demonstrated the ability to influence the physical world through the intangible. I wanted the two of you to be aware. I don't know why they only speak to me, but we must assume any of us is susceptible. I cannot imagine a defense against such an attack. Even so, be on your guard."

Lacrael and Brant said nothing as they worked through the consequences of this new information. Kaiser moved ahead again, giving them a semblance of privacy as they walked together.

"The high king couldn't have picked a stranger oracle," Brant said when Kaiser was out of earshot.

"He must have his reasons, even if they don't make sense to us," Lacrael said.

Brant tried to resume their friendly conversation, but Lacrael was no longer in the mood. He lapsed into hurt silence when she did not respond to his attempts.

Kaiser's revelation of his hostile dream had shaken Lacrael. One of the most comforting things that her grandfather had taught her was that the high king watched over his faithful. For those that believed, High King Rowen protected them from the sight and influence of the tyrant Abimelech. Kaiser's most recent dream was a direct contradiction of that teaching.

While she walked, Lacrael conducted an exhaustive review of everything she had learned from Garlang. There must be an explanation, she just needed to find it. Circumstances that challenged belief were an opportunity to fortify her faith, not cast it aside. Deep in thought, with her grandfather's voice speaking in her mind, Lacrael hiked through the trees with Brant at her side.

Chapter 35

SORRELL MOVED FAST ON the dirt highway. She walked hard, not stopping to rest even as the sun rose high overhead and most travelers paused to wait out the worst heat of the day. Lacking both food and money, she had no choice but to press on and hope she could somehow acquire them in the city of Parda.

In the late afternoon of the same day she escaped the forest, Sorrell reached Parda. She hesitated only briefly, worried about how it looked for her to walk through the streets in her tarnished military uniform. It would not go unnoticed, but she did not have a choice.

Upon entering the town, Sorrell was surprised to find it almost deserted. Almost every home and place of business was boarded up. The streets were empty of even beggars and vagrants, which was quite unusual for a border province in a newly conquered territory.

Sorrell turned a corner and found herself in front of a civic building repurposed as a Coriddian army garrison. Great banners of black and gold fluttered in the breeze. In spite of everything that had happened, the colors of the Coriddian empire still brought a lump to her throat. Here was a rock to which she could cling amidst the maelstrom that threatened to pull her under.

Feeling bold now that she was on familiar ground, Sorrell strode towards the garrison. She found a single bored guard standing in front of the steps. The man straightened up when he saw her coming. A brief look of panic filled his eyes as he scanned her dirty uniform. By her bearing, he would mark her as someone with authority. Sorrell would be impressed if he correctly identified the naval insignia for an admiral.

"Ah, a fine afternoon to you... ma'am?" the soldier said when Sorrell came to a stop before him.

She decided to ignore the question mark on the end of his greeting.

"I'm Admiral Sorrell, and I'm in dire need of aid," Sorrell said. "Take me to your garrison command, immediately."

The soldier's eyes widened at her name. Of course he knew who she was. Everyone did.

"Forgive me, ma'am," the soldier said, addressing her as an officer with confidence now. "The commander isn't here. He and most of the garrison, along with the entire town, have marched to meet the emperor's procession."

"Explain yourself," Sorrell said. "What procession is this you speak of?"

"The emperor himself is coming to Linstall. He's leading a grand ceremonial campaign to announce the formal conquest of this country. They'll only be a few days away by now."

Sorrell could not believe her good fortune. The emperor was near. But close behind that thought came the realization that if this new development cut her journey short, it would save Mazareem time too. She swore under her breath.

"I must reach the emperor as soon as possible," Sorrell said. "Who is your acting superior? Bring me to them at once."

"Yes, ma'am," the soldier said. "Follow me, if you please."

The soldier turned and climbed the stone stairs that led to the front door. Sorrell followed close behind. Inside, they wandered through the almost empty building until they reached a small office on the ground floor. Within, Sorrell found an old sergeant with his boots up on a desk. He was taking a nap.

The door guard cleared his throat, and the sergeant cracked an eye in their direction. It took him a second to register Sorrell's presence, and when he did, he almost fell out of his chair as he leapt to his feet.

"This is Admiral Sorrell, sergeant," the soldier said. "She's requested the attendance of the acting garrison commander."

All the blood drained from his face, and the sergeant snapped to attention. He opened his mouth to speak, but Sorrell cut him off with a wave of her hand.

"I don't need to know your name, and I'll forget what I saw here as long as you give me what I need as quickly as possible," Sorrell said.

"Yes, ma'am," the sergeant said, relief flooding his voice. "How can I help?"

"I need a horse, some money, and a few days supplies. I have to reach the emperor's procession before he arrives here."

"Not a problem," the sergeant said with a nod. "Soldier, grab a kit and meet us in the stables."

"Yes, sergeant," the soldier said before stepping from the room.

"If you'll come this way, the stables are in the rear of the building," the sergeant said.

Soon, Sorrell was standing beneath the crude roof of a hastily constructed stable. Most of the stalls were empty, but at the very end of the row, a few warhorses were munching on hay.

"All we've got left are extra cavalry mounts," the sergeant said. "They're not the most pleasant of creatures. Can you handle one of them, ma'am?"

"Of course, sergeant," Sorrell said. "Now be quick about it."

Sorrell watched and waited as the sergeant ordered the solitary stable hand to saddle and prepare a horse for departure. While the man worked, the soldier from the front door appeared with a fully loaded infantry pack. Sorrell took the satchel with a smile and a word of thanks.

The first thing Sorrell did was to lower the pack to the ground and root around inside for the foodstuffs. She found a strip of dried meat, hard bread, and some cheese wrapped in cloth. She devoured all three under the incredulous gaze of the sergeant.

Minutes later, the stable hand had finished preparing the horse, and he led it over to where Sorrell stood. She closed the pack and secured it behind the saddle. The animal's back was almost as high as she was tall, so she accepted the stable hand's help in getting mounted. She did not intend to get off the horse until she reached her destination. The horse pranced and tossed its head, unhappy about the unfamiliar rider. Sorrell patted the animal's neck to reassure it.

"If they've stayed on schedule, the emperor's procession should just be passing Togen today or tomorrow," the sergeant said from below.

"You have my thanks, sergeant," Sorrell said, looking down at the man. "And in the future, save the naps for your own time."

The sergeant turned red with embarrassment. He snapped a formal salute as Sorrell trotted the horse out of the yard. Sorrell returned the salute automatically. In the street outside the stable, the horse's shoes clattered on the cobblestones. The warhorse tried to resist Sorrell's direction at first, but she was having none of his attitude. After a few minutes of testing each other's will, they reached an understanding. Begrudgingly, the great animal let Sorrell take the lead.

As sister to the emperor and scion of the royal family, Sorrell was an accomplished equestrian, but this beast was far more animal than she was used to riding. She sensed the coiled power between her legs, the massive strength ready to be unleashed in a cavalry charge. The horse trotted through the deserted streets with disdain, every step echoing sharply as if to say this common chore of carrying a rider from one point to another was beneath it.

Sorrell kept a tight hold on the reins while they were still in the confines of the city. In a few hours perhaps she would have the courage to let the horse run. But even at a gentle trot, they covered ground far faster than she could walk. She had a hard time believing the stamina of such a magnificent creature could ever fail.

She had almost made it out of the city when a man stepped out from between two buildings, waving his arms at her. He looked distressed, and he was calling her by name. Surprised and alarmed, Sorrell brought her horse to a halt. Other than the soldiers at the garrison, this was the first person she had encountered in Parda.

"Admiral Sorrell!" the man said breathlessly. "Thank the emperor himself that I found you."

"What is it that you need?" Sorrell said. "Do I know you?"

"Not yet you don't," the man said with a sneer.

The shifting of the horse beneath her was the only warning Sorrell got. She turned to look at what had disturbed the animal, and at the same instant, a loop of rope fell over her head and landed on her shoulders. Before Sorrell could react, the rope went tight. The loop cinched closed. Someone on the other end of the rope gave it a terrible yank, and Sorrell went head over heels off the back of the horse.

Sorrell landed hard on the street. Stars exploded in her vision. The wind went out of her chest. Her skin bled as the noose dug into her throat—she could not breathe. Above her head, she heard someone slap the horse on the rump and tell it to run off. Several pairs of booted feet appeared in her vision.

Rough hands grabbed Sorrell's arms and feet and carried her into a nearby building. They deposited her in a corner. Someone loosened the noose around her neck. She took a ragged, choking breath.

"She don't look like much, for an admiral," a voice said.

"You've always had terrible taste in women," another voice answered.

Sorrell pushed herself to her hands and knees. She waited a moment for the world to stop spinning, and when it did, she sat up and leaned against the wall at her back. Her assailants ignored her as they continued to talk amongst themselves. There were four of them. Four filthy, nasty-looking men, each of them well armed and armored. Deserters or mercenaries, Sorrell guessed.

"Aren't we supposed to kill her now?" one of the men said.

"And throw away this golden opportunity?" the man who seemed to be the leader said. "This is Admiral Sorrell, pearl of the Coriddian Navy, blood kin to the emperor himself. Think of the ransom we could get for her!"

"But we was paid to put her down."

"This is why I'm in charge and you're not, you stupid arse. We'll hold her captive for a few days, just like we promised, and then we'll see about getting paid. There's no way the emperor will leave his own sister to rot. That creepy old corpse that hired us never needs to know."

There could only be one person that would have hired these men to watch for Sorrell. Mazareem. At the thought, the frustration and helplessness that had clawed at her for the past week came rushing back. Here, again, she was at the mercy of unforeseen consequences beyond her control.

Sorrell snarled. She was not as helpless as fate seemed to demand. The power within her surged, responding to her need without prompting. Sorrell let it fill her. She still was not certain of the extent of her new abilities, but every time she drew on them, it felt easier and more intuitive.

Almost trembling with unreleased energy, Sorrell got to her feet. Carefully, so as not to arouse suspicion, she removed the rope from around her neck. This got the bandits' attention.

"Don't get any ideas," the leader said. "Play by our rules, and we'll ransom you whole. Make trouble, and we'll deliver you in pieces."

"You know who I am," Sorrell said, her voice hard. "So you shouldn't be surprised about what happens next. I've killed men whose boots you're not fit to kiss in single combat. I've sailed into storms of metal and fire and come out the other side every time. I've laid low entire empires. My freedom isn't yours to take. Step aside or die."

The brigands were good. They took her threats seriously. Exhibiting the ease and confidence of experienced fighters, they drew their weapons and took up positions that cut Sorrell off from any escape.

"Don't be a bleedin' fool," the leader said. "You're down four to one. You've got no weapon. Maybe you know how to fight, but this isn't the deck of one of your fancy ships. Did you think we'd line up and take turns fighting you in an honorable duel?"

One of the other bandits snickered at this.

In answer, Sorrell let the power blossoming inside her manifest itself. Crystal blue ice flowed from her right hand, taking the shape of the weapon most familiar to her. In the blink of an eye, she held a long, thin rapier, the frozen blade glistening in the light. Sorrell shifted her feet and dropped into a sword fighting stance.

"A formal duel is reserved for officers possessed of both poise and grace," Sorrell said. "Killing the four of your will be as inconsequential as tossing a bucket of fish guts over the rail."

"Steady lads," the leader said. "It's just some silly trick."

The leader lunged forward while he was still talking, sword raised to test Sorrell's guard. She let the man's blade touch her rapier and slide down its length. With a twist, she diverted his thrust away from her body. At the same time, she turned the point of her rapier into the shoulder of his sword arm.

Enchanted ice pierced flesh—the bandit leader staggered back. The wound was not deep, but he clawed at his shoulder like he was in terrible pain.

"C-c-cold!" he stammered through chattering teeth.

The other three attackers paused, unwilling now to feel the touch of Sorrell's strange blade. She capitalized on their hesitation. Launching off her back foot, Sorrell executed a perfect lunging thrust, skewering the bandit leader through the heart. His mouth opened in a frozen scream, and he crumpled to the floor. He did not bleed.

Sorrell pivoted to face the remaining three kidnappers. They looked concerned, but they did not panic. One of them had a shield, and he stepped forward to draw Sorrell's attention. The other two started to shift around to either side of her. In a few seconds, they would have her surrounded.

She needed more than a rapier. In a flash, memories of long hours training in the dueling hall gave her the answer. There, she had specialized in an unorthodox fighting style that caught her opponents off guard. In response to her unspoken command, a second weapon took shape in her left hand. Sorrell felt the glacial grip of a chain whip take shape beneath her fingers. Like the weapon of her youth, the whip had a hundred connected links, only they were ice instead of metal. The length of the whip lay coiled on the floor at her feet, wood freezing solid instantly where it touched.

The man with the shield advanced. Sorrell stabbed at him with her rapier, forcing him to keep his guard up. She knew she had to keep the initiative or they would overpower her. The men trying to flank her advanced a few steps, and Sorrell had no choice but to dance backwards. She felt the wall close behind her.

She had no more ground to give, and no time to spare. Sorrell launched a desperate attack. She aimed a leaping thrust at the man on her right. As Sorrell anticipated, he was ready for this, and he easily parried. In one smooth motion, she pivoted and lashed out with the whip. The man on her left had thought to strike at her when she overcommitted her attack. Her whip caught him flat-footed.

Icy coils caught the bandit's blade and wrapped around his forearm. He screamed as the terrible cold burned through his leather armor. Sorrell gave the whip a jerk. She had expected to pull him off balance. Instead, his arm shattered into a thousand shards of ice.

Sorrell did not have time to wonder at this. The man with the shield was on top of her. He kept his guard up and tried to bull-rush her into the wall. The iron boss of the shield slammed into her side. Sorrell grunted in pain. She planted her feet on the floor and twisted away at the last second—the man crashed into the wall behind her.

Before the man could recover, Sorrell whirled and pierced him through the back. Her glacial rapier slid in and out of his body as easily as if she were stabbing water. He collapsed. Sorrell turned to face her remaining attacker.

The last brigand stood between her and the door. His sword was up, but the fight had gone out of his eyes. On the floor at his feet, the man with the ruined arm was moaning and crying.

"What *are* you?" the bandit said.

"You can purchase your miserable life by telling the world," Sorrell said. "Tell them that I'm Sorrell Pyreshade, admiral in the Coriddian Navy, and the next emperor of the Coriddian Empire." The power coursing through her body filled her with elation. Nothing could stand in her way. No one could deny her.

The man backed away from her, never lowering his sword. He glanced at the injured man at his feet but thought better of trying to help. When he reached the door, the only unscathed brigand turned on his heel and ran.

Sorrell dismissed the enchanted weapons from her hands. They turned to water and splashed to the floor. She looked at the bodies at her feet. The entire engagement had not lasted longer than a minute or two.

"P-p-please, help me," the one-arm man pleaded from the floor.

Without a second glance, Sorrell strode from the room and back into the daylight. There was no sign of the fourth bandit. She hoped he would travel far, spreading the word of what had happened here. To her relief, her horse had only wandered several hundred feet down the street.

It took Sorrell a few tries to get back onto the huge animal, but soon, she was mounted again and had herself turned towards the outskirts of the city. In a sudden rush, the adrenaline drained out of her system, and Sorrell found herself shaking in the saddle.

Her fortune had started to turn. Fate had tried to deal her another bad hand, and Sorrell had refused to play. Mazareem's gambit had failed, and he was next. With a thought, Sorrell summoned the rapier back into her hand. She smiled to herself as she inspected the glittering sword.

She would cut out Mazareem's frozen heart with a blade of ice.

Chapter 36

MAZAREEM MADE GOOD TIME after leaving Parda. Traveling on horseback gave his battered body a much-needed respite. He drank rationed portions of the blood he had harvested, mixed with shavings from Abimelech's scale, and let his body do its healing work.

The closer he drew to the city of Togen, the more crowded the roads became. It seemed that everyone in this part of the world had heard about the emperor's grand procession, and they were all flocking to his imperial banner. For most of the poor country folk, there was money to be made. For those with influence and power, it was a chance to be visible at a monumental event that was sure to go down in history.

As far as Mazareem was concerned, they were all fools. A thousand years of life brought with them a new perspective; It was hard to perceive the institutions of the world as anything other than transitory. An empire as mighty as Coriddia seemed fragile and finite when viewed through the lens of eternity. These people bickered and fought over scraps of a dying beast. Their hard-won spoils would rot, and they would perish along with them.

Despite his recovering health, Mazareem found himself in a foul mood. Viatrix would be expecting him. No doubt, she would want a full report as soon as possible. Mazareem detested all of Abimelech's agents. That they held power over him was a source of constant vexation. Viatrix, in particular, was a trial for Mazareem. At least in Northmark, the dragon spawn knew enough of his reputation to fear him. Here, Mazareem's name meant nothing.

Two days out of Parda, Mazareem encountered a patrol of soldiers that signified the outer perimeter of the emperor's campaign. The soldiers questioned him, but they let him pass when he produced the writ of authority. There were so many people heading in the same direction that the patrol could not hope to stop them all. Mazareem stood out, because he was one of the only travelers on horseback.

After passing the perimeter, it took Mazareem two hours to reach the camp itself. Finally, he climbed the last hill and looked down into a wooded valley. The emperor's expedition stretched out before him. For almost as far as the eye could see, tents, wagons, and piles of supplies dominated the landscape. Tens of thousands of people had made the procession their temporary home, and as Mazareem watched, hundreds more trickled in from the surrounding roads and forest.

It put Mazareem in mind of some of Rowen's most ostentatious displays of power. At the height of his influence, the self-proclaimed high king had loved to parade around his kingdom. Rowen had said it was for the benefit of the people, but Mazareem had watched him bask in their adoration like it was a tonic that sustained him.

Annoyed by the intrusion of unwanted memories, Mazareem kicked his horse down the hill. From the vantage point of elevation, the camp had looked huge, but that did not do it justice. It swallowed him as he descended, and it felt like he was entering a bustling city.

Mazareem's horse trotted past open-air shops, makeshift kitchens selling all manner of food, blacksmiths hard at work on wheel and anvil, acting troupes cavorting about on hastily erected stages, and he even saw a physician who had set up a stall. In a rare display of congeniality, the rich and poor mingled together, shoulder to shoulder. Mazareem smirked to himself. The honest would attract the dishonest. No doubt, just out of sight, a legion of pickpockets were making themselves wealthy here.

The emperor's official campaign force was separated from the rabble by a low wooden palisade. Soldiers stood guard at regular gaps in this fence, a mere formality rather than a true measure of security. On the other side of this barrier, the royal colors of the emperor's pavilion shone brilliantly in the noonday sun. Smaller tents, those of attending senators, merchants, and nobles, surrounded the emperor's mountain of splendid canvas. Behind those, the orderly white rows of army tents stretched off into the distance.

Every few days, all of this was torn down, packed away, and carried a few miles before being put up again. At this rate, Mazareem estimated it would be weeks before the emperor reached the Linstall border.

He was forced to suffer the scrutiny of the Coriddian soldiers a second time when he crossed through the palisade. This close to his destination, Mazareem was growing impatient, but he managed to restrain himself. Soon, he was sitting on his horse before the grand pavilion where the emperor held temporary court.

Glad to be out of the saddle at last, Mazareem lifted a leg over the pommel and lowered himself down to the ground. A young boy, clad in Coriddian livery, appeared from nowhere to take the reins.

"I'll feed and brush her for you, sir," the boy said. "When will you be needing her again?"

"I won't," said Mazareem. "Put her into tonight's stew for all I care."

The boy went pale. Mazareem did not wait to see how the lad would respond. He strode towards the entrance to the pavilion, which would rival a small palace in a lesser realm. Great wooden poles, at least thirty feet high, sat on either side of the doorway, mimicking stone pillars. Suspended from these giant stakes, rich fabrics of gold and scarlet formed a wall that rippled in the breeze. Mazareem suspected that the cost of the canvas alone would bankrupt Northmark.

Royal guards stood before the tent, their gold and black breastplates glinting in the sun. The gaudy uniform of the emperor's grenadiers matched the ridiculous tent they guarded. They stood like statues, the handles of their wicked-looking halberds grounded in the earth at their feet. A richly dressed attendant stepped out from between the silent sentinels to address Mazareem.

"The emperor and his mother aren't receiving visitors at this time," the attendant said. "You may, ah, return in the morning, if you wish an audience."

"I'm here on official business," Mazareem said, thrusting forward the imperial writ for a third time.

With a show of annoyance, the attendant accepted the writ and then took his time inspecting it. After much longer than it should have taken, the man finally looked up.

"While you no doubt think your errand terribly important, you must understand that the emperor employs a thousand agents just like you," the attendant said. "If they could call on him at any time, night and day, why, he'd never have time to govern the empire. That's why we have a schedule. Now, if you don't mind, I'm a very busy man."

The attendant made to hand the piece of paper back to Mazareem.

"Show it to Viatrix," Mazareem said. He had to struggle to keep a snarl out of his voice. "If she learns you denied me entry, she'll have your eyes in a jar."

At the mention of the royal mother, the man took an involuntary step back. "Perhaps—perhaps the emperor's mother is free to see you," he said. "Let me go inquire."

"You do that," Mazareem said.

Mazareem waited while the attendant disappeared into the tent. The guards never moved or spoke. He wondered if the human faces were real or if the scales of dragon spawn hid beneath the surface. Within minutes, the attendant returned. He was almost falling over himself in his haste to usher Mazareem inside.

"The royal mother will see you!" the attendant said, gesturing Mazareem forward. "How fortuitous that she's available on such short notice. Please don't tell her I gave you any difficulty, kind sir. I was only trying to guard her precious time."

"I'll ask her to only pluck one of your eyes out," Mazareem said.

The attendant shuddered and glanced back to see if Mazareem was joking. He must not have found humor on Mazareem's face, because he did not speak again. Mazareem followed him into the provisional palace.

Inside, the canvas roof of the tent swept up and away in a many-sided cathedral ceiling. A lush black carpet traced the path from the entrance to the throne in the middle of the room. Set on a small stone dais, the gilded onyx throne of the Coriddian emperor sat beneath an opening in the roof above. Sunlight from the noon sun streamed down, illuminating the dais and leaving the rest of the room in shadow.

It was wasted grandeur, because the throne sat empty, and the room was deserted. Behind the throne, partitions of canvas hung from the roof to create private quarters at the back of the tent.

Wringing his hands with every step, the attendant led Mazareem towards these rooms. He stopped short next to an opening behind the dais and indicated that Mazareem should enter. Mazareem brushed aside the thin cloth that functioned as a door and stepped through. The attendant did not follow.

On the other side, Mazareem found another throne, no less ornate than the first. And this throne was occupied. Viatrix sat upon her royal seat, watching Mazareem approach with amusement. The room around her was an exercise in excess. Marble sculptures, priceless paintings, and treasures of ancient antiquity were displayed in positions of prominence. Something crunched under Mazareem's foot, and he looked down to discover that precious gems had been scattered on the floor like common stones.

Viatrix had dropped the illusion of magic that made her appear human. She stared at Mazareem with reptilian eyes, her smile exposing wicked teeth in her long, scaly snout. Here in the privacy of her personal sanctuary, Viatrix reveled in her true nature.

Mazareem stopped ten feet from the throne. He waited for Viatrix to address him, as was customary.

"I do so loathe the human form," Viatrix said. "To wear it is to become a worm. Will you writhe in the dirt for me, little worm?"

"There are limits to my patience," Mazareem said.

"You'll not speak to me in defiance!" Viatrix said. "By Abimelech's decree, I rule in this realm. My word is absolute. Or have you forgotten that my hand is the one on your leash?"

"You're all the same," Mazareem said. "A little distance, a little power, and you succumb to the delusion that Abimelech favors you the most over all your brothers and sisters. What is all this trash you've surrounded yourself with? You're just a tool, spent and easily discarded, the same as me. If our master wanted me dead, I'd die. If he wanted me to grovel, I'd live on my knees. While I'm still useful, your threats mean nothing."

"Your impudence will be your undoing," Viatrix said, her voice almost a hiss. "Report and begone, before I decide to add you to my collection."

Mazareem recounted the final moments of the *Golden Dawn*, leaving out no detail. He described the capture and then escape of Sorrell. Preferring not to admit weakness to Viatrix, Mazareem neglected to mention being shot through the eye. The less she knew about his inhuman powers, the better. Let her assume he could be dealt with easily.

"Sorrell only escaped because she has become a magus," Mazareem said, concluding his report. "If she practices, her powers will grow by the day. By now, she should be a formidable opponent."

"You dare to stand before me and admit your failure?" Viatrix said. "Not only does Sorrell still live, she's now an even greater threat. I don't have to be her dead mother to know that she'll come straight for me to demand an accounting. You were supposed to *eliminate* her, not *empower* her!"

"Even a neophyte magus is dangerous. I was in no position to oppose her. With time, and preparation, I can engage her on my terms."

"I hear the pride in your voice, the inclination towards self-preservation. A tool you may be, but you're flawed and unreliable. Would Sorrell still live if you weren't so preoccupied with saving your own skin? You should have purchased my safety and the pleasure of Abimelech with your life. That you didn't, renders you a traitor."

Mazareem stiffened. Would Viatrix dare to act against him? Abimelech's seal should protect him, but Northmark was worlds away. This far from the seat of Abimelech's power, Viatrix might think she could get away with attacking Mazareem.

"Your judgements mean nothing," Mazareem said. "My purpose in coming to this realm wasn't to protect you. As I told you before departing on the *Celestial,* I came here at our master's command to hunt two other magi. Now there are three. They must all die, but I cannot spend my life to kill only one of them. Or do you put your needs above those of your father?"

Viatrix's clawed hands gripped the arms of the throne as she struggled to control her fury. "The day will come, little worm, when *he* will tire of you, and on that day, I'll be there to watch you suffer. I shall feast on the marrow of your bones."

"You'll have to get in line," Mazareem said. "Now that we've set that aside, can we get back to the task at hand? If you're right and Sorrell's coming here, we should prepare to meet her. She won't be more than a day or two behind me."

"No more words from you," Viatrix said, raising a hand to silence Mazareem. "You had your chance. Now it's my turn. I'll prove to Abimelech that he has no need to employ a wretch like you. His true children are all he needs. Return to him and admit your failure. Let's see if he's inclined to be lenient towards his favorite pet."

They both knew Abimelech's reward for failure was pain.

"It's been hundreds of years since a magus appeared in this realm," Mazareem said. "Where I'm from, we put them down every decade. You're not equipped to fight her. Let me do what Abimelech sent me here to do."

"Are you still talking?" Viatrix said. "I only hear the mewling cries of a pitiful maggot as it wriggles under my foot. Away with you, little worm. If I see you again, I'll squish you myself."

Mazareem clamped his mouth shut. His mouth filled with saliva as he imagined Viatrix's dragon blood on his tongue. It had been so long since he had properly fed. Viatrix stared at Mazareem with undisguised contempt. She was daring him to defy her.

Only with supreme effort did Mazareem let his anger go. Now was not the time. He turned on his heel and stalked out of the room. The attendant was waiting for him back in the main throne room, but Mazareem brushed the man aside. His long legs carried him across the open space and out the front of the pavilion. He did not stop until he had crossed the barricade that separated the royal encampment from the rest of the commoners.

Once back in the camp proper, Mazareem stopped to get his bearings. Despite Viatrix's confidence in her ability to deal with Sorrell, Mazareem could not leave her to her own devices. He still had to answer to Abimelech for what happened here, and Mazareem suspected that if Sorrell came seeking Viatrix, the other two magi would not be far behind.

Chaos bombarded Mazareem from all sides. He could not tolerate this many people. Incessant noise and motion filled his senses no matter where he looked. Several children dashed passed, screaming as they chased each other. One of them bumped into his leg, and Mazareem felt expert little hands searching for something to steal. They found nothing.

He needed to get away. He needed some time and space to think. Seeing no better option, Mazareem started walking towards a nearby hill that looked over the procession.

Mazareem's head cleared as he climbed the incline. The sound of ten thousand voices was reduced to a dull roar. As he left the floor of the valley behind, Mazareem found himself walking under the forest canopy. At the top of the hill, he was hidden from view below by a screen of trees. There were others up here, seeking their own forms of privacy, but they gave him his space and he gave them theirs.

Content in the cool shade, Mazareem sat with his back against a towering oak. He closed his eyes. To take on three magi, he needed an advantage. Back in the kingdom of Haverfell, he knew every town, bog, forest, and quarry. In the thousand years of his life, he had charted the ley lines of the land and learned where the barrier between the physical and spiritual realms were weakest. Armed with that knowledge, he had hunted down magi in Abimelech's service, released from his dungeon every ten years to ply his morbid trade.

Here, in this foreign realm, Mazareem was blind. He had visited it before, in the rare circumstances when Abimelech loosened his leash, but it was still unfamiliar ground. Not the sort of place you wanted to do battle with a deadly foe.

Eyes still closed, Mazareem scratched a sigil in the earth beneath his right hand. His long, pale finger drew the symbol of an open, watching eye, with the sun, the moon, a crown, and the head of a dragon surrounding it like the four points of a compass. That done, he lifted one of the bottles of blood from his bandolier, unstopped it, and poured a few drops on the spell.

Mazareem watched the blood fill the lines in the dirt, and with a flash of the faintest green light, the enchantment took effect. Behind his eyes, Mazareem's vision expanded. He looked beyond the corporeal world and into the metaphysical. The realm of spirits unfolded before him. In this place, he took on the form of a great carrion bird.

On ethereal wings, Mazareem lifted himself above the treetops. The roiling mass of humanity below had attracted an equal number of demons and imps. They danced and cavorted as they had their fun with their unwitting prey. Mazareem shut them out. There was no help to be found there.

Mazareem scanned the horizon, searching for something, anything, that he could use. To his surprise, he found it quite near to the camp. Just a little way to the south, the overwhelming echo of recent death drew his attention. Mazareem shuddered as the faint wailing of a thousand tormented souls washed over his consciousness.

Not wanting to stay in the spirit realm any longer than necessary, Mazareem dismissed the spell and returned to the physical world. After waiting a moment for his normal sight to return, Mazareem got to his feet. He looked up and considered the position of the sun as its light filtered down through the trees. By his estimate, he still had a few hours of daylight. That should be more than enough time to investigate his findings.

Following the spine of the hilltop, Mazareem headed south. He walked parallel to the valley below until he was above the spot from his vision. It was no more than a mile or two from the emperor's camp. Spurred on by his curiosity, Mazareem descended back into the grassy plain that split the undulating forest.

He stood on the edge of the tall grass and strained his senses. Why had he perceived so much pain in this place? Mazareem walked a short way out into the field. He stopped when his foot hit something hard. At his feet, he found a rusted shield. A few paces from that, he spied a broken sword.

A slow smile spread across Mazareem's face. This was a battlefield. The stench of death was gone, and the grass had grown high to hide it, but a great conflict had been fought here within the last year. Perhaps it had been the site of one of the first skirmishes between Coriddia and Linstall.

This was far better than Mazareem could have hoped for. He could use this, although preparation would take time. Confident now, Mazareem moved back to the tree line and began to search for a suitable place to work. The spell would be complex, and he needed enough dirt to draw it out uninterrupted.

Night fell, but Mazareem hardly noticed. He finally found a suitable patch of earth and was standing over it contemplating where to start. His thoughts were disturbed by the sound of a large animal in the brush behind him. Whatever it was, it was coming straight towards him.

Annoyed, Mazareem turned and waited to see what would appear. A few seconds later, Worm's hulking form materialized out of the shadows. The hound held Mazareem's staff in his jaws.

Mazareem actually laughed. The sound surprised him. He had not realized how much he missed his faithful companion. Worm padded up to him on huge paws, and Mazareem knelt to scratch the dog under the chin.

"You're just in time, old boy," Mazareem said as he took the staff from Worm. "I'm about to show this realm what us worms are capable of."

Chapter 37

SORRELL TRAVELED FAST FOR two days after leaving Parda. A few hours out of the town, she felt confident enough to give the horse his head, and the animal did not disappoint. His effortless gallop devoured the distance between her and Togen. She only stopped for a few hours each night to rest. Speed was critical, but Sorrell needed to arrive ready to act. Being exhausted from several days of sleepless riding would do her no good.

On the afternoon of the second day, Sorrell encountered the first signs of the emperor's procession. The highway, almost deserted up to this point, was getting crowded with people on foot. They were all heading the same direction as Sorrell. She slowed her horse to a canter, frustrated that it might take hours to cover the last few miles.

After another mile, Sorrell was stopped by a patrol of soldiers. They were questioning people at random on the road, and she was an obvious target on her borrowed warhorse. The captain in charge of the squad gave her tattered naval uniform a dubious look. At his command, the five other soldiers moved to block Sorrell's advance.

Sorrell looked down at the man. On the left breast of his armor, a brilliant red falcon, the symbol of his legion, shone vibrant in the sunlight. This was a captain in General Argrave's command. Sorrell almost shouted for joy. Argrave was one of her most prominent conspirators in the army. If he was in charge of this campaign, Viatrix's fate was sealed.

"That's a cavalry mount," the captain said. "How did you come by it?" His tone was not harsh, but it was not friendly either.

"I know I'm a mess, captain," Sorrell said in her best admiral's voice. "I'm Admiral Sorrell of his excellency's navy. I borrowed this horse from the garrison in Parda. It's imperative that I reach General Argrave without delay."

This was not the answer the captain had been expecting. He took a long moment to consider whether he believed her or not. Sorrell approved. Argrave recruited only the best.

"If I let you pass and it turns out you're lying, it'll be my back under the whip," the captain said. "There's room on that beast for two of us. Help me up, and I'll escort you to the general. If he doesn't verify your story, I'll be placing you under arrest."

"That suits me," Sorrell said. She offered a hand to help the man up.

The captain grasped Sorrell's outstretched arm, and with a grunt, she helped him climb onto the now annoyed warhorse.

"Keep watching the road," the captain told his soldiers. "I'll be back in an hour or two."

They gave him a nod and a salute, and Sorrell kicked the horse to start him back down the road. Instead of wrapping his arms around her waist, the captain leaned back, his palms on the horse's rump.

"You said you were at the Parda garrison?" he said. "Did you speak with Captain Gaston? He's the commander there. We go way back."

Sorrell smiled at the captain's obvious attempt to catch her in a lie. No doubt, Captain Gaston did not exist.

"You'll not root out a falsehood, captain," Sorrell said. "I am who I say I am, and the general will confirm it."

At this, the captain did not speak again other than to give her simple directions. Soon, they were trotting through a wide valley between forest-covered hills. Sorrell heard the emperor's procession long before she saw it. If she had not known better, she would have thought they were drawing near to a thriving town.

They turned the last bend in the road, and the sprawling camp stretched out before them. Sorrell's mouth fell open. She had been on campaign before, but she had never seen anything like this. There were thousands upon thousands of people, and even more trickled in as Sorrell and the captain approached. From where she sat on the horse, Sorrell could not see any sign of the emperor's pavilion or a military presence. It looked like they had stumbled across some unholy combination of an open-air market and a fair in the middle of the countryside.

"Swing around to the left," the captain said from behind her. "It'll be faster if we go around instead of through. The legion's camp is on the other side."

To comply with the captain's prompting, Sorrell pulled on the reins and diverted the warhorse into the grass. They circumvented the camp, avoiding the crush of humanity that had filled the valley. Sorrell could not tear her eyes away as they trotted by. The entire population of Parda would not even be noticed here. Everywhere she looked, she saw signs of revelry. People were celebrating the fall of Linstall with reckless abandon.

Presently, Sorrell spotted the brilliant canvas of the emperor's pavilion, and behind it, the ordered lines of the legion's tents. She felt a moment of panic at the thought that Viatrix or her brother might see her. The black and gold of her navy uniform was distinctive.

There was nothing she could do about it now. She could only hope that if they did see her, they would not recognize her.

"Captain, I'm feeling weak," Sorrell said, doing her best to feign exhaustion. "Would you please put your arms around me so that I don't fall?"

"Uh, certainly, if you need me to," the captain said.

He scooted forward and put his arms awkwardly around her waist. Sorrell leaned back into him with a grateful sigh. She sensed the captain's unease, but he did not protest. Now, if anyone looked at them, they would see two lovers enjoying a leisurely ride. It had to be enough of a disguise.

They made it to the military section of the encampment without a cry going up, and Sorrell breathed a sigh of relief. With his own hands on the reins, the captain guided the horse to the general's personal tent.

"My thanks, captain," Sorrell said. "For the escort and the support."

"Don't thank me yet," the captain said. "We still have to confirm your story."

Sorrell slid down from the horse. She turned to help the captain down, but he refused her assistance. Their close physical proximity had bothered the man and renewed his distrust of her.

The captain entered the general's tent, and Sorrell stepped in after him. General Argrave looked up from a piece of parchment he had been reading. His mouth dropped open when he saw Sorrell. He recovered quickly.

"Sorry for the interruption, general," the captain said, snapping to attention with a salute. "We intercepted this woman on the northern road. She claims to be Admiral Sorrell, and she requested an immediate audience with you. I escorted her here to confirm her story."

"I commend your caution, captain," Argrave said after returning the salute. "But in this case, it was unnecessary. This is indeed Admiral Sorrell in the flesh. You're dismissed; I can handle things from here."

"Yes, sir!" the captain said. He saluted again, spun in place, and marched from the tent.

As soon as they were alone, Argrave got up from behind his desk and moved to the door. He glanced outside and then lowered the canvas hanging to give them some privacy. That done, he returned to his seat.

"You're the last person I expected to see this day," Argrave said. "I don't know if your timing is perfect or terrible."

Sorrell sank into the chair opposite Argrave. The thin cushion beneath her backside felt luxurious after two long days on horseback.

"I traveled as quickly as I could to get here," Sorrell said. "I've been betrayed, general. My mother tried to have me assassinated. When that failed, her minion tried to take command of my ship. In the process, he murdered one of my most trusted officers and several of my crew."

Argrave listened intently to her words, but he did not respond immediately. He rested an elbow on the arm of his chair and held his chin in his hand as he considered Sorrell's story.

"If what you say is true, it warrants a swift and decisive response," Argrave finally said.

"What's this skepticism?" Sorrell said, incredulous. "I speak nothing less than the whole truth."

"It's not that I don't believe you. But there has been… a recent, unforeseen development."

Argrave slid the document he had been reading across the desk towards Sorrell. "I received this only moments before you arrived," he said. "It's from the desk of your mother. The ink isn't even dry yet. I've been ordered to distribute the news to the entire procession. Riders have already been dispatched to Coridal to spread it through the rest of the empire."

Sorrell picked up the paper and scanned its contents. Her heart seized in her chest as she read. Viatrix was publicly denouncing Sorrell as a traitor. More than that, her mother was accusing her of madness, claiming that Sorrell had gone insane and believed herself touched by the gods. The edict offered a kingly sum for any information that led to Sorrell's capture.

"She's getting desperate," Sorrell said as she slammed the paper down on the desk. "It's not on the timetable we anticipated, but we expected she'd try to attack my reputation."

"I must admit, an accusation of mental instability is a masterstroke," Argrave said. "When this edict gets out, I guarantee some of your supporters will think twice about standing by your side to oppose Viatrix. The rich and powerful like predictable returns. The risk that you might be descending into insanity will add an element of volatility to your character that will chase the more cautious away."

By the tone of Argrave's voice, Sorrell sensed his own indecision. The confidence she had carried into the general's tent vanished in an instant. Sorrell sat straighter in her chair. When she spoke again, she tried to keep the tension she felt out of her voice.

"Are you burdened with this same caution, general?" Sorrell said.

Argrave looked up to meet her gaze. Chin still in hand, he contemplated her for a long minute before answering. "I didn't get to where I am today without being prudent," he said at last. "In my career, I've made my reputation by being decisive. I loathe inaction. But I always consider the facts before I act. Here are the facts as I see them: One, you've appeared in my camp on a borrowed horse, alone, and in a disheveled state. Two, you've told me an incredible story of murder and betrayal that I have no way of corroborating. And three, that you've come to me at all implies you desire my immediate and complete commitment to whatever it is you wish to do.

"Put yourself in my seat for a moment. Would you risk your ship and all of those under your command if I came to you in the same way? Be honest with me. My reasons for wanting to depose Viatrix and your puppet of a brother remain the same, but perhaps the time is no longer right. If your unfortunate tale is true, you've suffered a major setback. Wouldn't it be wiser to retreat to a position of safety where you can lick your wounds and ascertain who still stands with you?"

While Argrave spoke, Sorrell battled against the panic rising in her breast. The entire world seemed to be slipping away from her. How could she make him understand that the time to act was now without appearing reckless?

"You don't have all the facts, general," Sorrell said. "My mother seeks to undermine me because she fears me. Does this look like madness to you?"

Sorrell raised her right hand, open palm upturned. At her beckoning, she summoned the ice. It flowed and lengthened, taking on the shape of a rapier, which Sorrell snatched out of the air when it was fully formed. She stood, flourished the blade, and taking a risk, offered it hilt first to Argrave.

Argrave had gone pale. He stood to take the enchanted weapon from her hand, and to Sorrell's relief, it did not turn to water the second it left her hand. Argrave grimaced at the terrible coldness wafting off the frozen rapier. He quickly lowered it to the desk where he could inspect it.

"What sort of trick is this?" Argrave said. "How did you manage it?"

"It's no trick," Sorrell said.

For Argrave's benefit, she called more ice into her fingers. A javelin took form in her hand. Sorrell raised her arm and threw the icy missile into the earth on the far side of the tent. It pierced the ground and stuck fast. Argrave sat down hard. He looked lost.

"How did you come by this power?" Argrave said. "How long have you had it? This is straight out of ancient legend. I never believed those silly stories."

"I don't know how or why it was given to me," Sorrell said. "But I've only had it for about a week now. I'd not make a public claim to be blessed by the gods, yet I can see how it would be advantageous for people to think I was. I wouldn't dissuade them of the notion, if it helped put me on the throne."

"And you can prove it beyond a doubt...," Argrave said. "The people will eat this up. Viatrix's only chance is to capture you and suppress all knowledge of your powers." The wheels of his mind were turning now, and Sorrell sensed that the man was coming back around to her side.

"What do you intend to do?" Argrave said, finally looking up from the rapier on the desk.

"How many of her own men did Viatrix bring?" Sorrell said.

"About fifty of the emperor's grenadiers. A token force only. If necessary, she's relying on my soldiers to be the muscle behind this campaign."

"Are your men trustworthy?"

"Will they act against the emperor and his mother, do you mean? Aye, they'll do as I order. Their loyalty is to me first and the government second. I've always been careful to recruit men who have no love for being ruled over."

"We'll not get a better opportunity than this. Viatrix is outnumbered fifty to one, she's not expecting me here, and she's cut off from the support she'd have in the capital. I want you to summon as many troops as you can on such a short notice and come with me to confront her. She can contemplate her future from behind the bars of a cell."

"That seems rash," Argrave said, some of his caution returning. "With this new power of yours, we could rally an unopposable force to our banner. In time, Viatrix and your brother might abdicate of their own accord. If we act now, we risk being painted as usurpers. The populace is happy. The emperor is showering them with wealth and accolades as he travels the countryside. To dethrone him here might turn the narrative against us."

"The time is now, general," Sorrell said, her voice hard. "If you step back from this moment, you'll only delay the inevitable. And I'll not soon forget your cowardice. I can be a powerful ally, or I can be a terrible enemy. The choice is yours."

Sorrell's words hung in the air between them, both invitation and challenge. She had made her play, now it was up to Argrave. If he refused to act, Sorrell would have to go into hiding. She would survive the bitter disappointment, but it would set her back by months or even years. Sorrell held Argrave's gaze, doing her best to radiate confidence in her manifest destiny.

"There's a proverb of the common man that has long appealed to me," Argrave said. "They like to say, 'don't wait until the iron is hot to strike, but instead, make the iron hot through repeated striking.' I can see the truth of this in you. Very well, admiral, I'll help you. Give me ten minutes, and I'll have a troop ready."

Argrave rose from his seat and exited the tent in haste. Sorrell watched him go with barely concealed elation. Before the sun set this day, she would be emperor of the Coriddian empire. This close to the realization of her lifelong ambition, the thought seemed alien to her. Sorrell smiled to herself. There would be plenty of time to acclimate to her new role.

True to his word, the general returned within the quarter hour. Sorrell stood when she heard him re-enter the tent. They stared at one another for a moment, both of them aware that they were fast approaching the point of no return.

"If it pleases the admiral, I'd like to accompany her to call on the emperor and his mother," Argrave said.

"Very well, general," Sorrell said with a nod and a grim smile. "After you."

Argrave turned and swept aside the hanging that covered the tent door. Sorrell followed him into the daylight. Outside, a hundred of Argrave's soldiers stood in tight formation. They were arrayed as if they were going into battle. Each man carried a large, wicked-looking pike. On the edges of the formation, the troop's sharpshooters cradled rare and expensive muskets.

A soldier stepped forward and offered Argrave a plumed helmet. The general donned the helm, and with a nod to Sorrell, took the lead position in front of the troop. Sorrell moved to stand beside the general.

Argrave set the soldiers in motion with a shout. Sorrell marched next to Argrave at their head. The royal pavilion was not far from the military section of the encampment, and within a few short minutes, they were passing into the shadow of the massive royal tent.

Marching to a silent cadence, Argrave kept the men moving in time as they made a wide circle around the mountain of rich canvas. The sound of a hundred coordinated footfalls could not be ignored. People stopped and stared. At the front of the pavilion, they found a line of petitioners waiting in front of the yawning entrance. Her brother was holding court.

Surprised by their sudden appearance, the crowd gave way before Sorrell and Argrave. People scrambled to get out of the path of the armed soldiers. Sorrell heard the first few cries of alarm and confusion. In front of the opening that led into the makeshift throne room, two royal grenadiers in gold and black livery crossed their halberds to stop Sorrell's and Argrave's advance. A surprised attendant appeared from inside.

"What's the meaning of this?" the attendant said. "I hope you—"

He stopped speaking when his gaze fell on Sorrell. He stammered and took a step backwards. No words would come, and he jerked himself around and vanished back into the tent.

"Step aside or be stepped over," Sorrell said to the two royal guards blocking the way.

Their impassive faces turned to regard each other, and after a long heartbeat, they lowered their weapons and moved away from the entrance. Sorrell did not hesitate. General Argrave at her side, a hundred loyal soldiers at her back, she strode into the emperor's temporary throne room.

Chapter 38

SORRELL FELT LIKE A conquering hero. Not even the fiercest battle in her long and decorated career could match the rush of adrenaline she experienced when marching into the emperor's pavilion. Against all odds, she was about to claim a resounding victory that would echo throughout history.

Inside the grand tent, a crowd of commoners had gathered to bring their pleas before the emperor. Stationed around the perimeter at regular intervals, ten to twenty of the emperor's grenadiers watched over the proceedings. An insignificant number compared to the hundred soldiers at Sorrell's back.

Confident that she would be unopposed by martial force, Sorrell turned her attention at last to the dais where her mother and brother sat. She had avoided looking at them the moment she entered, savoring the thought of the shock on their faces.

Her brother sat on his onyx throne, resplendent in his simple white uniform. His brow was knitted in confusion. Viatrix, the royal mother, sat on his right atop a smaller but no less ornate throne. Sorrell slid her gaze to the left, ready to meet her mother's hatred head-on.

Sorrell stopped in her tracks. She stopped so suddenly that the soldiers behind her ran into her. Where she had expected to see the face of her mother, she found a monster. Instead of the pale, wrinkled flesh of a middle-aged woman, the *thing* sitting in her mother's throne was covered in black scales. Eyes like colored jewels bisected by a sliver of the abyss stared at Sorrell. Long, ebony claws gripped the arms of the throne instead of fingers. The beast had a long snout like a lizard, and Sorrell saw rows of jagged teeth beneath upturned lips. If such a creature could smile, this abomination was smiling at her.

Argrave had stopped with Sorrell. He took one look at her face—his hand went to the hilt of the sword at his side.

"What is it?" Argrave said, scanning the room for an immediate threat.

"She's—she's a monster!" Sorrell said, hand raised to point at the creature sitting on her mother's throne. The power inside her swelled, screaming at her to use it. Sorrell struggled to stay in control. Her vision swam.

Argrave glanced at Viatrix and then back at Sorrell. He looked as confused as the emperor.

At a hand signal from Viatrix, the royal guards behind the dais stepped forward. They were inhuman too, lizard-men covered in scales instead of skin.

"They're all monsters!" Sorrell said.

Argrave's confusion was giving way to concern. His soldiers had taken up formation behind him and Sorrell. They waited to see what happened next.

"General Argrave, what fortuitous turn of events is this?" Viatrix said. "Not two hours ago did I convey to you my concern over Sorrell's well-being, and now here you are with her at your side. This is certainly unexpected, I must say."

"Silence, fiend," Sorrell said. "Who are you and what have you done with my mother?"

Sorrell stalked forward to stand before the dais. The creature's voice sounded just like Viatrix. It was jarring to hear her mother's voice issue forth from such a monstrous mouth.

"Why, whatever do you mean, child?" Viatrix said. "Here I sit in the flesh for all to see. Who else could I be?"

Without conscious prompting, the ice rapier had appeared in Sorrell's hand. The room gasped in awe.

"You're a beast, a demon," Sorrell said. "I don't know what pit you crawled from, but I'm here to send you back to it."

Viatrix looked over Sorrell's shoulder at Argrave. "As you can see, general, my daughter is unwell. This strange power that has possessed her has robbed her of her senses. I fear she's a danger to herself and everyone around her."

"Admiral, answer me truthfully," Argrave said, his voice grim. "What is it that you see here?"

"They're not human," Sorrell said, gesturing at Viatrix and the monstrous grenadiers. "They wear scales like snakes instead of skin. By the depths, they're walking, talking lizards!"

"You're to be commended for bringing her here straightaway," Viatrix said, still speaking to Argrave. "Now, for her own safety, please place my daughter under arrest."

"What?" Sorrell said, caught off guard. "No!" She whirled to face Argrave. For the first time since laying eyes on Viatrix, it dawned on Sorrell that no one else could see the royal mother's true appearance. If they did, they would all share in Sorrell's horror.

"I'm sorry, admiral," Argrave said. "This is for your own good." The general's gaze held a mixture of pity and sadness.

Sorrell could not believe it. Five minutes ago, they had been about to take control of an empire together. Now, he was going to arrest her for mental incompetence.

"You're making a grave mistake," Sorrell said.

"I fear I almost did," Argrave said. "Now, it's time to undo my foolishness. Admiral Sorrell, you're under arrest by order of Viatrix, the royal mother. For all our sakes, please come peacefully."

"I won't be taken," Sorrell snarled. She jerked her left hand, and the chain whip formed of frozen links flashed into existence. Rapier and whip in hand, Sorrell faced down Argrave and his soldiers.

"Let my guards handle her, general," Viatrix said from behind Sorrell. "This is a family matter. There's no need to risk your own men."

Argrave nodded and took a step back, effectively washing his hands of the matter. Sorrell whirled towards the dais, where Viatrix's soldiers were already advancing. The guards from the perimeter of the tent were closing in too. In a few seconds, Sorrell would be surrounded.

Viatrix's smile widened. Furious, Sorrell touched the power inside her, the power that was crying out for her to unleash it. This close to her goal, she refused to be denied. Sorrell exploded into motion. Her feet barely touched the floor as she lunged forward.

She ducked inside the thrust of a halberd and stabbed at her attacker's breastplate. The blade of her rapier struck true, but it did not penetrate the gold and black armor. It glanced off to the side, leaving a wicked scratch. Tendrils of frost spider-webbed across the metal from the site of the impact.

The shock of the blow traveled up Sorrell's arm, and she made a mental note that her enchanted weapons had limits. Before the guard recovered, Sorrell snapped the whip at the lizard-man's feet. Frigid links wrapped around his armored shins with a dull clinking sound and stuck fast. Sorrell yanked, and the guard's lower legs burst into chunks of frozen armor and flesh. He let out a reptilian shriek as he toppled to the ground.

Sorrell twirled without looking, swinging the chain out wide behind her. Her reckless maneuver caught the second guard by surprise. He tried to block the whip with his forearm, but he was too slow. It wrapped around his scaly head. The lizard-man staggered backwards, hands raised to claw at his face. He died after taking the second step. Jagged icicles filled his gaping mouth. Sorrell released the whip and let him fall—his head shattered when it hit the floor.

Another chain already in hand, Sorrell turned to face the soldiers advancing from the edges of the tent. They were more cautious than their fallen comrades. None of them were eager to rush into the range of Sorrell's deadly frozen weapons.

One of the soldiers feinted forward, halberd extended. Sorrell flicked her whip towards the guard. He jumped back, catching the attack on the shaft of his weapon. Seizing the opportunity, a second guard charged in, the shining point of his halberd aimed at Sorrell's unarmored midsection.

Sorrell let go of the whip and twisted at the same time, bringing her rapier up. She let her assailant's momentum carry him onto the sword. The rapier's killing point found the soldier's armpit and pierced deep into his chest. His dead weight sagged against Sorrell. She let him slide off her and onto the floor.

"That's enough!" Argrave said, his voice cutting across the melee.

The royal guards and Sorrell both paused. Argrave had ordered his sharpshooters to load their muskets. They now stood with their weapons aimed at Sorrell.

"Unless you can freeze musket balls midair, I suggest you stand down," Argrave said.

Breathing heavily, Sorrell faced Argrave and his gunmen. In the grips of a fierce battle-rage, she was tempted to dare Argrave to fire. But there were twenty shooters, and it would only take one bullet to kill her. She refused to die here. Not without killing Mazareem first.

Disgusted, Sorrell dismissed the icy weapons in her hands. They splashed to the floor, the last few droplets clinging to her fingers. Viatrix's guards wasted no time. A heartbeat later, an armored arm was wrapped around Sorrell's throat and the point of a dagger pressed hard into her back.

"Do you want her dead, sire?" the guard said, his reptile mouth hissing next to Sorrell's ear.

"No, no, nothing so dramatic," Viatrix said, waving a dismissive hand. "Her fangs are pulled. Now all that's left is to try and find help for what ails her."

"What ails me is that you still live," Sorrell said. She spat in Viatrix's direction. The arm around her throat clamped down. Sorrell gagged.

"I'm sure you don't mean that, child. General, my men will see to her keeping. You're dismissed. And your assistance here will not go unrewarded."

"The royal mother is too kind," Argrave said. He gave a little bow, turned on his heel, and ordered his men to follow him out of the pavilion.

Sorrell watched him go in despair. She added his name to the quickly growing list of people that would someday answer for their betrayal. The guard who held her wrestled Sorrell around to face the dais.

Next to Viatrix, the emperor looked on in dumbfounded dismay. "Sister, what have you done?" he said.

"Be silent, my son," Viatrix said. "I'll take care of this. Take her into the back and lock her up. One of the cages from the kennel should suffice. I want her guarded around the clock. She must not escape. Watch her with a musket at all times. If you see ice, shoot her."

"As you command, sire," the guard holding Sorrell said.

Sorrell tried to speak, but the soldier jerked her about so hard that he squeezed the wind out of her throat. She wheezed as the lizard-man half-carried, half-dragged her towards the rear of the royal pavilion. Viatrix was addressing the stunned crowd, but Sorrell could not make out what the woman was saying.

The imperial grenadiers pressed around her on all sides. If she tried to fight, Sorrell would be dead before one of her icy weapons could take shape. They dragged her into a small room at the back of the grand tent. Other than a single torch, the room was empty. The guards waited in silence. They did not relax their vigilance for an instant.

Soon, the exterior canvas wall of the tent rustled, and a gauntleted hand raised the cloth enough to slide something inside. It was a cage meant for a dog. It was perhaps big enough for Sorrell to crawl inside of and turn around in.

A hand on each of Sorrell's shoulders forced her to her knees. In front of her, the door to the cage hung open. One of the guards planted a boot on her backside and gave her a violent shove. Sorrell had to duck her head to avoid smashing into the top of the iron enclosure. Once she was inside, the door was closed and locked behind her.

Sorrell twisted her body around, tucking her legs into her chest in the cramped space so that she could turn and face the front. She was forced to stay on all fours. There was not enough room to lie down, and the cage was too low for her to sit upright. Beneath her hands and knees, the hard metal bars pressed painfully against her skin. She tried lying on her side, but that was worse.

A solitary guard stayed in the room to watch over her. The dark green scales on his face glinted in the torchlight. He wore a flintlock pistol at his hip. His reptilian eyes never moved from the cage—he never even blinked. Sorrell felt like a caged rat about to be fed to a snake.

Sooner than she expected, Sorrell's body was crying out in pain. She had never imagined that the simple act of being forced to kneel could be such torture. However, the physical agony was nothing compared to her shame and impotent rage.

The monster that was Viatrix had not chosen this form of imprisonment on a whim. To be caged like a filthy mongrel was almost more than Sorrell could bear. Tears filled her eyes and spilled down her cheeks, a mixture of fury and despair. Sorrell refused to let the guard hear her cry. She stifled the sobs that wanted to come.

How had she come to this? Two weeks ago, she had been an admiral, a captain on the empire's greatest ship, with Stone at her side and the future at her feet. It did not seem possible that all of that was gone now. Sorrell had been outmaneuvered at every turn. There were forces arrayed against her that she did not anticipate or understand.

Sorrell turned her head to the side so that she could look up at the lizard-faced guard. Not even in her wildest nightmares could she have dreamed up such a creature. Sorrell had told Argrave what she thought was the truth: she was not going mad. But now, Sorrell was no longer confident in herself. The simplest explanation was that her sanity was slipping.

A voice outside the room interrupted Sorrell's dismal contemplations, and a minute later, Viatrix stepped through the door. Viatrix dismissed the guard with a wave. They were alone, and the creature that used to be Sorrell's mother crouched in front of the cage.

"A cage suits you, I think," Viatrix said. "It illustrates the futility of your struggle and the consequences of your foolish ambition in a way that words never could."

"You're... not... my... mother," Sorrell said through gritted teeth. "What *are* you?"

"I've been a mother to you for fifteen years now," Viatrix said. "You never suspected a thing. The human that spawned you was quite a specimen. I'd have preferred to preserve her devious and scheming mind, but she never would have submitted to my authority. My only other option was to kill her and take her place. Perhaps we'll do the same with you. I've not yet decided."

"Why?" Sorrell said.

"Why does the predator hunt its prey?" Viatrix said. "Why does one always rise to rule above many? Because the weak serve the strong. This is the order of nature, the pattern of reality. My kind is superior to you frail humans. We wear a disguise because our numbers are few. But soon, very soon, we'll show our faces to the world, and your empire will grovel before us.

"You were the last piece of the puzzle. With you dealt with, I'll have complete control of your bloodline. I'd slit your throat here and now if I could, but it would look too suspicious. Your allies aren't the only ones plotting against me. Even now, I visit you to keep up the ruse that you're my daughter in truth. A few days in the cage will give you a fresh perspective. After that, perhaps we'll put you on a pyre. It'll be the highlight of our grand celebration. The people do so love to burn a traitor, especially one of royal lineage."

"They won't accept you," Sorrell said. "They'll see through your deception. You're a creature of darkness. The light of day will expose you for what you are."

Viatrix chuckled. "My master rules over both night and day. There's nothing under the sun that can defy me. The people will believe what I tell them, because I'll tell them what they want to believe. It's a pity you won't be around to watch. In another ten years, I'll have your mighty empire beneath my heel."

Before Sorrell could respond, Viatrix stood up to her full height. "I think that's enough time," Viatrix said. "The spies in my court will be satisfied that I commiserated with my imprisoned daughter. I'll tell them we're doing our best to help you, and that I'm making sure to take care of your every need. To that end, I'll have the guard bring you something to eat. You can thank me later."

Viatrix swept out of the room. The guard stepped inside and resumed his post. A few minutes later, a second guard appeared with a bowl of food. He unlocked the cage, placed the dish inside and then secured the door behind it. Sorrell stared down at the stinking meal. It was dog food in a bowl meant for a hound.

Sorrell pushed the dish into the far corner to try to get away from the smell. She would die before she ate that. Her stomach growled at the thought. Viatrix had said a lot and explained little. To get her mind off the pain, Sorrell replayed their conversation in her head.

She could not comprehend that her mother had been dead for fifteen years. Sorrell had hated her mother, but for this monster to have killed the real Viatrix to take on the mantle of royal mother, only stoked the anger burning in Sorrell's soul. It robbed her of the chance to prove her mother wrong, which had been Sorrell's driving motivation for as long as she could remember.

It had registered in Sorrell's mind that the creature pretending to be Viatrix had spoken of a master, but it did not seem important now. If Sorrell did not find a way to escape, the message was obvious: she would be publicly executed or secretly murdered. Sorrell had no intention of burning on a pyre or being put down like a sick dog.

First, she had to find a way to get out of this cage.

Chapter 39

LACRAEL, KAISER, AND BRANT traveled south as quickly as they could manage. They rested for only a few hours each night. On the second day after leaving the coast, they encountered a city. It looked deserted, but Kaiser had insisted that they go around. He had been adamant that they could not afford any sort of delay, and a foreign and potentially hostile town was sure to slow them down if they tried to pass through it.

Three days after leaving the city behind them, they started to encounter other travelers on the road. Soon, they were just another trio in a crowd, all heading in the same direction.

On the morning of the sixth day since they started searching for Sorrell, they were breaking their small camp and setting out on the road for another hard day of travel, when a man at a nearby fire waved them over.

"Just ignore him," Kaiser said as he tightened the straps of his pack.

"Five minutes won't cost us anything," Lacrael said. "We should talk to him and find out where all these people are going."

"Five minutes, no more," Kaiser said.

Lacrael had almost mastered the local language, so she took the lead. Kaiser and Brant walked a few steps behind her.

The man who had beckoned them over gave Lacrael a wide smile. He sat on a stump next to his fire. A wide-brimmed hat sat atop his head, and at his side was a pack stuffed with odds and ends. A kettle boiled over the low flames.

"A fine morning to the three of you," the man said. "Care to join me for a morning tea before setting your feet to the road?"

Lacrael glanced at Kaiser, who was frowning.

"We're on an important errand and don't have much time," Lacrael said. "But we thank you for the offer."

"That's too bad," the man said. "But I guess you're in a hurry to get to the execution, like the rest of us. A grim piece of work, that, but where there are crowds, there's money to be made."

"We've been traveling hard and haven't heard any news for days. What's this execution you speak of?"

The man looked surprised. "I reckon you're the only people in these parts who haven't heard. It's taken the countryside by storm. The emperor's sister, Admiral Sorrell herself, has been declared a traitor and arrested. They're going to burn her tomorrow morning. We've not executed anyone with fire for over a hundred years now. The whole gruesome spectacle will take place not a half-day's walk from here, in the valley just north of Togen."

Lacrael, Kaiser, and Brant digested this information in stunned silence.

Obviously curious, the man on the stump peered up at them. "You three okay? You look like maybe you need this drink more than I do."

Kaiser thrust the crude map Gustavus had drawn into Lacrael's hand. "Ask him if he can mark the location of the execution," he said next to her ear.

Lacrael knelt next to the man and showed him the hand-drawn map. "Can you show me where this will take place?"

"Well, sure," the man said. "Or you could just follow the horde. Everyone on the road is all headed to the same place."

He fished a burnt twig out of the fire and used the charcoal end to make a cross on the map. Lacrael stood up and passed the map back to Kaiser.

"Thanks for your help," Lacrael said.

"Not a problem," the man said with a wink. "I could never say no to a pretty lady. And if you get there before I do, save me a spot, will you? I can't walk as fast as you young bucks, but I still got a pack full of goods that need selling."

"I'll see what I can do," Lacrael said.

Kaiser had already set out down the road, and Lacrael had to cut the conversation short to run and catch up. Brant jogged along at her side.

"This is going to be harder than I thought," Kaiser said when the three of them were walking together again.

"You thought it was going to be easy?" Brant said.

Kaiser ignored the jab. In their six days on the road, Brant had almost returned to his old self, but with a few significant changes. One of them being that he was no longer intimidated by Kaiser. The second being that he was no longer shy about being interested in Lacrael. He possessed a new confidence that the shy Brant from Oakroot had lacked.

Lacrael's hand found Brant's, and he gave it a squeeze. They had not talked about this mutual affection growing between them. Kaiser's stern and constant presence had made sure of that. But they were enjoying each other's company, and every day on the road drew them closer together.

"The old man said a half-day's walk," Kaiser said. "For us, that should only be a couple of hours."

Kaiser picked up the pace. Lacrael let go of Brant's hand and concentrated on walking. Her legs were sore, but she was used to traveling with Kaiser by now. The man moved as if he had been shot from a cannon.

After a few more miles, the road became clogged with people. Everyone seemed to be carrying or pulling something to sell or the tools of their trade. Frustrated, Kaiser quit the road and moved up into the wooded hills. They made better time under the trees, and Kaiser made sure to keep the road in sight.

Sometime around noon, they reached their destination. The three of them climbed the last hill and looked down on a sprawling camp that dwarfed the city they had passed several days ago. Filthy smoke from a thousand fires hung over the encampment in a dark cloud. Travelers streamed in from all directions, adding their numbers to the multitude.

"There's more people down there than exists in all of Haverfell," Brant said in awe.

"How are we going to rescue Sorrell from *that?*" Lacrael said.

Kaiser did not respond. Instead, he pulled the spyglass he had borrowed from Gustavus from his pack. He raised it to his eye and inspected the procession beneath them.

"I can't see everything through the trees," Kaiser said after a moment. "But I know an unlit pyre when I see one. There's some military-looking tents next to it. That must be where they have Sorrell."

"That doesn't answer my question," Lacrael said.

"The problem isn't getting in," Kaiser said, still looking through the scope. "The hard part is getting out. There's only one thing I can think of that would rouse this many people and create a big enough distraction."

"What's that?" Brant said.

Kaiser lowered the spyglass and glanced at Lacrael. "Fire."

"Those are innocent people down there," Lacrael said.

"Some of them, maybe," Kaiser said. "But you don't need to kill anyone. All it would take is a few well-placed fireballs in the dry grass around the perimeter. I'll infiltrate the camp and find Sorrell. After nightfall, wait an hour, and then you can start your firework show. We'll use the chaos it causes to escape."

"Fire has a mind of its own," Lacrael said. "If I start this place burning, it might not stop."

"Do you have a better idea?"

Lacrael thought about it for a moment and then shook her head in resignation. "You know I don't."

"I'll make for the southern end of the camp once I have Sorrell," Kaiser said. "If we get split up, find me at the next spot marked on the map. That's where Gustavus will be."

Kaiser handed Lacrael the map. "I've got it memorized," he said.

Lacrael opened her mouth to speak, but Kaiser had already turned and started down the hill.

"The man never says goodbye," Brant said. "It's like he exists in a world where social decency was never invented."

"From what he's told me about his life as the tenth reaver, you might be closer to the truth than you know," Lacrael said.

"Do you think he can leave that life behind? Do you think a man can change?"

"You've changed, haven't you?"

"It depends on how you measure change. I've changed on the outside. But am I a different person now, after all that I've been through? I don't know. I'd like to think I was a good person before all this started. But who was Kaiser? Can a man come back from being a murderer and a tyrant?"

"What are you saying?"

"Do you trust him? I don't mean right this minute, but in the future. If we ever get back to our home in Haverfell, do you trust him to stand with us?"

Lacrael opened her mouth to answer in the affirmative, but the words would not come. She had never really thought about what might happen if they ever returned to Northmark and Kaiser's home.

"I trust him to do what's right for himself and his family," Lacrael said. "He's never done anything less, and he's always been honest about his motivations."

"And what happens when what's best for him is no longer best for us?" Brant said.

"Let's pray that never happens."

Chapter 40

KAISER ENTERED THE CAMP without difficulty. The mob accepted him without asking any questions. Rather than make straight for the pyre and Sorrell, he wandered through the stalls and roasting fires that had taken over the valley. He suspected a trap. Mazareem was still at large, and to Kaiser's frustration, their need to reclaim Sorrell was painfully transparent. All Mazareem had to do was watch and wait for them to make a move.

The attitude of the people reminded Kaiser of a festival. He saw smiling faces everywhere, even as they gossiped about the pending execution. As he meandered aimlessly through the throng, Kaiser searched for the hideous faces of dragon spawn. He did not see any, but that did not bring him relief. They had to be here somewhere, that much was certain.

After several hours of exploration, Kaiser picked a communal fire near the pyre and sat down to wait for nightfall. He had found nothing suspicious and could not see any evidence of Mazareem's presence. This bothered Kaiser more than if he had found an ambush lying in wait. The enemy that had been hunting them for over a year now would not pass this opportunity up.

Next to Kaiser, two men discussed tomorrow's execution.

"It just doesn't seem right to put her on a pile of sticks and light her up," the first man said. "We stopped burning people alive over a century ago for good reason. It's barbaric."

"It's symbolic, don't you see?" the second man said. "She's a Pyreshade. Death by fire is the ultimate insult to her lineage. Instead of eclipsing the sun, she'll be devoured by the flames. And anyway, a beheading just doesn't provide the same spectacle."

Kaiser accepted a bowl of stew from a serving girl and shoveled the food into his mouth. Lost in his own thoughts, he barely tasted it. He only noticed the bowl was empty when his wooden spoon clinked on the bottom.

While he listened to the men talk, Kaiser stared at the stacked wood around the tall stake that awaited Sorrell. He knew where and when he was, but something inside of him latched onto the idea that it was Mariel, his dead wife, that was set to die in the morning. Kaiser's hands trembled. He could not fail her again.

His thoughts were interrupted by a clamor coming from the direction of the pyre. The people sharing the fire with Kaiser surged to their feet and hurried towards the noise. Kaiser rose with them.

"What's happening?" Kaiser said to the man next to him.

"They're bringing out Sorrell," the man said. "They drag her out every night at dusk and give her the chance to confess to her crimes."

Kaiser let the crowd carry him to the flimsy wooden fence that separated the rest of the camp from the military section. From the tent next to the pyre, the one he suspected housed Sorrell, two soldiers clad in black and gold dragged a small cage with a length of rope. The cage did not move easily across the ground, and they were not gentle, jerking it with mighty heaves when it got stuck.

It took a few minutes for Kaiser to understand that Sorrell was locked in the tiny enclosure. She was curled up in a fetal position.

Despite the distance, Kaiser could see that she was filthy. He suspected they were not releasing her to relieve herself.

Sorrell was lying in the cage with her back to the crowd. Her brown hair was the same color that Mariel's had been, and a powerful rage gripped Kaiser as his heart tried to convince him that it was his wife being subjected to this terrible degradation.

The two soldiers wrestled the iron prison into position in front of the mob. People jeered and screamed, trying to provoke a reaction from Sorrell. She never moved. Only the near imperceptible rise and fall of her chest gave any indication that she was alive.

A richly dressed fop of a man climbed up to the speaking platform that had been assembled to address the crowd. He waved his hands for silence and cleared his throat before speaking.

"The time for confession is passed," the man said, his voice carrying out over the throng. "The traitor has refused to admit her wrongdoing. What mercy she may have purchased for herself is withdrawn. Tomorrow, we put a Pyreshade on the pyre. Let's pay our respects one last time. Now is the moment of her final humiliation!"

As the man spoke, servants carried baskets of rotten fruits and vegetables to the edges of the crowd. To indicate what was expected, the man on the platform raised an ugly tomato high over his head, held it for all to see, and then hurled it at Sorrell's cage. The squishy missile burst against the bars and showered Sorrell's head with pulp and juice.

Similarly armed, the mob joined in with gusto. A hail of soggy projectiles pelted Sorrell's enclosure. Her only response was to pull herself into a tighter ball. The people laughed and made sport of the event. An apple flew clean through the bars and hit Sorrell square in the back of the head, provoking a roar of amusement.

Kaiser watched, furious but helpless, as the baskets were emptied of their putrid contents. After the last piece of organic ammunition fell, the crowd calmed down. Sorrell's cage dripped with the remnants of rotten refuse. The people seemed to hold their breath as if they hoped for a reaction from Sorrell. There were mutterings of disappointment and disbelief when she did nothing.

Stepping forward with his hands raised, the orator addressed the crowd again while the soldiers pulled the cage back towards the tent. "Now that she's been properly basted, we'll cook her in the morning!"

A rumble of laughter rippled through the crowd. The man on the platform grinned at the reaction to his joke.

"The emperor has decreed that this grant event is to become a national holiday," the man said. "Celebrate in remembrance of the conquest of our enemies, both foreign and domestic!"

He favored the crowd with a flourish and a bow and then turned and descended the steps. Minutes later, the people started to dissipate, returning to their fires and tents to get ready for the night.

Back at the communal fire, Kaiser sat and tried to calm the turmoil in his soul. In his mind, he was back in Northmark, and Mariel was still alive. No matter how much he tried to reason with himself, he could not shake the feeling that he had just watched his wife be humiliated, not Sorrell.

Darkness descended upon the camp, although it failed to dim the light of an army of campfires. People relaxed as the ale and wine started to flow. Drunken songs filled the night sky, spreading from fire to fire as a thousand revelers added their voices. It was the beginning of a long night of riotous celebration that would culminate in Sorrell's burning.

Kaiser sat in the midst of all of this, tense as a taut bowstring. Any minute, Lacrael would act, and these people would get the conflagration they were clamoring for. Voices joined in happy carousal would turn to cries of lamentations.

No one else saw it, because no one else was looking for it. But Kaiser had not taken his eyes from the hill where he knew Lacrael and Brant were hiding. A tiny new flame winked into existence beneath the trees, unremarkable, at first, in a sea of campfires. This fire, however, did not stay small. It expanded rapidly until it was a great, swirling orb of flame. Still no one noticed.

Lacrael launched her first fireball at the far side of the valley, well away from anyone who might be hurt. The miniature sun streaked over the camp, leaving a searing orange trail in the sky in its wake. It detonated in the tall grass with a muted explosion. Fire licked greedily at the dry grass and began to spread immediately.

Around Kaiser, the drunken revelry had been replaced with stupefied silence. A cry went up when the second fireball appeared in the night sky.

"We're under attack!" a panicked woman shouted.

"It's them Linstall bastards, come to catch us with our pants down!" a man cried, brandishing a sword at the trees.

Kaiser waited for Lacrael to attack twice more before acting. By the time he moved towards Sorrell's tent, the camp had collapsed into chaos. Infantry, hastily summoned, were trying to form up and advance toward the source of the fireballs. The flames sparked in the weeds of the valley were threatening to turn into a wildfire, and the doomed merrymakers were doing everything in their power to move out of its path.

Crouched low to the ground and moving fast, Kaiser climbed over the fence and infiltrated the military section of the encampment. The soldiers outside Sorrell's tent never saw Kaiser coming. Their attention was on the hillside, not the camp itself. The first guard died with Kaiser's spectral blade in his back. Its glowing point pierced his heart and out the front of his chest. He made no sound as he died, but the rattling of his armor as he fell to the ground alerted the second guard.

Kaiser pivoted away from the dead soldier and lashed out with his sword. The second guard raised his halberd to ward off the blow. It was a futile defense. The ethereal edge of Kaiser's weapon sliced through the guard's halberd, gorget, and into his throat. Gurgling his last few breaths, the man fell backwards and lay still.

For an instant, Kaiser wondered if these soldiers were dragon spawn. But there was no time to check beneath their closed-face helmets. He slipped into the tent. A third guard inside stood watch over Sorrell. The soldier looked down in surprise at the glowing blade protruding from his chest before he died. This one was un-helmeted and confirmed Kaiser's suspicion. Reptilian eyes stared up at him, unseeing in death.

Sorrell was certain to have heard the commotion outside, but she still did not move. Kaiser knelt next to the cage and inspected the lock. With a touch of his ghostly scimitar, he sliced through the metal latch and swung the door open. Gently, Kaiser reached a hand towards Sorrell's head.

At Kaiser's touch, Sorrell flinched.

"It's okay," Kaiser said. "I'm here to get you out."

In response, Sorrell only ducked her head into her chest, away from Kaiser's fingers. Rather than try to reason with her, Kaiser crawled halfway into the cage, put his hands under Sorrell's arms, and pulled her out. Her ragged uniform was covered in filth.

She tried to fight him, but she was weak. On his knees, Kaiser wrapped his arms around Sorrell and weathered her feeble attempts to break free. She tired quickly. Sobbing, lungs heaving, Sorrell pressed her face into Kaiser's chest.

"Shhh," Kaiser said. "You're safe now. I've got you."

Sorrell looked up at his face for the first time. Her eyes seemed to have trouble focusing. "W-who?"

To his surprise, Kaiser realized that tears were spilling down his face.

"It's me, Mariel. I've come to save you at last."

Chapter 41

MAZAREEM WAS JOLTED FROM his meditation when the first fireball lit the sky. He had been waiting for days on a hilltop just south of the camp. All his preparations were complete; he only needed his quarry to appear. And now here they were. His pulse quickened at the thought.

"That's magus fire, boy," Mazareem said to Worm, who was slumbering on the earth at his side. "Now's our time. We'd best be at it."

Together, master and hound got to their feet and stretched stiff limbs. Neither of them had moved for three days and nights. When Mazareem could bend his knees and elbows again, he took up his staff and started down the hill. For the first mile, he had to use the staff to keep his balance, but soon the blood was flowing strongly again, and he could walk without help.

From the sounds coming from the direction of the camp, it sounded like Kaiser and his companions had launched an all-out assault in the bid to rescue Sorrell. Mazareem hoped that Viatrix and her forces would at least slow the magi down. He needed a little time to trigger the trap he had so carefully laid.

The two of them reached the grass-covered battlefield and moved towards the southern tree line. In the dark of night, Mazareem made straight for the spell he had carved in the dirt. The latent power of the magic called to him, demanding he either release it or erase it. He would have been able to find it in complete blackness. If he had been forced to wait much longer, the potency of the spell would have soured and become too dangerous to use.

Mazareem crouched to inspect the designs and symbols he had scratched in the earth. The faint moonlight provided just enough illumination to work by. With painstaking care, he corrected the errors caused by several days of neglect and made a few minor last-minute improvements where inspiration struck him.

Satisfied, and out of time, Mazareem stood up to his full height. He pulled his short dagger from his boot sheath. Hands held out above the dormant spell, he wrapped his left palm around the blade. A conjuration of this magnitude would require his own blood. Power could not be purchased without sacrifice.

"I read about this in a book once," Mazareem said to Worm. "Let's see if I got it right."

Mazareem drew the sharp edge of the dagger across his palm. Black ichor welled up from the wound. He squeezed his hand into a fist and let the tainted blood drip into the dirt.

The earth hissed where his blood touched. Ghastly green light, the color of chained souls, sprouted in smoky tendrils, reaching up towards the source of the blood gift. A terrible, clawing weight wrapped its icy fingers around Mazareem's spirit.

"My soul isn't on the table this day," Mazareem said only with monumental effort. His voice trembled under the strain.

The questing intelligence inspected the spell, and when it understood the intent, Mazareem sensed both amusement and approval. This magic would work, as long as Mazareem finished the invocation properly.

"I call to you, lost souls of the damned," Mazareem said into the night. "Return to the world of the living. Return to take the vengeance you were denied in death. Rise, rise and serve your master. I am Mazareem the Vulture, dread Keeper of the Last Watch. I summon you in the name of Abimelech, who bestowed upon me those titles. Heed my will and obey!"

Mazareem's voice strengthened as he spoke, and he finished the ritual with his bleeding fist raised above his head and his words booming out across the empty battlefield. At his feet, the spell blazed in a brilliant green flash of light and the earth drank his lifeblood.

Possessed of a mind of its own, the ghostly radiance leapt up from the intricate furrows carved in the dirt and drifted out across the dark field. Every few feet, it reached down to touch the ground, like a phantom farmer planting some sinister seed. Mazareem stopped counting at a hundred. The spectral illumination danced as it spread the length and width of the valley, kissing the scene of battle a hundred, then a thousand times.

A moan whispered over the top of the grass, a moan from beyond the grave. The wordless groan started low, but it grew and grew until it was a deafening howl. A thousand tongueless mouths screamed their rage at a world that had been stolen from them.

Mazareem shivered as the withering wail washed over his soul. The sound itself possessed power. It demanded a surrendering of mortality, a capitulation to the tomb. It wanted to inflict suffering as it had suffered. Worm raised his massive muzzle and howled, adding his canine voice to the dirge.

In front of them, in the first place the searching light had touched, a skeletal fist punched up through the earth of the battlefield.

"Let's see what our friends think of our new army," Mazareem said.

Chapter 42

SORRELL CLUNG TO KAISER with all her strength. He carried her through the pandemonium caused by Lacrael's fireballs. No one stopped them or gave them a second look. Uncontrolled fire was spreading fast and would soon engulf the entire valley. The soldiers had abandoned trying to find the source of the attack and had rallied to the emperor. They were now carving a path through the panicked horde of his subjects, trying to get him to safety.

Kaiser moved fast, even with Sorrell in his arms. Every footfall jolted a little more sense into her. Sorrell had thought to escape on her own, but she had not anticipated the terrible toll that days of abuse and neglect would take on her body. In the last twenty-four hours, she had given up and decided to die. Now that she had been delivered, Sorrell's mind struggled to catch up to the sudden and unexpected reversal of fortune.

Most of the procession had fled north out of the valley to escape the wildfire, but there were still thousands of people making their way south. Kaiser joined them. At what had been the perimeter of the camp, he stopped and turned in a slow circle, obviously looking for someone or something. A short distance away, on the incline of the nearest hill, he found what he was searching for. Lacrael and Brant were waving to get his attention.

"We're almost out of this," Kaiser said to Sorrell.

Battling against the flow of the mob, Kaiser cut across their path to reach Lacrael and Brant. When they were reunited, the two of them drew near to assess Sorrell's condition.

"Is she hurt?" Lacrael said.

"They had her locked in a dog cage," Kaiser said. "She must have been in there for days, because she can't walk."

Sorrell turned her head towards Lacrael and Brant. She was having trouble keeping a thought in her head, but one question demanded to be asked.

"Why did you come for me?" Sorrell said.

"We can talk about that when we're safe," Kaiser said. "We've got minutes before that fire reaches us."

Before any of them could speak to form a plan of action, a new sound cut across the bedlam. Screams filled the night sky, and they were not coming from the direction of the camp. Shouts of horror rang out from the south.

The four of them turned to look, and to their surprise, they saw the fleeing horde turning against itself. Those who had ventured further down the valley were now fighting and clawing to come back towards the fire. But the press of bodies trying to move south prevented them.

"What the devil?" said Brant.

From the hill above them, a few terrified men and women came sprinting down. They almost tripped and fell in their haste to get away from the forest.

"There's death in the woods!" a man screamed at them as he ran by. "Don't go into the trees!"

Sorrell twisted her neck to look up at the tree line. Kaiser shifted himself so she could see better. More people came running out of the darkness beneath the trees, their shadows mimicking their frantic movements in the light of the fire. One man, bleeding and dying, fell and tried to rise again, but he did not have the strength.

"That man's been gutted with a blade," Kaiser said.

The fallen man's killer stepped into the light cast by the raging fire. Sorrell gasped. It was a skeleton. It walked upright like a man, but there was no flesh on its body. Scraps of mail hung in tattered remnants from its bones, and it carried a rusted sword in its hand. Pale green fire burned in empty eye sockets.

Those twin points of light regarded the four of them for a heartbeat. The skeleton appeared to be searching for something. It unhinged its jaw and screeched at them. Sorrell did not know how it produced sound without a throat or lungs, but the noise hit her with almost physical force. From the forest and valley, the risen soldier's cry was answered by a thousand other tormented voices.

"I think that thing was looking for us," Brant said.

The undead warrior charged. It moved with surprising speed, bones clacking together in a hideous rattle as it plummeted down the hill. Lacrael raised a hand, open palm upturned and shot a lance of fire through the monster's naked skull. Shards of bone exploded in every direction as the skeleton's head disappeared in a puff of smoke. It did not slow the thing down. Three strides later, it was almost on top of them.

"Brant!" Lacrael said.

Reckless in a way the living cannot match, the skeleton covered the remaining distance in a savage lunge, sword extended before it as it tried to skewer Lacrael. The thing was blind, but still incredibly dangerous. Lacrael backpedaled, twisting away from the rusted blade.

Brant stepped forward, before the fiend recovered its balance, and caught the skeleton's sword arm in his huge hand. The reanimated soldier seemed to anticipate this. It released the weapon from its hand at the same instant that it pulled away from Brant.

Brant was left holding a disembodied arm. In the same motion, the revenant snatched the sword out of the air before it hit the ground with its remaining arm. It stabbed at Brant's bare stomach.

"No!" Lacrael screamed.

Kaiser dropped Sorrell to the ground and jumped forward—he was far too slow. Sorrell was certain that Brant was finished, but the big man never flinched. He caught the jagged blade in his free hand. His muscles bulged as he took the full weight of the undead creature's attack with a single arm. No matter how hard the fiend flailed, it could not drive the point of the sword into Brant's skin. Blood seeped from between Brant's fingers, yet he did not yield an inch.

Spectral scimitars in hand, Kaiser sliced into the back of the skeleton. Three quick crosscuts turned the monster into a pile of bones. They fell to the earth in a clatter, twitching, but no longer a threat.

Brant released the enemy's sword and let it drop. He inspected his wounded hand, and as the four of them watched, the bleeding stopped and the skin knit itself back together. Brant grunted in surprise.

"That's new," Brant said.

Lacrael and Kaiser were breathing hard. Sorrell looked up at the three of them from the dirt. She opened her mouth to speak, but the words abandoned her when ten more skeletons appeared from beneath the trees. These did not hesitate. They charged down the slope, weapons raised, haunted eyes burning with hatred.

"Stay together!" Kaiser shouted. "Fight as a unit. Don't let them reach Sorrell."

Kaiser leapt forward to meet the attack—Lacrael and Brant followed his command without question. The undead assault crashed into them. Fire blossomed from Lacrael's fingers as she launched fireball after fireball. Kaiser's shining swords sang in the light of the rising moon. Brant pummeled their skeletal attackers, his fists a blur.

Sorrell cursed her helplessness. She tried to stretch her legs, but they cried out in pain. Muscles trembled as they tried and failed to obey. Her back throbbed from being forced to stoop in the cage for three days.

Down in the valley below the hill they were fighting on, the sounds of violence caused Sorrell to turn her head. She stared in horror. A thousand risen skeletons had formed a shieldwall and were tearing into the mob. The people trampled each other to get away from the undead battle line. They would rather face the fire than die on the blades of that cursed army.

It was clear from the enemy's advance that they were trying to reach Sorrell and her protectors. The four of them were trapped. By Sorrell's estimate, they had only minutes before they were completely surrounded. Kaiser, Lacrael, and Brant were barely holding the line beneath the trees. If the main force reached them, they would be overwhelmed.

On the opposite side of the valley, a dark figure moved on the hillside, directing the revenant army like a dread general. At his side stalked a hound the size of a horse. Sorrell did not need the light of day to recognize Mazareem. Her heart hammered in her chest. She had been terrified to touch the power within her the past three days. Viatrix would have killed her at the first sign of ice. But now Sorrell reached out for it. She needed a way to strike out at Mazareem. If

Sorrell was to die here, she would drag that wretched fiend down into the underworld with her.

The power answered Sorrell's plea, stronger than ever before. She gasped. Something was different. This time the energy that filled her had a will, a desire of its own. A voice spoke in her mind, telling her that it could help, it could show her how to defeat Mazareem. Sorrell reached out for that hope, frantic to claim any advantage. The entity pulled back from Sorrell's desperation, taking the power with it. It wanted something from her first. It wanted surrender.

Sorrell consented without hesitation. She was about to die. What did it matter if she gave a part of herself to this strange presence inside her? Sorrell sensed approval, and the power came rushing back. A new intuition flooded Sorrell's mind, and she understood instinctively the magnitude of her new abilities.

Rapier and whip formed in her hands, but the conjuring did not stop there. A suit of armor materialized out of thin air, wrapping Sorrell's body in overlapping plates of ice. The bitter cold felt wonderful against her skin. In an instant, the pain disappeared. Sorrell jumped to her feet. To her surprise, the armor itself supported her battered body, lending her strength well beyond her normal means. The frozen armor seemed to be weightless.

Sorrell turned and looked up the hill at where her companions held the line. They were fighting for their lives. For every skeleton they felled, another two rose up to take its place. The three of them were being driven back, forced to give ground before the relentless onslaught of the undead.

None of the others had noticed Sorrell's transformation. She briefly thought about going to their aid, but she discarded that idea as soon as it popped into her head. Their only hope was to stop the risen army before it swarmed them, and Sorrell might be the only one who could do it.

Overhead, storm clouds swirled in the night sky. They appeared to be forming directly over the battlefield. Jagged bolts of lightning flashed in the darkness, each streak punctuated by a great crack of thunder. Sorrell jumped when the lightning slashed down and detonated in the midst of the skeletons in front of Kaiser. The undead screamed as shards of splintered bone flew in every direction.

So Kaiser controlled the lightning like she did the ice. Sorrell did not have time to dwell on this—the last few stragglers of the mob had fallen before the skeleton shieldwall, and the enemy now marched towards her unobstructed. Sorrell took a deep breath and plunged down the hill towards the horde of animated dead.

In the last few feet before crashing into the enemy's raised shields, Sorrell planted her foot on a rock and launched herself into the air. Her heart dropped into her stomach as she soared into the sky. She did not know her own strength in this new armor. A thousand pairs of burning eyes looked upward to track her flight. Sorrell landed hard in the middle of the skeleton army, bones of the enemy fracturing under her fall.

Rusted swords and spears stabbed at Sorrell—her enchanted armor absorbed every blow without taking a scratch. She struck with her rapier and lashed out with her chain whip. The enemy reared back from Sorrell's initial assault, but they surged forward again an instant later.

Sorrell's frozen blade touched a ribcage, and the skeleton fell to pieces, its torso dropping to the ground as a solid block of ice. Her whip wrapped around a raised shield, shattering both bone and steel when she yanked it back. Sorrell tried to keep the rapier extended in front of her, but the enemy pressed in, denying her the space to fight. The whip in her left hand was useless if she could not swing it.

Seeing no other options, Sorrell dismissed her conventional weapons and summoned chunks of ice around her clenched hands.

The frozen armor flowed, morphing to form twin mauls around her fists. In a frenzy, the mass of skeletons tried to crush her under their sheer weight, throwing themselves at her in a mad rush.

Sorrell hammered at the enemy. She caught a skeleton mid-air, her frozen mace smashing its skull to dust. Her left hand plowed through a torso, snapping ribs like they were kindling. They could not stand before her. Their attacks buffeted her from all sides, but Sorrell's armor held strong. She waded through their ranks, fists flying, slivers of ice filling the air as she pulverized bone.

In the middle of the enemy force, Sorrell could not see how her companions fared, but she hoped she had purchased them a bit of breathing space. She definitely had the attention of the skeleton soldiers. Sorrell clobbered her way towards Mazareem, determined to visit her icy vengeance on him.

The power flowing through her body was intoxicating. Through it all, Sorrell felt the strange presence inside her, almost as if a specter stood with her on the battlefield. Where Sorrell struck, it mirrored her, adding its weight to the blow. She sensed that this entity sustained her armor and gave her the strength to keep up her assault. On her own, Sorrell would have never made it this far.

As the bones piled up beneath Sorrell's inexorable advance, the enemy changed tactics. The revenants let go of their weapons, and instead of trying to kill Sorrell, they started trying to restrain her. Boney fingers scrabbled against the icy plates of her armor. Sorrell struck out blindly in an attempt to get free of the grasping hands behind her. But no matter how hard she fought, there was no escape.

She made it a few more steps before the weight became too much. A hundred skeletal hands dragged her down towards the dirt. The combined burden of the undead army forced Sorrell to her knees. She braced her hands against the earth, using every bit of her enhanced strength to stay upright as the skeletons piled onto her back. A skull stared at her, an inch from her face. The thing's jaws snapped open and closed as it tried to chew through her helmet of ice.

Sorrell forced her head up. The ranks of the enemy were parting, forming a long corridor for Mazareem. He was coming fast, a gigantic, hideous hound at his side. Sorrell grit her teeth. She was not going to die like this, and not by Mazareem's hand.

A quiet whisper in Sorrell's mind showed her a way to strike back. It also showed her the cost. It would take every bit of power she could summon, and it would leave her completely drained. She could kill Mazareem, but it would leave her vulnerable and exposed. Sorrell accepted the risk without a second thought.

The presence that had been Sorrell's mystical shadow since donning the enchanted armor receded for a heartbeat. She waited, panting under the strain of holding herself out of the dirt. All around her, the skeleton fiends wailed for her blood. Mazareem was near now. He would reach Sorrell within seconds.

Like an avalanche, the power inside Sorrell burst forth from her soul. She screamed as frigid talons reached down into the core of her being. Frozen tears leaked from her eyes and stuck to her cheeks. She had become a living weapon, a conduit for terrible magic.

Mazareem hesitated. Sorrell's icy armor erupted. The mass of skeletons on her back were flung away like snowflakes in a gust of wind. Wave after wave of living ice radiated outward from Sorrell's prone form. It swept over the earth, faster than a horse could run, devouring everything in its path. In the span of a few seconds, the undead army was transformed from a thousand armed soldiers to a field of frozen statues.

Sorrell stopped breathing. The cold was absolute. She felt as if she had *become* ice. Now that the power had gone out of her, her body had forgotten the warmth of life. Sorrell lowered herself to the ground and lay on her back. She was not scared, only tired. So tired.

Far above her head, the thunderstorm raged. A weak smile formed on Sorrell's lips. She had always liked storms. Consciousness started to fade, and she watched the sky with a sense of detached peace. Thunder rumbled so hard it shook the earth, but Sorrell barely noticed. A thousand spears of lightning lanced down, every bolt seeking a single frozen skeleton. The enemy army vanished in a cloud of shrapnel, ice and bone glittering in the light of the wildfire.

It was so pretty. Sorrell tried to reach a hand toward the scintillating mist, but her body would not obey. She could not even blink her eyes. Stone's face appeared in her mind. He smiled at her. At least she had taken Stone's killer with her to the grave. Sorrell held onto this thought, confident it would be her last.

Another face thrust itself into her vision. This annoyed Sorrell, because it blocked her view of the sky. It took her a few long heartbeats to realize this new face was not a part of her dying imagination. It was Lacrael, and she stared down at Sorrell with concern.

Lacrael's mouth moved, but Sorrell did not hear a word the other woman said. Kaiser and Brant's face joined Lacrael's, hovering above Sorrell's head. Lacrael placed an open palm on Sorrell's chest and closed her eyes.

Heat flowed into Sorrell. It started beneath Lacrael's hand, and from there, it saturated Sorrell's body. With renewed feeling came intense pain. The tears frozen on Sorrell's cheeks melted, opening the floodgates for more to fall. Sorrell squeezed her eyes shut and tried not to scream. Her muscles cramped as they thawed.

When Lacrael finally pulled her hand back, Sorrell was breathing again. Her breaths came in ragged gasps, but she was alive. Kaiser knelt next to her and helped Sorrell into a sitting position.

"Can you stand?" Kaiser said.

Sorrell only shook her head. She did not even have the strength to speak. Kaiser understood. Gently, he put an arm under her legs, and supporting her back with the other, he lifted her off the ground.

Kaiser, Lacrael, and Brant discussed what to do next, but Sorrell was too fatigued to follow the conversation. Instead, she searched the field for any sign of Mazareem's corpse. She searched in vain. There was nothing left of the skeleton horde. If Mazareem had fallen here, he had been reduced to frozen dust along with his risen minions.

Sorrell's companions must have reached a decision, because they started moving south again. She tried to stay awake, but exhaustion soon claimed her. Sorrell passed out in Kaiser's arms. The last thing she remembered was the pristine moon in the now clear sky, and beneath it, a sea of fire, blood, and ice.

Chapter 43

KAISER CARRIED SORRELL THROUGH the night and well into the next day. He wanted to put as much distance as possible between them and the scene of destruction they had left behind. The nearest rendezvous point to reunite with Gustavus was only a day and a half's walk away, but Kaiser had to call a halt in the late afternoon. He could not haul Sorrell any further without a few hour's rest.

Though they did not say it, Kaiser knew Lacrael and Brant needed rest as well. They found a dried-out streambed that would conceal them from all but the most diligent of searchers and lowered their packs to the ground. A narrow trickle of water wound its way through the dirt at their feet. Kaiser sat Sorrell down as gently as he could manage. She had been asleep since the battle.

"Is she going to be okay?" Brant said.

"She'll be fine," Kaiser said. "I suspect that was the first time she tapped into her powers to the fullest. It takes practice. The first time I did it, I was wiped out for days. You were there, remember?"

"I suppose I was," Brant said after thinking about it. "That seems like so long ago. I can carry her too, you know. There's no reason to wear yourself out."

"I'll carry her," Kaiser said, the tone of his voice leaving no room for argument. "I just need a few hours of sleep."

No matter how hard he tried, Kaiser could not sever the link his heart had created between Mariel and Sorrell. As they had walked through the night, he would catch himself thinking he held Mariel in his arms. Every time Kaiser discovered that he had deceived himself, the pain was almost too great to bear, but in the light of day, he could not bring himself to move from Sorrell's side.

Brant raised both his hands in a placating gesture. He exchanged a glance with Lacrael, which Kaiser chose to ignore. Kaiser pulled the crude map Gustavus had given them from his pack. Lacrael had returned it to him in the night. He unfolded the parchment and made his best guess as to their current position.

"I think we're somewhere near here," Kaiser said, touching the map with a finger for Lacrael and Brant's benefit. "I had hoped to make it to the nearest cove, here, to meet Gustavus and the ship. But we'll never reach it before he moves on now. His next stopping point is only a few miles further down the coast. We'll sleep for a few hours, walk through the rest of the night, and we should reach the inlet just as Gustavus arrives in the morning."

Lacrael and Brant nodded their agreement. The two of them moved a little ways down the streambed until they found a comfortable spot. Together, they lay down, Brant with his arm around Lacrael, and her with her back snuggled close into his chest. Kaiser watched this, surprised at the jealousy he felt.

Forcibly dismissing such an immature reaction, Kaiser lowered himself to the ground next to Sorrell. He lay with his back to her and did his best to put her out of his mind. With the ease of a veteran soldier, Kaiser let slumber claim him. He was asleep within minutes.

Kaiser was not surprised when he opened his eyes to a dream of the same streambed he lay sleeping in. His three companions were gone. In their place, a hooded stranger sat on the far bank, regarding Kaiser. He knew instantly that this was not Umbris. The stranger looked haggard and disheveled. Usually strong and confident, the man's hands trembled slightly. Under Kaiser's scrutiny, the stranger clasped his hands to hide their shaking.

In the dream, Kaiser sat up. "You're nothing if not predictable," he said.

The stranger acted as if he had not heard Kaiser.

"I've expended too much of myself in this realm," the stranger said. His voice was almost a whisper. Kaiser strained his hearing to understand what the man said. "The enemy never expected me to risk so much, and that's the only reason we've prevailed. But the cost may be our undoing in the end.

"I fear this may be the last time I can visit you in a long while. The tyrant is close. Even now, he's sniffing outside my hiding place. I must flee or be discovered. The time is not yet right to fight. Listen well, Kaiser of Northmark, for the outcome of my fate may rest with you. You must escape this realm with all haste. As my power wanes, so will yours, and the enemy is powerful here. You must quit this place, while you still can. However, always remember that as long as I remain free, some of your abilities will endure. If there comes a day when the gifts I've given abandon you entirely, you will know that I'm defeated and the cause is lost. Pray that day never comes."

Kaiser listened to the stranger's words, but he could not shake the sense of wrongness about the dream. Something was different this time. In a flash of insight, Kaiser realized what it was. The warmth and sincerity that had characterized the stranger's earlier visits was gone. In its place, Kaiser perceived only calculated ambition and self-interest. Perhaps in his weakness, the stranger's true motivations were showing through.

"You're not the only one to visit my dreams spouting riddles and dire prophecies," Kaiser said.

The hooded stranger reacted to this news with a visible jerk. "If the enemy has reached you here, then I'm weaker than I thought. Stay vigilant. Find the fourth champion, finish the task, and you can make your family whole again."

As he spoke these last words, the stranger faded from sight. A few seconds later, he disappeared entirely. Kaiser was left alone in the dream. Unlike the other times the stranger visited him, he had to figure out how to get out himself. Kaiser concentrated on sleep, and the dream started to recede. Soon enough, he was resting peacefully again. His last thought before unconsciousness was of his family.

Kaiser woke four hours later, his eyes opening in response to his mental clock telling him he had slept long enough. The dream was the first thing he recalled, and he lay there for a moment, considering the implications. Gustavus and Lacrael were not going to be happy. The enemy was closing in, and the ally that had carried them this far, the one advantage they possessed, was stepping back and leaving them on their own.

Chapter 44

SORRELL STIRRED. SHE OPENED her eyes to find that Kaiser had rolled over to look at her. Something in his eyes made her pause. He looked at her with such longing, and she sensed such emptiness in him, that she almost reached out to caress his face.

"I feel like I had a mountain dropped on me," Sorrell said.

"It will pass," Kaiser said. "Your body will adjust to the new demands."

"You carried me all night," Sorrell said. It was not a question.

"Yes," Kaiser said.

"I remember… odd fragments. You spoke someone else's name."

"I'll wake the others," Kaiser said. He jumped to his feet before Sorrell finished her thought.

Lacrael and Brant both woke at Kaiser's hand on their shoulders. Brant looked fresh and rested, but Lacrael spent several minutes rubbing the sleep out of her eyes. While Lacrael stretched and yawned, Kaiser leaned close to have a word with Brant.

Sorrell did not hear what they said, but the result was that when they resumed their trek, Brant was to carry her instead of Kaiser. Brant wrinkled his nose as he and Lacrael approached Sorrell. He whispered something in Lacrael's ear, who nodded and moved to kneel next to her.

"We should get you cleaned up a bit before we move on," Lacrael said. "Can you stand?"

"I can try," Sorrell said.

Lacrael offered her a hand, and with help, Sorrell managed to hobble to the pitiful stream in the middle of the ravine. Kaiser and Brant walked a short distance into the trees to give them privacy. Carefully, Lacrael helped Sorrell peel her rancid clothes from her skin. Sorrell hissed in pain as the clinging fabric pulled at her raw flesh.

"We've nothing else for you to wear, but we can at least rinse these out," Lacrael said.

Too sore to properly clean herself, Sorrell sat quietly under Lacrael's ministrations. Lacrael did her best, her tender fingers washing the worst of the grime and refuse away. When Sorrell was as clean as possible given the circumstances, Lacrael helped her back into her damp uniform.

"Thank you," Sorrell said. "I had forgotten what it felt like to be human."

"Don't mention it," Lacrael said with a smile. "You're amongst friends now. We may seem like a dysfunctional bunch, but we look out for each other."

Kaiser and Brant returned, and after taking a few minutes to eat some dried meat and bread from their packs, the four of them set out. Brant picked up Sorrell as if she weighed nothing. Sorrell tried and failed to catch Kaiser's attention. She had upset him somehow. He was doing his best to ignore her.

They hiked through the night, heading west until they reached the sea and then following it south. All they had to do was keep the ocean on their right, which made navigation simple. Twice, they had to detour inland to avoid a rocky stretch of coastline, but for the most part, it was easy going.

Kaiser stayed well ahead of the others. Frustrated by his behavior, Sorrell gave up trying to talk to him. Instead, she counted the inlets and coves they passed, ticking them off from her memory of the map. At the fifth one, Kaiser slowed his pace to let the other three catch up.

"The next cove should be where we find Gustavus," Kaiser said. "We'll be away with the tide."

"On my ship," Sorrell said.

"You're free to discuss the finer points of ownership with Gustavus, once we're on board," Kaiser said. "For now, let's focus on reaching it."

In the next hour, the sun rose over the tops of the trees to the east, and they could see out over the ocean to the west. It looked like it was going to be a clear, cool day. The weather put Sorrell in mind of home, and she was about to say as much, when the peaceful dawn was shattered by the thunder of cannons.

Ahead of them, a rocky hill rose out of the forest, and Kaiser sprinted up this rise to get a view of the water. He skidded to a halt when he reached the top. Lacrael and Brant scrambled up next to Kaiser. Still in Brant's arms, Sorrell raised a hand to shield her eyes from the light as she peered out at the scene.

At their feet, a steep cliff plunged down into the sea where waves crashed around jagged boulders. From this vantage point, Sorrell could see for miles to the south and west.

About a mile away and closing fast, the *Celestial* was making for the inlet at full speed. Her silver sails shone brilliantly in the rays of morning sun that were just cresting the treetops. Behind the *Celestial*, a trio of warships were in close pursuit. Sorrell recognized them. She knew each by name. A second volley of cannon fire echoed across the water, and puffs of smoke rose from the bow guns of the enemy vessels.

"Those are Coriddian frigates," Sorrell said. "He should have known better than to think he could sail down the coast in a stolen ship and go unnoticed."

"He's not slowing down," Lacrael said.

They watched in disbelief as the *Celestial*'s prow cut through the water, its path never wavering from the short strip of beach at the far end of the cove. The Coriddian pursuers turned their ships parallel with the shore, both to bring the rest of their guns to bear and to avoid a suicidal crash. The enemy held their fire, waiting to see if Gustavus was actually going to scuttle the *Celestial*.

The *Celestial* plowed through the shallows and slammed into the shore with a tremendous crash. The force of the impact snapped the makeshift masts that had been repaired only days earlier. Water rushed into the punctured hull. Sorrell winced, and Kaiser swore.

"They need more of a rescue than we do," Sorrell said.

Tiny figures appeared on the *Celestial*'s deck and flung themselves into the sea. They struggled towards the shore, desperate to get away from the wreck and into the safety of the forest. Out on the water, the Coriddian frigates resumed their bombardment. Cannon shot splashed in the surf next to the *Celestial*'s floundering crew.

"Can you chase those ships off with your fire?" Brant said to Lacrael.

In answer, Lacrael stepped forward, hands raised to summon a fireball. She closed her eyes and concentrated, but nothing happened. After a moment, she took a step back, a look of confusion and fear on her face.

"The fire won't come," Lacrael said. "I can feel the power inside me, but it won't answer my call."

"We're all tired and in desperate need of rest," Kaiser said. "I don't think I could summon lightning right now if my life depended on it."

Lacrael shook her head, ready to argue. Sorrell cut her off, a hand raised to point down at the beach.

"Look, there's Gustavus," Sorrell said.

Gustavus had reached the shore. A few of his crew struggled through the surf behind him. Sorrell spotted the slight form of a girl fighting through the waves, and Kaiser looked ready to hurl himself into the sea from the clifftop.

"Come on, Tarathine, stay with Gustavus," Kaiser said.

The rest of the *Celestial's* sailors had scattered, every man and woman making a mad dash for the trees. Gustavus moved in that direction, but a cannon ball exploding in the sand in front of him diverted his path.

To escape the threat of the enemy's guns, Gustavus led his doomed band into the rocks of the nearby cliff. They disappeared into the shadows between the boulders.

"What's he thinking?" Brant said. "They'll be trapped in there!"

Two of the enemy frigates were approaching the beach while the third hung back, guns firing at random to keep Gustavus pinned down behind the rocks.

"In a few minutes, this place is going to be crawling with marines," Sorrell said.

"We've got to get down there," Kaiser said.

"We'll be trapped along with them," Lacrael said.

"My daughter's down there," Kaiser said. "And Gustavus is the only one who knows where to find the next portal. I'm going. Stay here if you like."

Kaiser did not wait for an answer. He ran along the top of the cliff until he found a spot he could safely descend. He ducked down and disappeared from view.

"This is madness," Sorrell said.

"There's nowhere else to go," Lacrael said. "If we don't stay together, we're lost."

Lacrael and Brant followed Kaiser down the steep slope. Brant slid most of the way, doing his best to hang onto Sorrell. They reached the bottom out of breath and covered in scrapes and bruises. Sorrell expected to be fired on any second, but either the frigate did not notice them or decided they were not worth the effort. Whatever the reason, she let out a sigh of relief when they reached the beach unscathed.

The four of them crept along the rocky shoreline until they reached the last place they had seen Gustavus. They ducked when a cannonball screamed through the air. It smashed into the cliff side above their heads—stinging chips of stone rained down on their shoulders. The deformed iron lump of shot hit the ground with a solid *thunk* in front of Kaiser.

To Sorrell's surprise, instead of finding Gustavus and Tarathine huddled down behind a boulder, they discovered the mouth of a cave. Kaiser ducked inside without a second thought, and it almost cost him his life. Gustavus lunged out of the darkness, cutlass raised to pin Kaiser to the wall. At the last instant, Gustavus recognized him and diverted his attack to let the blade glance harmlessly off the stone.

"By the stygian depths, man," Gustavus said. "I almost killed you!"

"I'd have that sword out of your hand before it touched me," Kaiser said, patting Gustavus's shoulder.

Lacrael, Brant, and Sorrell crowded in behind Kaiser.

"So you found her," Gustavus said when he saw Sorrell.

"Of course we did," Kaiser said. "Your end of the bargain was getting us out of here. What happened?"

"The damned Coriddian Navy happened, that's what. We ran into a patrol at sunset yesterday. I couldn't answer their signals properly, so they decided to board us or blow us out of the water. They chased us all night."

Tarathine appeared from the back of the cave and ran into Kaiser's arms. She buried her head into his chest, and Kaiser hugged her tight to himself. Niad stepped forward, along with two sailors whose names Sorrell did not know.

"Between three frigates, they'll have over a hundred marines," Sorrell said. "If we don't surrender, they'll smoke us out."

The muted roar of another cannon volley rumbled through the cave.

"We can't scrap our way out of this one," Kaiser said. "We need rest before our magic returns to full strength."

"I've still got fight in me," Brant said. "I don't know if I can hold off a hundred soldiers, but I can slow them down. We just need a way to escape this cave."

"This isn't the dead end you think it is," Gustavus said.

Every head turned to look at Gustavus.

"Those rendezvous points I marked on the map weren't random," Gustavus said. "Each of those coves and inlets has a hidden portal, placed by the order of dragon slayers a thousand years ago. They used this shoreline to navigate between the realms."

"There's a portal in here?" Kaiser said. "You brilliant bastard, why didn't you say so right away?"

"Because while I remember the locations of these portals, I've no idea where they'll drop us. I can't read the script on the ancient maps. I only know the symbol for the portals. And the sign marking this one is strange, unlike all the rest. It has extra text beneath it. If I had to guess, I'd say it's a warning."

"What does the symbol for this portal look like?" Lacrael said, her voice filled with dread.

"It's a black, twisted star, and beneath it are what look like the dunes of a desert," Gustavus said.

"That's the sign of my homeland. That's the mark of Vaul. Whatever happens, we can't go through that portal."

The cannon fire had stopped. Gustavus risked a peek outside the cave. When he returned, he looked worried.

"They're forming up on the beach," Gustavus said.

"We don't have a choice," Kaiser said, meeting Lacrael's terrified gaze.

Lacrael shook her head. "You don't understand. Vaul is a place of pestilence. It's been consumed by death. I'd rather die here than go through that portal."

"But the rest of us would prefer to live," Kaiser said. "And if that portal takes us to your homeland, we'll need your help to survive. We've come this far. Don't give up now."

Brant handed Sorrell to Kaiser and then moved closer to Lacrael and spoke so that only she could hear. Lacrael raised a trembling hand to her mouth. Brant stepped back and gave Kaiser a small nod.

"Will you help us?" Kaiser said.

"Y-yes," Lacrael said, all emotion drained from her voice. "But don't forget what I said: it would be better for us to die in this cave."

"Show us the portal," Kaiser said to Gustavus.

Beckoning for them to follow him, Gustavus moved to the back of the cave. Away from the faint sunlight shining through the entrance, the rest of the grotto was lost in darkness. Gustavus pulled an amulet out of his shirt, slipped it off, and held it over his head. Somewhere in front of them, a faint green luminescence glowed in response to the amulet.

Careful not to stray from Gustavus's steps, their small party navigated the dark stone floor until they stood before a door of swirling light. Runes inscribed in the rock formed the frame of the portal, and they were carved in a flowing, interwoven ancient script that made them look like vines. Only when Kaiser leaned in close to inspect it did Sorrell realize that the vines were composed of individual symbols of some lost language.

The runes pulsed with the same green light of the portal, which slowly rotated on its side in the middle of the doorway. Above this, the twisted star Gustavus had mentioned shone down on them.

Voices outside the cave made it clear they were out of time.

"We'll see you on the other side," Kaiser said. He moved towards the portal.

Sorrell twisted violently in Kaiser's arms. He had no choice but to stop and set her on the floor. For the first time in days, she stood on her feet without help or support.

"You're not taking me through that," Sorrell said.

Kaiser stood between Sorrell and the portal. Tarathine clung to his side.

"If you don't come with us, the only other way out is with them," Kaiser said, pointing to the mouth of the cave.

"I'm an admiral in the Coriddian Navy, sister to the emperor, and next in line to the throne of the empire," Sorrell said. "I can't just abandon my home and leave all that behind. I don't even know who you people are."

"We're the people who rescued you from that empire. They had you locked in a dog cage and were going to cook you on a stake, or did you forget that part?"

Sorrell had no ready response. Kaiser was right. If she did still have allies in the empire, she had no way to reach them. The marines on the beach would take her into custody and return her to Viatrix. There was only one way to keep her freedom—she had to go through the portal. Her world was collapsing, but Sorrell needed something, anything, to latch onto. She needed to believe that this was not the end.

"Is your word worth a damn?" Sorrell said.

"I'd spend my life before I went back on it," Kaiser said.

"Then promise me, promise me we'll return someday. I'll not flee the field of battle in disgrace, but if we retreat to live to fight another day, that I can do."

"If it's in my power to bring you back, I will. Now if you've made up your mind, we have to go."

Sorrell heard the sincerity in Kaiser's voice. They shared a bond that she did not understand, but she knew instinctively that she could trust him. She had no other choice.

"I won't be carried any further," Sorrell said. "I'll face my fate on my own two feet."

Kaiser nodded and extended an open hand. Sorrell took it, grateful for his assistance despite her bold words. Together, they stood in front of the portal. She took a deep breath.

Sorrell stepped into the swirling light.

Epilogue

MAZAREEM SAT ATOP A cliff overlooking the sea. A gentle ocean breeze caressed his cheek, and the warmth of the noonday sun covered his body like a comfortable blanket. Far below, the brilliant blue ocean sparkled in the sunlight. Mazareem noticed none of this beauty.

Worm was gone. The hound had saved his master, leaping in front of Sorrell's icy blast at the last instant. Mazareem had escaped with his life and nothing else. There were not many injuries that would render Worm beyond repair, but complete disintegration was definitely one of them.

Sadness was an emotion lost to Mazareem, but he would miss the hound's company. Worm had been a more honest and loyal companion than any human Mazareem had ever met. Perhaps someday, when he had the time and leisure to return to his studies, he could improve on Worm's design.

Mazareem had used every bit of the resources and power at his disposal to track and destroy the magi, and he had been thwarted at every turn. And yet, Abimelech was not angry. This fact bothered Mazareem, for his master did not allow failure. The only conclusion

Mazareem could reach was that Abimelech did not consider his efforts a failure, but Mazareem did not understand why.

It had been days since his quarry disappeared, vanished through yet another portal. Abimelech had visited Mazareem last night with instructions. As before, Mazareem was to follow. His mission had not changed. And as before, Abimelech told him where they had gone, but not how to get there.

This time, however, Mazareem contemplated disobedience. Kaiser and his companions had escaped to Vaul. Of the four realms that made up creation, Mazareem was not allowed to enter Vaul. He had been banished, long ago.

She ruled there, and she had sworn to destroy him if he ever set foot in her realm again. Abimelech was a protection, of sorts, from her vengeance, but Mazareem did not trust even his master's power to save him if he ventured into Vaul.

Mazareem sighed. If he ran, where could he go? There was no escape from the reach of Abimelech's ravening claws. Mazareem had set his feet on this path a thousand years ago. He could not abandon it now, not when the chance at true immortality still remained. Abimelech bred dragon princes in secret, the beating heart of which could free Mazareem from the tyrant's curse. He would have what he was owed.

But he was weary. So weary. It was hard to hold on to the hunger and zest for never-ending life after a millennium of service. To Mazareem's lament, in these moments of weakness, he could find nothing else on which to ground himself. He had forgotten any other purpose or goal. His relentless pursuit of immortality defined him, down to the very bedrock of his being.

And yet... thoughts of Vaul, memories of *her*, whispered of the path not taken. It brought Mazareem back to a time when the future was still full of potential and he remembered what freedom tasted like.

Mazareem could not remember her name. Her last words to him had been a curse, a vile enchantment that stripped her from his recollection. Over the long years, Mazareem had reconstructed a picture of her in his mind, but he knew it was flawed. It was an image of who she used to be, not who she became. The woman whose memory Mazareem held onto was long dead.

It was time, Mazareem decided, to return to Vaul. It might end in his death, but he wanted to see her again, after all these years. He wanted to discard the delusion and etch her true face into his memory. Rowen's bride. The only woman Mazareem had ever loved.

— —

Saredon sat at an ornate wooden table in the room that was now his home. He had not been allowed to leave the room since he had arrived a week ago, but every possible comfort he could want for had been provided. The appointments of the apartment were even richer and more extravagant than what he had enjoyed as a child of the tenth reaver. After six hard months living on the street, Saredon felt a strange sense of guilt to be sitting in the lap of luxury again.

On the table before him, a breakfast fit for royalty had been served. Saredon picked at the food. It was far too much for one boy to eat. He had been told by his priestess guardian that today was a special occasion, to expect a special visitor sometime in the early morning. Saredon was too excited to have much of an appetite.

The priestesses had been nothing but kind and gentle with him, and Saredon was certain that Ursais had been mistaken about them. If only the old man had given them a chance, maybe he would still be alive and in good health.

The sturdy wooden door creaked as someone pushed it open. Saredon looked up from his plate. His eyes found the face of the visitor—he forgot to breathe. It was his mother. She was alive! His mother looked just as she had on the last day Saredon had seen her, down to the same green dress.

Saredon's chair fell over with a crash as he launched himself out of it. He almost tripped and fell flat on his nose when he ran around the table. Tears were spilling down his cheeks by the time he reached the open arms of his mother. Saredon buried his face into the folds of her dress. She smelled strange, but Saredon did not care.

They held that embrace for a long time until Saredon stopped sobbing. His mother caressed his head while he cried. Saredon let six months of fear, grief, and agony pour out. When at last he was done, his mother put her hands on his shoulders and gently pushed him back so that she could look down into his face.

Saredon smiled up at her through his tears. She smiled back, and Saredon's heart soared.

"I'm sorry you've had to suffer," his mother said. "You were never supposed to get lost in the city. I had to fake my own death to save myself, and your father was going to flee with you and your sister until the danger was past. When we found out that you hadn't escaped with them, we started searching. I'm so glad we finally found you."

She led him back to the table, and together they sat and shared breakfast. While they ate, Saredon's mother asked him all sorts of questions about his time on the streets, and he happily told her story after story about his exploits. In particular, she wanted to know a lot about Ursais and Garius, and if they had any other friends in the slums. Saredon answered to the best of his ability, basking in the affection and approval of his mother.

When they finished the meal, his mother stood up from the table.

"I'm very busy right now, so I can only stay with you for a short while," she said. "But I promise, I'll visit you every day. You've got to stay in this room a little while longer, just until it's safe. Soon, you can come and live with me, and we'll start picking up the pieces of the life we lost."

Panic stabbed through Saredon at the thought of losing his mother again, but her warm smile chased away all his fears.

"You're safe here, don't worry," she said, pausing at the open door. "I'll make sure the priestesses take good care of you."

"I love you, mother," Saredon said.

"I love you too, my son," his mother said.

— —

The woman who appeared to be Saredon's mother exited the room and shut the door behind her. She stopped at a mirror in the hall. Frowning at her reflection, she reached down the front of her dress and pulled out a small, painted portrait of Mariel. She inspected the picture for a moment and then looked back at her face in the mirror. She concentrated, and her face shifted, morphing into a better approximation of Mariel.

She smiled at herself. This would get easier with practice, and anyway, the boy had not noticed that anything was amiss. In time, he would know only her face as his mother.

Read the next book in the series!

Lacrael never intended to return home like this.

Cast into the realm of Vaul against her will, she is forced to don a disguise to avoid being recognized. In a world where the air itself can kill and the people worship death, Lacrael must lead the others to safety through a hostile empire filled with treachery, deceit, and murder…

The Shrouded King series continues in The First Champion. Read it here on Amazon!

About the Author

Sandell Wall is a computer programmer/business analyst by trade. He lives in Michigan with his wonderful wife and two rambunctious children. He has embarked on a personal quest to write a million words. This book represents the halfway point of that quest. *The Coriddian Adimral* is his fifth book and his triumphant return to writing. He hopes his readers enjoyed the book. He is excited to keep writing and to create new worlds for his readers to explore!

You can visit his website at http://www.sandellwall.com. He would love it if you stopped by and said hi!

www.ingramcontent.com/pod-product-compliance
Lightning Source LLC
Chambersburg PA
CBHW060147260626
47160CB00001B/157